RAYMOND CHANDLER'S
TROUBLE IS
MY BUSINESS

RAYMOND CHANDLER'S
TROUBLE IS MY BUSINESS

ARVIND ETHAN DAVID, ILIAS KYRIAZIS, CRIS PETER

FOREWORD BY BEN H. WINTERS

PANTHEON BOOKS · NEW YORK

Library of Congress Cataloging-in-Publication Data

Names: David, Arvind Ethan, author. | Kyriazis, Ilias, 1978– artist. | Peter, Cris, colorist. |
Esposito, Taylor, letterer. | Chandler, Raymond, 1888–1959. Trouble is my business.
Title: Raymond Chandler's Trouble is my business / Arvind Ethan David, Ilias Kyriazis, Cris Peter ;
lettering by Taylor Esposito.
Other titles: Trouble is my business
Description: New York : Pantheon Books, 2025.
Identifiers: LCCN 2024031628 (print) | LCCN 2024031629 (ebook) | ISBN 9780553387599 (hardcover) |
ISBN 9780553387605 (ebook)
Subjects: LCSH: Marlowe, Philip (Fictitious character)—Comic books, strips, etc. | Private investigators—California—
Los Angeles—Comic books, strips, etc. | Los Angeles (Calif.)—History—20th century—Comic books, strips, etc. |
LCGFT: Detective and mystery comics. | Noir comics. | Graphic novel adaptations. | Graphic novels.
Classification: LCC PN6727.D325 R39 2025 (print) | LCC PN6727.D325 (ebook) |
DDC 741.5/973—dc23/eng/20240719
LC record available at https://lccn.loc.gov/2024031628
LC ebook record available at https://lccn.loc.gov/2024031629

www.pantheonbooks.com

Jacket illustration by Ilias Kyriazis and Cris Peter
Jacket design by Madeline Partner
Book design by John Kuramoto
Written by Arvind Ethan David
Pencils and ink by Ilias Kyriazis
Colors by Cris Peter
Letters by Taylor Esposito for Ghost Glyph Studios
Produced by Brittany Chapman-Holman

Printed in China
First Edition

9 8 7 6 5 4 3 2 1

This book is dedicated to Arthur Herman Gilkes (1849–1922), Master of Dulwich College, and to Margaret Ann Kaloo (1945–2022), founder and Principal of elc International School.

Gilkes influenced many students in his leadership of Dulwich College. He was known particularly for his empathetic teaching of Latin and Greek, his passion for perfectly constructed sentences, and his unexpected use of simile and metaphor.

Two of his pupils took these lessons especially to heart. Their names were P. G. Wodehouse and Raymond Chandler. Dulwich's two libraries are named for them, and Gilkes's legacy is secure in every line they wrote.

Born nearly a hundred years after Gilkes, Margaret Kaloo, a Scottish educationalist and force of nature, settled in Malaysia and founded what has become its preeminent private school. Thousands of pupils have benefited from her determination to unlock their full potential.

One of those students was me.

By coincidence, three of Margaret's grandsons attended Dulwich College, where they spent a lot of time in the Wodehouse and Chandler libraries.

Teachers matter.

—Arvind Ethan David
August 2024

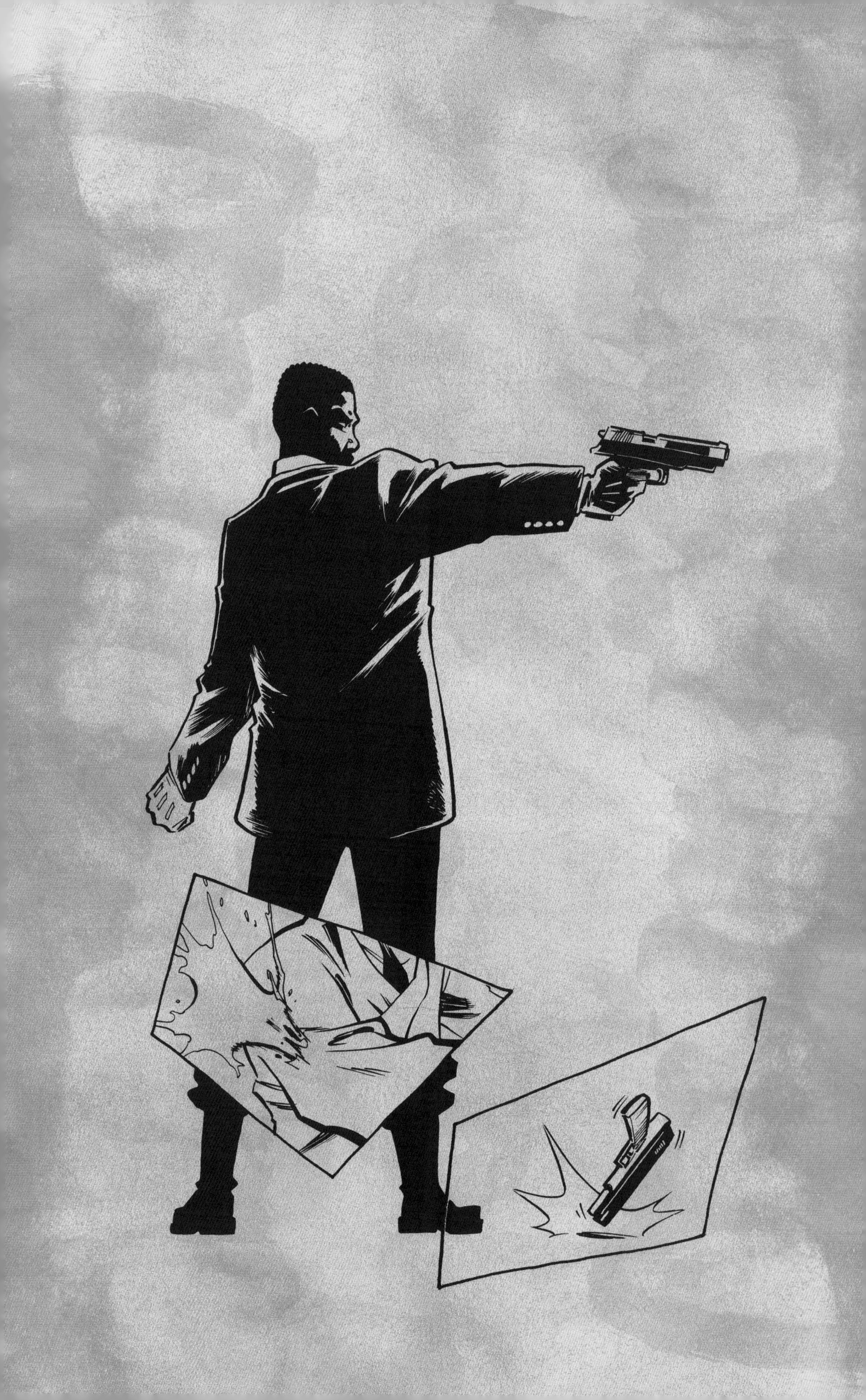

FOREWORD

Trouble Is My Business, in its original form, begins with a classic piece of Raymond Chandler business: a cool, cynical, and viciously colorful bit of description, in this case of the female sleuth trying to pawn off a case onto Philip Marlowe. "Anna Halsey was about two hundred and forty pounds of middle-aged, putty-faced woman in a black tailor-made suit. Her eyes were shiny black shoe buttons, her cheeks were as soft as suet and about the same color."

The illustrated version you hold in your hands, in one of several artful deviations from the original structure, starts instead with a prelude. We meet Chandler's femme fatale, the sultry and conniving Miss Harriet Huntress—*God, that name!*—as the little girl she once was, confronted with the horror of her father's suicide. The creators of the graphic novel start with a literary gambit, relieving Marlowe of his primacy and launching the story with the origin of one of the antagonists.

This maneuver is the first clue to the question I want to pose, by way of starting this foreword:

Why? Why adapt this particular story into a graphic novel?

Sorry, mugs—trick question.

Because there doesn't have to be a reason. There needn't be a "reason" to transform *Trouble Is My Business* from prose classic to comic book, any more than a reason was needed to transform *The Great Gatsby* into a Broadway musical or *The War of the Worlds* into a radio serial or *Peter Pan* into a stage play, or *Murder on the Orient Express* into a few different movies, to name several of several million examples.

I am aware of those who plant hands on hips and huff about this sort of thing whenever their favorite book is turned into a show, say, or a graphic novel.

Well, what's the point of that? (cry the huffers) *It doesn't add anything!*

Or even—and this is really rich—*You're ruining the original.*

It should go without saying that it is impossible to retroactively ruin a piece of art, especially a great work of art. If your love for your favorite book is so brittle that the mere existence of some subsequent artist's take will crumble it, well . . . remind me not to fall in love with you.

As to that other quibble, that the adaptation doesn't *add* anything, I would argue that the adaptation necessarily adds something—it adds itself. By its mere existence, a new imagining of an older work serves to remind us of the value of the original. Whatever the underlying ideas or themes are of that first work, it reconstitutes them in a new period, a new aesthetic environment, and through the transmogrifying lens of new artistic ideas. At the very least, even a bad adaptation does the good work of reminding us what is striking or powerful about the original.

Patricia Highsmith's *The Talented Mr. Ripley* has now been made for the screen three times that I know of, two films and one TV show, and though I have things I loved and hated about all of these versions they could make a new iteration every year and I would watch every one of them. Why? Because I am a lifelong fan of *Ripley,* I find the original profoundly interesting, and anything that is added to the penumbra of work emanating out from it will be of interest to me.

(Side note: speaking of adaptation and of Highsmith, it was Chandler who wrote the first draft of the film version of *Strangers on a Train* . . . a draft Hitchcock supposedly hated so much he dropped it in the garbage can in Chandler's presence. Showbiz!)

Trouble Is My Business, and really the whole Chandler noir universe, occupies the same elite level as Highsmith and *Ripley.* There is no adaptation, no version, no reimagining, that I won't at least be curious about. Thinking about Chandler, reimagining him, presenting him anew, will always be of interest, whether the results are good, bad, or indifferent.

In this case, the results are very, very good, and I think I know why.

Between the one-syllable humors of the comic strip and the anemic subtleties of the litterateurs there is a wide stretch of country, in which the mystery story may or may not be an important landmark.

That's Chandler himself in the introduction to a 1950 collection of his earlier stories, a collection titled and including *Trouble Is My Business*. In a characteristically sardonic and self-deprecating way, Chandler makes a case for the place of American detective fiction—what he calls "The *Black Mask* type of story," after the magazine—in the canon of what snobs call real literature.

Despite its humble origins, despite its rank commercial appeal, Chandler says, this is not just throwaway stuff. He dares the reader of 1950 to "look beyond the unnecessarily gaudy covers, trashy titles, and barely acceptable advertisements and recognize the authentic power" of these works.

And then, careful not to toot his own horn *too* loudly, Chandler offers a theory as to where that authentic power came from. Earlier forms of detective writing were "more or less passagework." In other words, the whole point of these things was to get to the end. "The denouement would justify everything." Whereas in this new kind of story, in the rain-swept alleys and gin joints where Chandler and his cohort were fashioning their new form, "the scene outranked the plot."

That's the source of that *authentic power*. Too many mysteries of that period (and, I'm sorry to report, too many now) were primarily or entirely concerned with the ending. They were ten-page-long crossword puzzles, where the point was to construct a clever series of clues which pointed to a clever solution. They weren't stories, they were questions, and all that mattered were answers, primarily to the question of, you know—*who did it?*

But Chandler understood what most of us know now: if the point of a story is just "who did it?" then the answer is going to be "who cares?"

It's not that he didn't care about crafting a complex and rewarding plot. To the contrary, he was excellent at it, as you'll soon experience as you follow Marlowe through *Trouble Is My Business*. It's just that the *plot*, to him, became secondary to the *style*. Every scene, every moment, should be crafted not just to plant a clue or advance the story, but for its own sake—what *feeling* was it trying to achieve?

This started with the nature of the hero, of course. The PI Philip Marlowe is a style unto himself. A brooding, articulate, alcoholic style, one that we so take for granted by now we forget how bracingly original Marlowe was when he strode onto the scene. Chandler's primary interest, in writing the man, was never in the things that Marlowe *discovered*, but in Marlowe *himself*. What did it feel like to be a man like that, to see the world as he did, this hard, dark, angry, drunk, inquiring, clever, hard-hitting, melancholy man?

What gave Chandler's writing its punch, what made it more than passagework, were not the twists and turns of the stories but his darkly hued, infinitely descriptive way of seeing the world: Ms. Huntress's eyes are "lapis-lazuli blue and the color of her hair was dusky red, like a fire under control but still dangerous."

Chandler, in other words, was writing for *color*.

And *color* is what Arvind Ethan David, Ilias Kyriazis, and Cris Peter have given us in their new imagining of the story. Some of the same colors; some new ones.

And I don't just mean that literally, although Peter's colors are satisfyingly moody, an interplay of darknesses reflecting the shadowy hearts of the players, with pops of yellow for oncoming headlights or booze bottles poking from gangsters' coats or the occasional curl of smoke.

But also the kind of color we get from that two-page prelude, set fifteen years in the past—or another narrative side road, a few pages later, that dips in and out of the heart of the quiet African American driver George Hasterman. These creators adeptly use the tools of their medium to find shadings, underlayers that Chandler didn't include; not because he didn't want to, or because he didn't think of it, but because that's not what he was up to. Marlowe was a first-person character, the idiomatic private "I," and so the colors that Chandler gave us were the colors that Marlowe could see.

But now, here, in this new form of *Trouble,* the authors allow us to see into new places, new corners of the house that Chandler built. They let us see around corners and into the past and (in a lovely final narrative intimation) into the future.

In that same introduction I mentioned above, Chandler self-deprecatingly dismisses the notion that his work would have the staying power of great novels he admired. "A classic is a piece of writing which exhausts the possibilities of its form and can hardly be surpassed," he says. "No story or novel of mystery has done that."

Here, Mr. Chandler, I must demur.

I would argue that even as this new version of *Trouble* would seem to take it a step backward, toward those "one-syllable humors of the comic strip," it actually adds to the case for Chandler's original as a literary classic: not a mere plot, but a trove of richly interesting characters whose violent intersections are not merely interesting, but emotionally satisfying and instructive.

There is no adaptation that doesn't add something. This one adds a lot.

—Ben H. Winters
Los Angeles

Ben H. Winters is the *New York Times* bestselling author of *Big Time*, *The Quiet Boy*, *Underground Airlines*, *Golden State*, and the Last Policeman trilogy. His books have won the Edgar Award, the Philip K. Dick Award, the Sidewise Award, and France's Grand Prix de l'Imaginaire. Ben also writes for television. He lives in Los Angeles with his family.

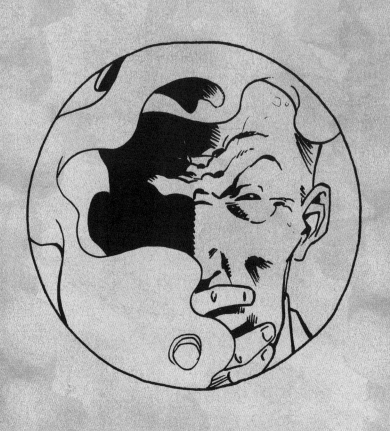

RAYMOND CHANDLER'S
TROUBLE IS
MY BUSINESS

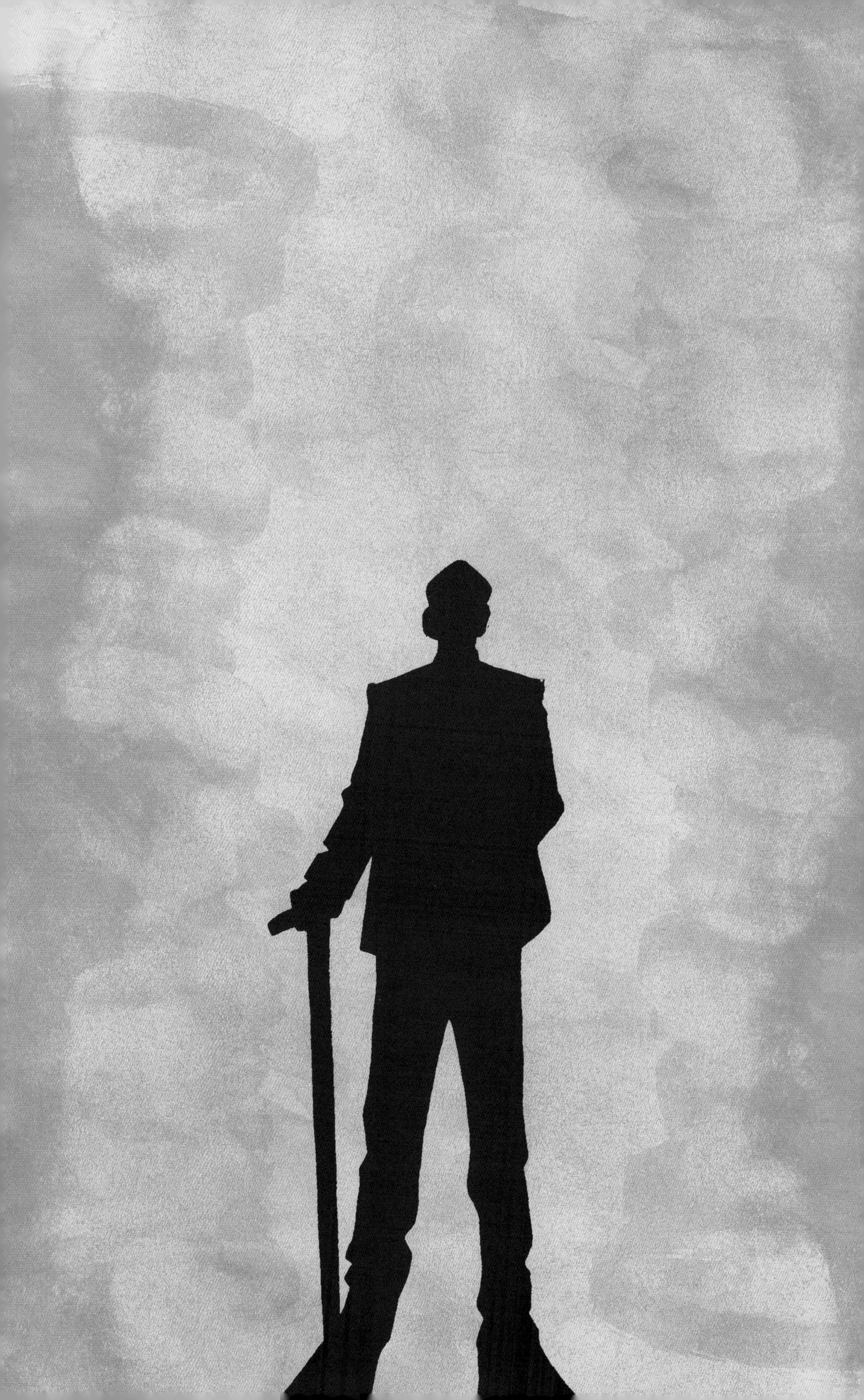

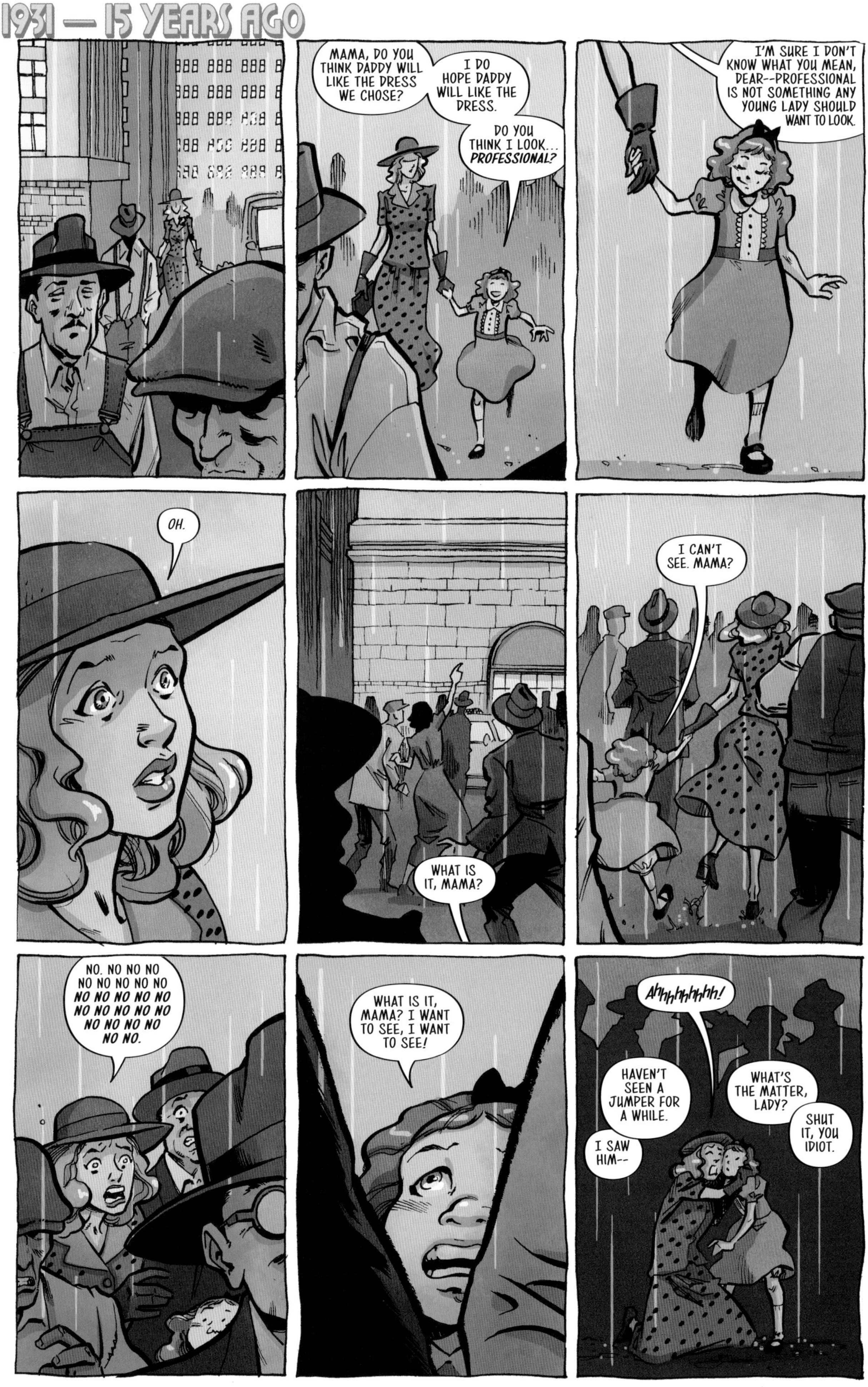
1931 — 15 YEARS AGO
MAMA, DO YOU THINK DADDY WILL LIKE THE DRESS WE CHOSE?
I DO HOPE DADDY WILL LIKE THE DRESS.
DO YOU THINK I LOOK... PROFESSIONAL?
I'M SURE I DON'T KNOW WHAT YOU MEAN, DEAR--PROFESSIONAL IS NOT SOMETHING ANY YOUNG LADY SHOULD WANT TO LOOK.
OH.
WHAT IS IT, MAMA?
I CAN'T SEE. MAMA?
NO. NO NO NO NO NO NO NO NO NO NO NO NO NO NO NO NO NO NO NO NO NO NO NO NO NO NO.
WHAT IS IT, MAMA? I WANT TO SEE, I WANT TO SEE!
Ahhhhhhhh!
HAVEN'T SEEN A JUMPER FOR A WHILE.
I SAW HIM--
WHAT'S THE MATTER, LADY?
SHUT IT, YOU IDIOT.

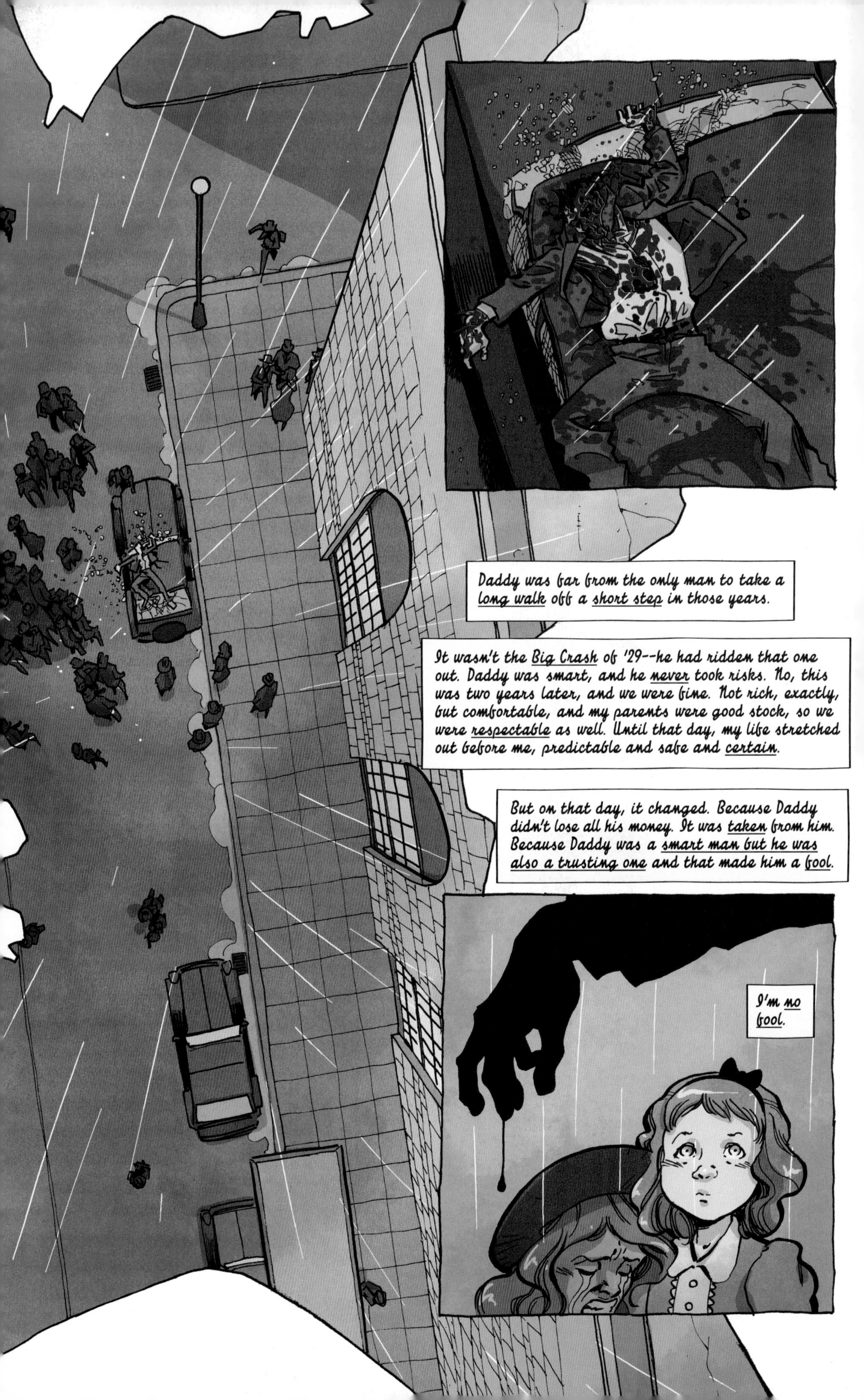
Daddy was far from the only man to take a long walk off a short step in those years.
It wasn't the Big Crash of '29--he had ridden that one out. Daddy was smart, and he never took risks. No, this was two years later, and we were fine. Not rich, exactly, but comfortable, and my parents were good stock, so we were respectable as well. Until that day, my life stretched out before me, predictable and safe and certain.
But on that day, it changed. Because Daddy didn't lose all his money. It was taken from him. Because Daddy was a smart man but he was also a trusting one and that made him a fool.
I'm no fool.

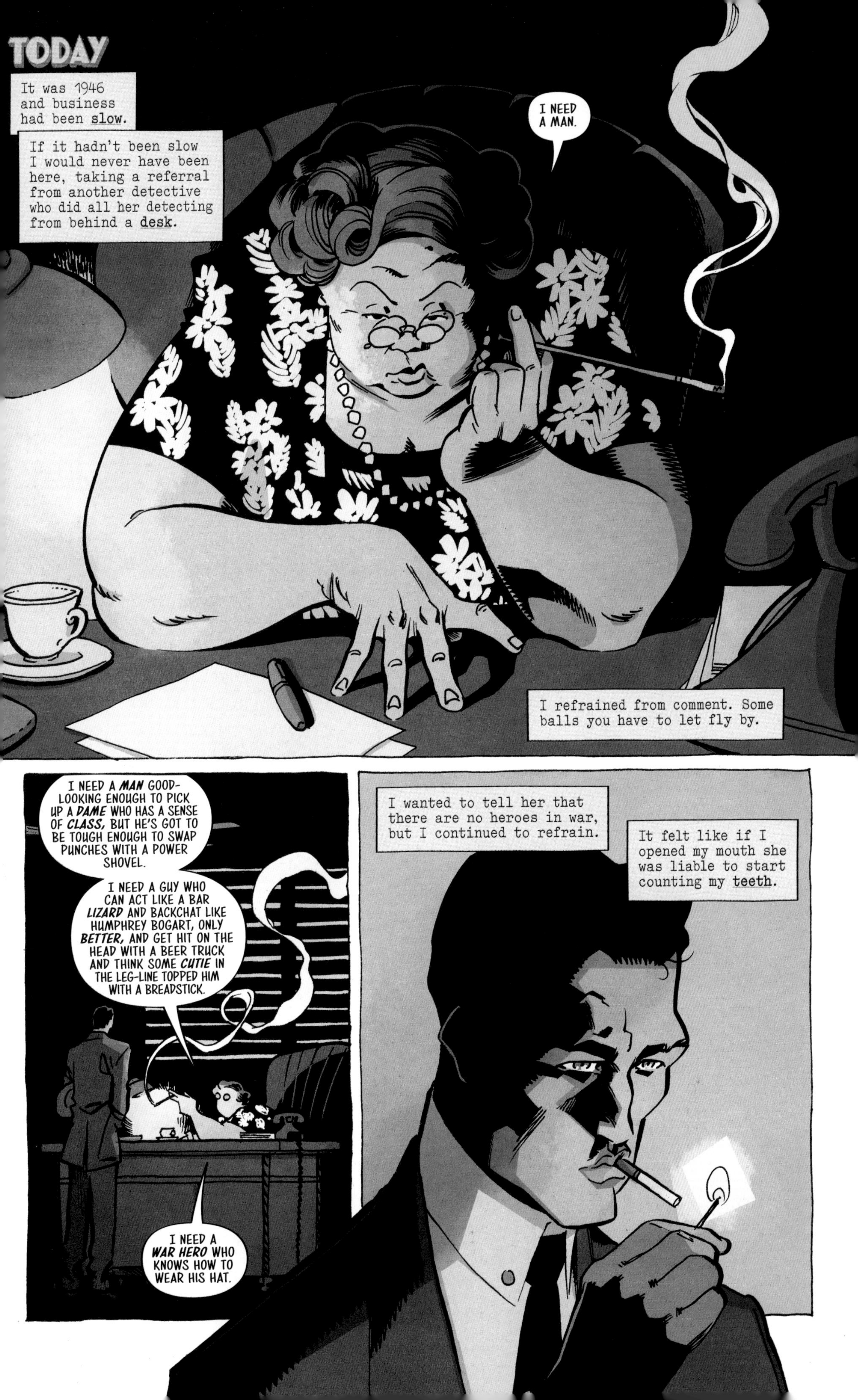
TODAY
It was 1946 and business had been slow.
If it hadn't been slow I would never have been here, taking a referral from another detective who did all her detecting from behind a desk.
I NEED A MAN.
I refrained from comment. Some balls you have to let fly by.
I NEED A MAN GOOD-LOOKING ENOUGH TO PICK UP A DAME WHO HAS A SENSE OF CLASS, BUT HE'S GOT TO BE TOUGH ENOUGH TO SWAP PUNCHES WITH A POWER SHOVEL.
I NEED A GUY WHO CAN ACT LIKE A BAR LIZARD AND BACKCHAT LIKE HUMPHREY BOGART, ONLY BETTER, AND GET HIT ON THE HEAD WITH A BEER TRUCK AND THINK SOME CUTIE IN THE LEG-LINE TOPPED HIM WITH A BREADSTICK.
I NEED A WAR HERO WHO KNOWS HOW TO WEAR HIS HAT.
I wanted to tell her that there are no heroes in war, but I continued to refrain.
It felt like if I opened my mouth she was liable to start counting my teeth.

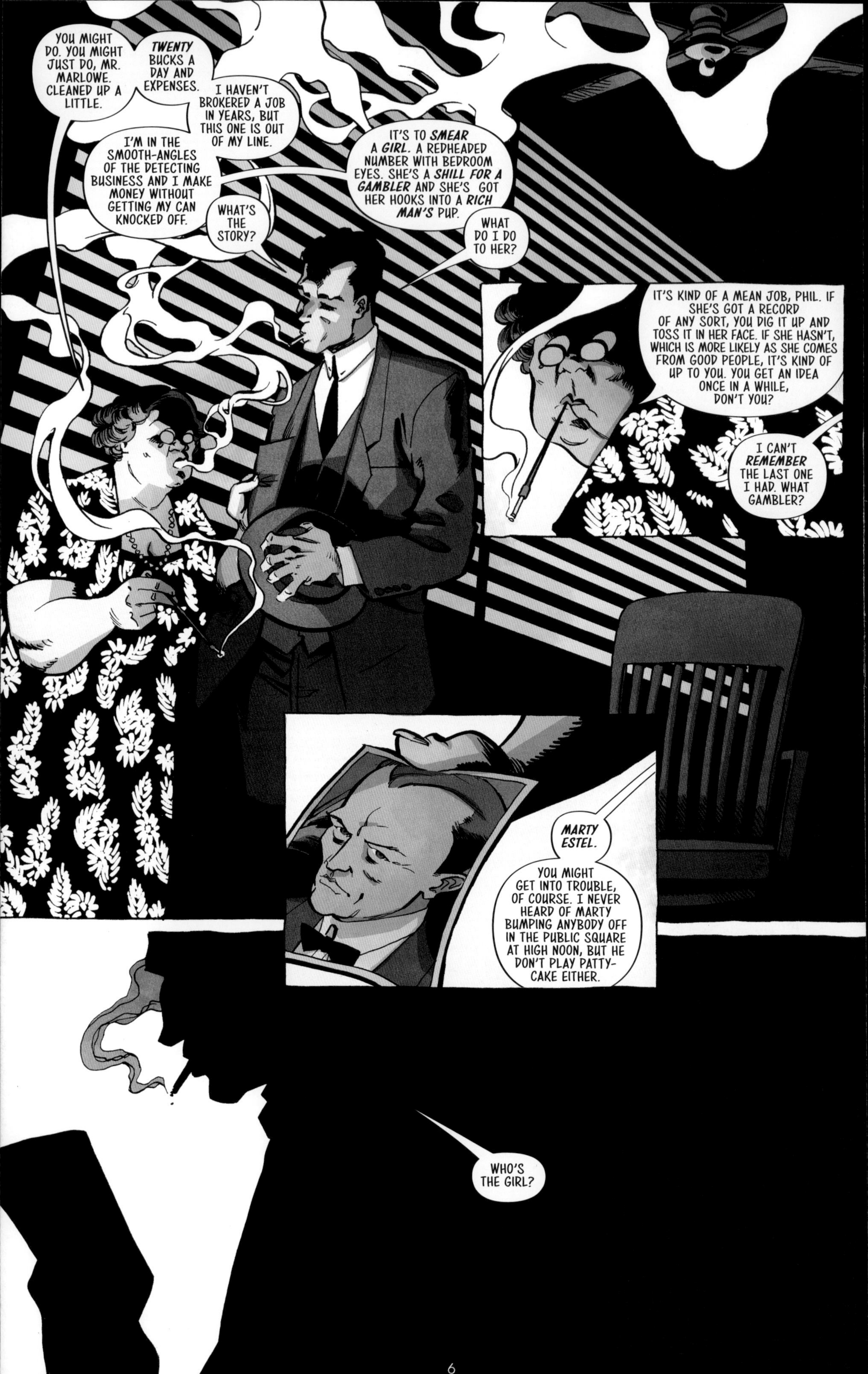

YOU MIGHT DO. YOU MIGHT JUST DO, MR. MARLOWE. CLEANED UP A LITTLE.
TWENTY BUCKS A DAY AND EXPENSES.
I HAVEN'T BROKERED A JOB IN YEARS, BUT THIS ONE IS OUT OF MY LINE.
I'M IN THE SMOOTH-ANGLES OF THE DETECTING BUSINESS AND I MAKE MONEY WITHOUT GETTING MY CAN KNOCKED OFF.
WHAT'S THE STORY?
IT'S TO SMEAR A GIRL. A REDHEADED NUMBER WITH BEDROOM EYES. SHE'S A SHILL FOR A GAMBLER AND SHE'S GOT HER HOOKS INTO A RICH MAN'S PUP.
WHAT DO I DO TO HER?
IT'S KIND OF A MEAN JOB, PHIL. IF SHE'S GOT A RECORD OF ANY SORT, YOU DIG IT UP AND TOSS IT IN HER FACE. IF SHE HASN'T, WHICH IS MORE LIKELY AS SHE COMES FROM GOOD PEOPLE, IT'S KIND OF UP TO YOU. YOU GET AN IDEA ONCE IN A WHILE, DON'T YOU?
I CAN'T REMEMBER THE LAST ONE I HAD. WHAT GAMBLER?
MARTY ESTEL.
YOU MIGHT GET INTO TROUBLE, OF COURSE. I NEVER HEARD OF MARTY BUMPING ANYBODY OFF IN THE PUBLIC SQUARE AT HIGH NOON, BUT HE DON'T PLAY PATTY-CAKE EITHER.
WHO'S THE GIRL?

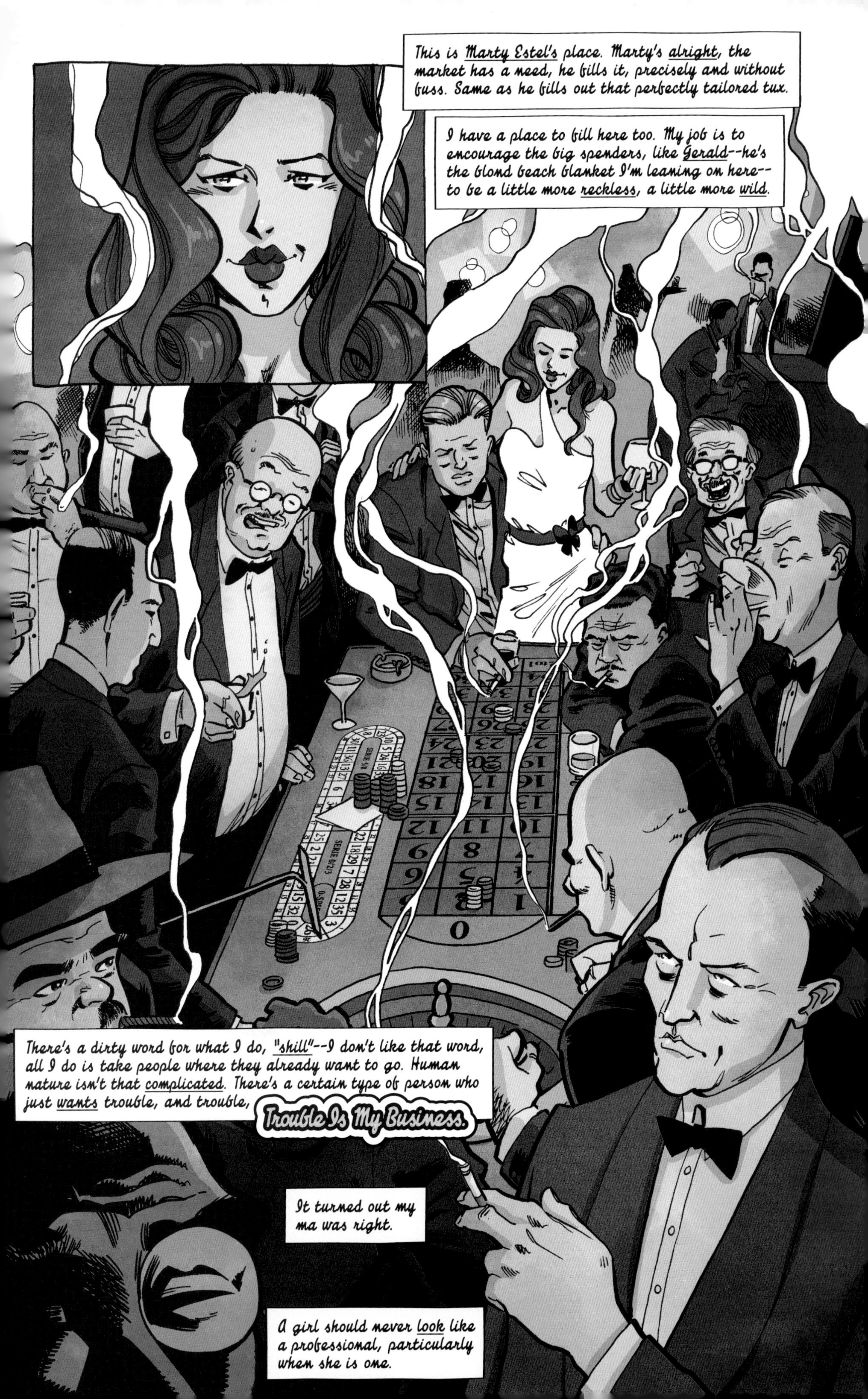
This is Marty Estel's place. Marty's alright, the market has a need, he fills it, precisely and without fuss. Same as he fills out that perfectly tailored tux.
I have a place to fill here too. My job is to encourage the big spenders, like Gerald--he's the blond beach blanket I'm leaning on here--to be a little more reckless, a little more wild.
There's a dirty word for what I do, "shill"--I don't like that word, all I do is take people where they already want to go. Human nature isn't that complicated. There's a certain type of person who just wants trouble, and trouble,
Trouble Is My Business.
It turned out my ma was right.
A girl should never look like a professional, particularly when she is one.

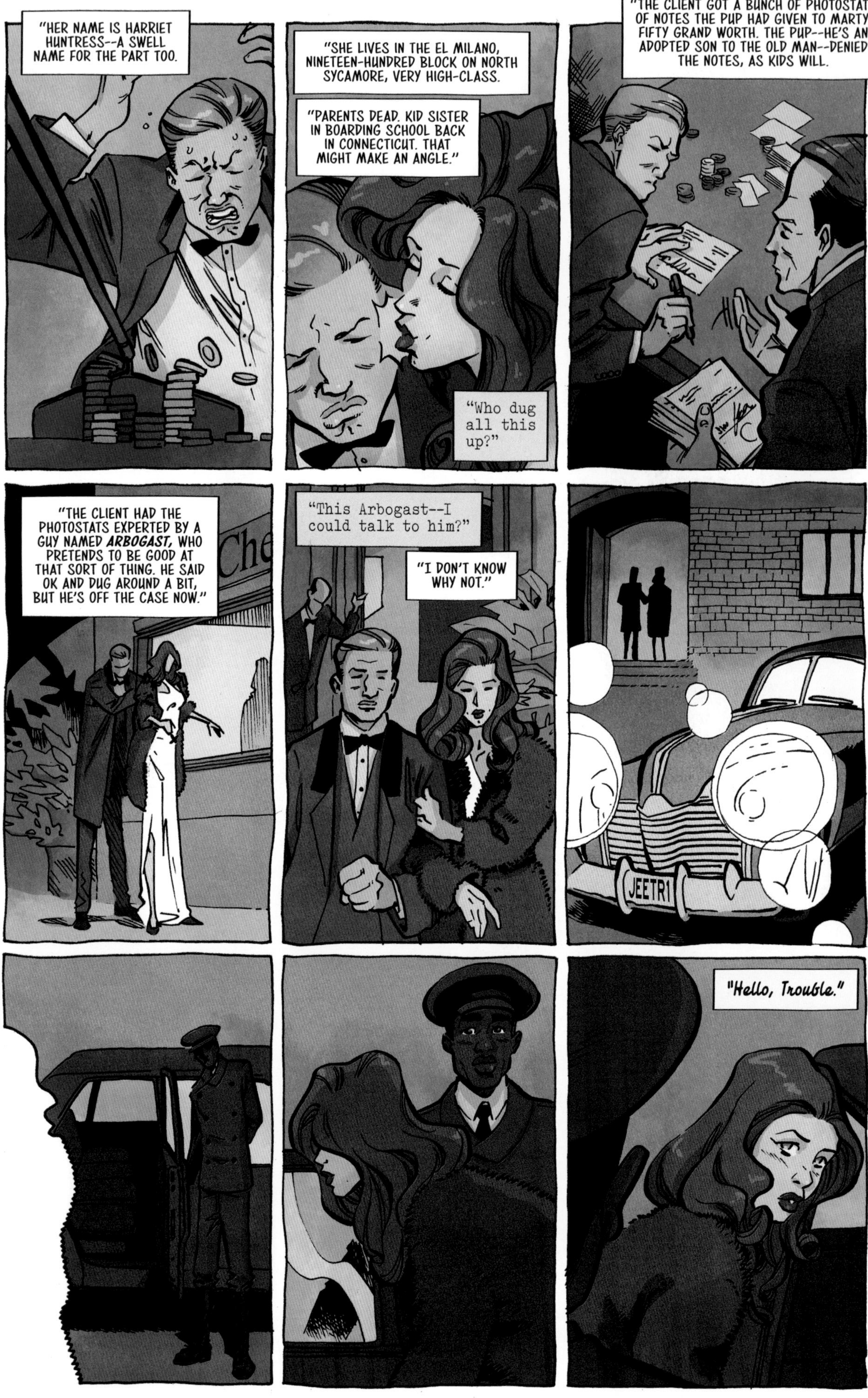
"HER NAME IS HARRIET HUNTRESS--A SWELL NAME FOR THE PART TOO.
"SHE LIVES IN THE EL MILANO, NINETEEN-HUNDRED BLOCK ON NORTH SYCAMORE, VERY HIGH-CLASS.
"PARENTS DEAD. KID SISTER IN BOARDING SCHOOL BACK IN CONNECTICUT. THAT MIGHT MAKE AN ANGLE."
"Who dug all this up?"
"THE CLIENT GOT A BUNCH OF PHOTOSTATS OF NOTES THE PUP HAD GIVEN TO MARTY. FIFTY GRAND WORTH. THE PUP--HE'S AN ADOPTED SON TO THE OLD MAN--DENIED THE NOTES, AS KIDS WILL.
"THE CLIENT HAD THE PHOTOSTATS EXPERTED BY A GUY NAMED ARBOGAST, WHO PRETENDS TO BE GOOD AT THAT SORT OF THING. HE SAID OK AND DUG AROUND A BIT, BUT HE'S OFF THE CASE NOW."
"This Arbogast--I could talk to him?"
"I DON'T KNOW WHY NOT."
JEETR1
"Hello, Trouble."

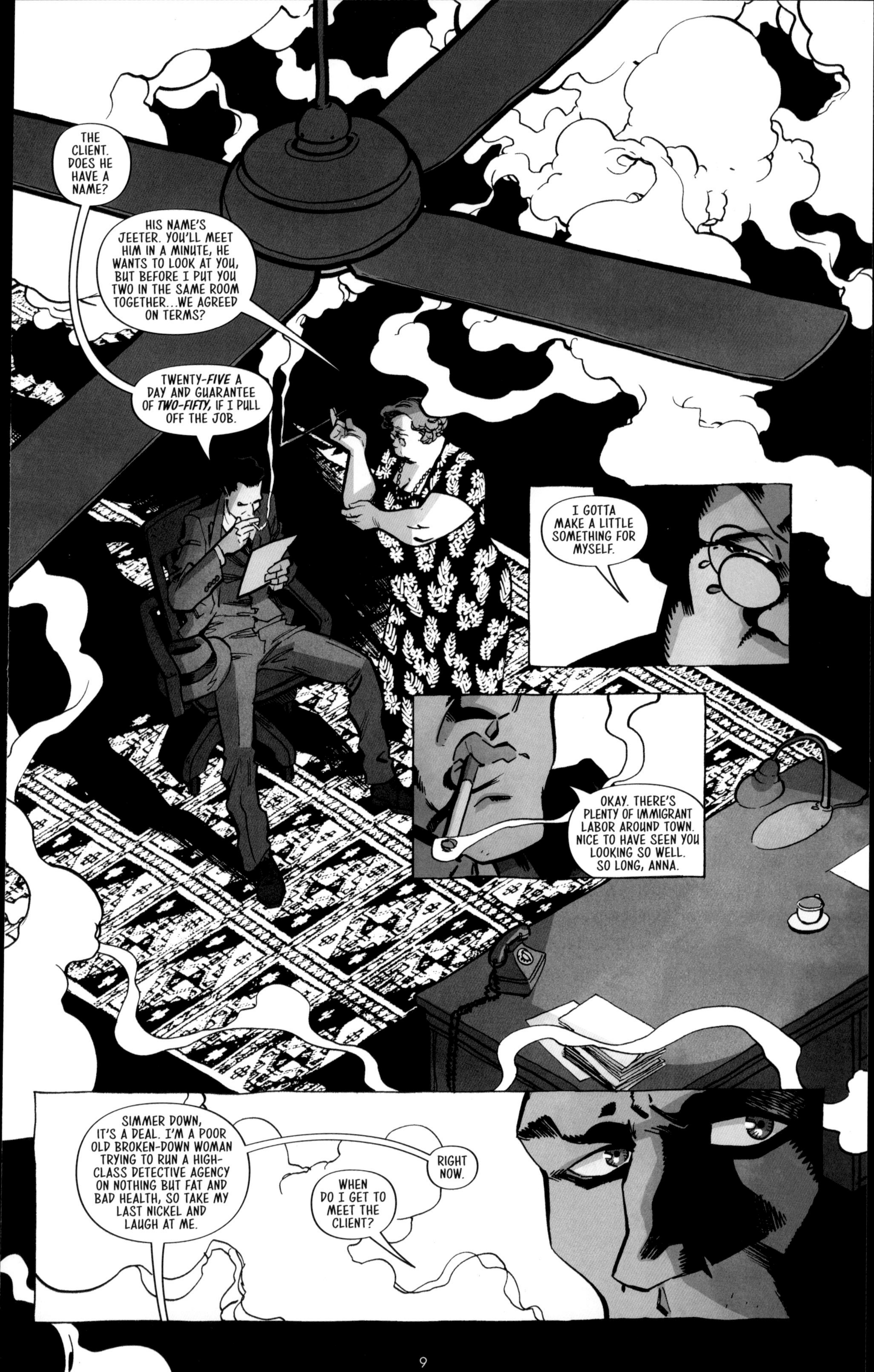
THE CLIENT. DOES HE HAVE A NAME?
HIS NAME'S JEETER. YOU'LL MEET HIM IN A MINUTE, HE WANTS TO LOOK AT YOU, BUT BEFORE I PUT YOU TWO IN THE SAME ROOM TOGETHER...WE AGREED ON TERMS?
TWENTY-FIVE A DAY AND GUARANTEE OF TWO-FIFTY, IF I PULL OFF THE JOB.
I GOTTA MAKE A LITTLE SOMETHING FOR MYSELF.
OKAY. THERE'S PLENTY OF IMMIGRANT LABOR AROUND TOWN. NICE TO HAVE SEEN YOU LOOKING SO WELL. SO LONG, ANNA.
SIMMER DOWN, IT'S A DEAL. I'M A POOR OLD BROKEN-DOWN WOMAN TRYING TO RUN A HIGH-CLASS DETECTIVE AGENCY ON NOTHING BUT FAT AND BAD HEALTH, SO TAKE MY LAST NICKEL AND LAUGH AT ME.
WHEN DO I GET TO MEET THE CLIENT?
RIGHT NOW.

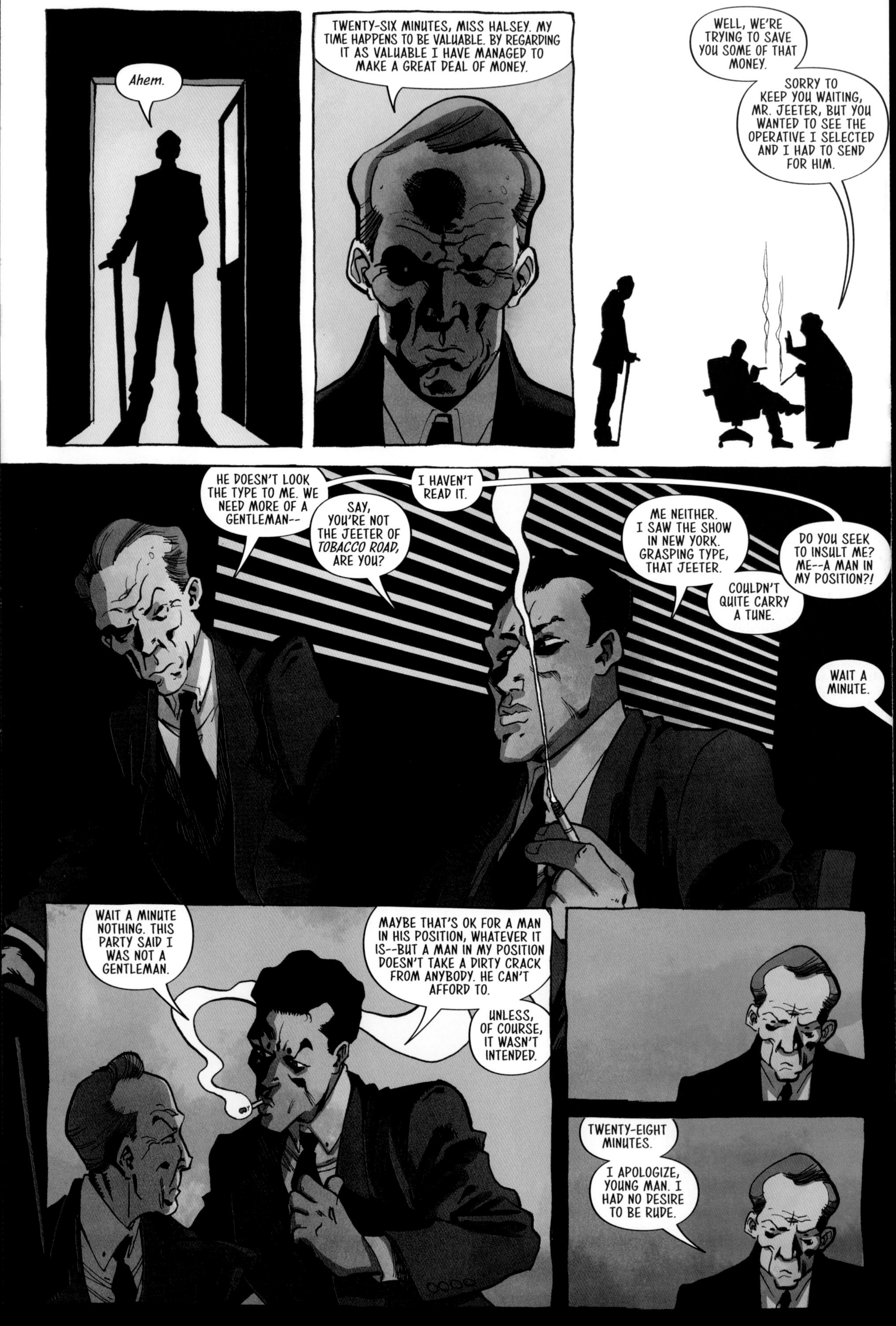
Ahem.
TWENTY-SIX MINUTES, MISS HALSEY. MY TIME HAPPENS TO BE VALUABLE. BY REGARDING IT AS VALUABLE I HAVE MANAGED TO MAKE A GREAT DEAL OF MONEY.
WELL, WE'RE TRYING TO SAVE YOU SOME OF THAT MONEY.
SORRY TO KEEP YOU WAITING, MR. JEETER, BUT YOU WANTED TO SEE THE OPERATIVE I SELECTED AND I HAD TO SEND FOR HIM.
HE DOESN'T LOOK THE TYPE TO ME. WE NEED MORE OF A GENTLEMAN--
SAY, YOU'RE NOT THE JEETER OF *TOBACCO ROAD,* ARE YOU?
I HAVEN'T READ IT.
ME NEITHER. I SAW THE SHOW IN NEW YORK. GRASPING TYPE, THAT JEETER.
COULDN'T QUITE CARRY A TUNE.
DO YOU SEEK TO INSULT ME? ME--A MAN IN MY POSITION?!
WAIT A MINUTE.
WAIT A MINUTE NOTHING. THIS PARTY SAID I WAS NOT A GENTLEMAN.
MAYBE THAT'S OK FOR A MAN IN HIS POSITION, WHATEVER IT IS--BUT A MAN IN MY POSITION DOESN'T TAKE A DIRTY CRACK FROM ANYBODY. HE CAN'T AFFORD TO.
UNLESS, OF COURSE, IT WASN'T INTENDED.
TWENTY-EIGHT MINUTES.
I APOLOGIZE, YOUNG MAN. I HAD NO DESIRE TO BE RUDE.

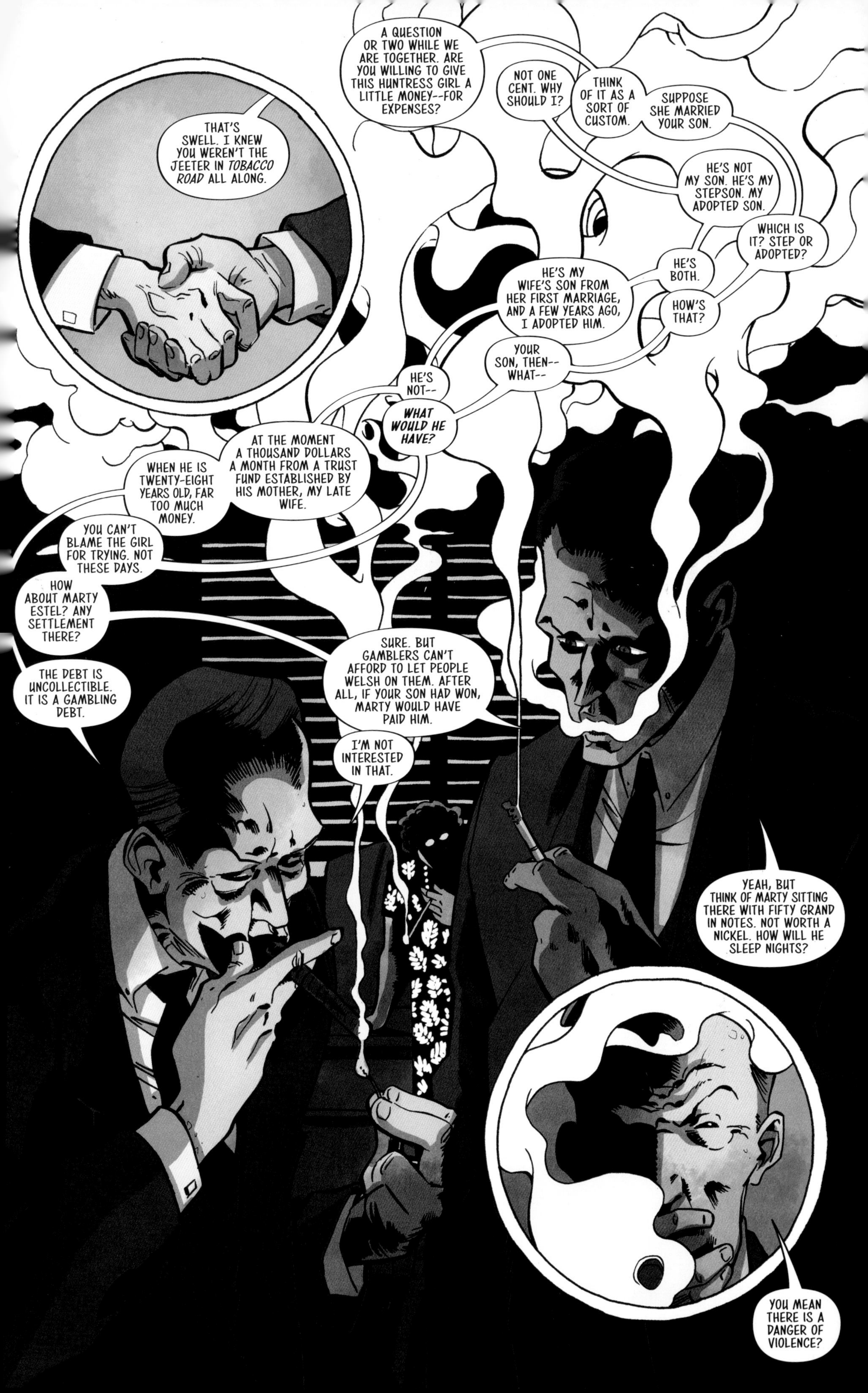
THAT'S SWELL. I KNEW YOU WEREN'T THE JEETER IN *TOBACCO ROAD* ALL ALONG.
A QUESTION OR TWO WHILE WE ARE TOGETHER. ARE YOU WILLING TO GIVE THIS HUNTRESS GIRL A LITTLE MONEY--FOR EXPENSES?
NOT ONE CENT. WHY SHOULD I?
THINK OF IT AS A SORT OF CUSTOM.
SUPPOSE SHE MARRIED YOUR SON.
HE'S NOT MY SON. HE'S MY STEPSON. MY ADOPTED SON.
WHICH IS IT? STEP OR ADOPTED?
HE'S BOTH.
HOW'S THAT?
HE'S MY WIFE'S SON FROM HER FIRST MARRIAGE, AND A FEW YEARS AGO, I ADOPTED HIM.
YOUR SON, THEN--WHAT--
HE'S NOT--
WHAT WOULD HE HAVE?
AT THE MOMENT A THOUSAND DOLLARS A MONTH FROM A TRUST FUND ESTABLISHED BY HIS MOTHER, MY LATE WIFE.
WHEN HE IS TWENTY-EIGHT YEARS OLD, FAR TOO MUCH MONEY.
YOU CAN'T BLAME THE GIRL FOR TRYING. NOT THESE DAYS.
HOW ABOUT MARTY ESTEL? ANY SETTLEMENT THERE?
THE DEBT IS UNCOLLECTIBLE. IT IS A GAMBLING DEBT.
SURE. BUT GAMBLERS CAN'T AFFORD TO LET PEOPLE WELSH ON THEM. AFTER ALL, IF YOUR SON HAD WON, MARTY WOULD HAVE PAID HIM.
I'M NOT INTERESTED IN THAT.
YEAH, BUT THINK OF MARTY SITTING THERE WITH FIFTY GRAND IN NOTES. NOT WORTH A NICKEL. HOW WILL HE SLEEP NIGHTS?
YOU MEAN THERE IS A DANGER OF VIOLENCE?

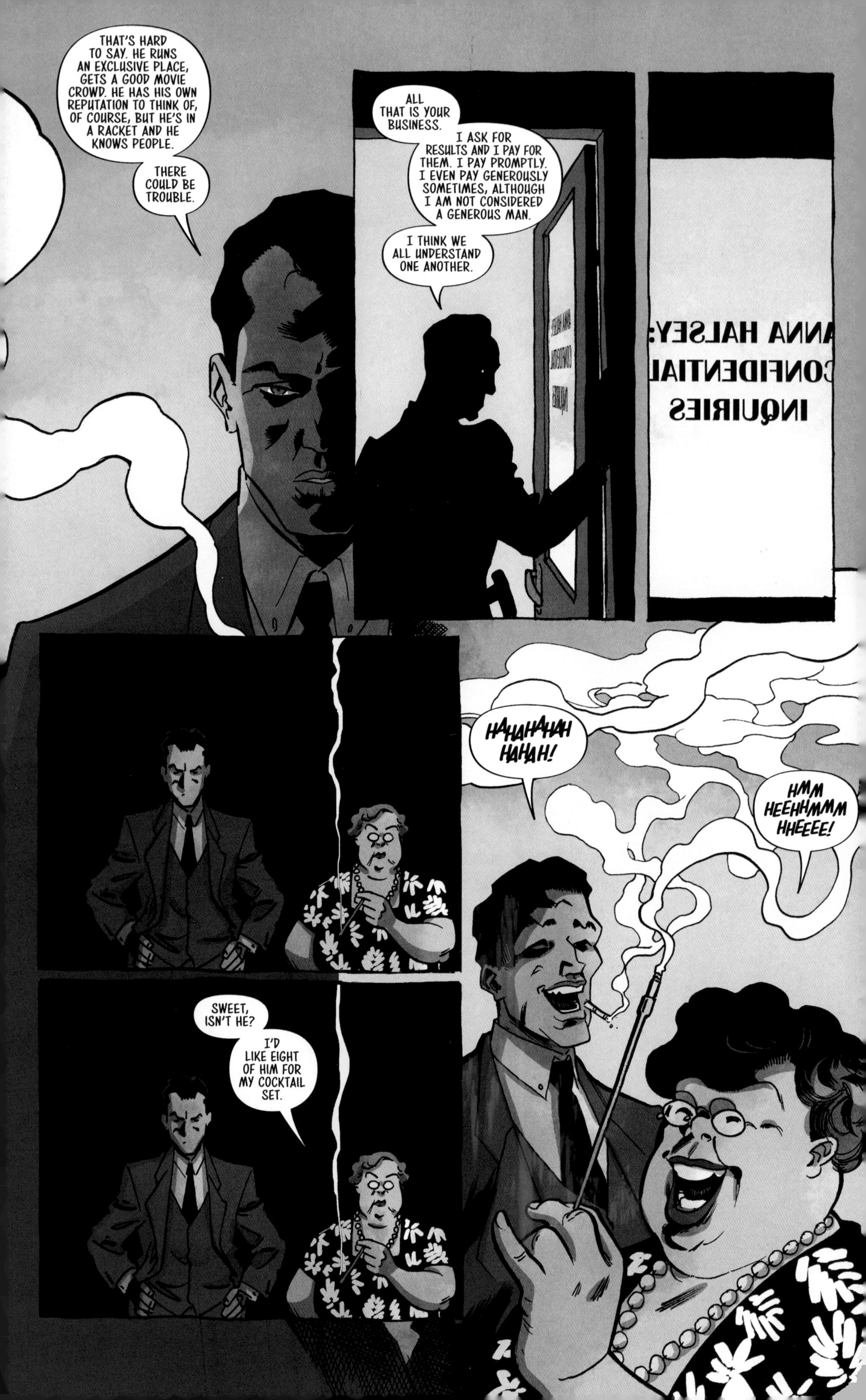
THAT'S HARD TO SAY. HE RUNS AN EXCLUSIVE PLACE, GETS A GOOD MOVIE CROWD. HE HAS HIS OWN REPUTATION TO THINK OF, OF COURSE, BUT HE'S IN A RACKET AND HE KNOWS PEOPLE.
THERE COULD BE TROUBLE.
ALL THAT IS YOUR BUSINESS.
I ASK FOR RESULTS AND I PAY FOR THEM. I PAY PROMPTLY. I EVEN PAY GENEROUSLY SOMETIMES, ALTHOUGH I AM NOT CONSIDERED A GENEROUS MAN.
I THINK WE ALL UNDERSTAND ONE ANOTHER.
ANNA HALSEY: CONFIDENTIAL INQUIRIES
SWEET, ISN'T HE?
I'D LIKE EIGHT OF HIM FOR MY COCKTAIL SET.
HAHAHAHAH HAHAH!
HMM HEEHHMMM HHEEEE!

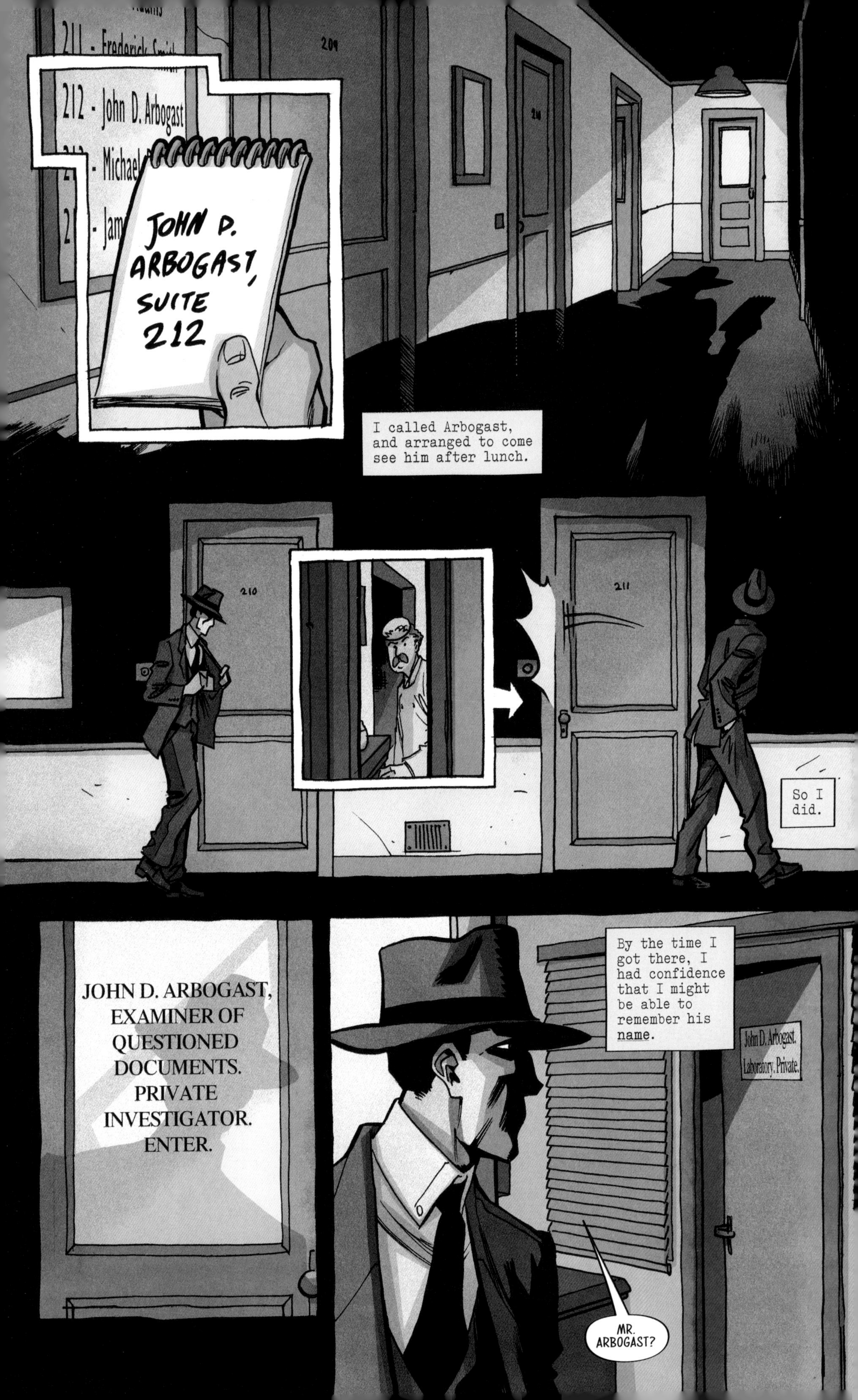

211 - Frederick Smith
212 - John D. Arbogast
Michael
JOHN D. ARBOGAST, SUITE 212
I called Arbogast, and arranged to come see him after lunch.
210
211
So I did.
JOHN D. ARBOGAST, EXAMINER OF QUESTIONED DOCUMENTS. PRIVATE INVESTIGATOR. ENTER.
By the time I got there, I had confidence that I might be able to remember his name.
John D. Arbogast. Laboratory. Private.
MR. ARBOGAST?

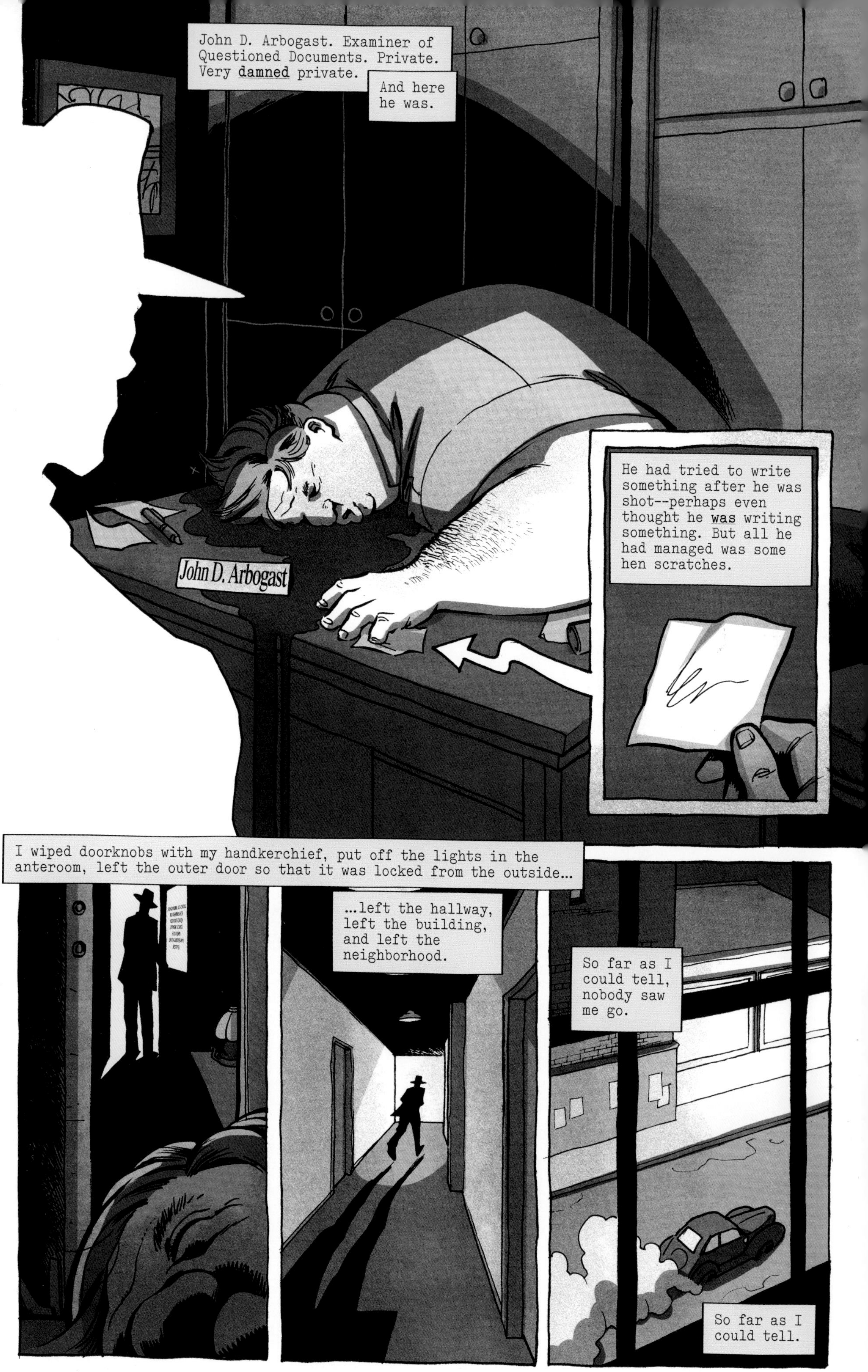
John D. Arbogast. Examiner of Questioned Documents. Private. Very damned private.
And here he was.
John D. Arbogast
He had tried to write something after he was shot--perhaps even thought he was writing something. But all he had managed was some hen scratches.
I wiped doorknobs with my handkerchief, put off the lights in the anteroom, left the outer door so that it was locked from the outside...
...left the hallway, left the building, and left the neighborhood.
So far as I could tell, nobody saw me go.
So far as I could tell.

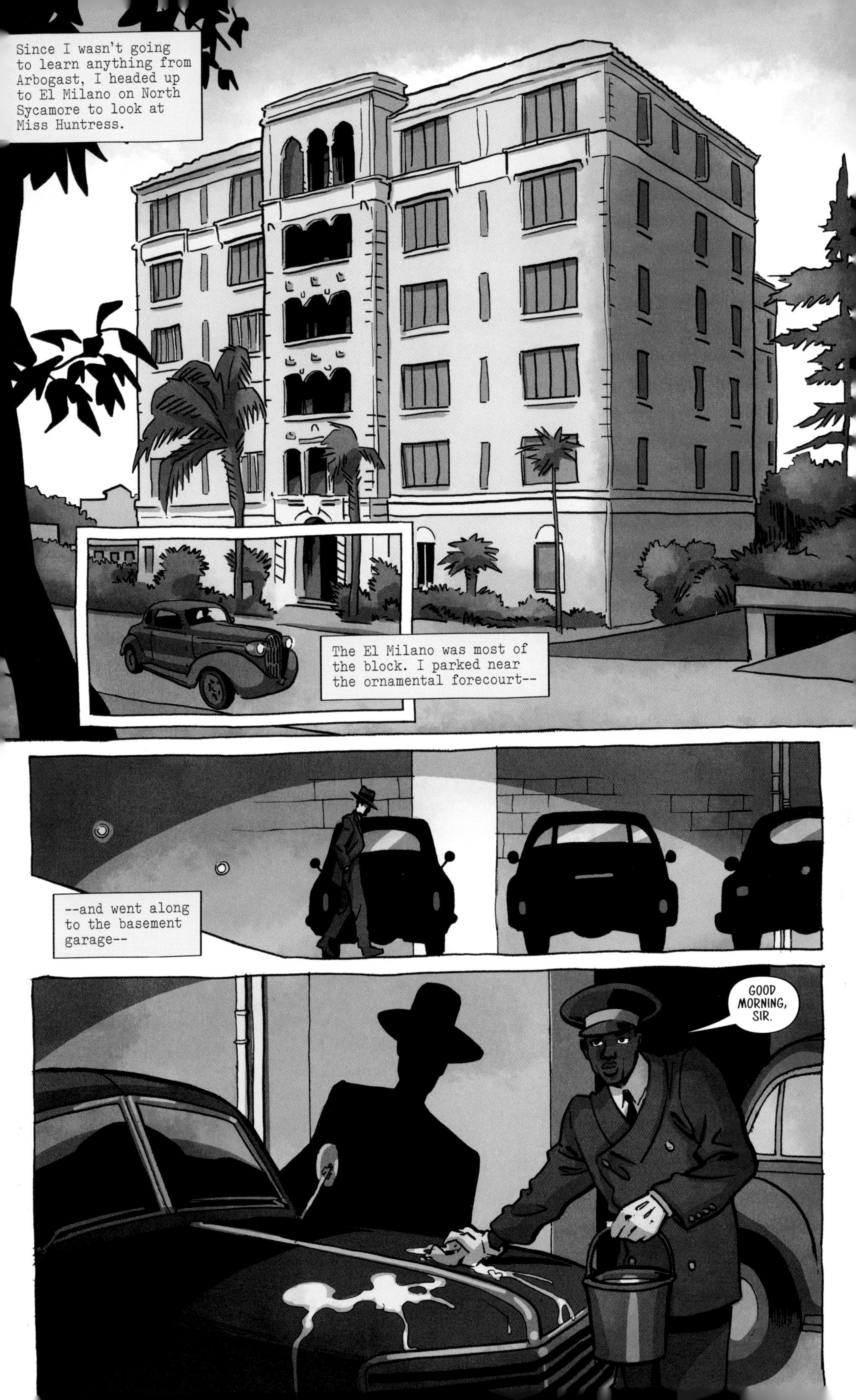
Since I wasn't going to learn anything from Arbogast, I headed up to El Milano on North Sycamore to look at Miss Huntress.
The El Milano was most of the block. I parked near the ornamental forecourt--
--and went along to the basement garage--
GOOD MORNING, SIR.

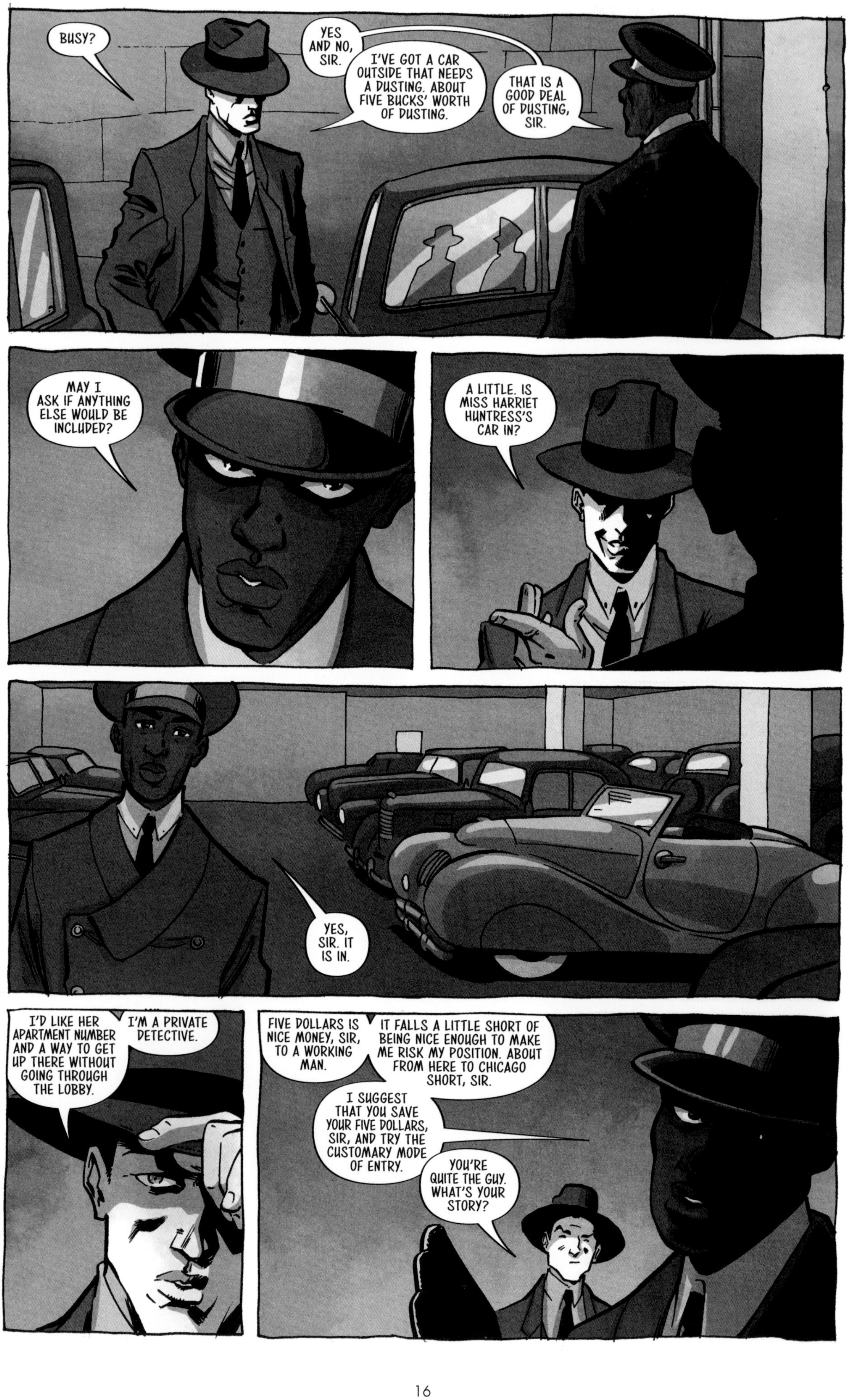
BUSY?
YES AND NO, SIR.
I'VE GOT A CAR OUTSIDE THAT NEEDS A DUSTING. ABOUT FIVE BUCKS' WORTH OF DUSTING.
THAT IS A GOOD DEAL OF DUSTING, SIR.
MAY I ASK IF ANYTHING ELSE WOULD BE INCLUDED?
A LITTLE. IS MISS HARRIET HUNTRESS'S CAR IN?
YES, SIR. IT IS IN.
I'D LIKE HER APARTMENT NUMBER AND A WAY TO GET UP THERE WITHOUT GOING THROUGH THE LOBBY.
I'M A PRIVATE DETECTIVE.
FIVE DOLLARS IS NICE MONEY, SIR, TO A WORKING MAN.
IT FALLS A LITTLE SHORT OF BEING NICE ENOUGH TO MAKE ME RISK MY POSITION. ABOUT FROM HERE TO CHICAGO SHORT, SIR.
I SUGGEST THAT YOU SAVE YOUR FIVE DOLLARS, SIR, AND TRY THE CUSTOMARY MODE OF ENTRY.
YOU'RE QUITE THE GUY. WHAT'S YOUR STORY?

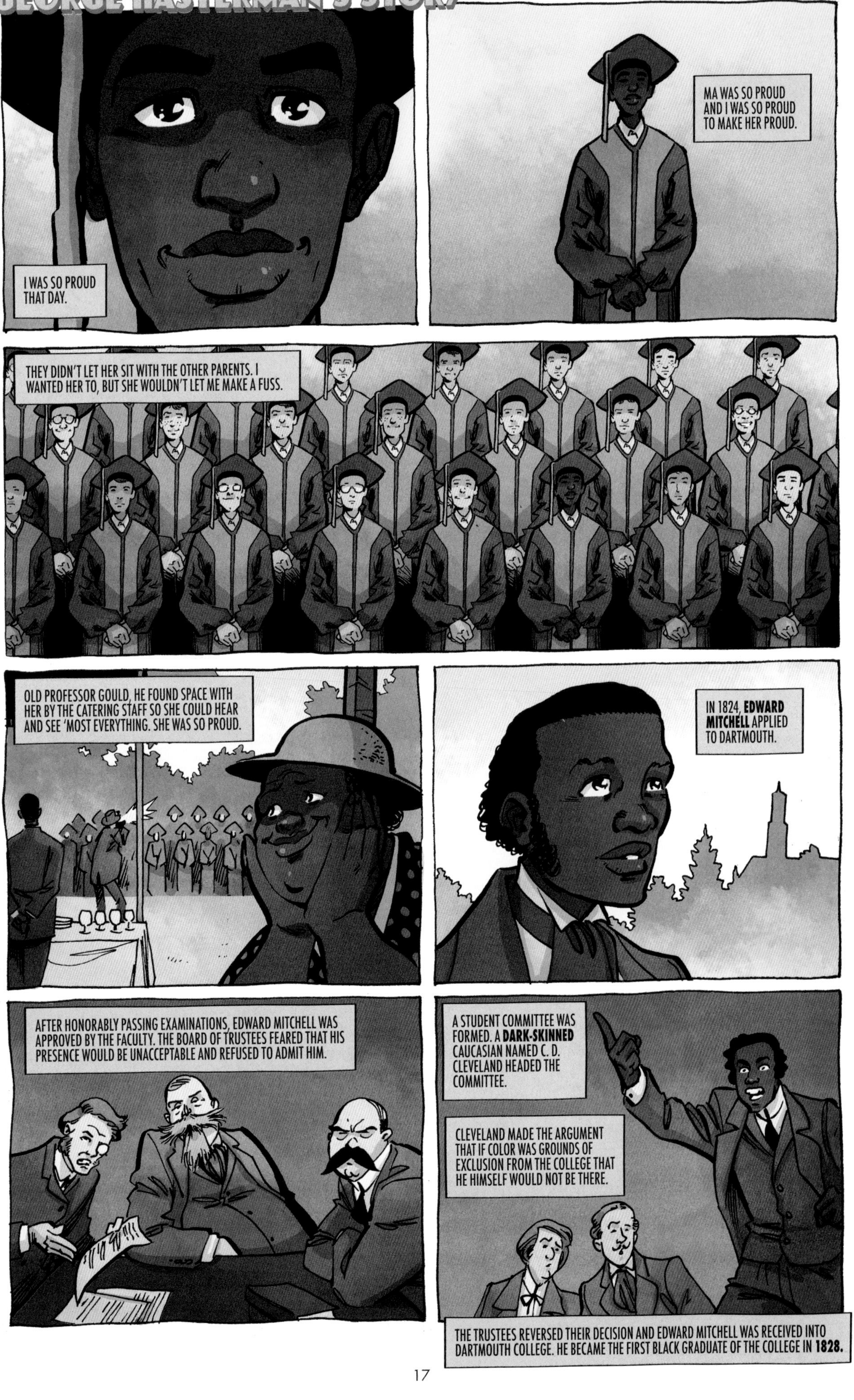
I WAS SO PROUD THAT DAY.
MA WAS SO PROUD AND I WAS SO PROUD TO MAKE HER PROUD.
THEY DIDN'T LET HER SIT WITH THE OTHER PARENTS. I WANTED HER TO, BUT SHE WOULDN'T LET ME MAKE A FUSS.
OLD PROFESSOR GOULD, HE FOUND SPACE WITH HER BY THE CATERING STAFF SO SHE COULD HEAR AND SEE 'MOST EVERYTHING. SHE WAS SO PROUD.
IN 1824, **EDWARD MITCHELL** APPLIED TO DARTMOUTH.
AFTER HONORABLY PASSING EXAMINATIONS, EDWARD MITCHELL WAS APPROVED BY THE FACULTY. THE BOARD OF TRUSTEES FEARED THAT HIS PRESENCE WOULD BE UNACCEPTABLE AND REFUSED TO ADMIT HIM.
A STUDENT COMMITTEE WAS FORMED. A **DARK-SKINNED** CAUCASIAN NAMED C. D. CLEVELAND HEADED THE COMMITTEE.
CLEVELAND MADE THE ARGUMENT THAT IF COLOR WAS GROUNDS OF EXCLUSION FROM THE COLLEGE THAT HE HIMSELF WOULD NOT BE THERE.
THE TRUSTEES REVERSED THEIR DECISION AND EDWARD MITCHELL WAS RECEIVED INTO DARTMOUTH COLLEGE. HE BECAME THE FIRST BLACK GRADUATE OF THE COLLEGE IN **1828.**

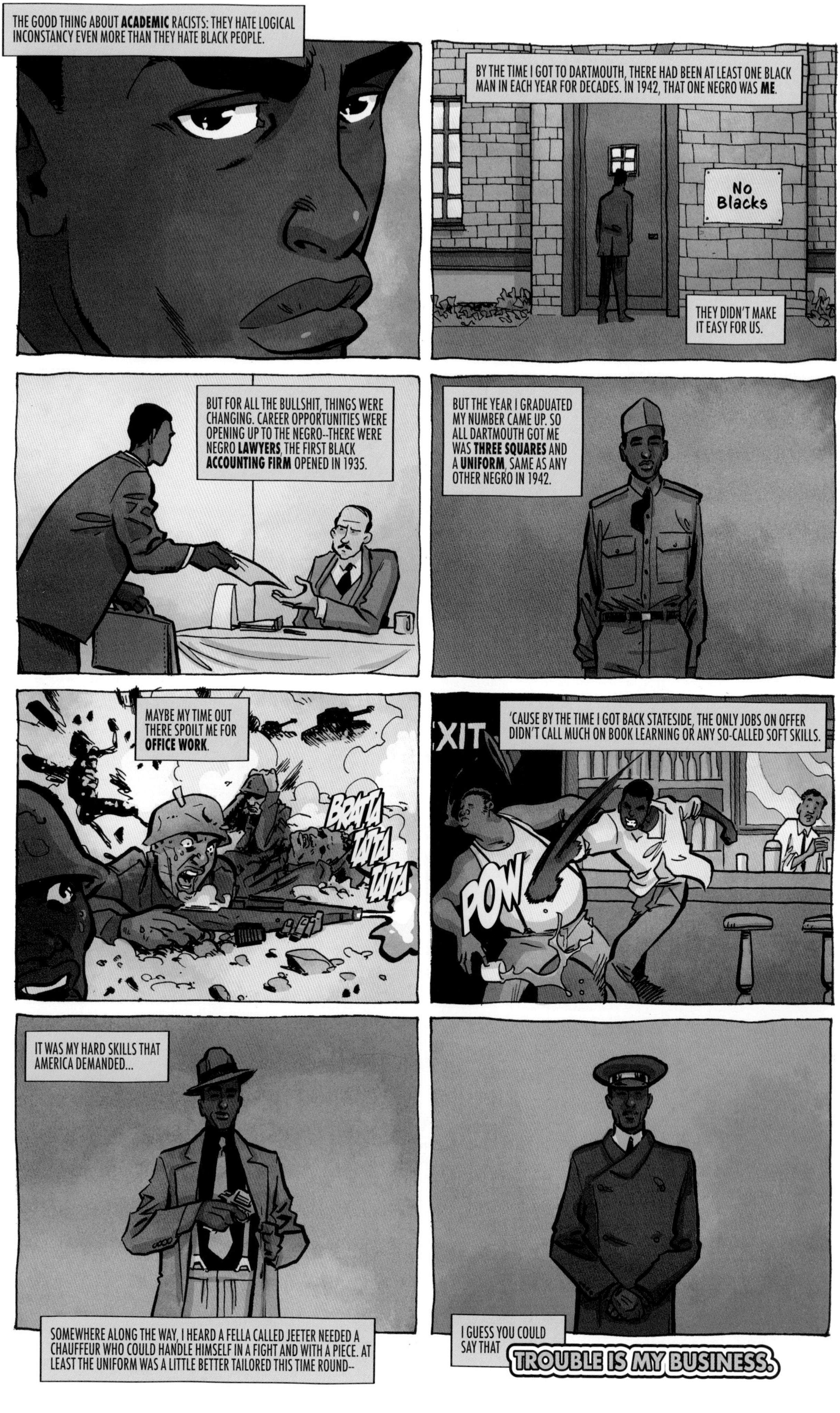
THE GOOD THING ABOUT ACADEMIC RACISTS: THEY HATE LOGICAL INCONSTANCY EVEN MORE THAN THEY HATE BLACK PEOPLE.
BY THE TIME I GOT TO DARTMOUTH, THERE HAD BEEN AT LEAST ONE BLACK MAN IN EACH YEAR FOR DECADES. IN 1942, THAT ONE NEGRO WAS ME.
No Blacks
THEY DIDN'T MAKE IT EASY FOR US.
BUT FOR ALL THE BULLSHIT, THINGS WERE CHANGING. CAREER OPPORTUNITIES WERE OPENING UP TO THE NEGRO--THERE WERE NEGRO LAWYERS, THE FIRST BLACK ACCOUNTING FIRM OPENED IN 1935.
BUT THE YEAR I GRADUATED MY NUMBER CAME UP. SO ALL DARTMOUTH GOT ME WAS THREE SQUARES AND A UNIFORM, SAME AS ANY OTHER NEGRO IN 1942.
MAYBE MY TIME OUT THERE SPOILT ME FOR OFFICE WORK.
BRATTA TATTA TATTA
'CAUSE BY THE TIME I GOT BACK STATESIDE, THE ONLY JOBS ON OFFER DIDN'T CALL MUCH ON BOOK LEARNING OR ANY SO-CALLED SOFT SKILLS.
EXIT
POW
IT WAS MY HARD SKILLS THAT AMERICA DEMANDED...
SOMEWHERE ALONG THE WAY, I HEARD A FELLA CALLED JEETER NEEDED A CHAUFFEUR WHO COULD HANDLE HIMSELF IN A FIGHT AND WITH A PIECE. AT LEAST THE UNIFORM WAS A LITTLE BETTER TAILORED THIS TIME ROUND--
I GUESS YOU COULD SAY THAT
TROUBLE IS MY BUSINESS.

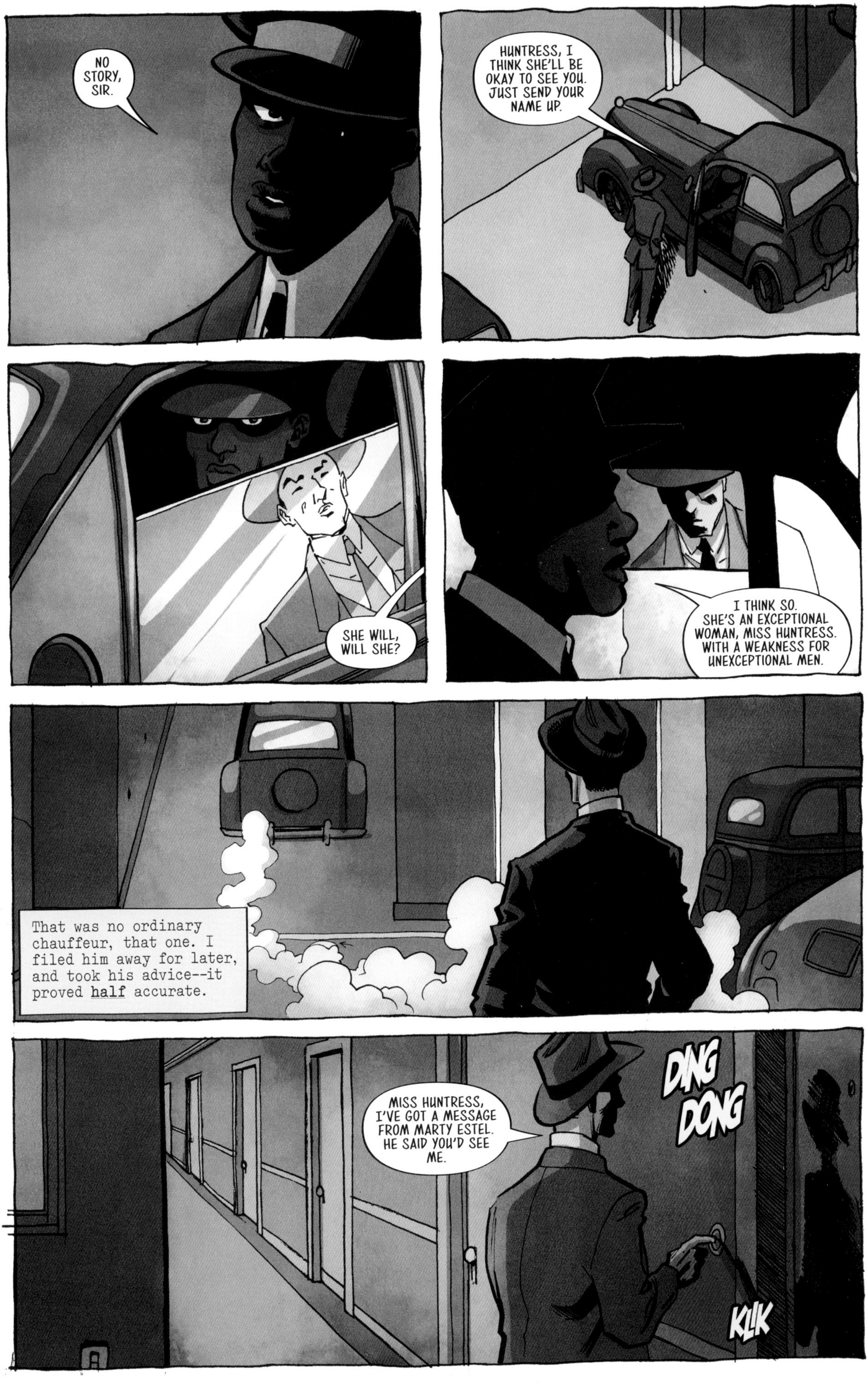

NO STORY, SIR.
HUNTRESS, I THINK SHE'LL BE OKAY TO SEE YOU. JUST SEND YOUR NAME UP.
SHE WILL, WILL SHE?
I THINK SO. SHE'S AN EXCEPTIONAL WOMAN, MISS HUNTRESS. WITH A WEAKNESS FOR UNEXCEPTIONAL MEN.
That was no ordinary chauffeur, that one. I filed him away for later, and took his advice--it proved half accurate.
MISS HUNTRESS, I'VE GOT A MESSAGE FROM MARTY ESTEL. HE SAID YOU'D SEE ME.
DING DONG
KLIK

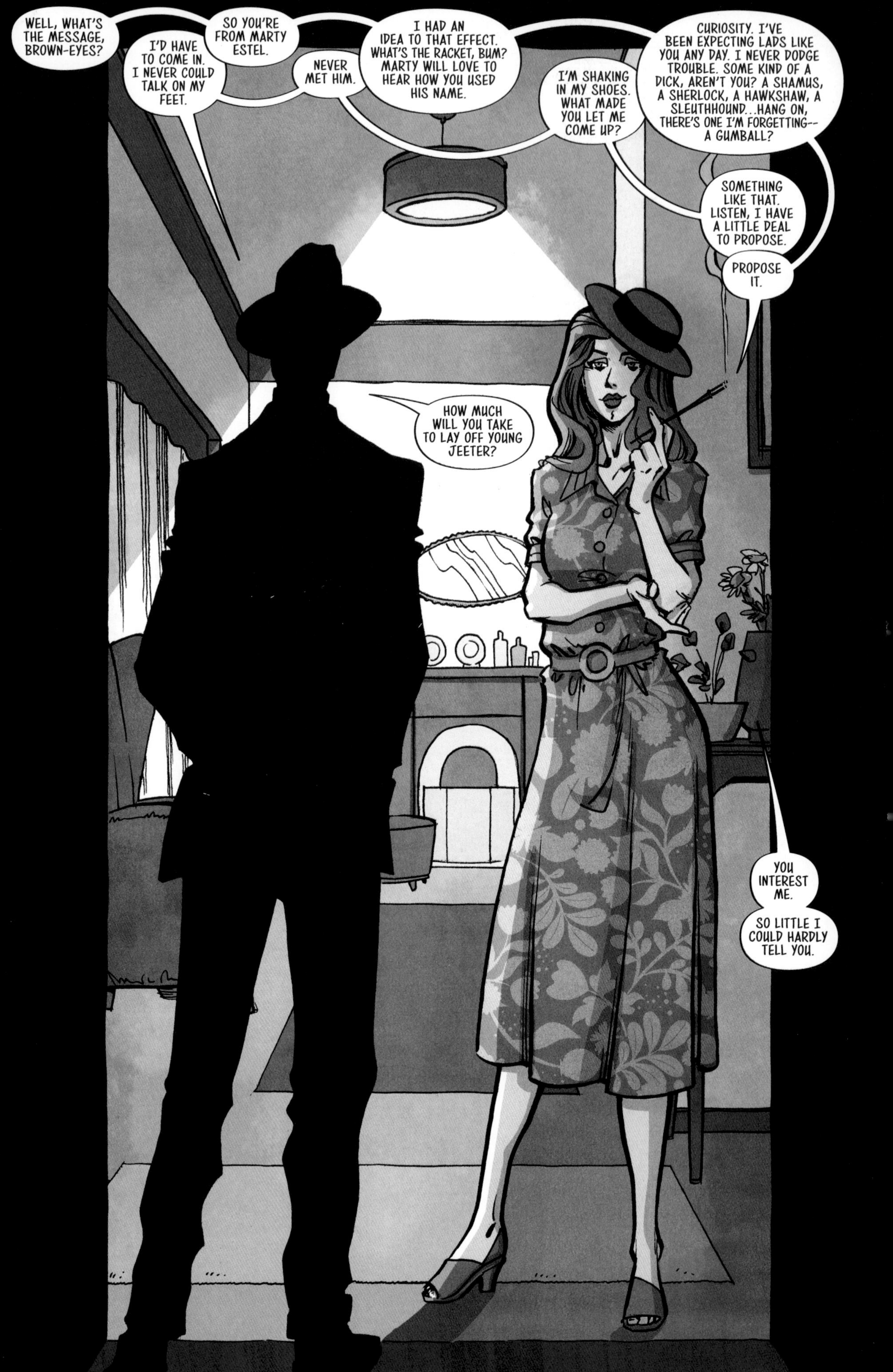

WELL, WHAT'S THE MESSAGE, BROWN-EYES?
I'D HAVE TO COME IN. I NEVER COULD TALK ON MY FEET.
SO YOU'RE FROM MARTY ESTEL.
NEVER MET HIM.
I HAD AN IDEA TO THAT EFFECT. WHAT'S THE RACKET, BUM? MARTY WILL LOVE TO HEAR HOW YOU USED HIS NAME.
I'M SHAKING IN MY SHOES. WHAT MADE YOU LET ME COME UP?
CURIOSITY. I'VE BEEN EXPECTING LADS LIKE YOU ANY DAY. I NEVER DODGE TROUBLE. SOME KIND OF A DICK, AREN'T YOU? A SHAMUS, A SHERLOCK, A HAWKSHAW, A SLEUTHHOUND...HANG ON, THERE'S ONE I'M FORGETTING-- A GUMBALL?
SOMETHING LIKE THAT. LISTEN, I HAVE A LITTLE DEAL TO PROPOSE.
PROPOSE IT.
HOW MUCH WILL YOU TAKE TO LAY OFF YOUNG JEETER?
YOU INTEREST ME.
SO LITTLE I COULD HARDLY TELL YOU.

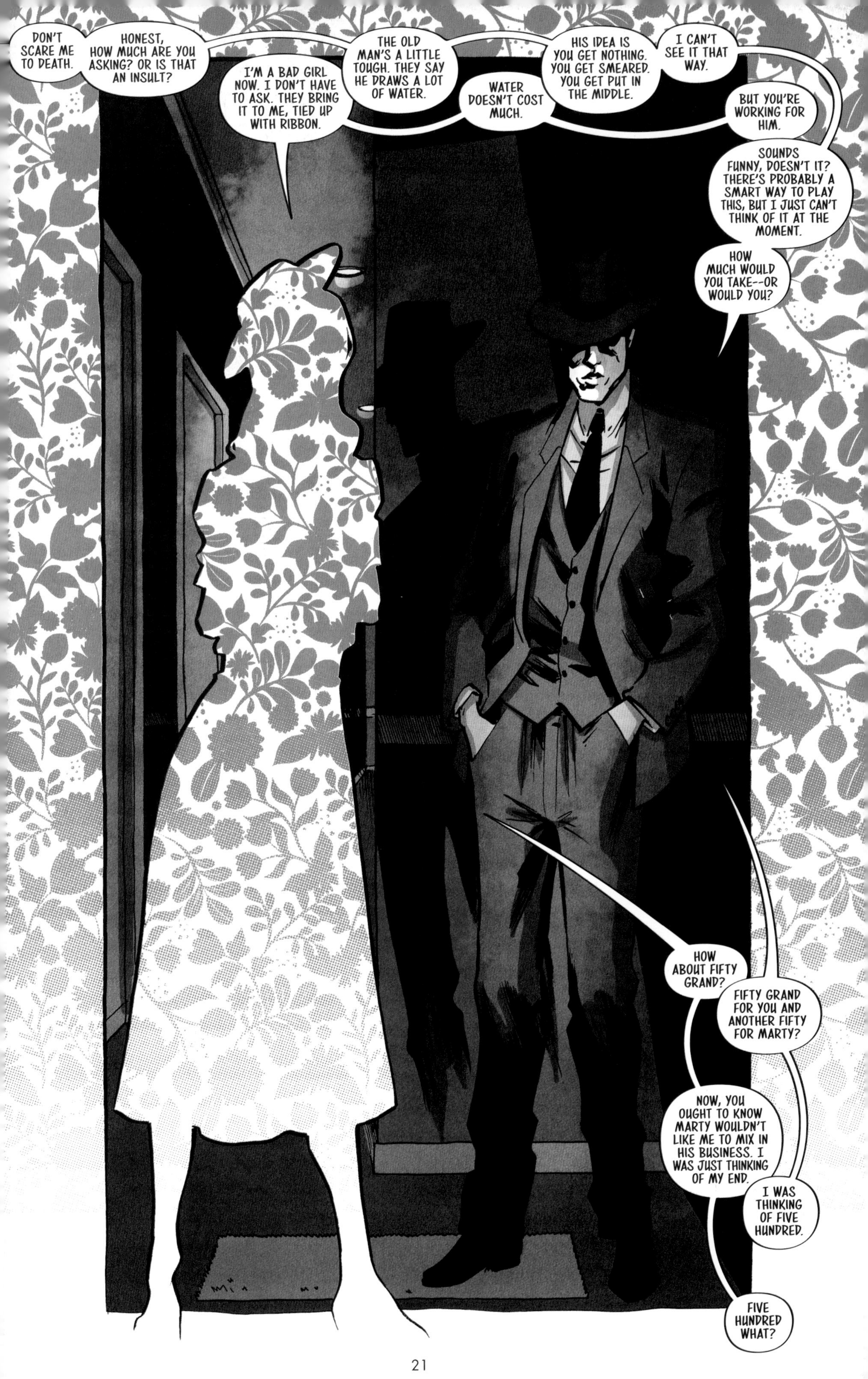
DON'T SCARE ME TO DEATH.
HONEST, HOW MUCH ARE YOU ASKING? OR IS THAT AN INSULT?
I'M A BAD GIRL NOW. I DON'T HAVE TO ASK. THEY BRING IT TO ME, TIED UP WITH RIBBON.
THE OLD MAN'S A LITTLE TOUGH. THEY SAY HE DRAWS A LOT OF WATER.
WATER DOESN'T COST MUCH.
HIS IDEA IS YOU GET NOTHING. YOU GET SMEARED. YOU GET PUT IN THE MIDDLE.
I CAN'T SEE IT THAT WAY.
BUT YOU'RE WORKING FOR HIM.
SOUNDS FUNNY, DOESN'T IT? THERE'S PROBABLY A SMART WAY TO PLAY THIS, BUT I JUST CAN'T THINK OF IT AT THE MOMENT.
HOW MUCH WOULD YOU TAKE--OR WOULD YOU?
HOW ABOUT FIFTY GRAND?
FIFTY GRAND FOR YOU AND ANOTHER FIFTY FOR MARTY?
NOW, YOU OUGHT TO KNOW MARTY WOULDN'T LIKE ME TO MIX IN HIS BUSINESS. I WAS JUST THINKING OF MY END.
I WAS THINKING OF FIVE HUNDRED.
FIVE HUNDRED WHAT?

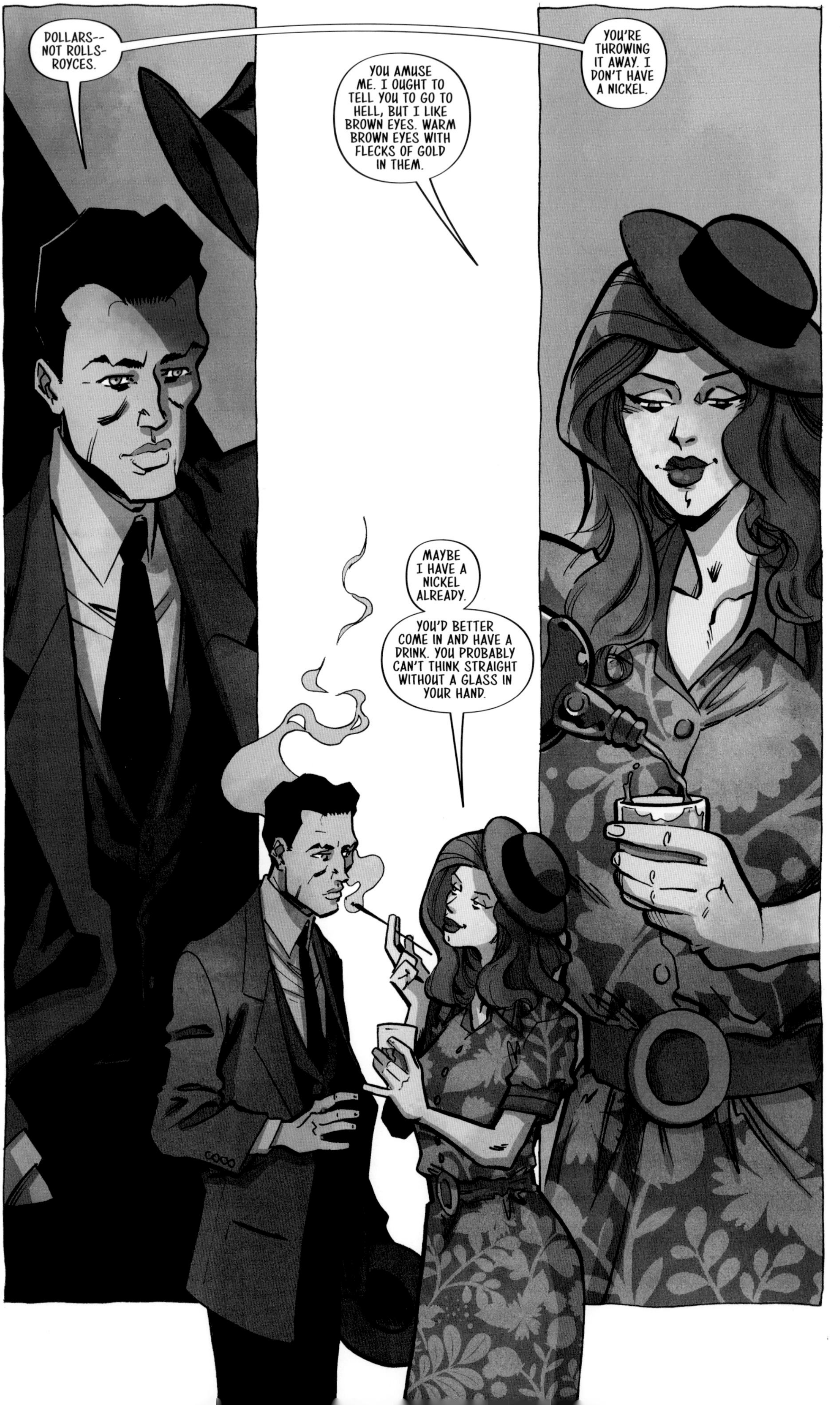
DOLLARS--NOT ROLLS-ROYCES.
YOU'RE THROWING IT AWAY. I DON'T HAVE A NICKEL.
YOU AMUSE ME. I OUGHT TO TELL YOU TO GO TO HELL, BUT I LIKE BROWN EYES. WARM BROWN EYES WITH FLECKS OF GOLD IN THEM.
MAYBE I HAVE A NICKEL ALREADY.
YOU'D BETTER COME IN AND HAVE A DRINK. YOU PROBABLY CAN'T THINK STRAIGHT WITHOUT A GLASS IN YOUR HAND.

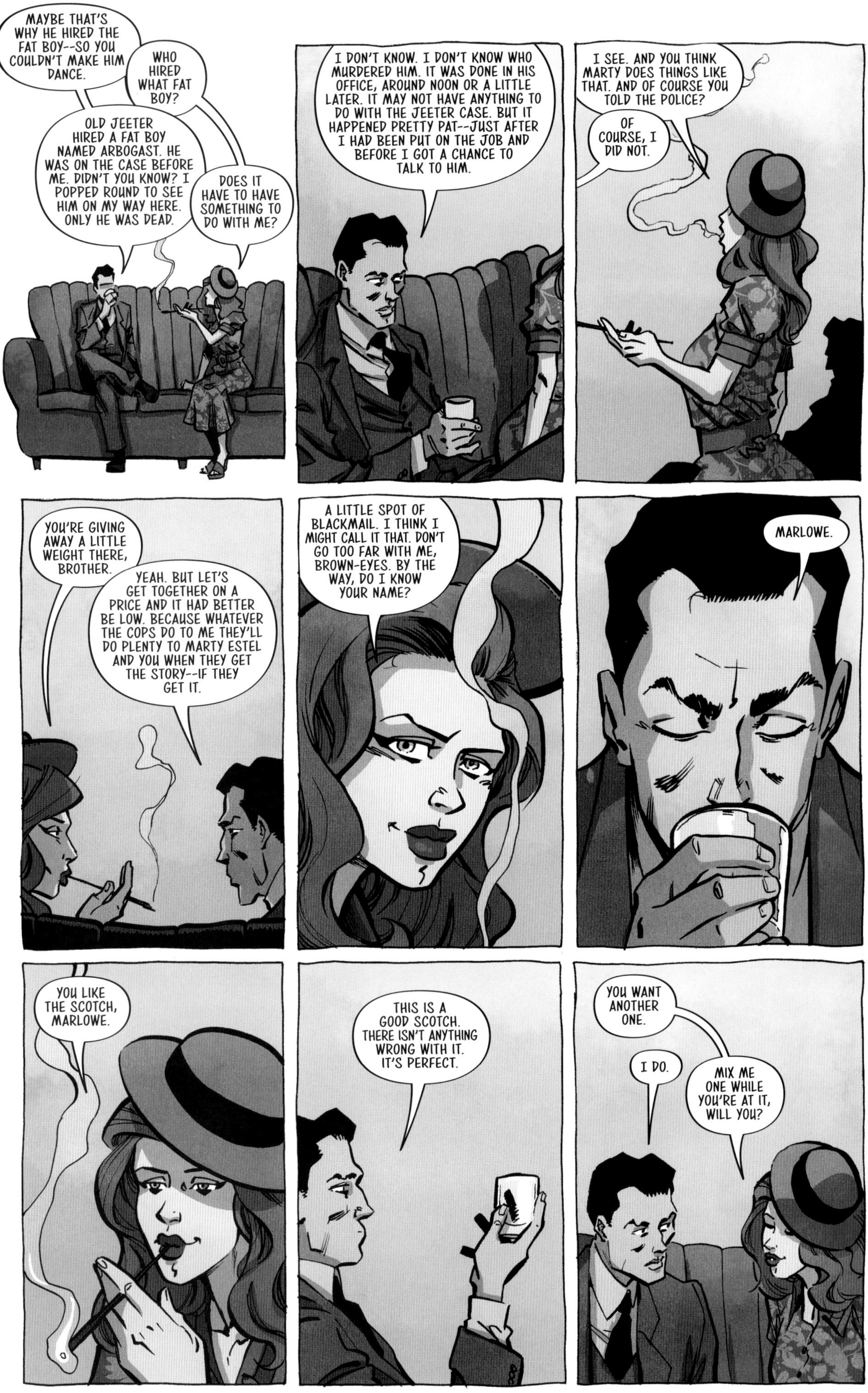
MAYBE THAT'S WHY HE HIRED THE FAT BOY--SO YOU COULDN'T MAKE HIM DANCE.
WHO HIRED WHAT FAT BOY?
OLD JEETER HIRED A FAT BOY NAMED ARBOGAST. HE WAS ON THE CASE BEFORE ME. DIDN'T YOU KNOW? I POPPED ROUND TO SEE HIM ON MY WAY HERE. ONLY HE WAS DEAD.
DOES IT HAVE TO HAVE SOMETHING TO DO WITH ME?
I DON'T KNOW. I DON'T KNOW WHO MURDERED HIM. IT WAS DONE IN HIS OFFICE, AROUND NOON OR A LITTLE LATER. IT MAY NOT HAVE ANYTHING TO DO WITH THE JEETER CASE. BUT IT HAPPENED PRETTY PAT--JUST AFTER I HAD BEEN PUT ON THE JOB AND BEFORE I GOT A CHANCE TO TALK TO HIM.
I SEE. AND YOU THINK MARTY DOES THINGS LIKE THAT. AND OF COURSE YOU TOLD THE POLICE?
OF COURSE, I DID NOT.
YOU'RE GIVING AWAY A LITTLE WEIGHT THERE, BROTHER.
YEAH. BUT LET'S GET TOGETHER ON A PRICE AND IT HAD BETTER BE LOW. BECAUSE WHATEVER THE COPS DO TO ME THEY'LL DO PLENTY TO MARTY ESTEL AND YOU WHEN THEY GET THE STORY--IF THEY GET IT.
A LITTLE SPOT OF BLACKMAIL. I THINK I MIGHT CALL IT THAT. DON'T GO TOO FAR WITH ME, BROWN-EYES. BY THE WAY, DO I KNOW YOUR NAME?
MARLOWE.
YOU LIKE THE SCOTCH, MARLOWE.
THIS IS A GOOD SCOTCH. THERE ISN'T ANYTHING WRONG WITH IT. IT'S PERFECT.
YOU WANT ANOTHER ONE.
I DO.
MIX ME ONE WHILE YOU'RE AT IT, WILL YOU?

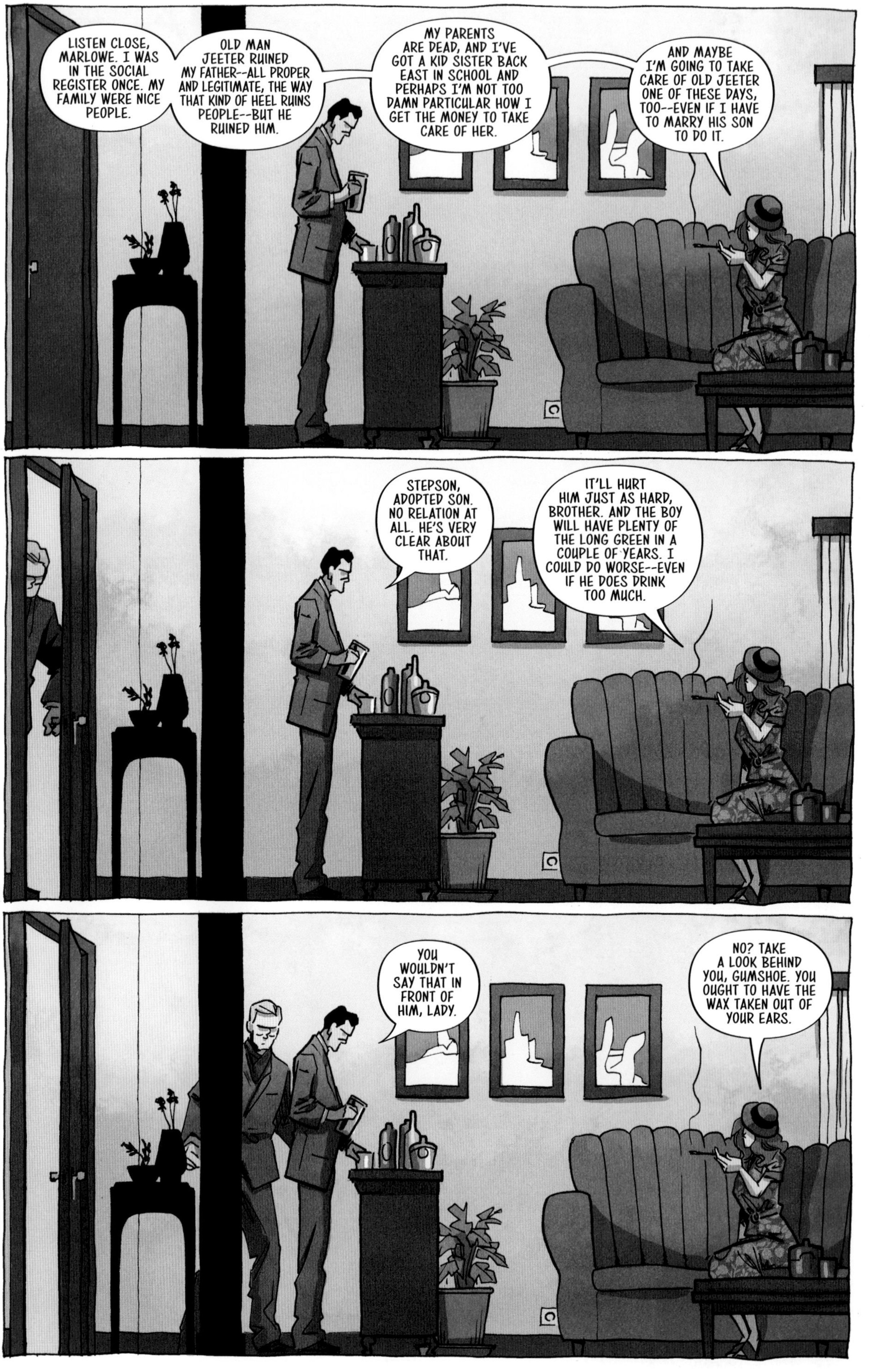
LISTEN CLOSE, MARLOWE. I WAS IN THE SOCIAL REGISTER ONCE. MY FAMILY WERE NICE PEOPLE.
OLD MAN JEETER RUINED MY FATHER--ALL PROPER AND LEGITIMATE, THE WAY THAT KIND OF HEEL RUINS PEOPLE--BUT HE RUINED HIM.
MY PARENTS ARE DEAD, AND I'VE GOT A KID SISTER BACK EAST IN SCHOOL AND PERHAPS I'M NOT TOO DAMN PARTICULAR HOW I GET THE MONEY TO TAKE CARE OF HER.
AND MAYBE I'M GOING TO TAKE CARE OF OLD JEETER ONE OF THESE DAYS, TOO--EVEN IF I HAVE TO MARRY HIS SON TO DO IT.
STEPSON, ADOPTED SON. NO RELATION AT ALL. HE'S VERY CLEAR ABOUT THAT.
IT'LL HURT HIM JUST AS HARD, BROTHER. AND THE BOY WILL HAVE PLENTY OF THE LONG GREEN IN A COUPLE OF YEARS. I COULD DO WORSE--EVEN IF HE DOES DRINK TOO MUCH.
YOU WOULDN'T SAY THAT IN FRONT OF HIM, LADY.
NO? TAKE A LOOK BEHIND YOU, GUMSHOE. YOU OUGHT TO HAVE THE WAX TAKEN OUT OF YOUR EARS.

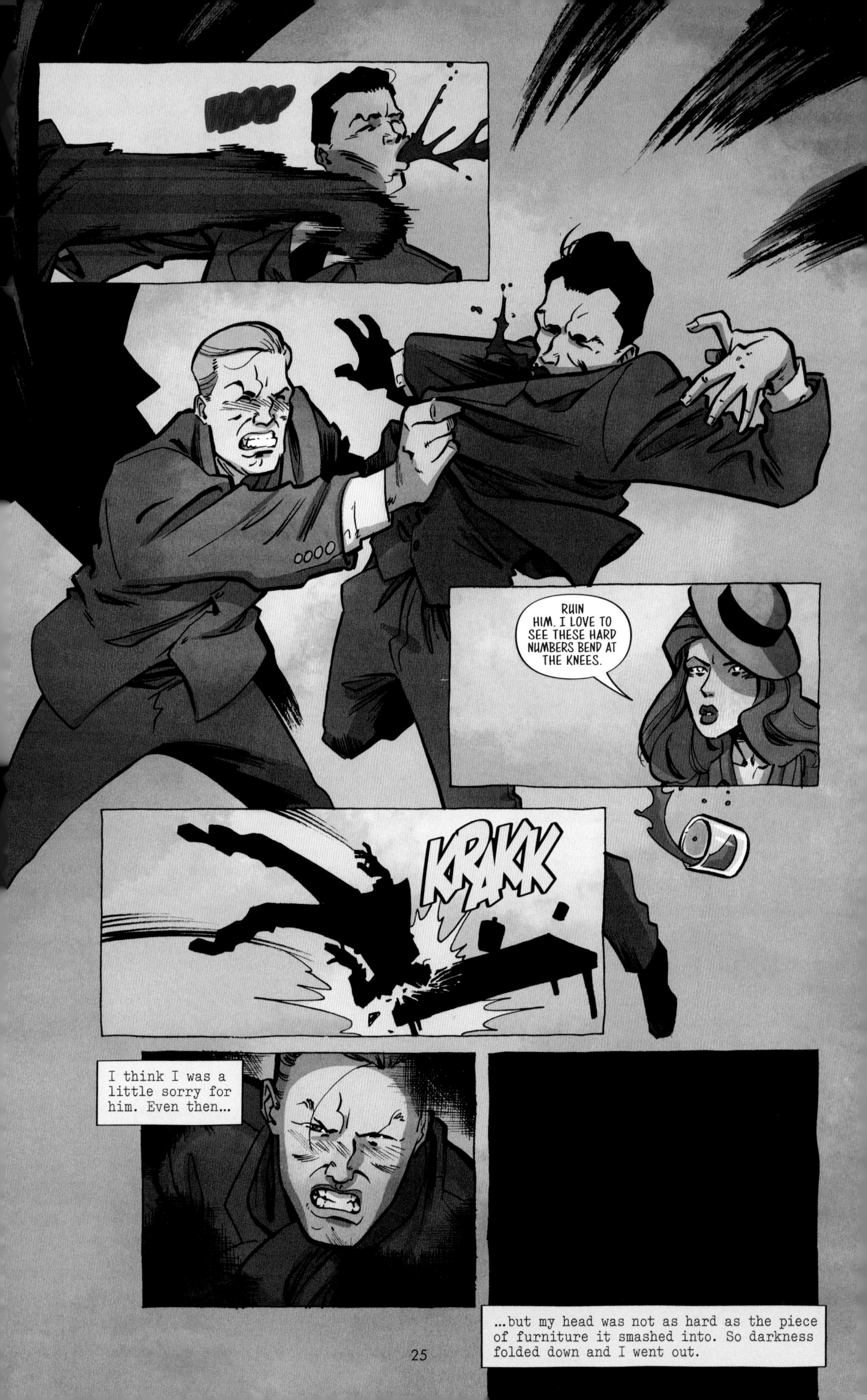
RUIN HIM. I LOVE TO SEE THESE HARD NUMBERS BEND AT THE KNEES.
KRAKK
I think I was a little sorry for him. Even then...
...but my head was not as hard as the piece of furniture it smashed into. So darkness folded down and I went out.

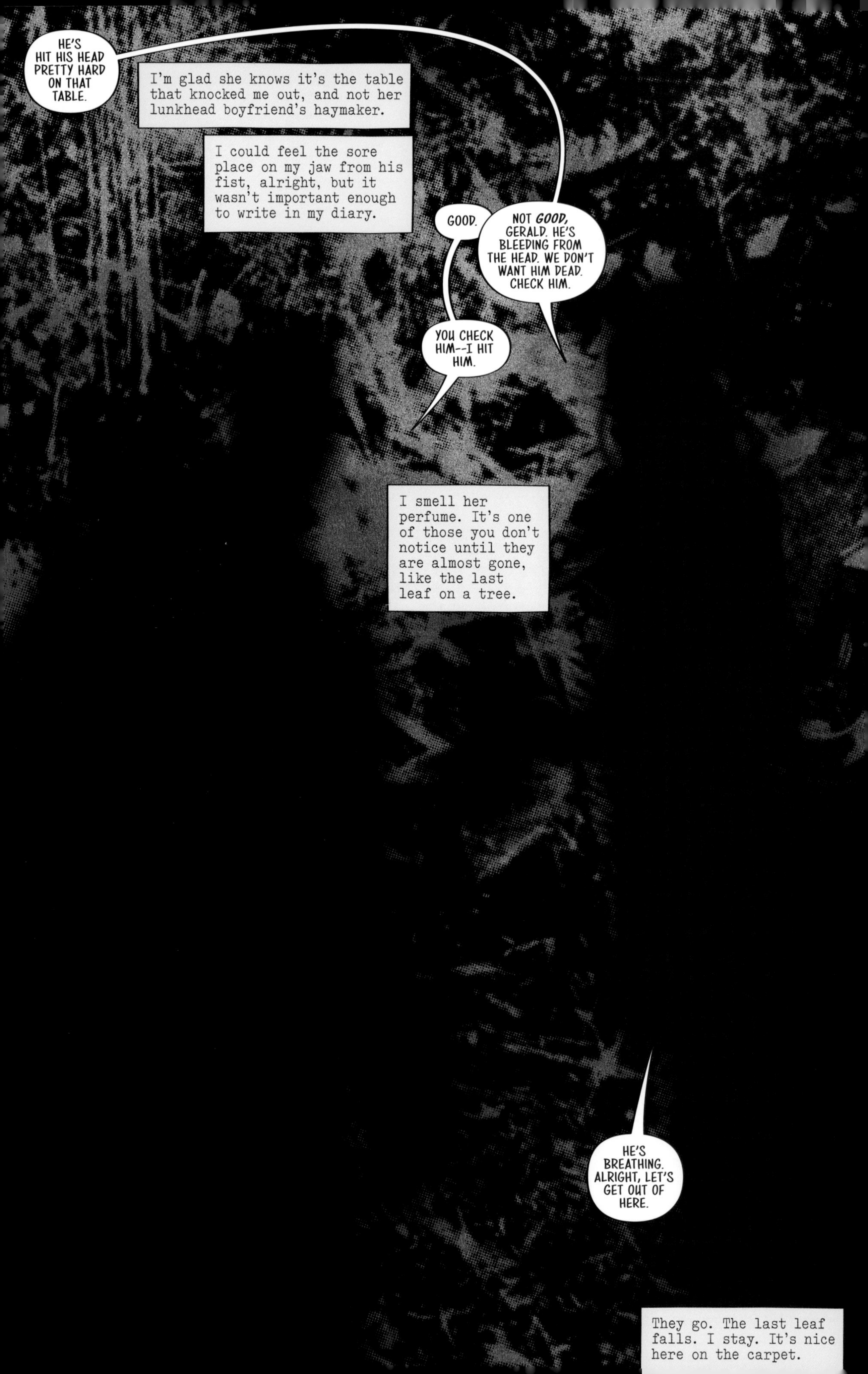
HE'S HIT HIS HEAD PRETTY HARD ON THAT TABLE.
I'm glad she knows it's the table that knocked me out, and not her lunkhead boyfriend's haymaker.
I could feel the sore place on my jaw from his fist, alright, but it wasn't important enough to write in my diary.
GOOD.
NOT *GOOD,* GERALD. HE'S BLEEDING FROM THE HEAD. WE DON'T WANT HIM DEAD. CHECK HIM.
YOU CHECK HIM--I HIT HIM.
I smell her perfume. It's one of those you don't notice until they are almost gone, like the last leaf on a tree.
HE'S BREATHING. ALRIGHT, LET'S GET OUT OF HERE.
They go. The last leaf falls. I stay. It's nice here on the carpet.

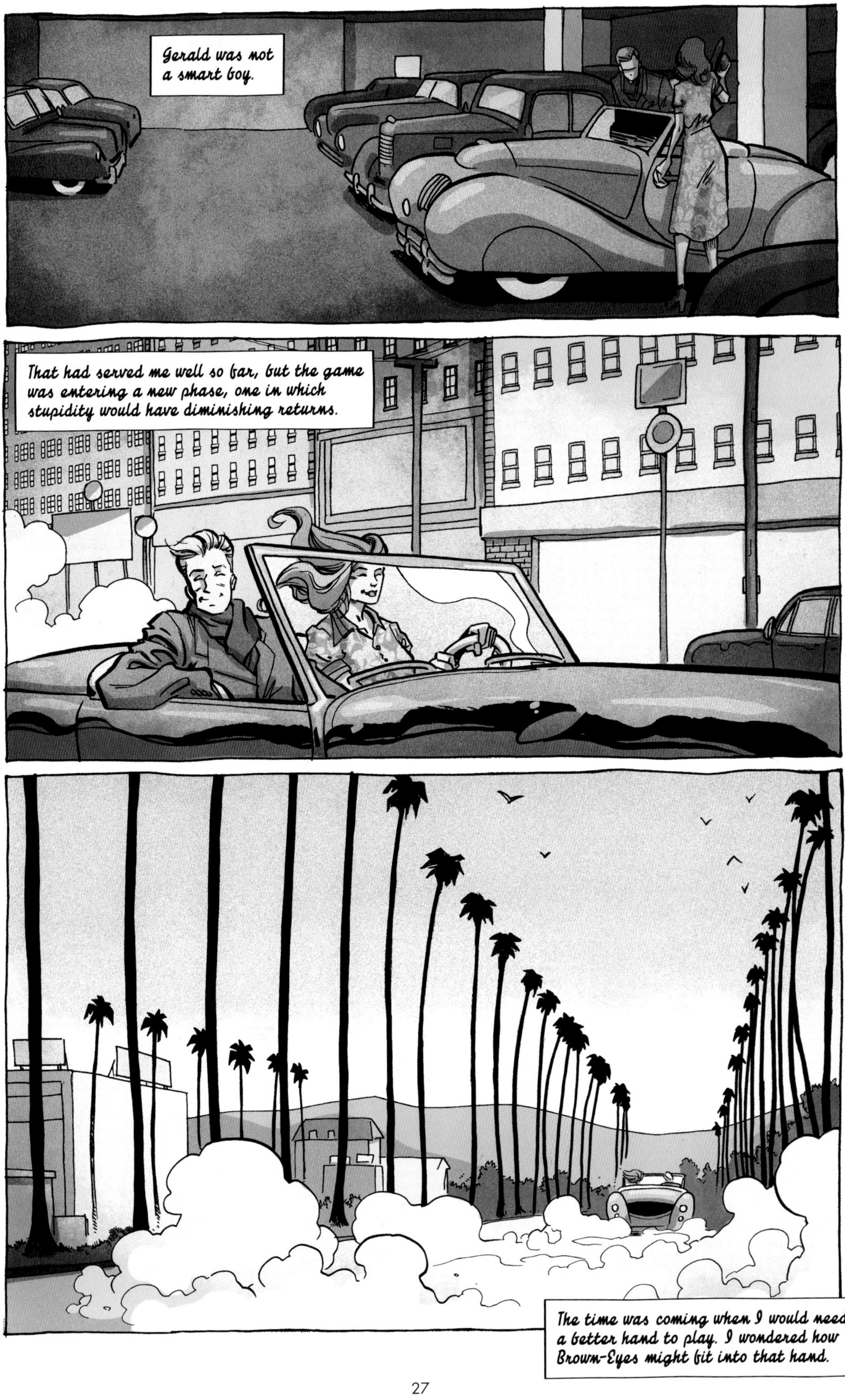
Gerald was not a smart boy.
That had served me well so far, but the game was entering a new phase, one in which stupidity would have diminishing returns.
The time was coming when I would need a better hand to play. I wondered how Brown-Eyes might fit into that hand.

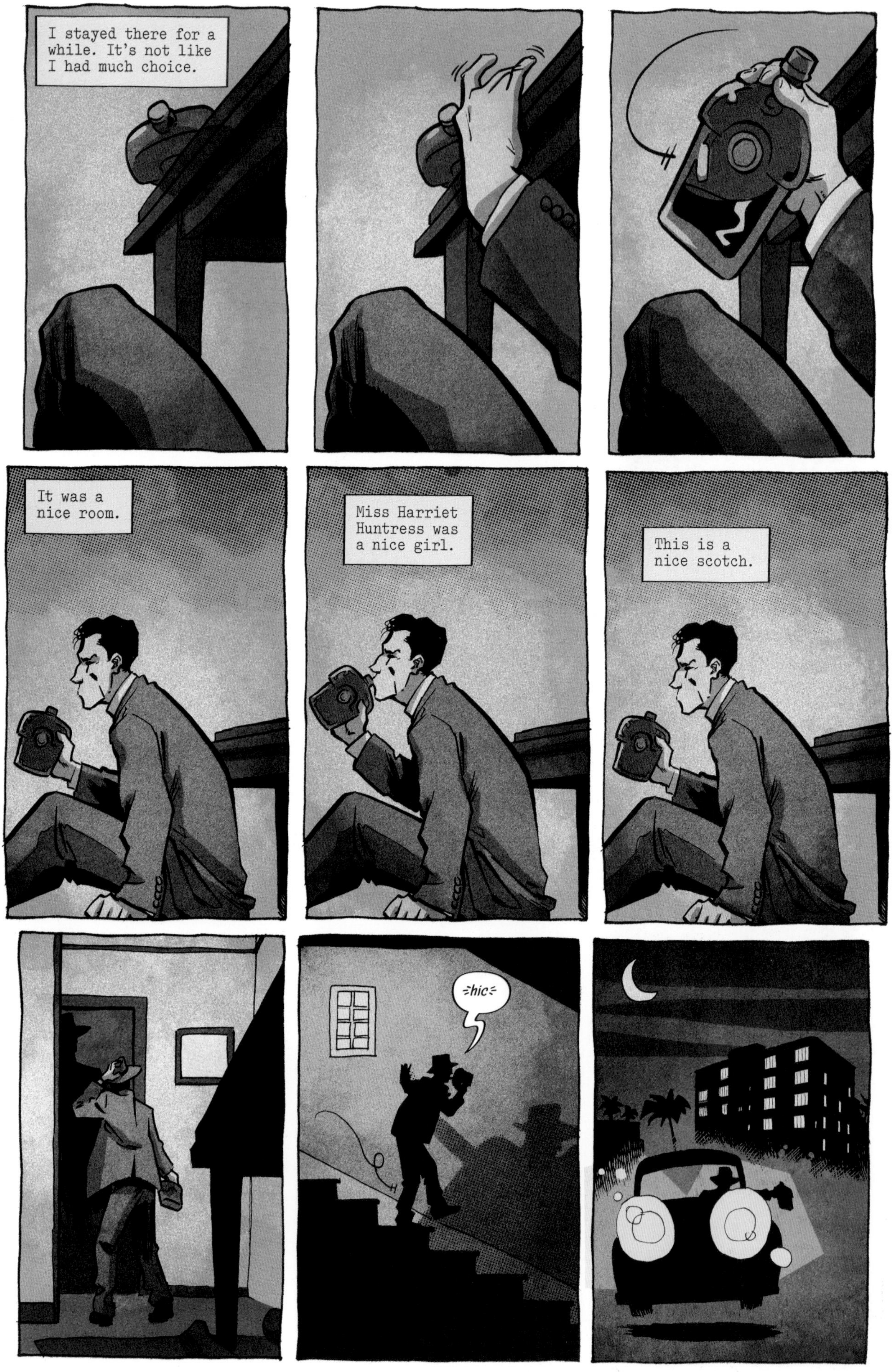
I stayed there for a while. It's not like I had much choice.
It was a nice room.
Miss Harriet Huntress was a nice girl.
This is a nice scotch.
hic

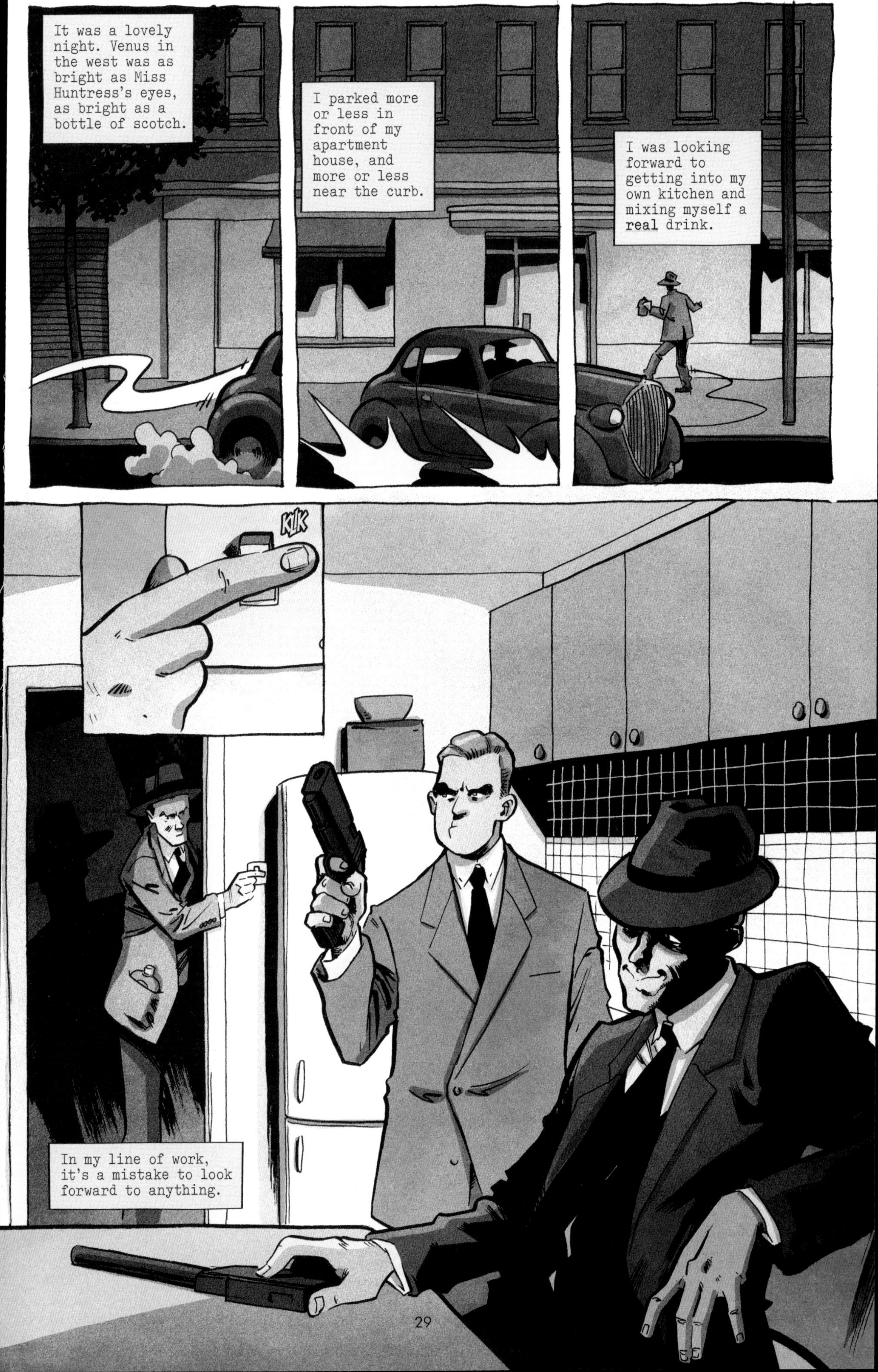

It was a lovely night. Venus in the west was as bright as Miss Huntress's eyes, as bright as a bottle of scotch.
I parked more or less in front of my apartment house, and more or less near the curb.
I was looking forward to getting into my own kitchen and mixing myself a **real** drink.
KLIK
In my line of work, it's a mistake to look forward to anything.

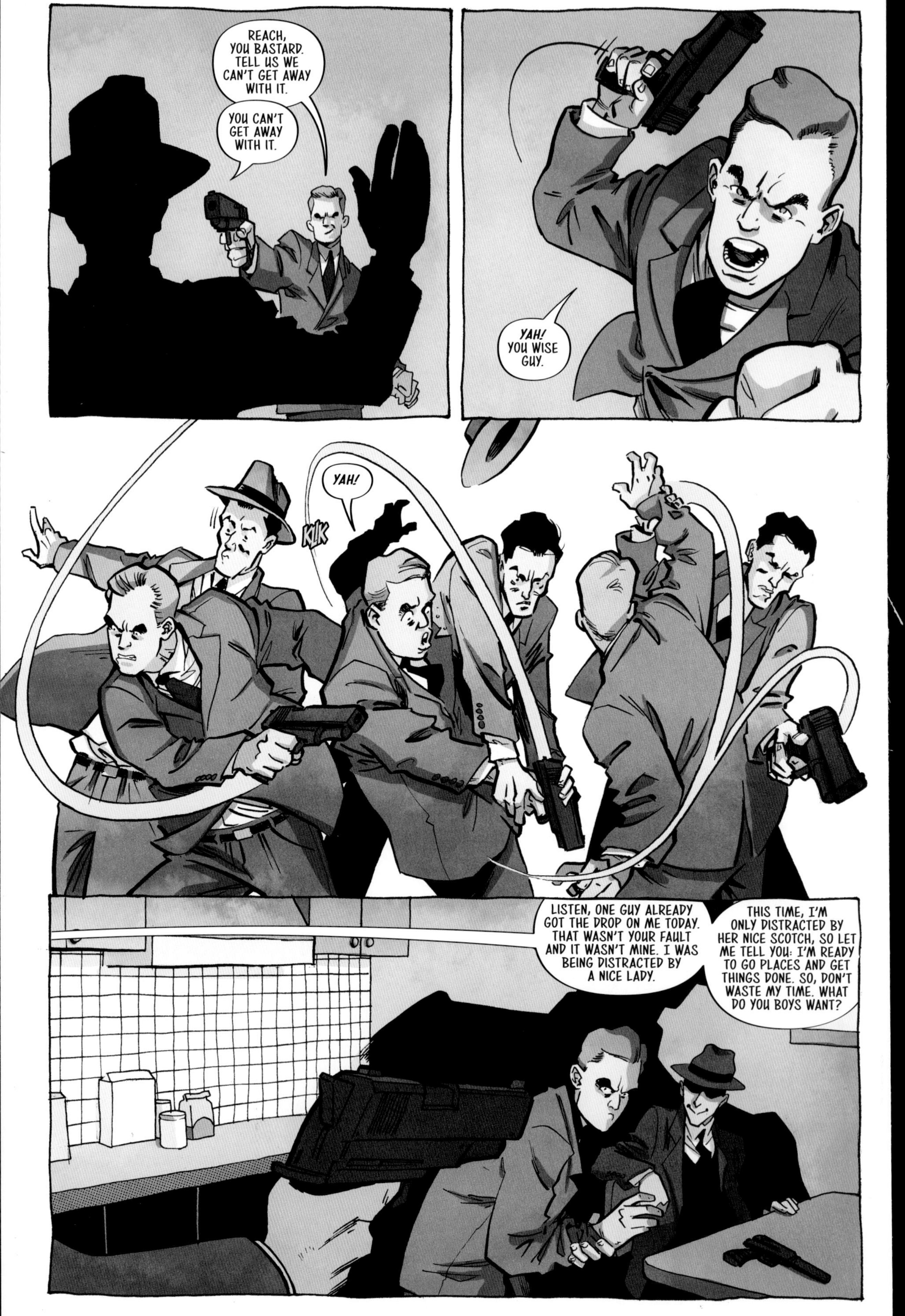
REACH, YOU BASTARD. TELL US WE CAN'T GET AWAY WITH IT.
YOU CAN'T GET AWAY WITH IT.
YAH! YOU WISE GUY.
YAH!
KLIK
LISTEN, ONE GUY ALREADY GOT THE DROP ON ME TODAY. THAT WASN'T YOUR FAULT AND IT WASN'T MINE. I WAS BEING DISTRACTED BY A NICE LADY.
THIS TIME, I'M ONLY DISTRACTED BY HER NICE SCOTCH, SO LET ME TELL YOU: I'M READY TO GO PLACES AND GET THINGS DONE. SO, DON'T WASTE MY TIME. WHAT DO YOU BOYS WANT?

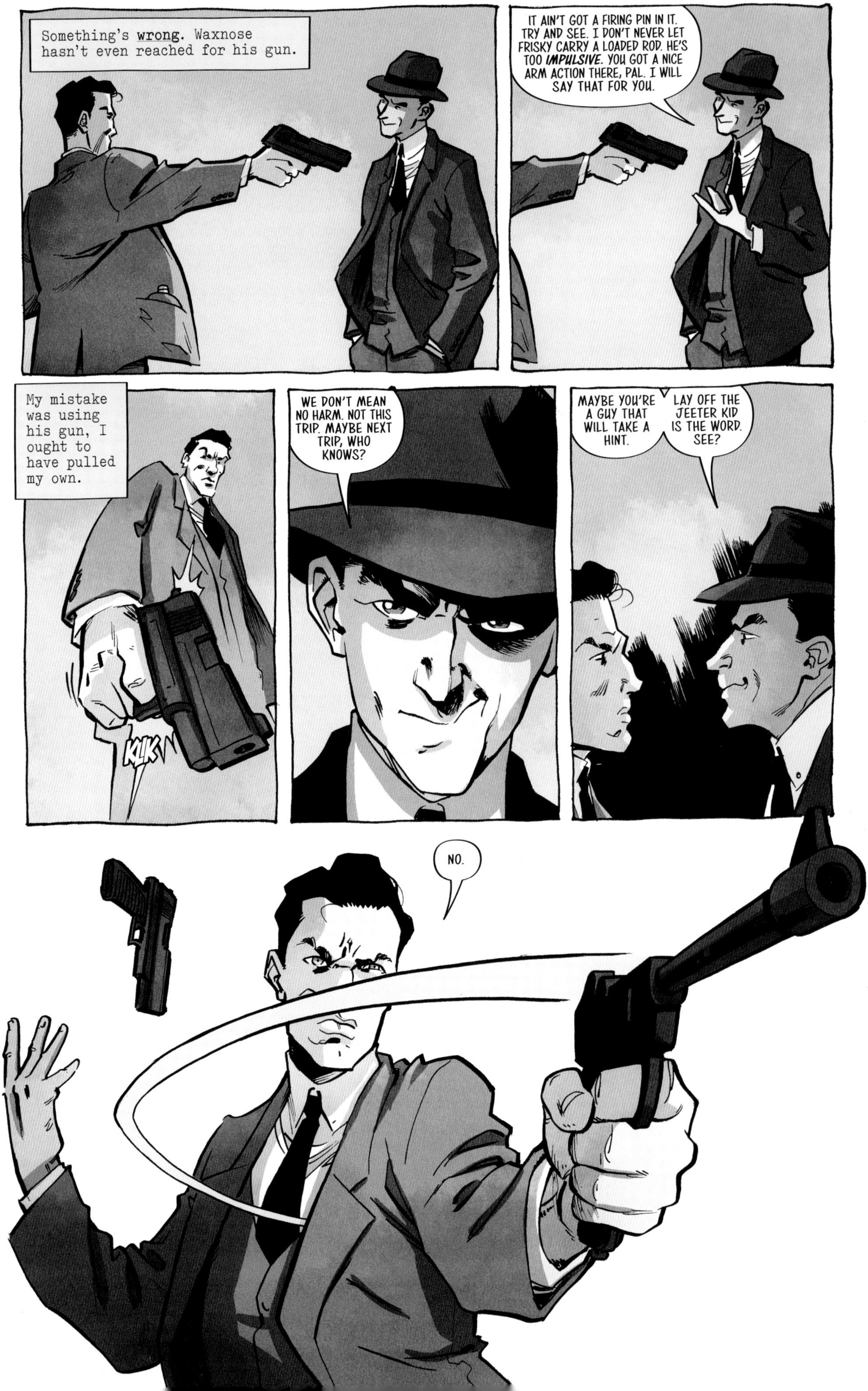
Something's wrong. Waxnose hasn't even reached for his gun.
IT AIN'T GOT A FIRING PIN IN IT. TRY AND SEE. I DON'T NEVER LET FRISKY CARRY A LOADED ROD. HE'S TOO IMPULSIVE. YOU GOT A NICE ARM ACTION THERE, PAL. I WILL SAY THAT FOR YOU.
My mistake was using his gun, I ought to have pulled my own.
KLIK
WE DON'T MEAN NO HARM. NOT THIS TRIP. MAYBE NEXT TRIP, WHO KNOWS?
MAYBE YOU'RE A GUY THAT WILL TAKE A HINT.
LAY OFF THE JEETER KID IS THE WORD. SEE?
NO.

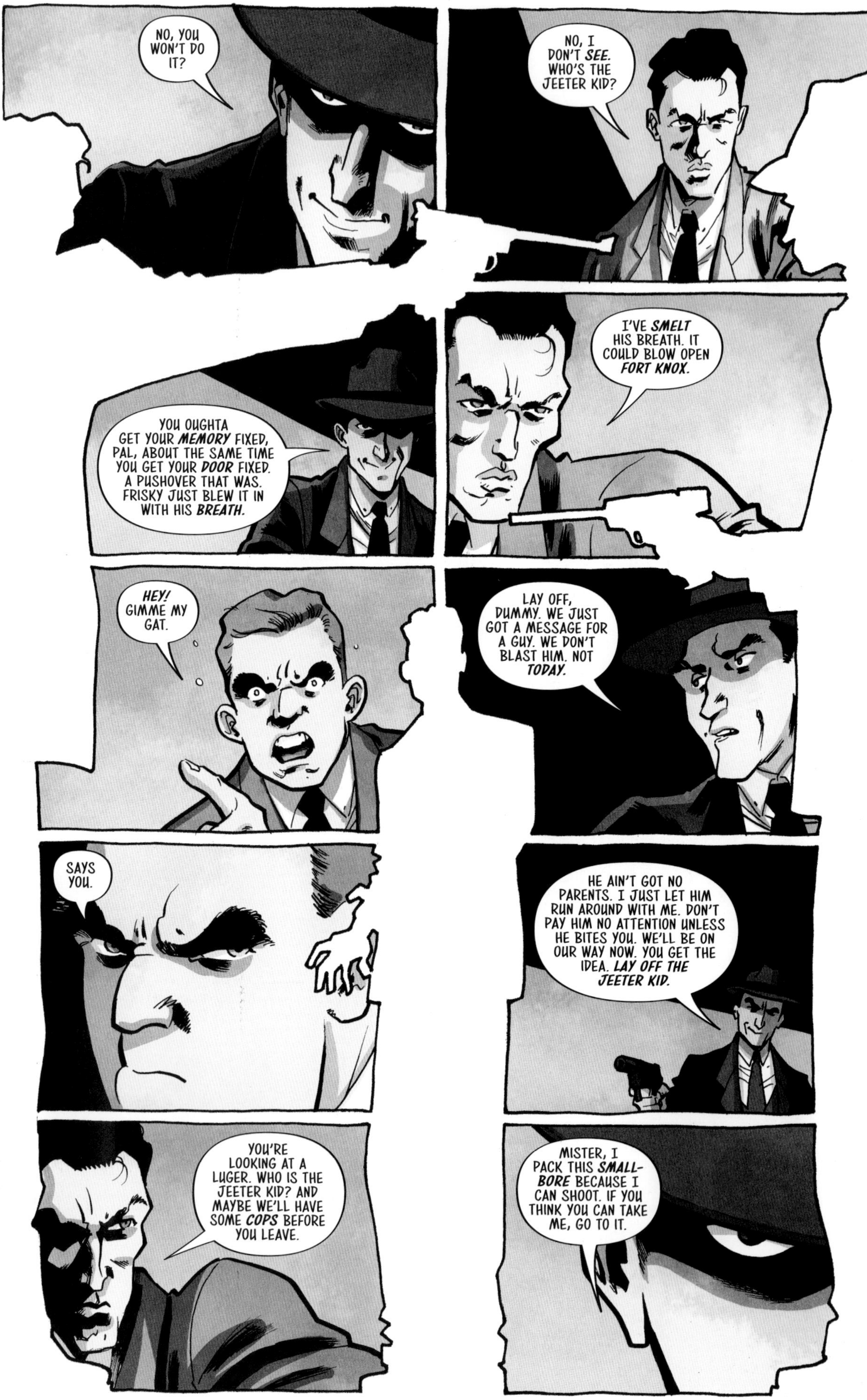
NO, YOU WON'T DO IT?
NO, I DON'T SEE. WHO'S THE JEETER KID?
YOU OUGHTA GET YOUR MEMORY FIXED, PAL, ABOUT THE SAME TIME YOU GET YOUR DOOR FIXED. A PUSHOVER THAT WAS. FRISKY JUST BLEW IT IN WITH HIS BREATH.
I'VE SMELT HIS BREATH. IT COULD BLOW OPEN FORT KNOX.
HEY! GIMME MY GAT.
LAY OFF, DUMMY. WE JUST GOT A MESSAGE FOR A GUY. WE DON'T BLAST HIM. NOT TODAY.
SAYS YOU.
HE AIN'T GOT NO PARENTS. I JUST LET HIM RUN AROUND WITH ME. DON'T PAY HIM NO ATTENTION UNLESS HE BITES YOU. WE'LL BE ON OUR WAY NOW. YOU GET THE IDEA. LAY OFF THE JEETER KID.
YOU'RE LOOKING AT A LUGER. WHO IS THE JEETER KID? AND MAYBE WE'LL HAVE SOME COPS BEFORE YOU LEAVE.
MISTER, I PACK THIS SMALL-BORE BECAUSE I CAN SHOOT. IF YOU THINK YOU CAN TAKE ME, GO TO IT.

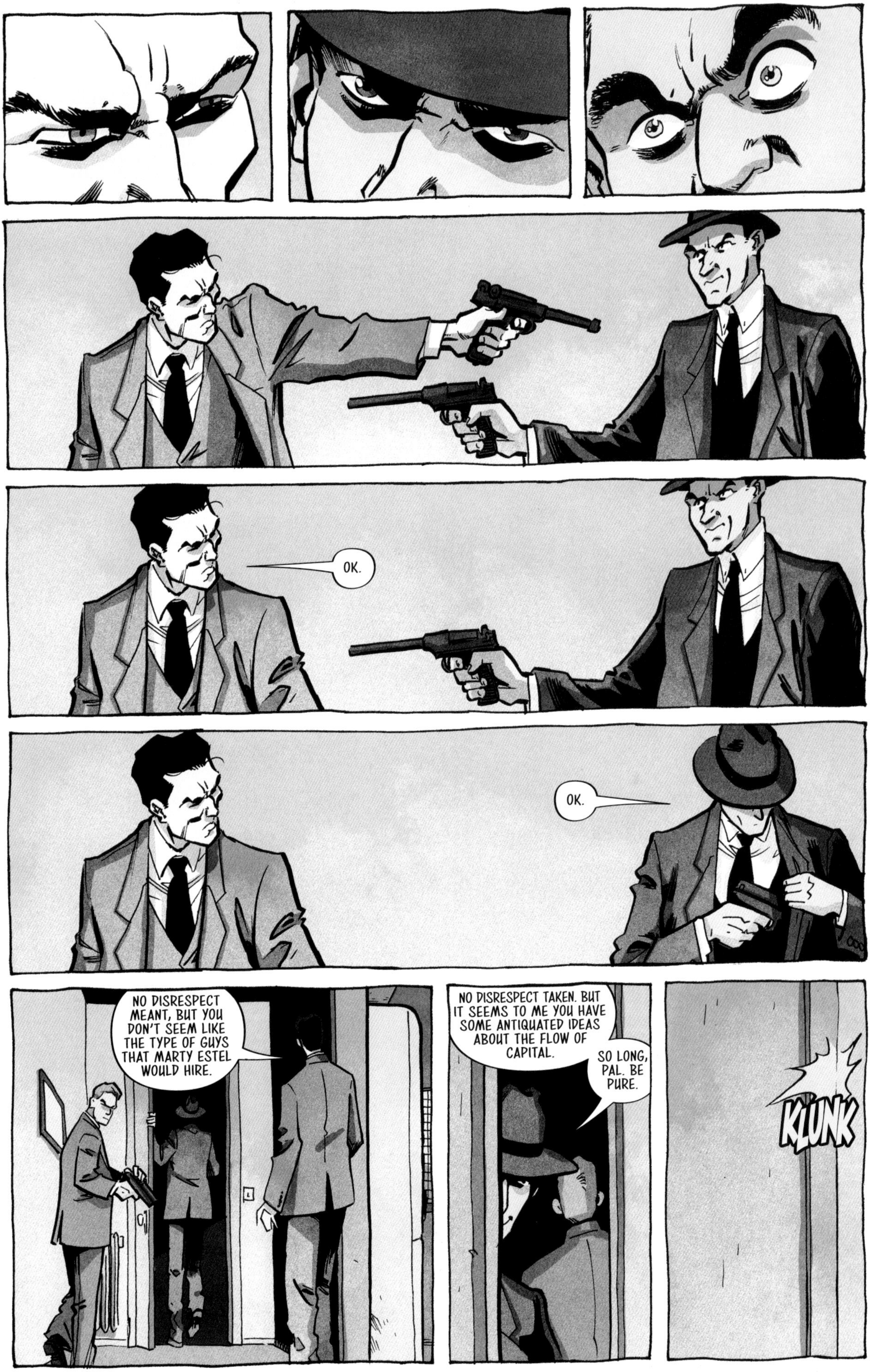
OK.
OK.
NO DISRESPECT MEANT, BUT YOU DON'T SEEM LIKE THE TYPE OF GUYS THAT MARTY ESTEL WOULD HIRE.
NO DISRESPECT TAKEN. BUT IT SEEMS TO ME YOU HAVE SOME ANTIQUATED IDEAS ABOUT THE FLOW OF CAPITAL.
SO LONG, PAL. BE PURE.
KLUNK

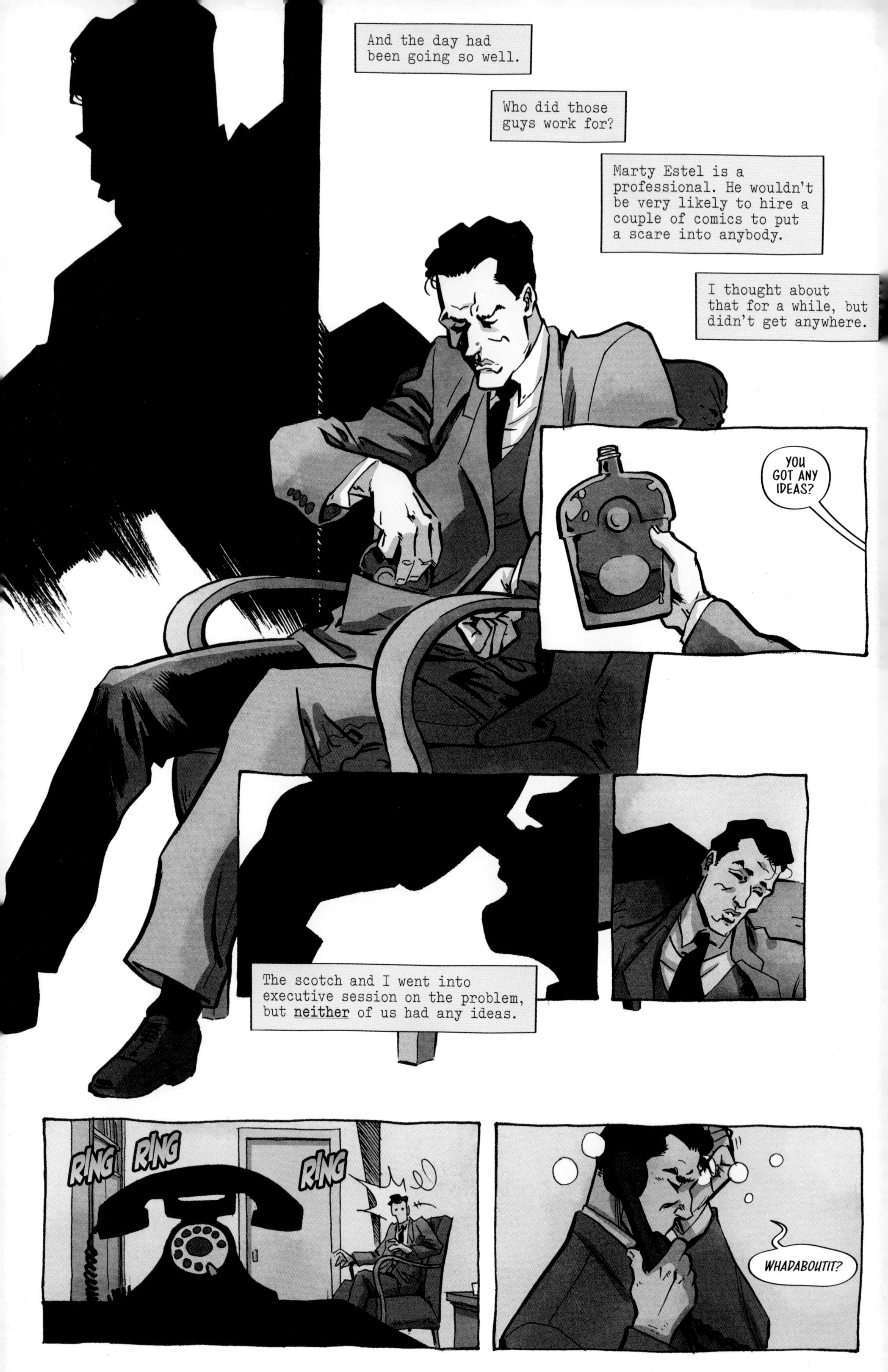

And the day had been going so well.
Who did those guys work for?
Marty Estel is a professional. He wouldn't be very likely to hire a couple of comics to put a scare into anybody.
I thought about that for a while, but didn't get anywhere.
YOU GOT ANY IDEAS?
The scotch and I went into executive session on the problem, but neither of us had any ideas.
RING RING
RING
WHADABOUTIT?

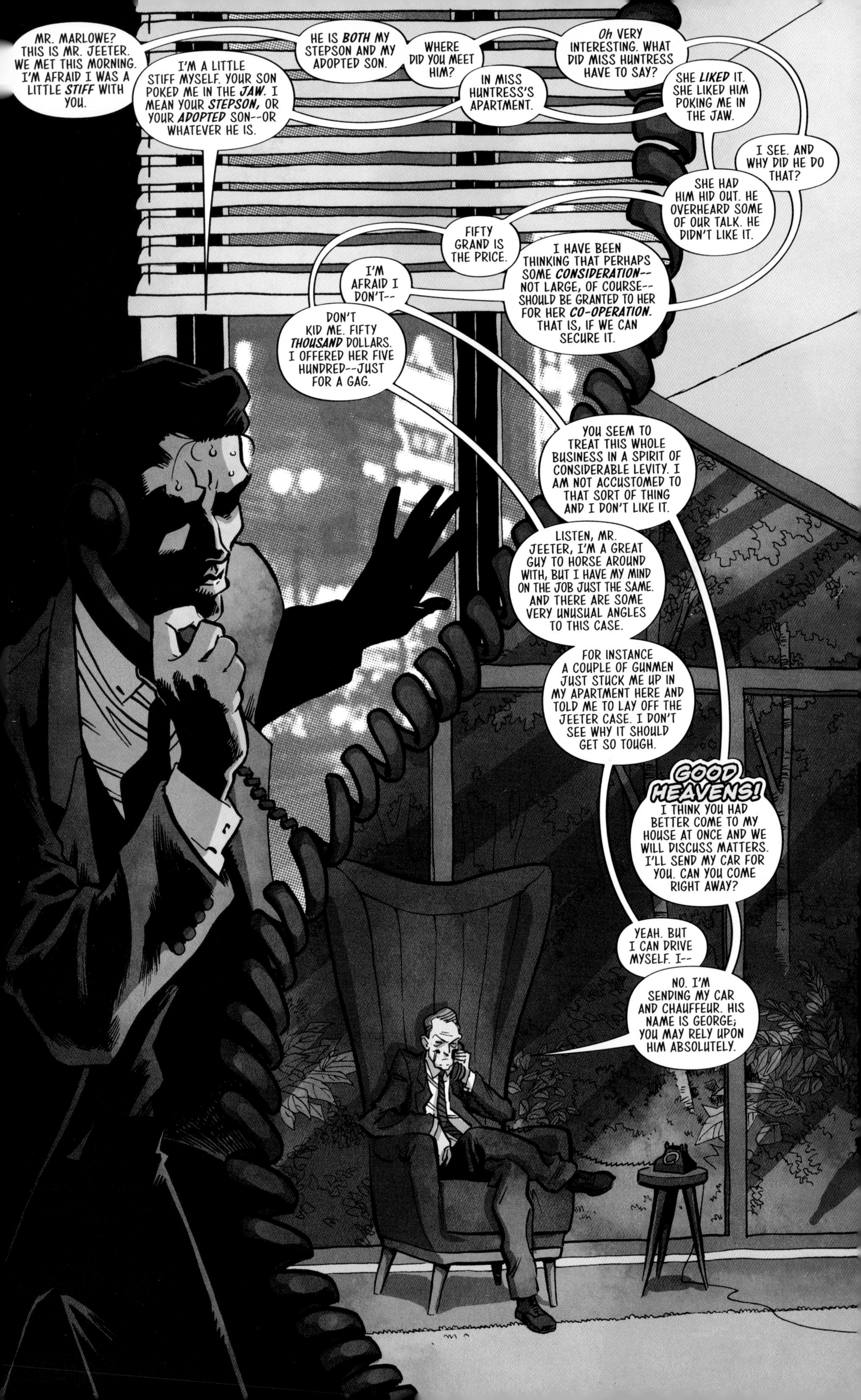
MR. MARLOWE? THIS IS MR. JEETER. WE MET THIS MORNING. I'M AFRAID I WAS A LITTLE STIFF WITH YOU.
I'M A LITTLE STIFF MYSELF. YOUR SON POKED ME IN THE JAW. I MEAN YOUR STEPSON, OR YOUR ADOPTED SON--OR WHATEVER HE IS.
HE IS BOTH MY STEPSON AND MY ADOPTED SON.
WHERE DID YOU MEET HIM?
IN MISS HUNTRESS'S APARTMENT.
Oh VERY INTERESTING. WHAT DID MISS HUNTRESS HAVE TO SAY?
SHE LIKED IT. SHE LIKED HIM POKING ME IN THE JAW.
I SEE. AND WHY DID HE DO THAT?
SHE HAD HIM HID OUT. HE OVERHEARD SOME OF OUR TALK. HE DIDN'T LIKE IT.
I HAVE BEEN THINKING THAT PERHAPS SOME CONSIDERATION--NOT LARGE, OF COURSE--SHOULD BE GRANTED TO HER FOR HER CO-OPERATION. THAT IS, IF WE CAN SECURE IT.
FIFTY GRAND IS THE PRICE.
I'M AFRAID I DON'T--
DON'T KID ME. FIFTY THOUSAND DOLLARS. I OFFERED HER FIVE HUNDRED--JUST FOR A GAG.
YOU SEEM TO TREAT THIS WHOLE BUSINESS IN A SPIRIT OF CONSIDERABLE LEVITY. I AM NOT ACCUSTOMED TO THAT SORT OF THING AND I DON'T LIKE IT.
LISTEN, MR. JEETER, I'M A GREAT GUY TO HORSE AROUND WITH, BUT I HAVE MY MIND ON THE JOB JUST THE SAME. AND THERE ARE SOME VERY UNUSUAL ANGLES TO THIS CASE.
FOR INSTANCE A COUPLE OF GUNMEN JUST STUCK ME UP IN MY APARTMENT HERE AND TOLD ME TO LAY OFF THE JEETER CASE. I DON'T SEE WHY IT SHOULD GET SO TOUGH.
GOOD HEAVENS! I THINK YOU HAD BETTER COME TO MY HOUSE AT ONCE AND WE WILL DISCUSS MATTERS. I'LL SEND MY CAR FOR YOU. CAN YOU COME RIGHT AWAY?
YEAH. BUT I CAN DRIVE MYSELF. I--
NO. I'M SENDING MY CAR AND CHAUFFEUR. HIS NAME IS GEORGE; YOU MAY RELY UPON HIM ABSOLUTELY.

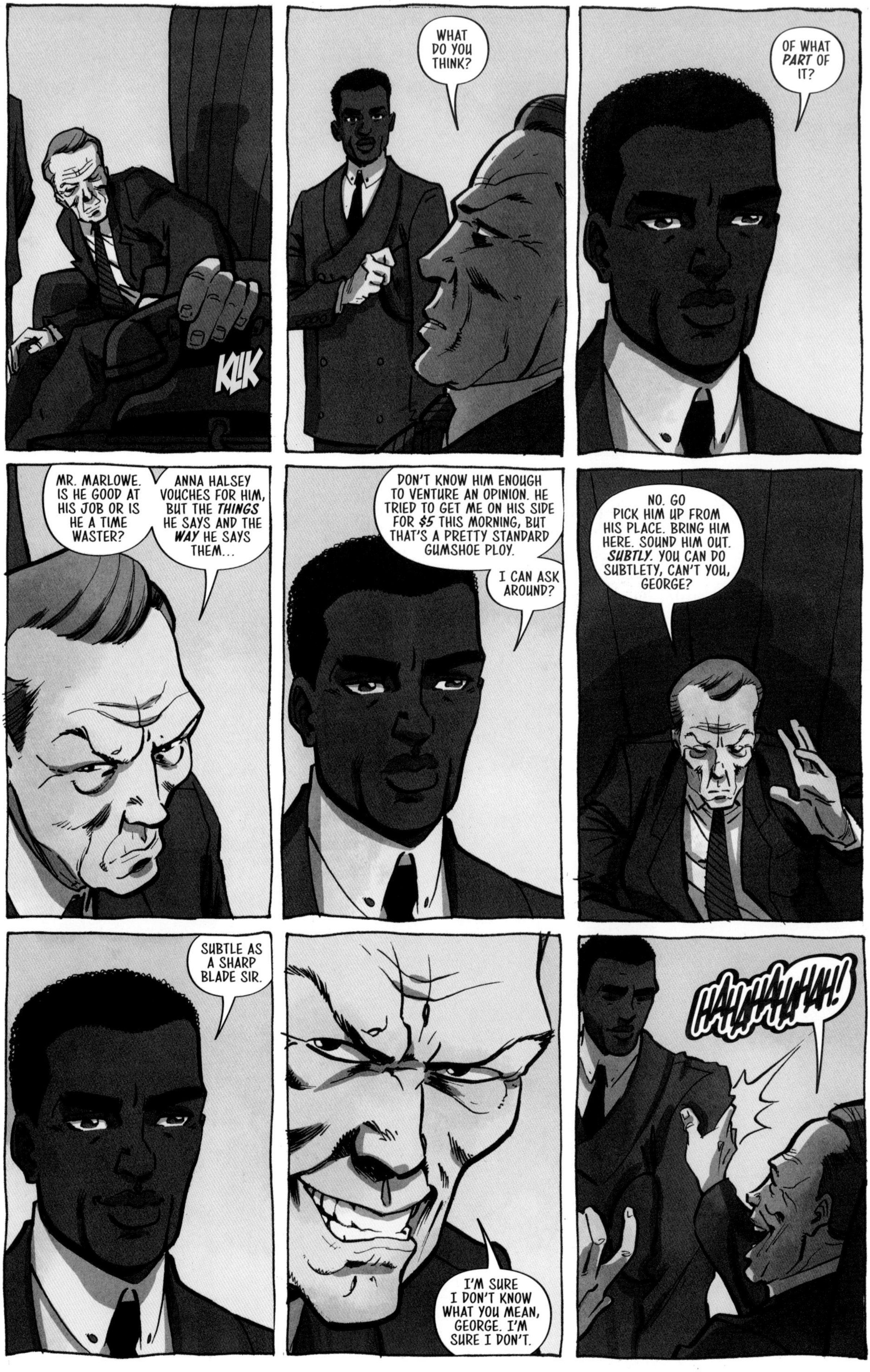
KLIK
WHAT DO YOU THINK?
OF WHAT PART OF IT?
MR. MARLOWE. IS HE GOOD AT HIS JOB OR IS HE A TIME WASTER?
ANNA HALSEY VOUCHES FOR HIM, BUT THE THINGS HE SAYS AND THE WAY HE SAYS THEM...
DON'T KNOW HIM ENOUGH TO VENTURE AN OPINION. HE TRIED TO GET ME ON HIS SIDE FOR $5 THIS MORNING, BUT THAT'S A PRETTY STANDARD GUMSHOE PLOY.
I CAN ASK AROUND?
NO. GO PICK HIM UP FROM HIS PLACE. BRING HIM HERE. SOUND HIM OUT. SUBTLY. YOU CAN DO SUBTLETY, CAN'T YOU, GEORGE?
SUBTLE AS A SHARP BLADE SIR.
I'M SURE I DON'T KNOW WHAT YOU MEAN, GEORGE. I'M SURE I DON'T.
HAHAHAHAHAH!

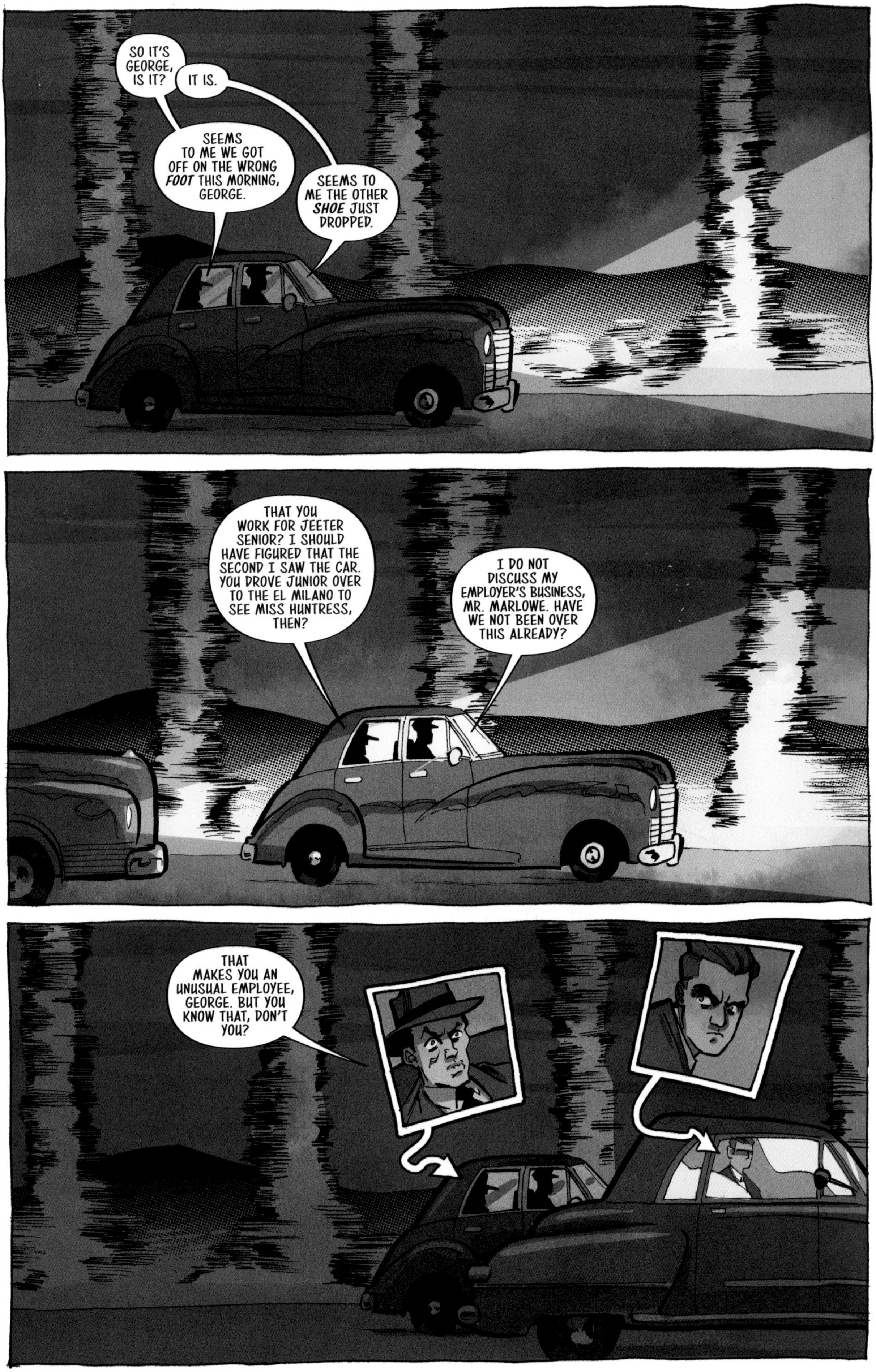
SO IT'S GEORGE, IS IT?
IT IS.
SEEMS TO ME WE GOT OFF ON THE WRONG *FOOT* THIS MORNING, GEORGE.
SEEMS TO ME THE OTHER *SHOE* JUST DROPPED.
THAT YOU WORK FOR JEETER SENIOR? I SHOULD HAVE FIGURED THAT THE SECOND I SAW THE CAR. YOU DROVE JUNIOR OVER TO THE EL MILANO TO SEE MISS HUNTRESS, THEN?
I DO NOT DISCUSS MY EMPLOYER'S BUSINESS, MR. MARLOWE. HAVE WE NOT BEEN OVER THIS ALREADY?
THAT MAKES YOU AN UNUSUAL EMPLOYEE, GEORGE. BUT YOU KNOW THAT, DON'T YOU?

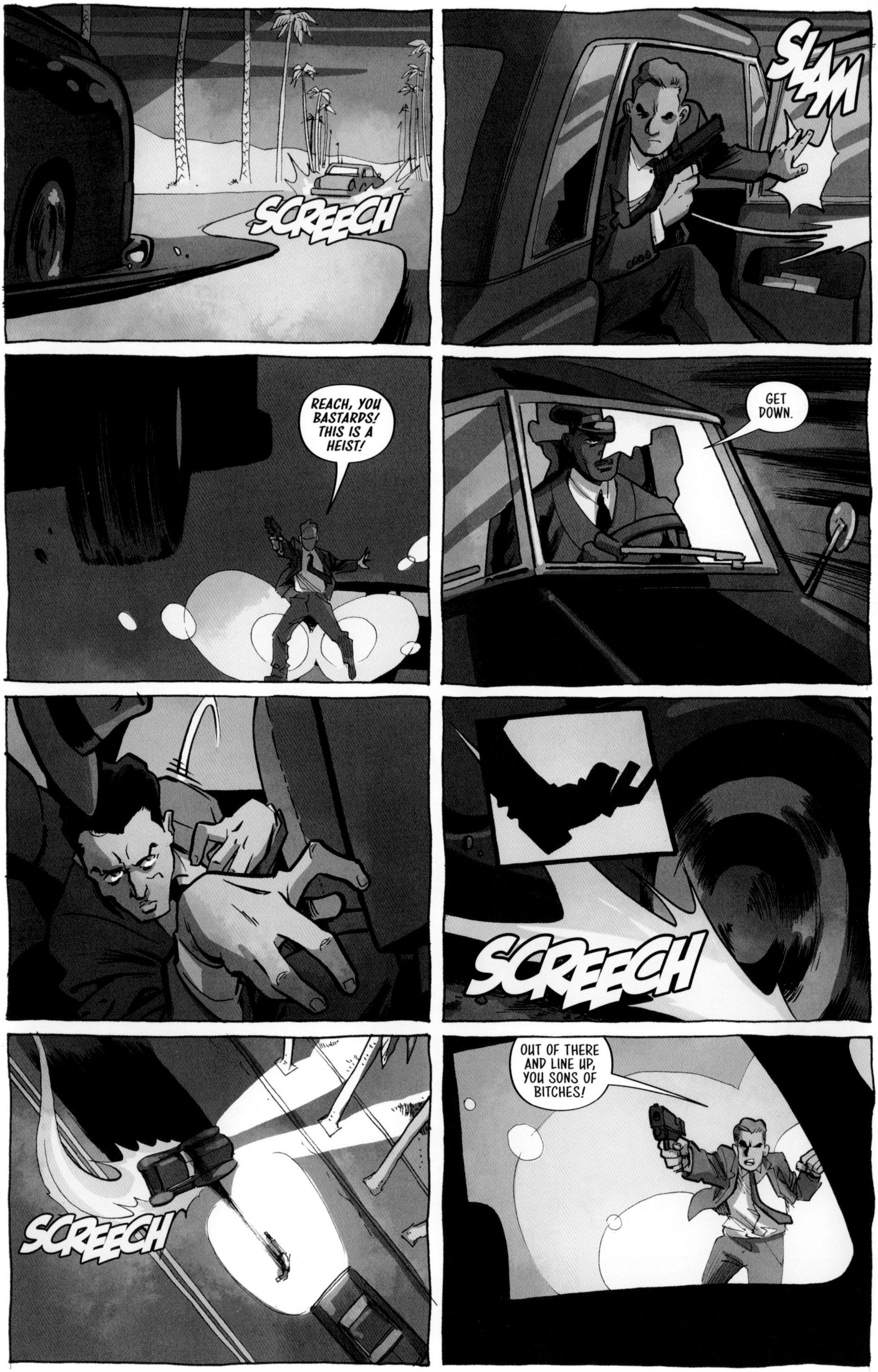
SCREECH
SLAM
REACH, YOU BASTARDS! THIS IS A HEIST!
GET DOWN.
SCREECH
SCREECH
OUT OF THERE AND LINE UP, YOU SONS OF BITCHES!

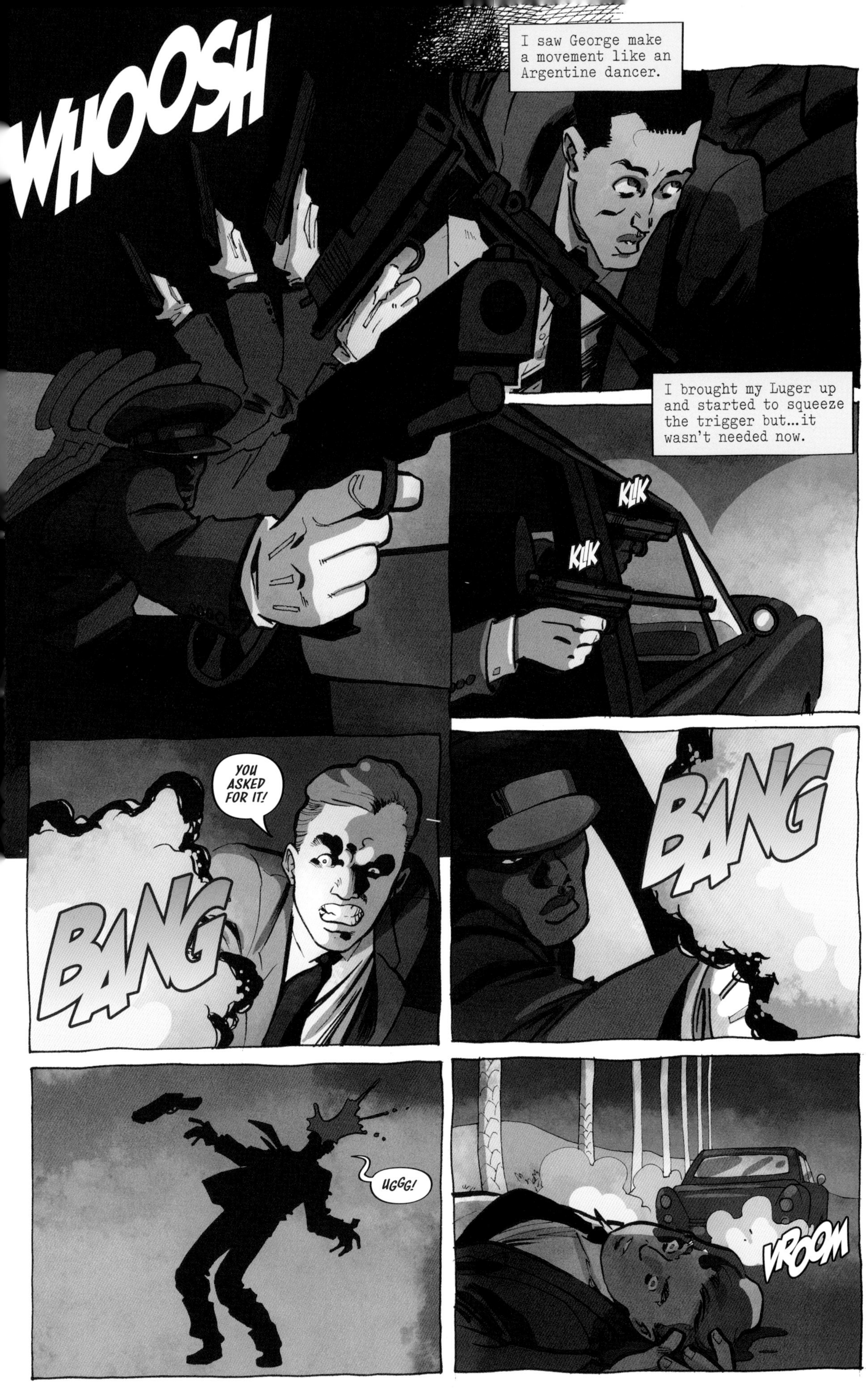
WHOOSH
I saw George make a movement like an Argentine dancer.
I brought my Luger up and started to squeeze the trigger but...it wasn't needed now.
KLIK
KLIK
YOU ASKED FOR IT!
BANG
BANG
UGGG!
VROOM

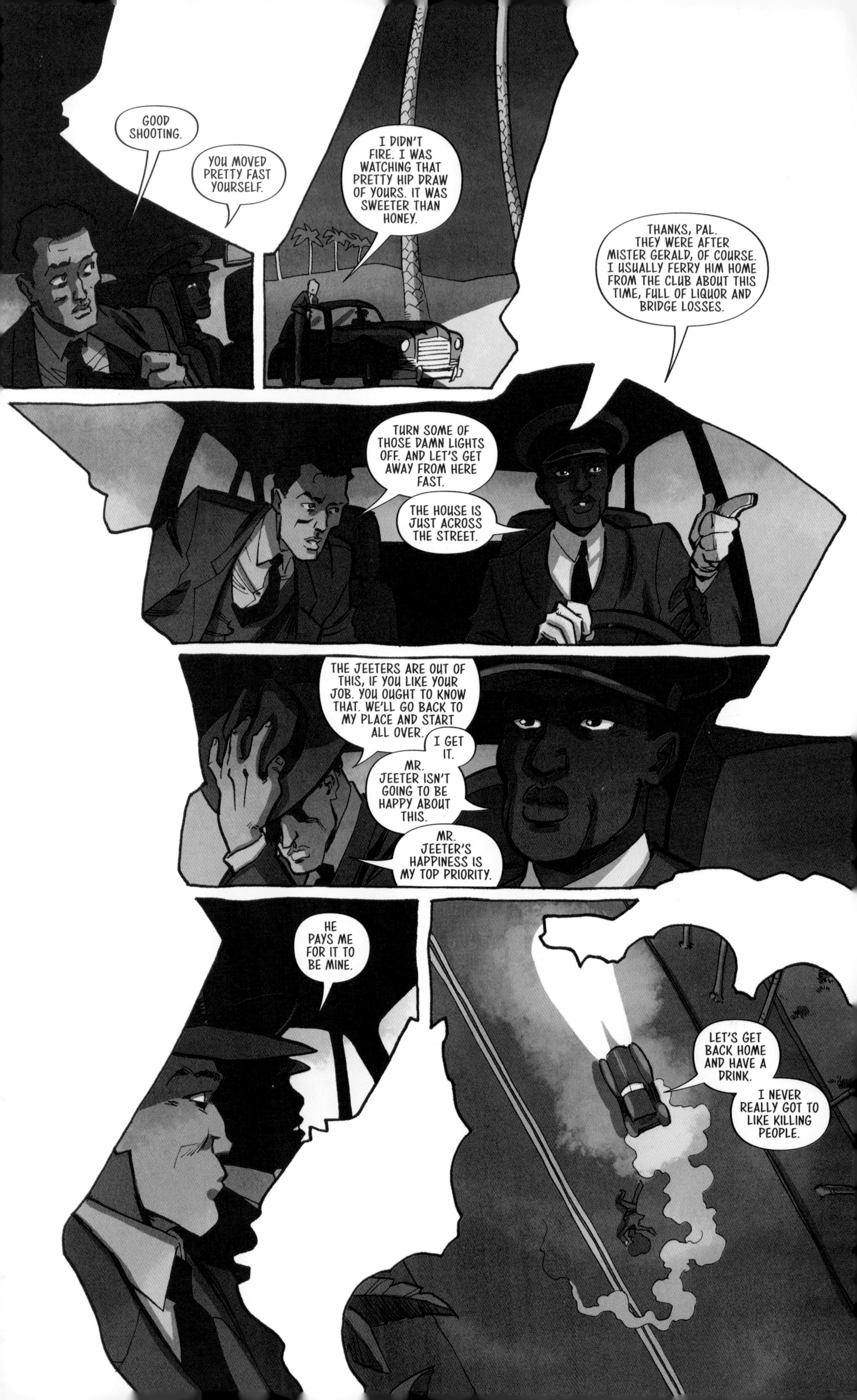
GOOD SHOOTING.
YOU MOVED PRETTY FAST YOURSELF.
I DIDN'T FIRE. I WAS WATCHING THAT PRETTY HIP DRAW OF YOURS. IT WAS SWEETER THAN HONEY.
THANKS, PAL. THEY WERE AFTER MISTER GERALD, OF COURSE. I USUALLY FERRY HIM HOME FROM THE CLUB ABOUT THIS TIME, FULL OF LIQUOR AND BRIDGE LOSSES.
TURN SOME OF THOSE DAMN LIGHTS OFF. AND LET'S GET AWAY FROM HERE FAST.
THE HOUSE IS JUST ACROSS THE STREET.
THE JEETERS ARE OUT OF THIS, IF YOU LIKE YOUR JOB. YOU OUGHT TO KNOW THAT. WE'LL GO BACK TO MY PLACE AND START ALL OVER.
I GET IT.
MR. JEETER ISN'T GOING TO BE HAPPY ABOUT THIS.
MR. JEETER'S HAPPINESS IS MY TOP PRIORITY.
HE PAYS ME FOR IT TO BE MINE.
LET'S GET BACK HOME AND HAVE A DRINK.
I NEVER REALLY GOT TO LIKE KILLING PEOPLE.

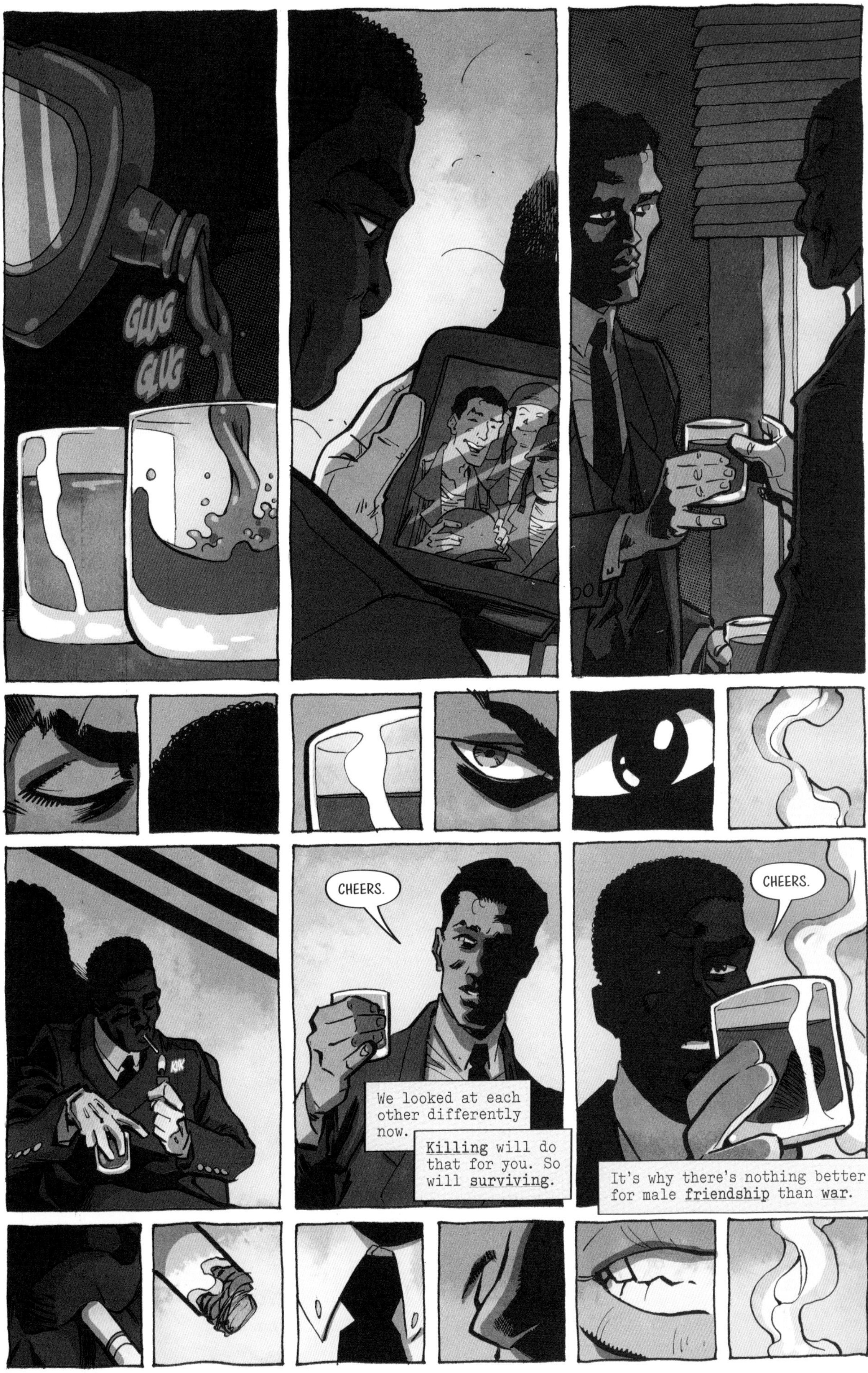
GLUG
GLUG
KLIK
CHEERS.
CHEERS.
We looked at each other differently now.
Killing will do that for you. So will surviving.
It's why there's nothing better for male friendship than war.

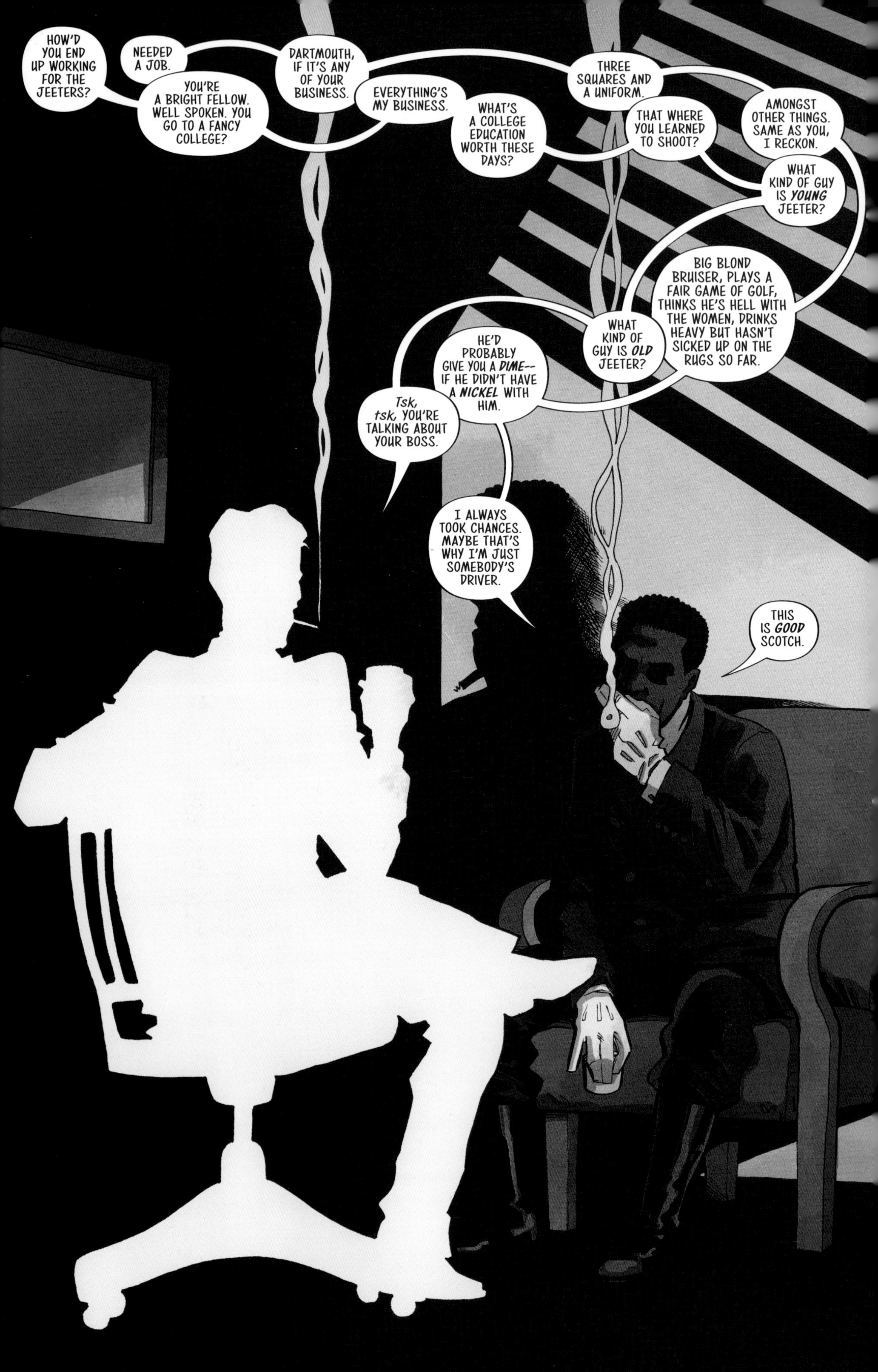
HOW'D YOU END UP WORKING FOR THE JEETERS?
NEEDED A JOB.
YOU'RE A BRIGHT FELLOW. WELL SPOKEN. YOU GO TO A FANCY COLLEGE?
DARTMOUTH, IF IT'S ANY OF YOUR BUSINESS.
EVERYTHING'S MY BUSINESS.
WHAT'S A COLLEGE EDUCATION WORTH THESE DAYS?
THREE SQUARES AND A UNIFORM.
THAT WHERE YOU LEARNED TO SHOOT?
AMONGST OTHER THINGS. SAME AS YOU, I RECKON.
WHAT KIND OF GUY IS *YOUNG* JEETER?
BIG BLOND BRUISER, PLAYS A FAIR GAME OF GOLF, THINKS HE'S HELL WITH THE WOMEN, DRINKS HEAVY BUT HASN'T SICKED UP ON THE RUGS SO FAR.
WHAT KIND OF GUY IS *OLD* JEETER?
HE'D PROBABLY GIVE YOU A *DIME--* IF HE DIDN'T HAVE A *NICKEL* WITH HIM.
Tsk, tsk, YOU'RE TALKING ABOUT YOUR BOSS.
I ALWAYS TOOK CHANCES. MAYBE THAT'S WHY I'M JUST SOMEBODY'S DRIVER.
THIS IS *GOOD* SCOTCH.

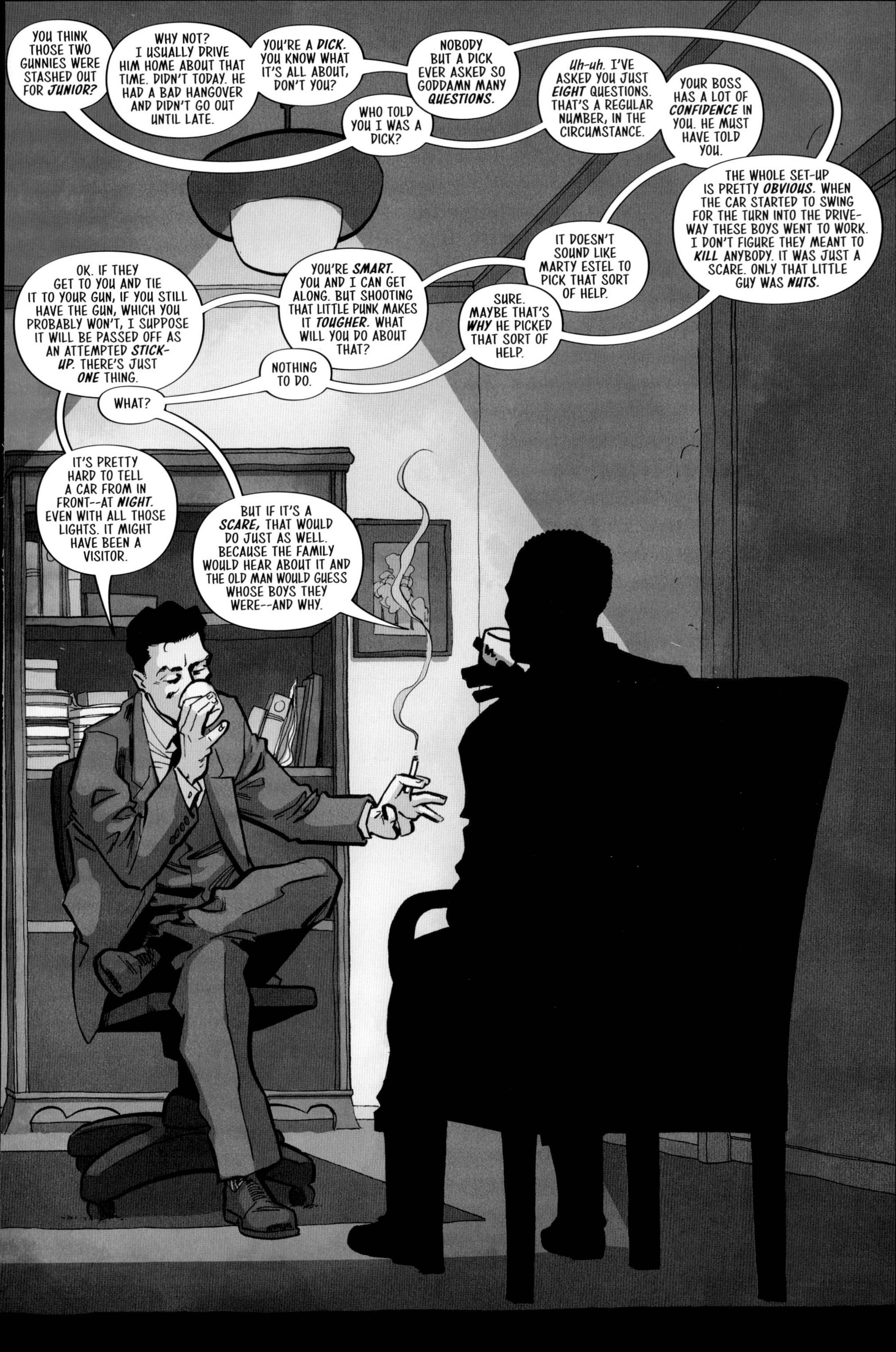
YOU THINK THOSE TWO GUNNIES WERE STASHED OUT FOR *JUNIOR?*
WHY NOT? I USUALLY DRIVE HIM HOME ABOUT THAT TIME. DIDN'T TODAY. HE HAD A BAD HANGOVER AND DIDN'T GO OUT UNTIL LATE.
YOU'RE A *DICK.* YOU KNOW WHAT IT'S ALL ABOUT, DON'T YOU?
WHO TOLD YOU I WAS A DICK?
NOBODY BUT A DICK EVER ASKED SO GODDAMN MANY *QUESTIONS.*
Uh-uh. I'VE ASKED YOU JUST *EIGHT* QUESTIONS. THAT'S A REGULAR NUMBER, IN THE CIRCUMSTANCE.
YOUR BOSS HAS A LOT OF *CONFIDENCE* IN YOU. HE MUST HAVE TOLD YOU.
THE WHOLE SET-UP IS PRETTY *OBVIOUS.* WHEN THE CAR STARTED TO SWING FOR THE TURN INTO THE DRIVEWAY THESE BOYS WENT TO WORK. I DON'T FIGURE THEY MEANT TO *KILL* ANYBODY. IT WAS JUST A SCARE. ONLY THAT LITTLE GUY WAS *NUTS.*
IT DOESN'T SOUND LIKE MARTY ESTEL TO PICK THAT SORT OF HELP.
SURE. MAYBE THAT'S *WHY* HE PICKED THAT SORT OF HELP.
YOU'RE *SMART.* YOU AND I CAN GET ALONG. BUT SHOOTING THAT LITTLE PUNK MAKES IT *TOUGHER.* WHAT WILL YOU DO ABOUT THAT?
NOTHING TO DO.
OK. IF THEY GET TO YOU AND TIE IT TO YOUR GUN, IF YOU STILL HAVE THE GUN, WHICH YOU PROBABLY WON'T, I SUPPOSE IT WILL BE PASSED OFF AS AN ATTEMPTED *STICK-UP.* THERE'S JUST *ONE* THING.
WHAT?
IT'S PRETTY HARD TO TELL A CAR FROM IN FRONT--AT *NIGHT.* EVEN WITH ALL THOSE LIGHTS. IT MIGHT HAVE BEEN A VISITOR.
BUT IF IT'S A *SCARE,* THAT WOULD DO JUST AS WELL. BECAUSE THE FAMILY WOULD HEAR ABOUT IT AND THE OLD MAN WOULD GUESS WHOSE BOYS THEY WERE--AND WHY.

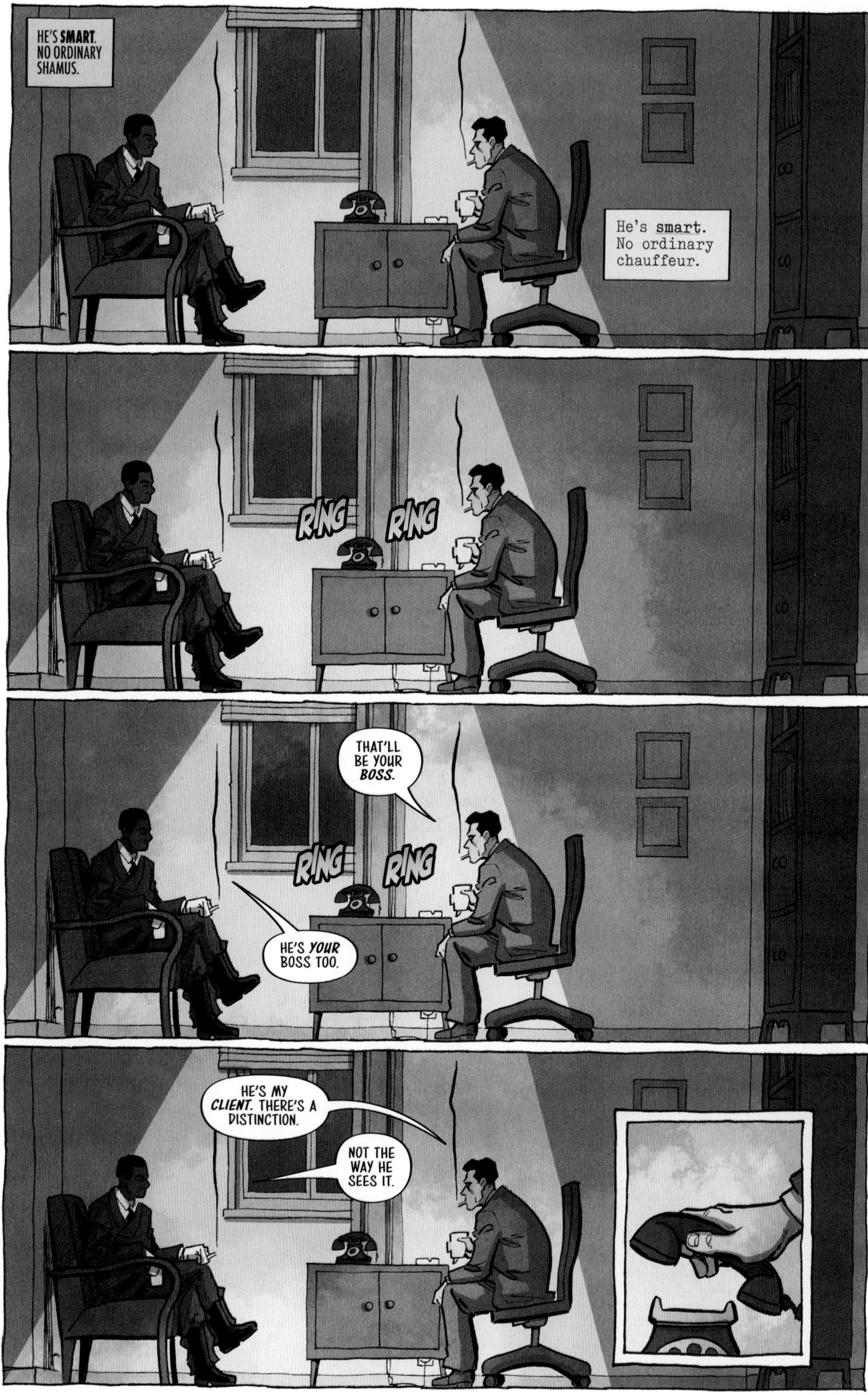
HE'S **SMART**. NO ORDINARY SHAMUS.
He's smart. No ordinary chauffeur.
RING RING
RING RING
THAT'LL BE YOUR *BOSS.*
HE'S *YOUR* BOSS TOO.
HE'S MY *CLIENT.* THERE'S A DISTINCTION.
NOT THE WAY HE SEES IT.

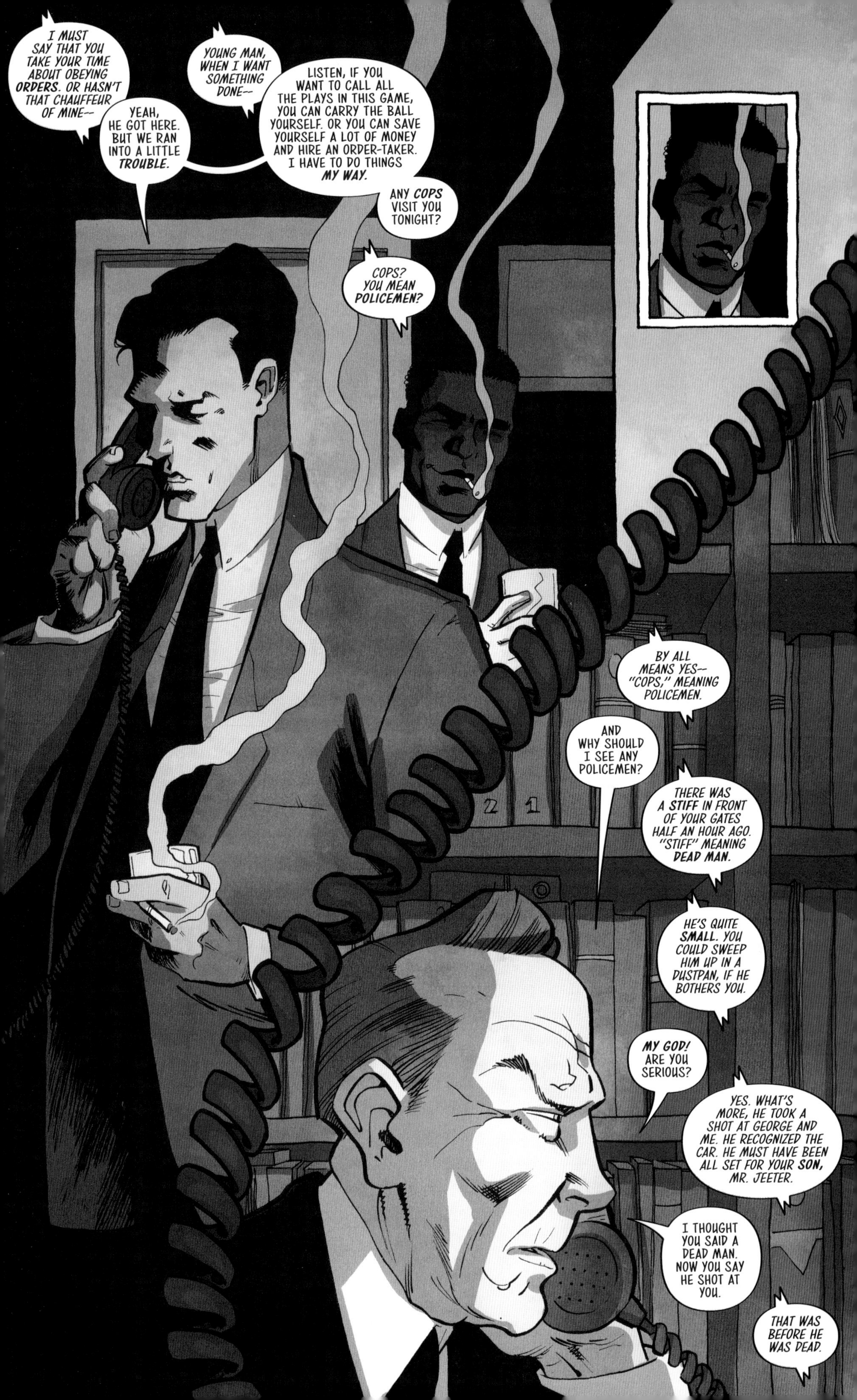
I MUST SAY THAT YOU TAKE YOUR TIME ABOUT OBEYING ORDERS. OR HASN'T THAT CHAUFFEUR OF MINE--
YEAH, HE GOT HERE. BUT WE RAN INTO A LITTLE TROUBLE.
YOUNG MAN, WHEN I WANT SOMETHING DONE--
LISTEN, IF YOU WANT TO CALL ALL THE PLAYS IN THIS GAME, YOU CAN CARRY THE BALL YOURSELF. OR YOU CAN SAVE YOURSELF A LOT OF MONEY AND HIRE AN ORDER-TAKER. I HAVE TO DO THINGS MY WAY.
ANY COPS VISIT YOU TONIGHT?
COPS? YOU MEAN POLICEMEN?
BY ALL MEANS YES-- "COPS," MEANING POLICEMEN.
AND WHY SHOULD I SEE ANY POLICEMEN?
THERE WAS A STIFF IN FRONT OF YOUR GATES HALF AN HOUR AGO. "STIFF" MEANING DEAD MAN.
HE'S QUITE SMALL. YOU COULD SWEEP HIM UP IN A DUSTPAN, IF HE BOTHERS YOU.
MY GOD! ARE YOU SERIOUS?
YES. WHAT'S MORE, HE TOOK A SHOT AT GEORGE AND ME. HE RECOGNIZED THE CAR. HE MUST HAVE BEEN ALL SET FOR YOUR SON, MR. JEETER.
I THOUGHT YOU SAID A DEAD MAN. NOW YOU SAY HE SHOT AT YOU.
THAT WAS BEFORE HE WAS DEAD.

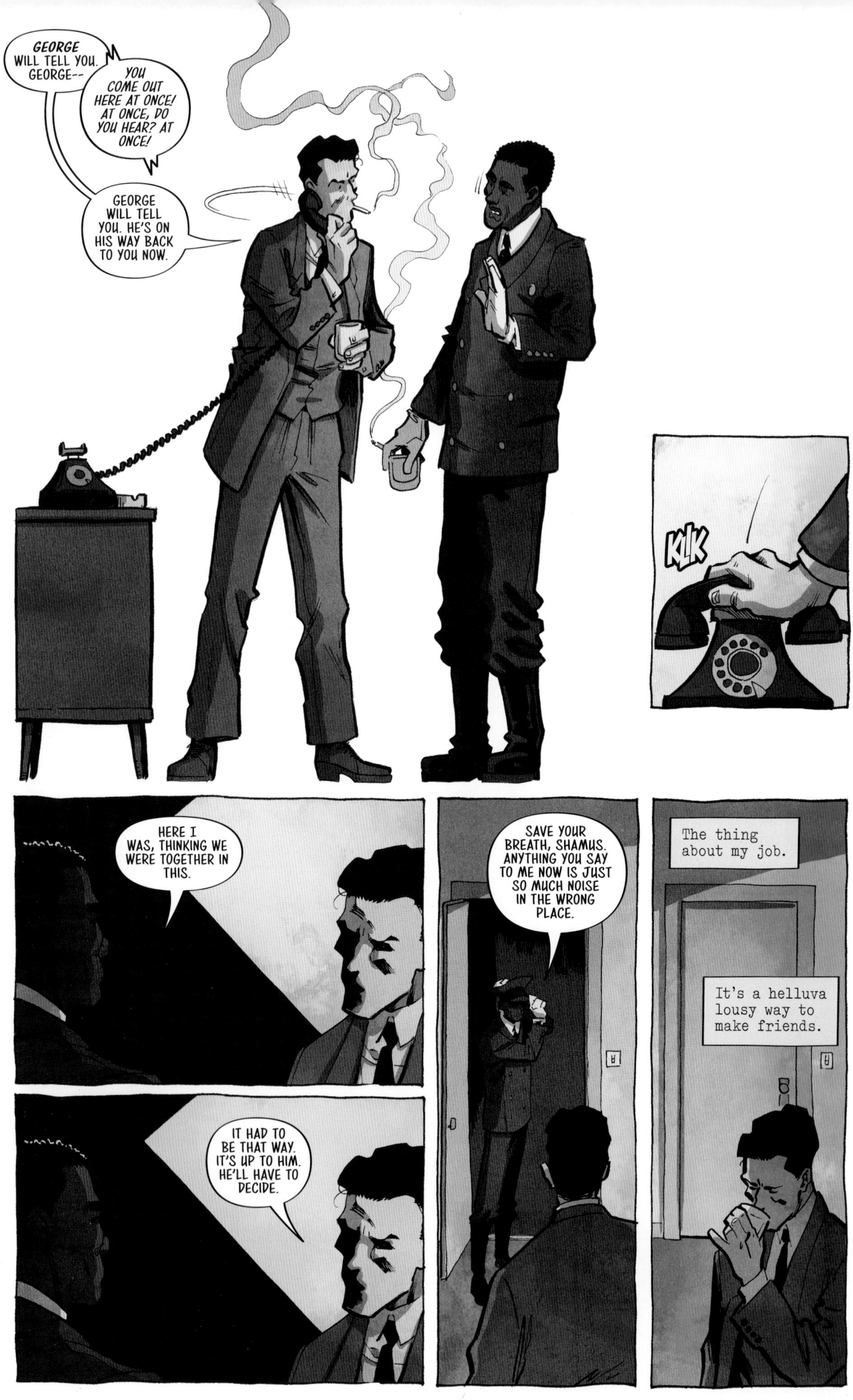
GEORGE WILL TELL YOU. GEORGE--
YOU COME OUT HERE AT ONCE! AT ONCE, DO YOU HEAR? AT ONCE!
GEORGE WILL TELL YOU. HE'S ON HIS WAY BACK TO YOU NOW.
KLIK
HERE I WAS, THINKING WE WERE TOGETHER IN THIS.
IT HAD TO BE THAT WAY. IT'S UP TO HIM. HE'LL HAVE TO DECIDE.
SAVE YOUR BREATH, SHAMUS. ANYTHING YOU SAY TO ME NOW IS JUST SO MUCH NOISE IN THE WRONG PLACE.
The thing about my job.
It's a helluva lousy way to make friends.

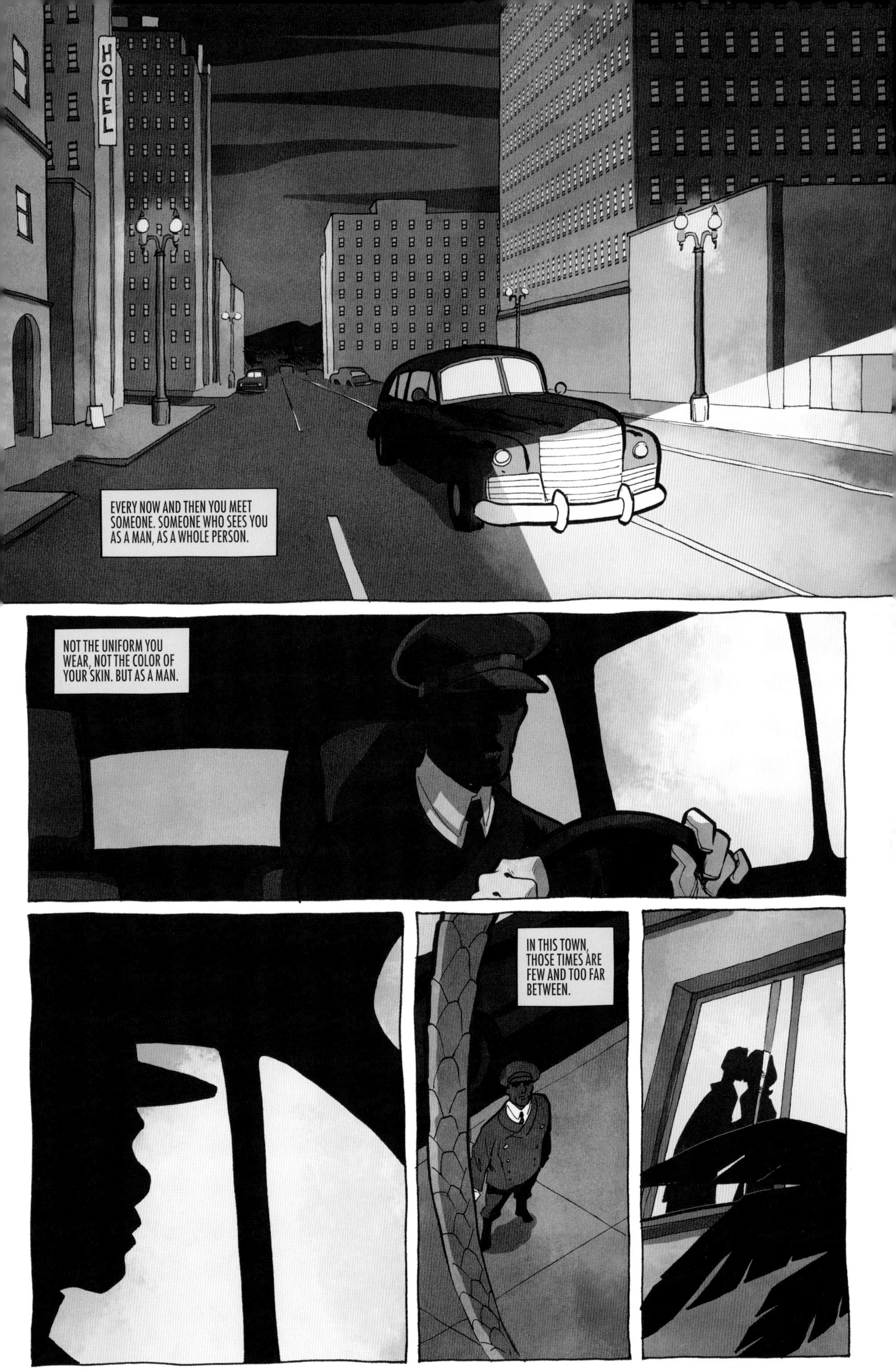
EVERY NOW AND THEN YOU MEET SOMEONE. SOMEONE WHO SEES YOU AS A MAN, AS A WHOLE PERSON.
HOTEL
NOT THE UNIFORM YOU WEAR, NOT THE COLOR OF YOUR SKIN. BUT AS A MAN.
IN THIS TOWN, THOSE TIMES ARE FEW AND TOO FAR BETWEEN.

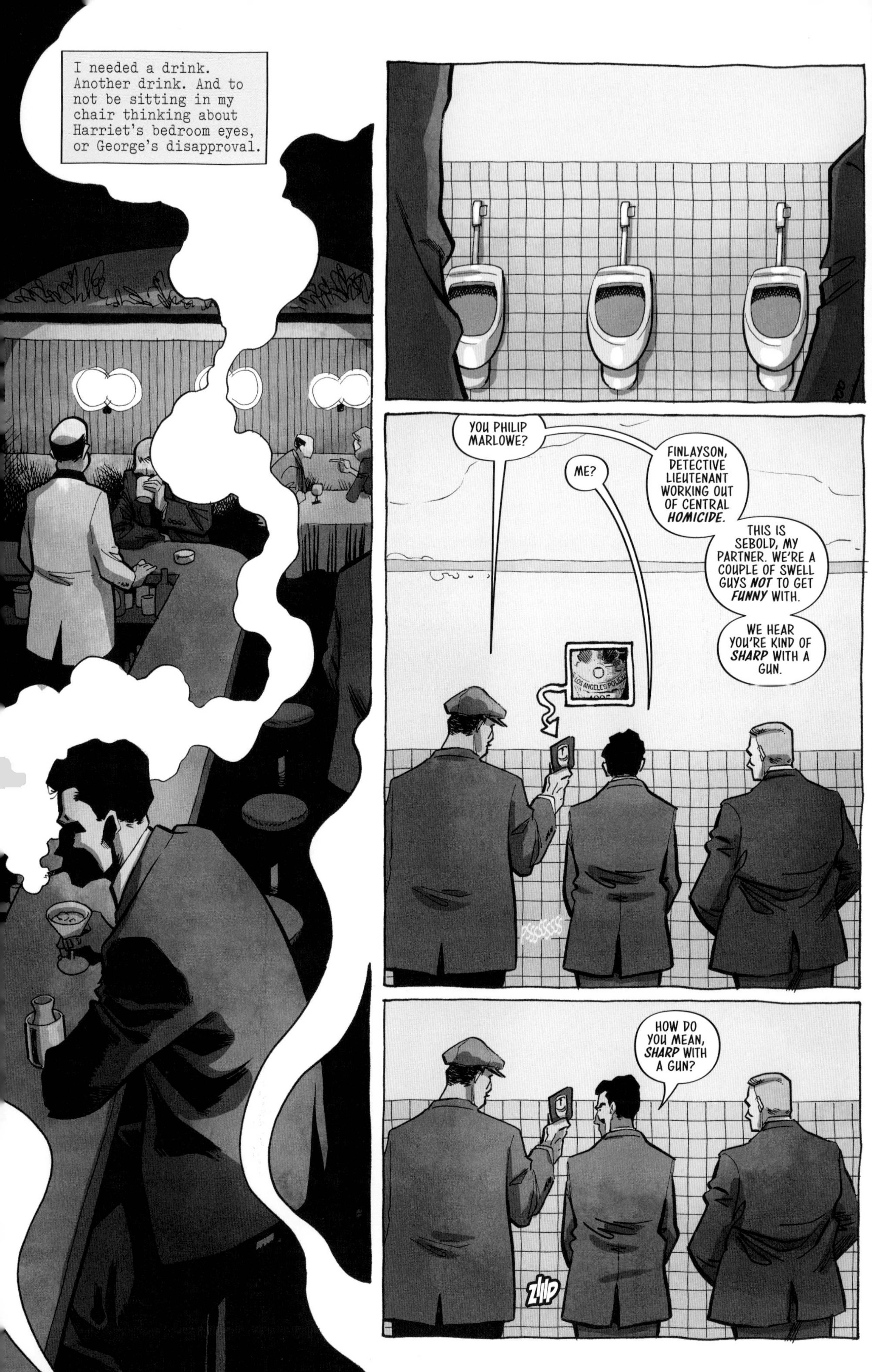

I needed a drink. Another drink. And to not be sitting in my chair thinking about Harriet's bedroom eyes, or George's disapproval.
YOU PHILIP MARLOWE?
ME?
FINLAYSON, DETECTIVE LIEUTENANT WORKING OUT OF CENTRAL **HOMICIDE.**
THIS IS SEBOLD, MY PARTNER. WE'RE A COUPLE OF SWELL GUYS **NOT** TO GET **FUNNY** WITH.
WE HEAR YOU'RE KIND OF **SHARP** WITH A GUN.
LOS ANGELES POLICE
PSSSSSSSS
HOW DO YOU MEAN, **SHARP** WITH A GUN?
ZIIP

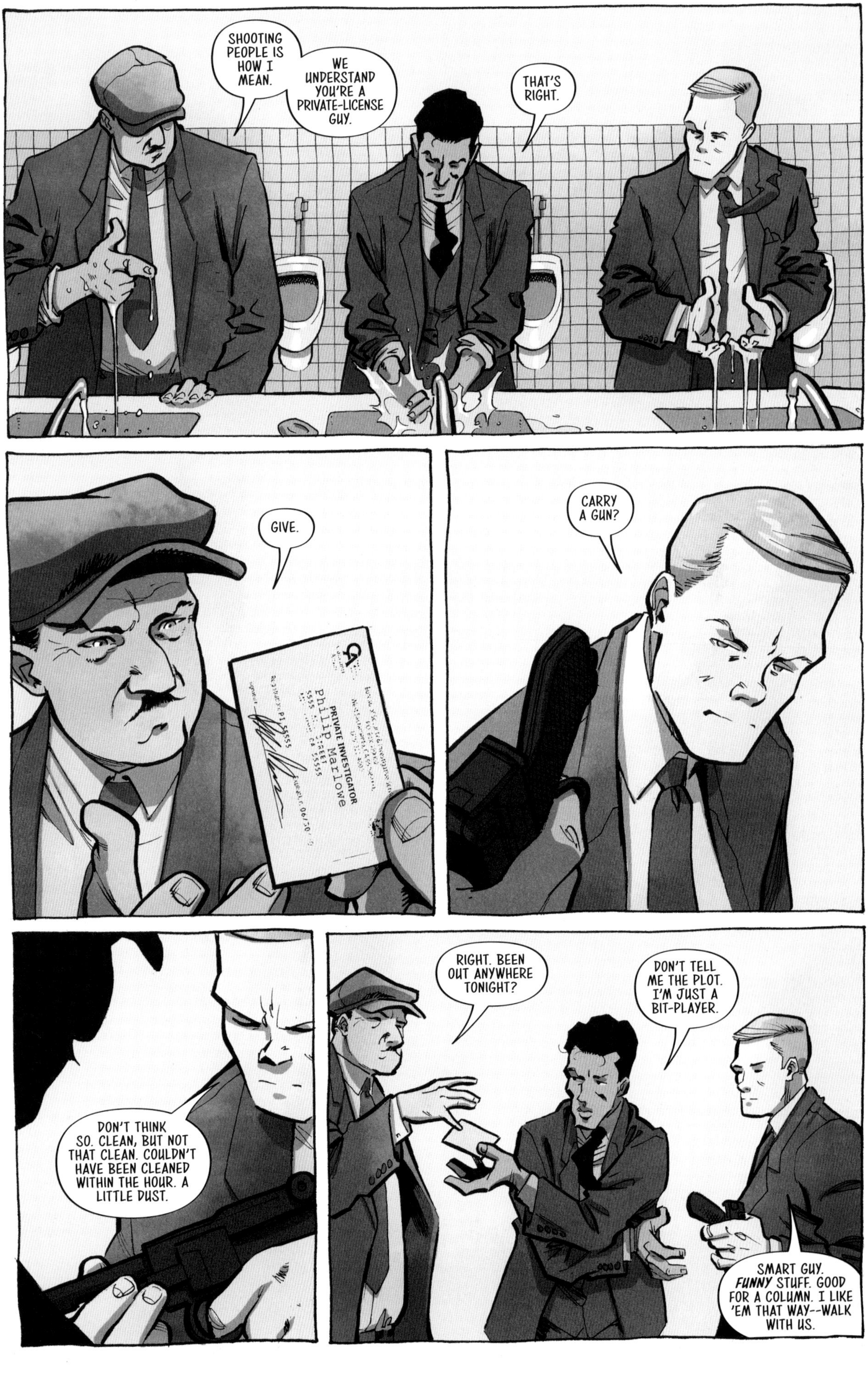

SHOOTING PEOPLE IS HOW I MEAN.
WE UNDERSTAND YOU'RE A PRIVATE-LICENSE GUY.
THAT'S RIGHT.
GIVE.
PRIVATE INVESTIGATOR
Philip Marlowe
CARRY A GUN?
DON'T THINK SO. CLEAN, BUT NOT THAT CLEAN. COULDN'T HAVE BEEN CLEANED WITHIN THE HOUR. A LITTLE DUST.
RIGHT. BEEN OUT ANYWHERE TONIGHT?
DON'T TELL ME THE PLOT. I'M JUST A BIT-PLAYER.
SMART GUY. ***FUNNY*** STUFF. GOOD FOR A COLUMN. I LIKE 'EM THAT WAY--WALK WITH US.

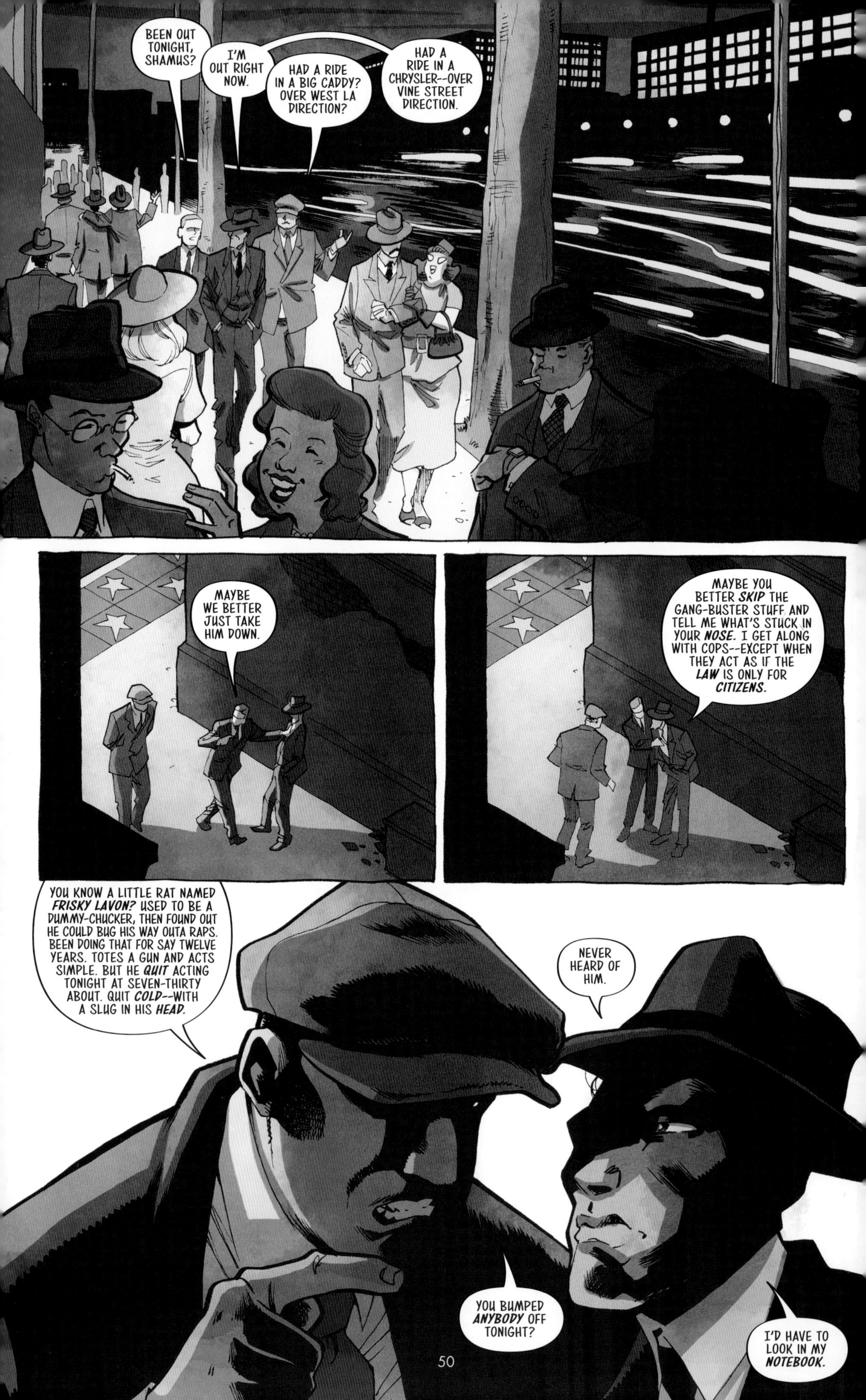
BEEN OUT TONIGHT, SHAMUS?
I'M OUT RIGHT NOW.
HAD A RIDE IN A BIG CADDY? OVER WEST LA DIRECTION?
HAD A RIDE IN A CHRYSLER--OVER VINE STREET DIRECTION.
MAYBE WE BETTER JUST TAKE HIM DOWN.
MAYBE YOU BETTER SKIP THE GANG-BUSTER STUFF AND TELL ME WHAT'S STUCK IN YOUR NOSE. I GET ALONG WITH COPS--EXCEPT WHEN THEY ACT AS IF THE LAW IS ONLY FOR CITIZENS.
YOU KNOW A LITTLE RAT NAMED FRISKY LAVON? USED TO BE A DUMMY-CHUCKER, THEN FOUND OUT HE COULD BUG HIS WAY OUTA RAPS. BEEN DOING THAT FOR SAY TWELVE YEARS. TOTES A GUN AND ACTS SIMPLE. BUT HE QUIT ACTING TONIGHT AT SEVEN-THIRTY ABOUT. QUIT COLD--WITH A SLUG IN HIS HEAD.
NEVER HEARD OF HIM.
YOU BUMPED ANYBODY OFF TONIGHT?
I'D HAVE TO LOOK IN MY NOTEBOOK.

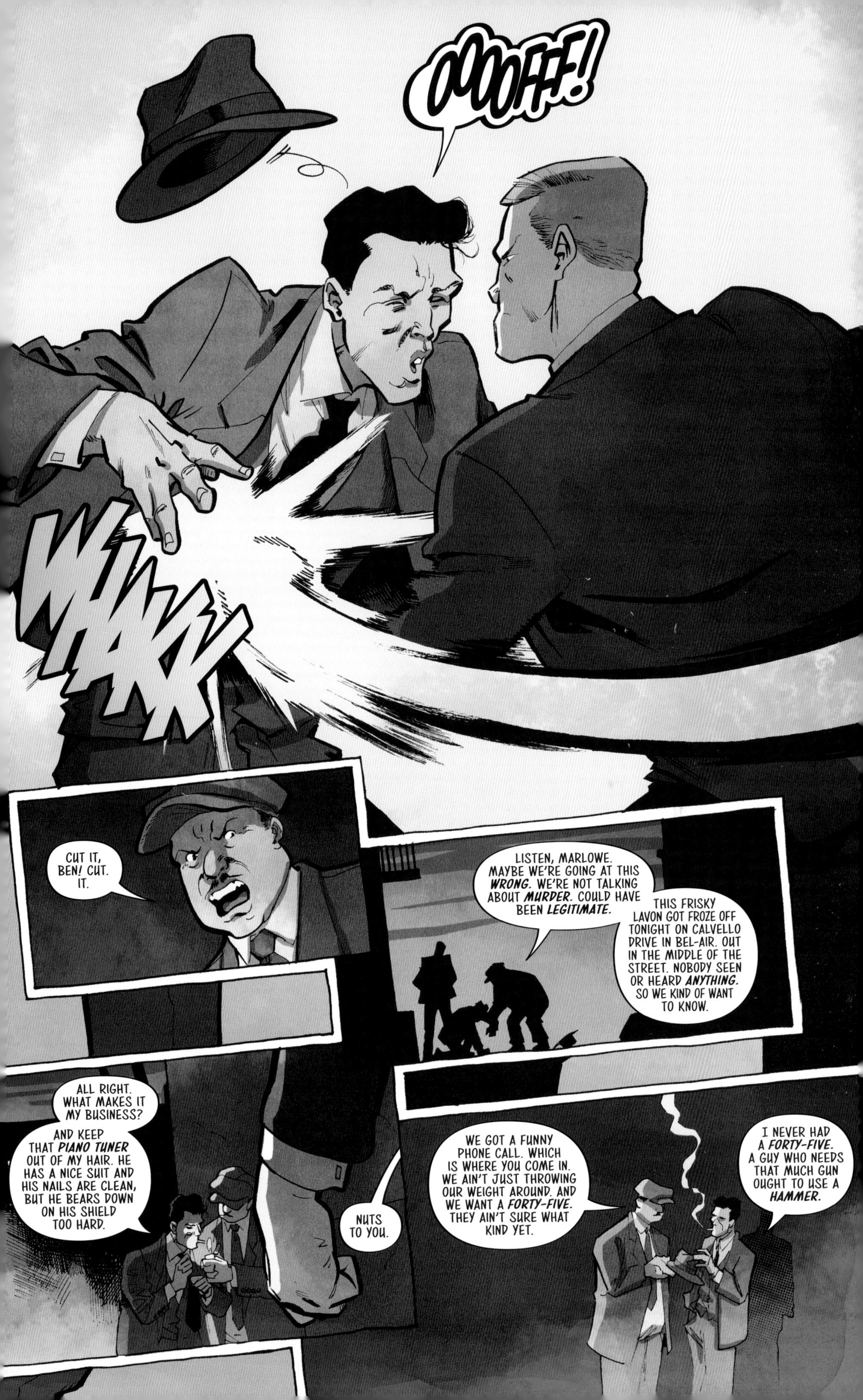
OOOOFFF!
WHAK!
CUT IT, BEN! CUT. IT.
LISTEN, MARLOWE. MAYBE WE'RE GOING AT THIS *WRONG.* WE'RE NOT TALKING ABOUT *MURDER.* COULD HAVE BEEN *LEGITIMATE.*
THIS FRISKY LAVON GOT FROZE OFF TONIGHT ON CALVELLO DRIVE IN BEL-AIR. OUT IN THE MIDDLE OF THE STREET. NOBODY SEEN OR HEARD *ANYTHING.* SO WE KIND OF WANT TO KNOW.
ALL RIGHT. WHAT MAKES IT MY BUSINESS?
AND KEEP THAT *PIANO TUNER* OUT OF MY HAIR. HE HAS A NICE SUIT AND HIS NAILS ARE CLEAN, BUT HE BEARS DOWN ON HIS SHIELD TOO HARD.
NUTS TO YOU.
WE GOT A FUNNY PHONE CALL. WHICH IS WHERE YOU COME IN. WE AIN'T JUST THROWING OUR WEIGHT AROUND. AND WE WANT A *FORTY-FIVE.* THEY AIN'T SURE WHAT KIND YET.
I NEVER HAD A *FORTY-FIVE.* A GUY WHO NEEDS THAT MUCH GUN OUGHT TO USE A *HAMMER.*

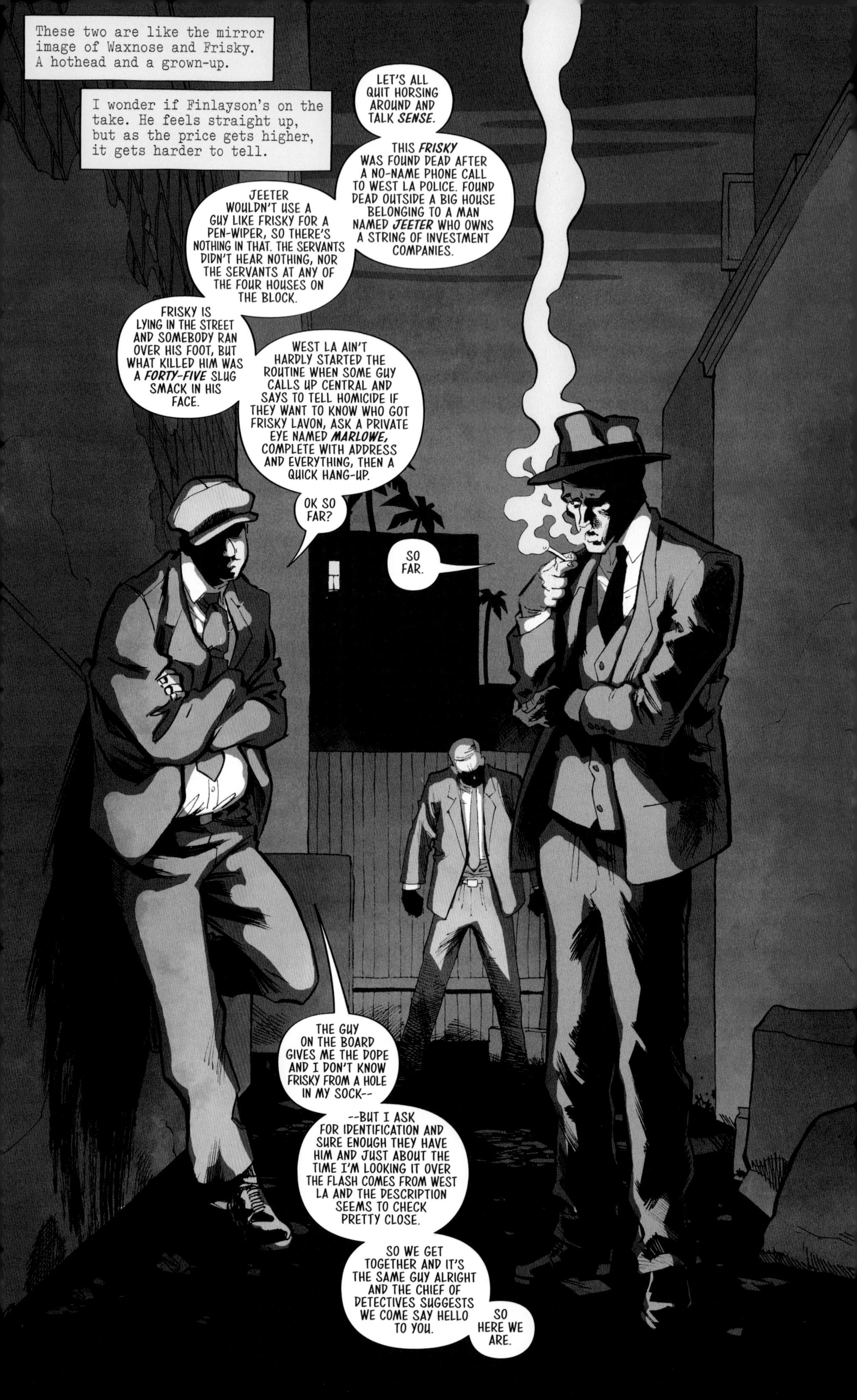

These two are like the mirror image of Waxnose and Frisky. A hothead and a grown-up.
I wonder if Finlayson's on the take. He feels straight up, but as the price gets higher, it gets harder to tell.
LET'S ALL QUIT HORSING AROUND AND TALK SENSE.
THIS FRISKY WAS FOUND DEAD AFTER A NO-NAME PHONE CALL TO WEST LA POLICE. FOUND DEAD OUTSIDE A BIG HOUSE BELONGING TO A MAN NAMED JEETER WHO OWNS A STRING OF INVESTMENT COMPANIES.
JEETER WOULDN'T USE A GUY LIKE FRISKY FOR A PEN-WIPER, SO THERE'S NOTHING IN THAT. THE SERVANTS DIDN'T HEAR NOTHING, NOR THE SERVANTS AT ANY OF THE FOUR HOUSES ON THE BLOCK.
FRISKY IS LYING IN THE STREET AND SOMEBODY RAN OVER HIS FOOT, BUT WHAT KILLED HIM WAS A FORTY-FIVE SLUG SMACK IN HIS FACE.
WEST LA AIN'T HARDLY STARTED THE ROUTINE WHEN SOME GUY CALLS UP CENTRAL AND SAYS TO TELL HOMICIDE IF THEY WANT TO KNOW WHO GOT FRISKY LAVON, ASK A PRIVATE EYE NAMED MARLOWE, COMPLETE WITH ADDRESS AND EVERYTHING, THEN A QUICK HANG-UP.
OK SO FAR?
SO FAR.
THE GUY ON THE BOARD GIVES ME THE DOPE AND I DON'T KNOW FRISKY FROM A HOLE IN MY SOCK--
--BUT I ASK FOR IDENTIFICATION AND SURE ENOUGH THEY HAVE HIM AND JUST ABOUT THE TIME I'M LOOKING IT OVER THE FLASH COMES FROM WEST LA AND THE DESCRIPTION SEEMS TO CHECK PRETTY CLOSE.
SO WE GET TOGETHER AND IT'S THE SAME GUY ALRIGHT AND THE CHIEF OF DETECTIVES SUGGESTS WE COME SAY HELLO TO YOU.
SO HERE WE ARE.

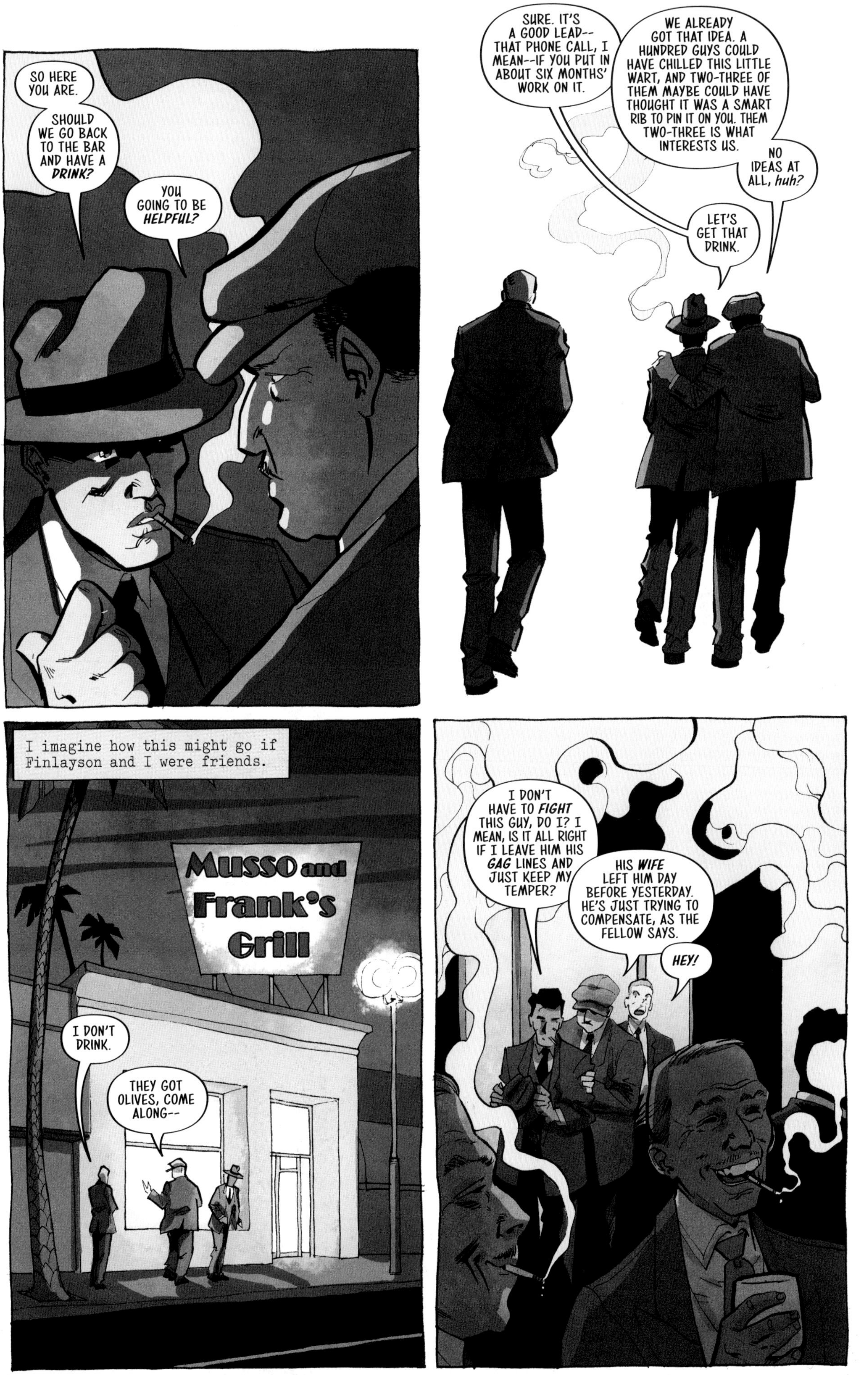
SO HERE YOU ARE.
SHOULD WE GO BACK TO THE BAR AND HAVE A *DRINK?*
YOU GOING TO BE *HELPFUL?*
SURE. IT'S A GOOD LEAD--THAT PHONE CALL, I MEAN--IF YOU PUT IN ABOUT SIX MONTHS' WORK ON IT.
WE ALREADY GOT THAT IDEA. A HUNDRED GUYS COULD HAVE CHILLED THIS LITTLE WART, AND TWO-THREE OF THEM MAYBE COULD HAVE THOUGHT IT WAS A SMART RIB TO PIN IT ON YOU. THEM TWO-THREE IS WHAT INTERESTS US.
NO IDEAS AT ALL, *huh?*
LET'S GET THAT DRINK.
I imagine how this might go if Finlayson and I were friends.
MUSSO and Frank's Grill
I DON'T DRINK.
THEY GOT OLIVES, COME ALONG--
I DON'T HAVE TO *FIGHT* THIS GUY, DO I? I MEAN, IS IT ALL RIGHT IF I LEAVE HIM HIS *GAG* LINES AND JUST KEEP MY TEMPER?
HIS *WIFE* LEFT HIM DAY BEFORE YESTERDAY. HE'S JUST TRYING TO COMPENSATE, AS THE FELLOW SAYS.
HEY!

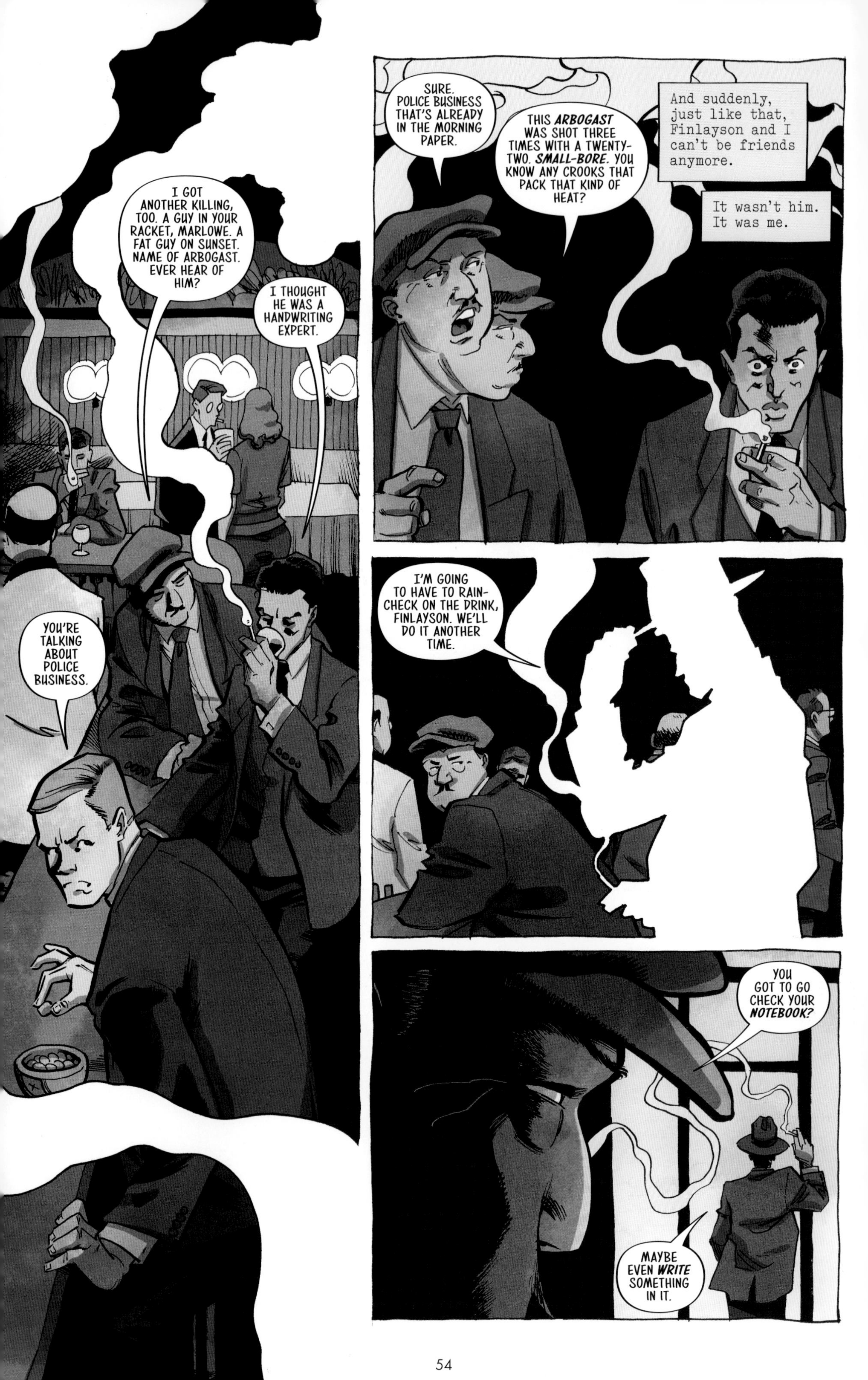
I GOT ANOTHER KILLING, TOO. A GUY IN YOUR RACKET, MARLOWE. A FAT GUY ON SUNSET. NAME OF ARBOGAST. EVER HEAR OF HIM?
I THOUGHT HE WAS A HANDWRITING EXPERT.
YOU'RE TALKING ABOUT POLICE BUSINESS.
SURE. POLICE BUSINESS THAT'S ALREADY IN THE MORNING PAPER.
THIS ARBOGAST WAS SHOT THREE TIMES WITH A TWENTY-TWO. SMALL-BORE. YOU KNOW ANY CROOKS THAT PACK THAT KIND OF HEAT?
And suddenly, just like that, Finlayson and I can't be friends anymore.
It wasn't him. It was me.
I'M GOING TO HAVE TO RAIN-CHECK ON THE DRINK, FINLAYSON. WE'LL DO IT ANOTHER TIME.
YOU GOT TO GO CHECK YOUR NOTEBOOK?
MAYBE EVEN WRITE SOMETHING IN IT.

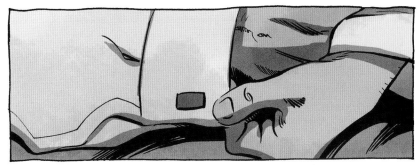

Arbogast was killed with a **small-bore** gun. A twenty-two. By someone who knew how to shoot.

I had met someone like that earlier **today**.

Now the next question was who was Waxnose working for?

I agreed with George that Waxnose and Frisky didn't feel like the kind of goons that Marty Estel would hire.

Also, why would you hire the same people to tell me to **leave off** Gerald and then have those **same people** shoot at Gerald?

None of this was **adding** up.

So I put on my monkey suit and went to see Marty.

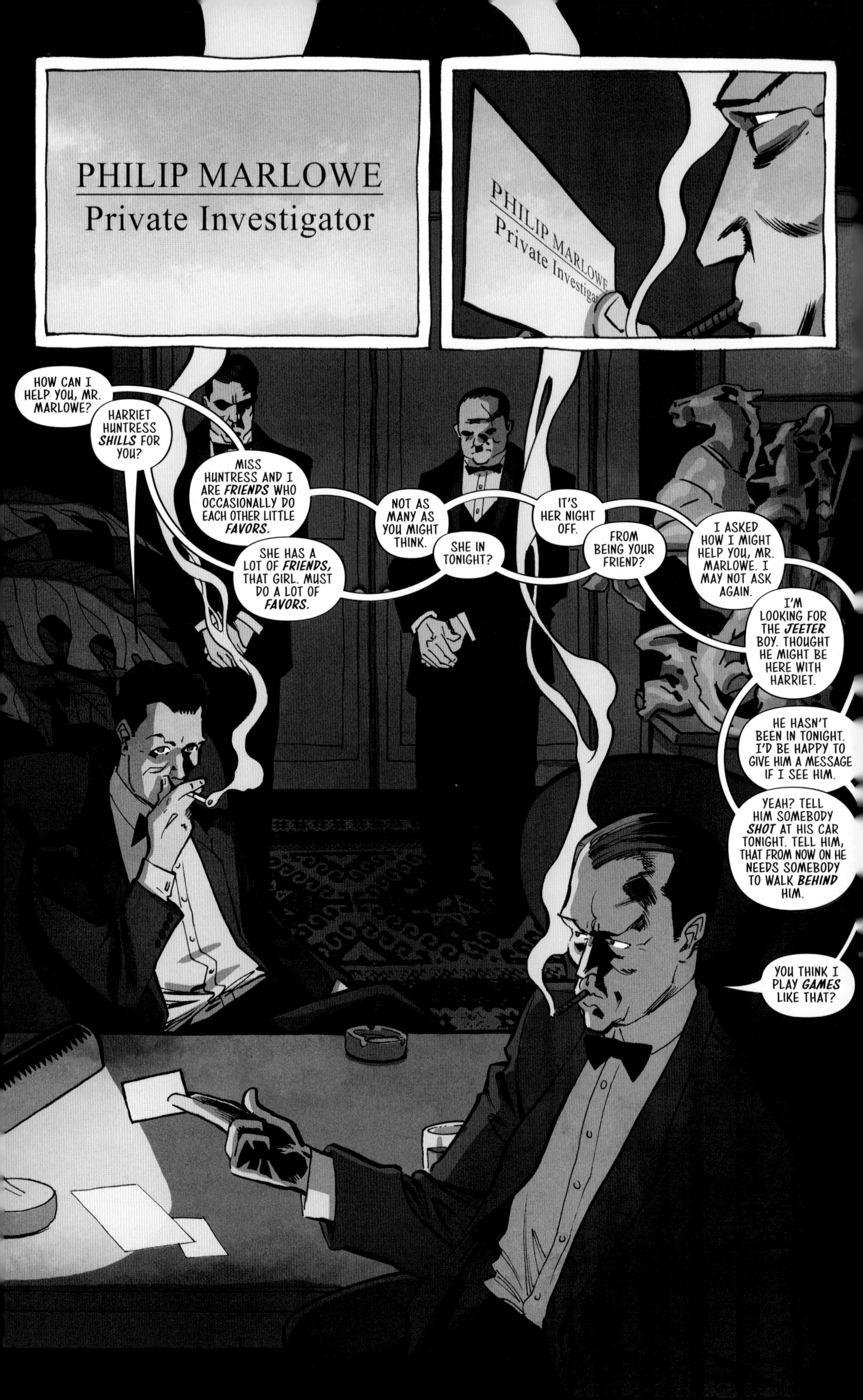
PHILIP MARLOWE
Private Investigator
PHILIP MARLOWE
Private Investigat
HOW CAN I HELP YOU, MR. MARLOWE?
HARRIET HUNTRESS SHILLS FOR YOU?
MISS HUNTRESS AND I ARE FRIENDS WHO OCCASIONALLY DO EACH OTHER LITTLE FAVORS.
SHE HAS A LOT OF FRIENDS, THAT GIRL. MUST DO A LOT OF FAVORS.
NOT AS MANY AS YOU MIGHT THINK.
SHE IN TONIGHT?
IT'S HER NIGHT OFF.
FROM BEING YOUR FRIEND?
I ASKED HOW I MIGHT HELP YOU, MR. MARLOWE. I MAY NOT ASK AGAIN.
I'M LOOKING FOR THE JEETER BOY. THOUGHT HE MIGHT BE HERE WITH HARRIET.
HE HASN'T BEEN IN TONIGHT. I'D BE HAPPY TO GIVE HIM A MESSAGE IF I SEE HIM.
YEAH? TELL HIM SOMEBODY SHOT AT HIS CAR TONIGHT. TELL HIM, THAT FROM NOW ON HE NEEDS SOMEBODY TO WALK BEHIND HIM.
YOU THINK I PLAY GAMES LIKE THAT?

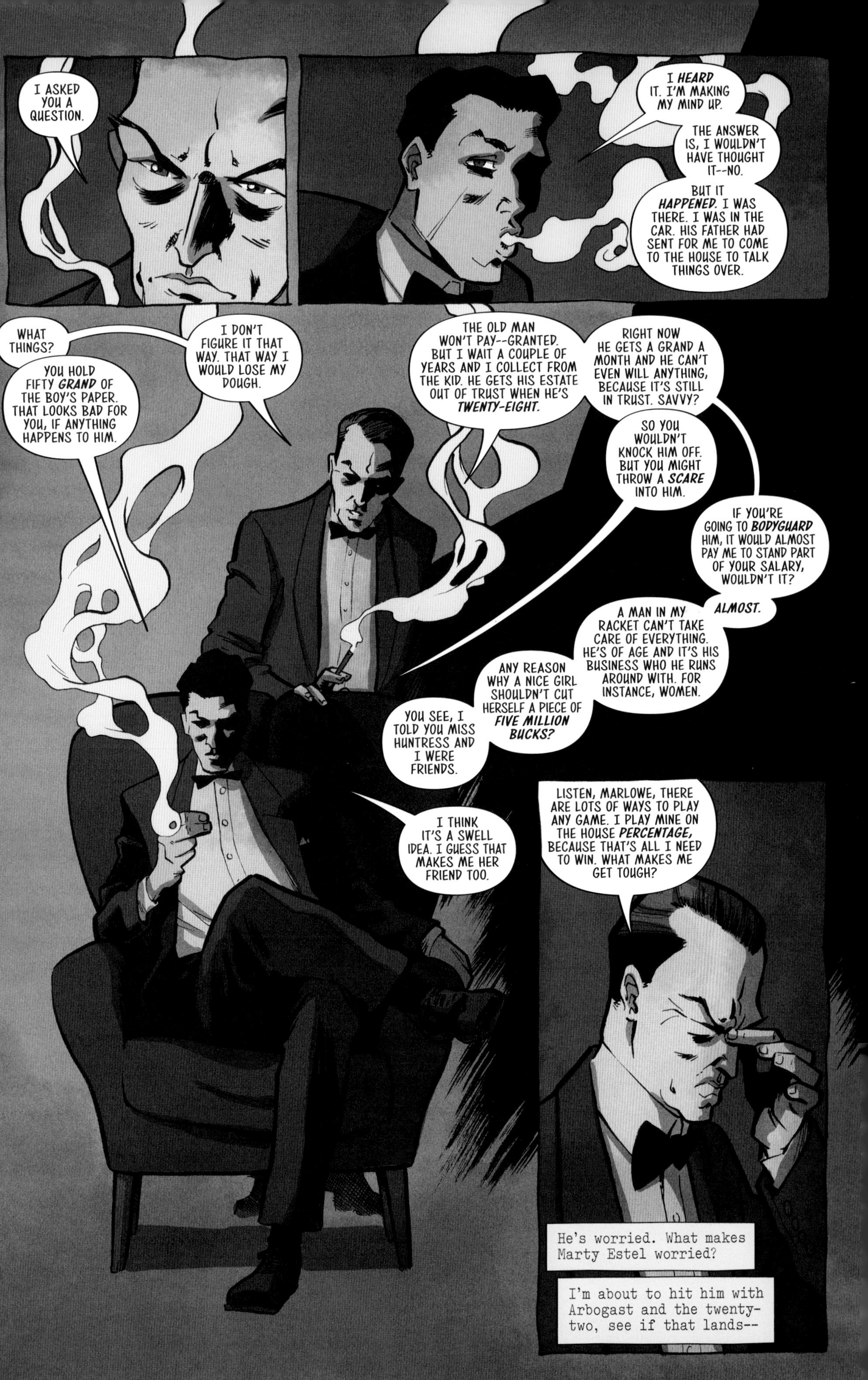

I ASKED YOU A QUESTION.
I HEARD IT. I'M MAKING MY MIND UP.
THE ANSWER IS, I WOULDN'T HAVE THOUGHT IT--NO.
BUT IT HAPPENED. I WAS THERE. I WAS IN THE CAR. HIS FATHER HAD SENT FOR ME TO COME TO THE HOUSE TO TALK THINGS OVER.
WHAT THINGS?
YOU HOLD FIFTY GRAND OF THE BOY'S PAPER. THAT LOOKS BAD FOR YOU, IF ANYTHING HAPPENS TO HIM.
I DON'T FIGURE IT THAT WAY. THAT WAY I WOULD LOSE MY DOUGH.
THE OLD MAN WON'T PAY--GRANTED. BUT I WAIT A COUPLE OF YEARS AND I COLLECT FROM THE KID. HE GETS HIS ESTATE OUT OF TRUST WHEN HE'S TWENTY-EIGHT.
RIGHT NOW HE GETS A GRAND A MONTH AND HE CAN'T EVEN WILL ANYTHING, BECAUSE IT'S STILL IN TRUST. SAVVY?
SO YOU WOULDN'T KNOCK HIM OFF. BUT YOU MIGHT THROW A SCARE INTO HIM.
IF YOU'RE GOING TO BODYGUARD HIM, IT WOULD ALMOST PAY ME TO STAND PART OF YOUR SALARY, WOULDN'T IT?
ALMOST.
A MAN IN MY RACKET CAN'T TAKE CARE OF EVERYTHING. HE'S OF AGE AND IT'S HIS BUSINESS WHO HE RUNS AROUND WITH. FOR INSTANCE, WOMEN.
ANY REASON WHY A NICE GIRL SHOULDN'T CUT HERSELF A PIECE OF FIVE MILLION BUCKS?
YOU SEE, I TOLD YOU MISS HUNTRESS AND I WERE FRIENDS.
I THINK IT'S A SWELL IDEA. I GUESS THAT MAKES ME HER FRIEND TOO.
LISTEN, MARLOWE, THERE ARE LOTS OF WAYS TO PLAY ANY GAME. I PLAY MINE ON THE HOUSE PERCENTAGE, BECAUSE THAT'S ALL I NEED TO WIN. WHAT MAKES ME GET TOUGH?
He's worried. What makes Marty Estel worried?
I'm about to hit him with Arbogast and the twenty-two, see if that lands--

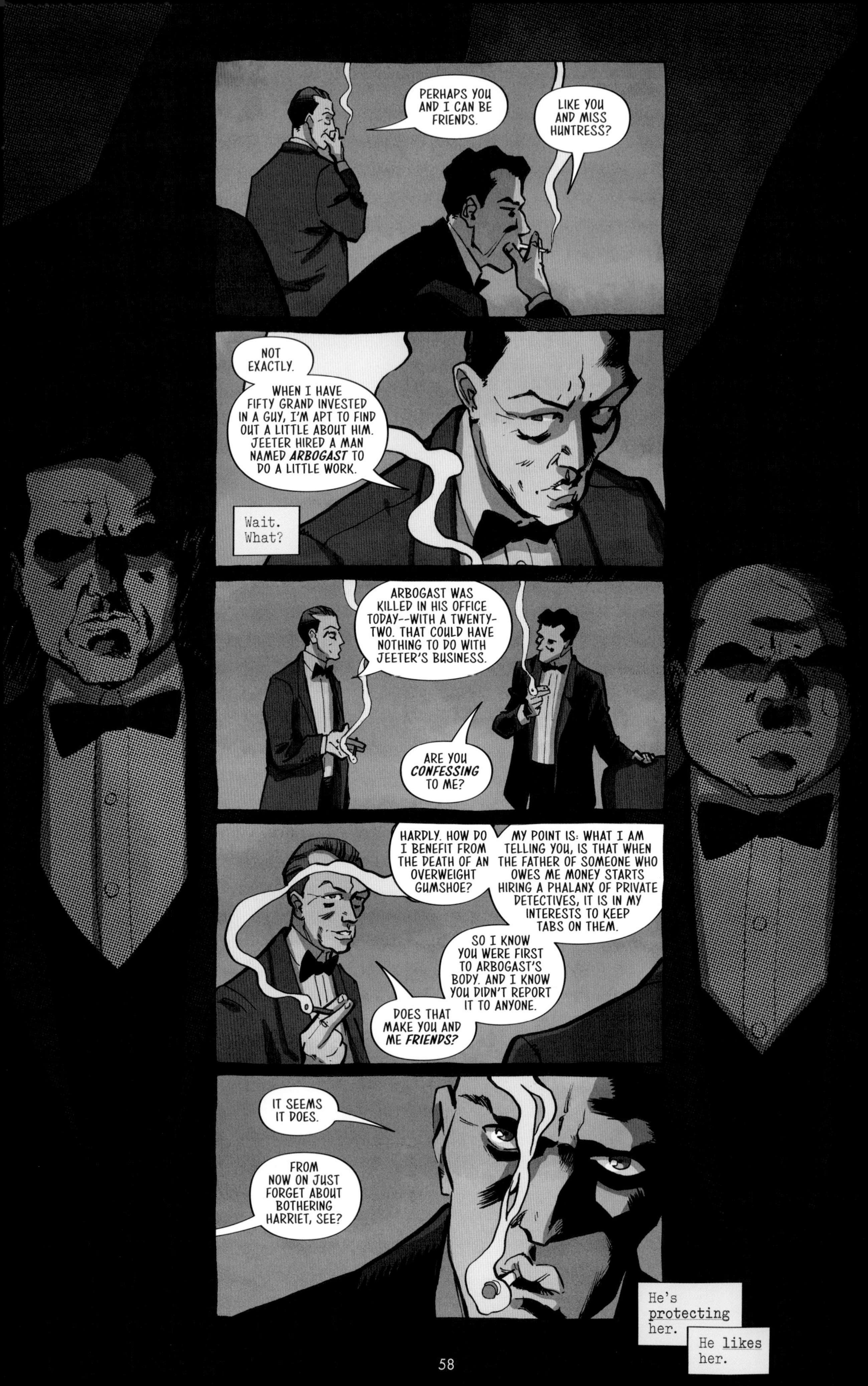
PERHAPS YOU AND I CAN BE FRIENDS.
LIKE YOU AND MISS HUNTRESS?
NOT EXACTLY.
WHEN I HAVE FIFTY GRAND INVESTED IN A GUY, I'M APT TO FIND OUT A LITTLE ABOUT HIM. JEETER HIRED A MAN NAMED ARBOGAST TO DO A LITTLE WORK.
Wait. What?
ARBOGAST WAS KILLED IN HIS OFFICE TODAY--WITH A TWENTY-TWO. THAT COULD HAVE NOTHING TO DO WITH JEETER'S BUSINESS.
ARE YOU CONFESSING TO ME?
HARDLY. HOW DO I BENEFIT FROM THE DEATH OF AN OVERWEIGHT GUMSHOE?
MY POINT IS: WHAT I AM TELLING YOU, IS THAT WHEN THE FATHER OF SOMEONE WHO OWES ME MONEY STARTS HIRING A PHALANX OF PRIVATE DETECTIVES, IT IS IN MY INTERESTS TO KEEP TABS ON THEM.
SO I KNOW YOU WERE FIRST TO ARBOGAST'S BODY. AND I KNOW YOU DIDN'T REPORT IT TO ANYONE.
DOES THAT MAKE YOU AND ME FRIENDS?
IT SEEMS IT DOES.
FROM NOW ON JUST FORGET ABOUT BOTHERING HARRIET, SEE?
He's protecting her.
He likes her.

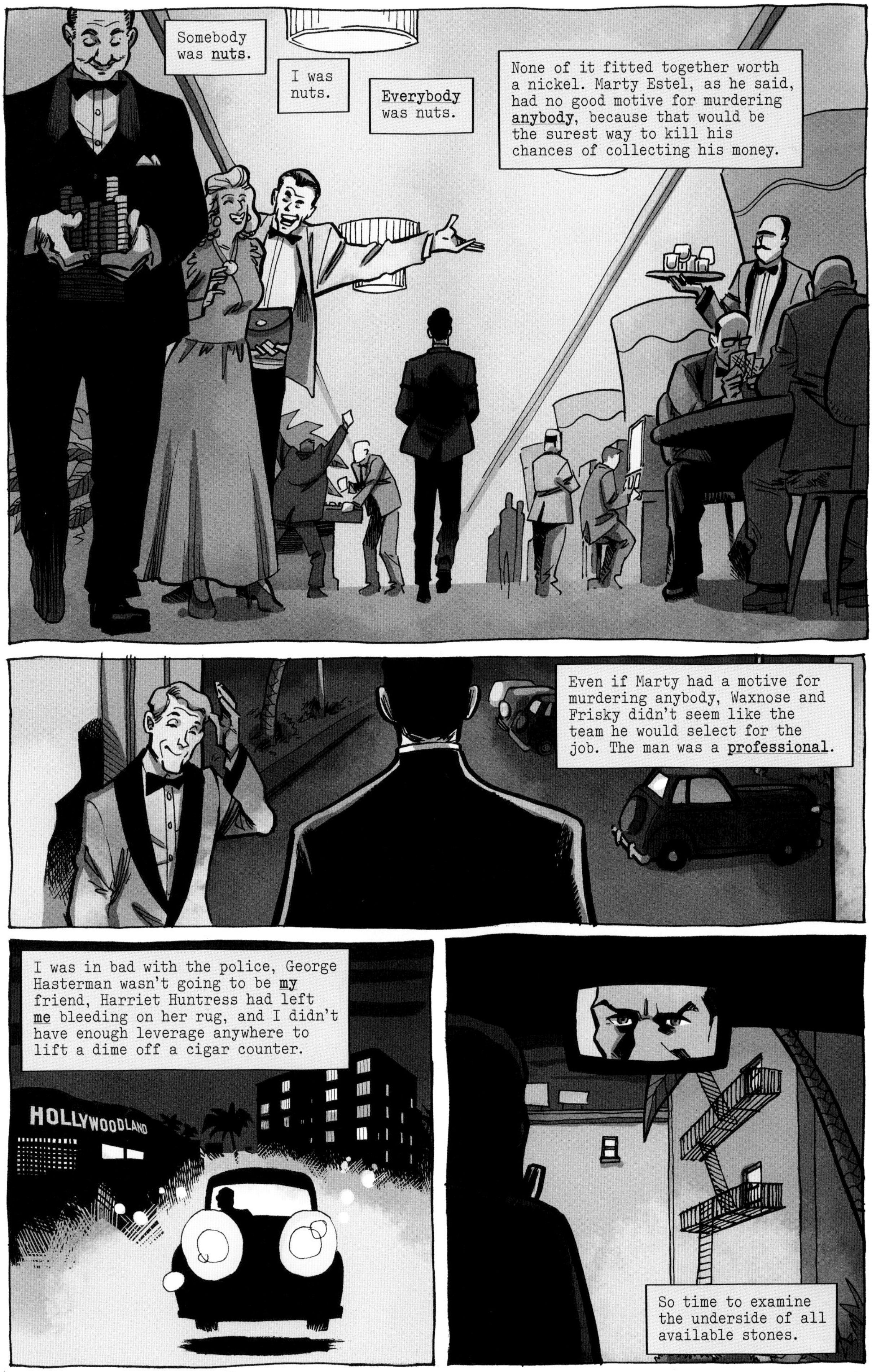
Somebody was nuts.
I was nuts.
Everybody was nuts.
None of it fitted together worth a nickel. Marty Estel, as he said, had no good motive for murdering anybody, because that would be the surest way to kill his chances of collecting his money.
Even if Marty had a motive for murdering anybody, Waxnose and Frisky didn't seem like the team he would select for the job. The man was a professional.
I was in bad with the police, George Hasterman wasn't going to be my friend, Harriet Huntress had left me bleeding on her rug, and I didn't have enough leverage anywhere to lift a dime off a cigar counter.
HOLLYWOODLAND
So time to examine the underside of all available stones.

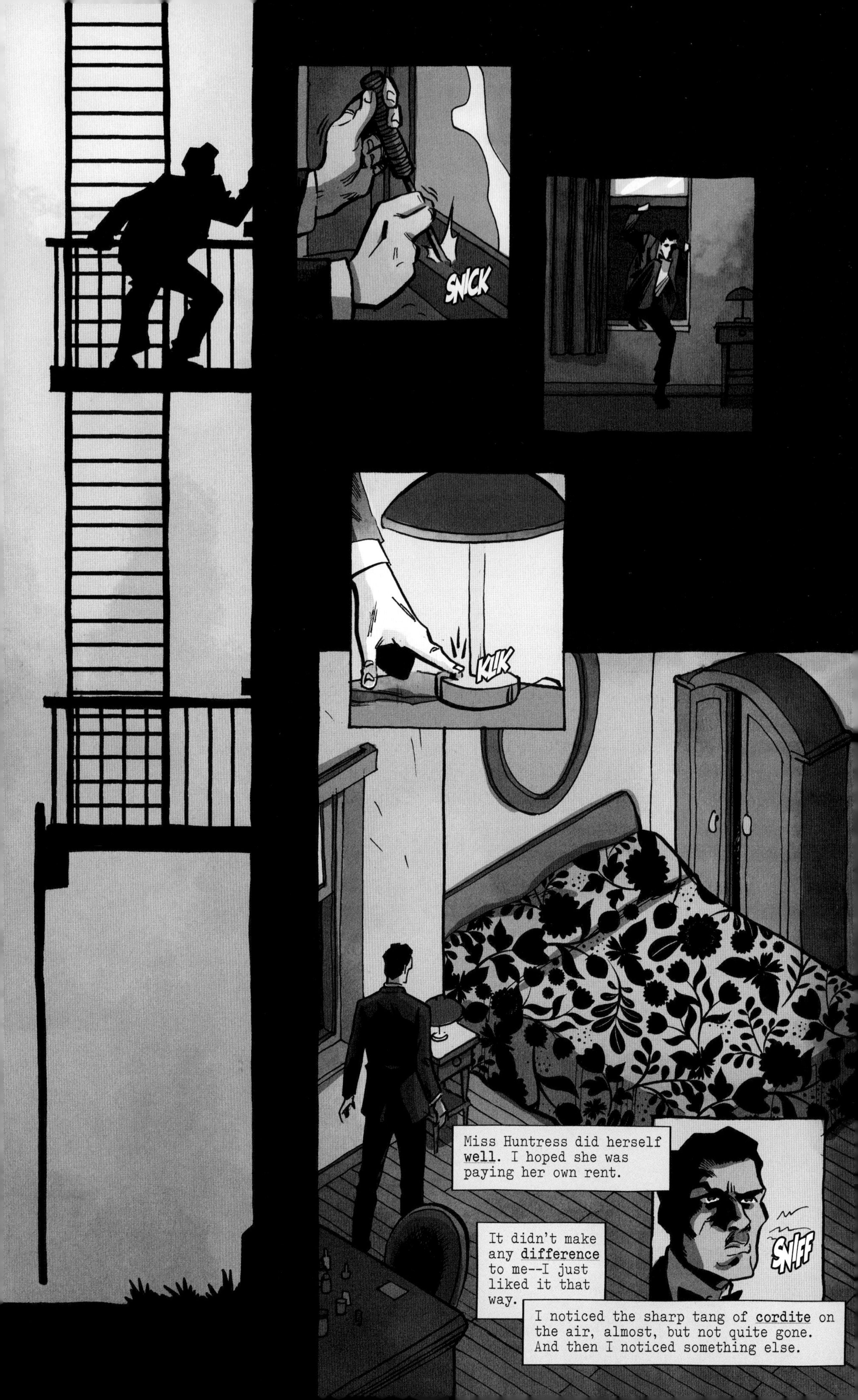

SNICK
KLIK
Miss Huntress did herself well. I hoped she was paying her own rent.
It didn't make any difference to me--I just liked it that way.
SNIFF
I noticed the sharp tang of cordite on the air, almost, but not quite gone. And then I noticed something else.

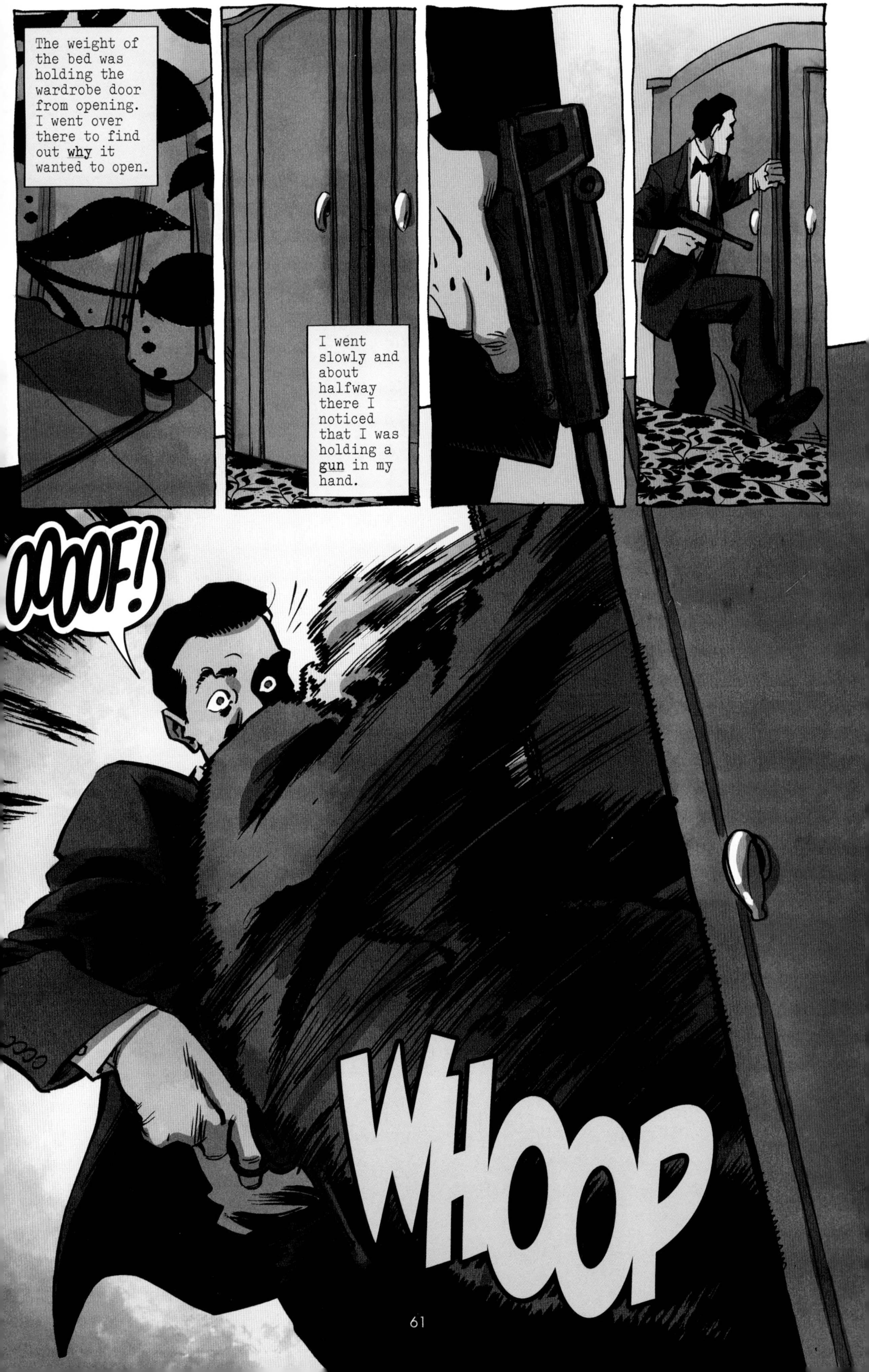
The weight of the bed was holding the wardrobe door from opening. I went over there to find out **why** it wanted to open.
I went slowly and about halfway there I noticed that I was holding a **gun** in my hand.
OOOOF!
WHOOP

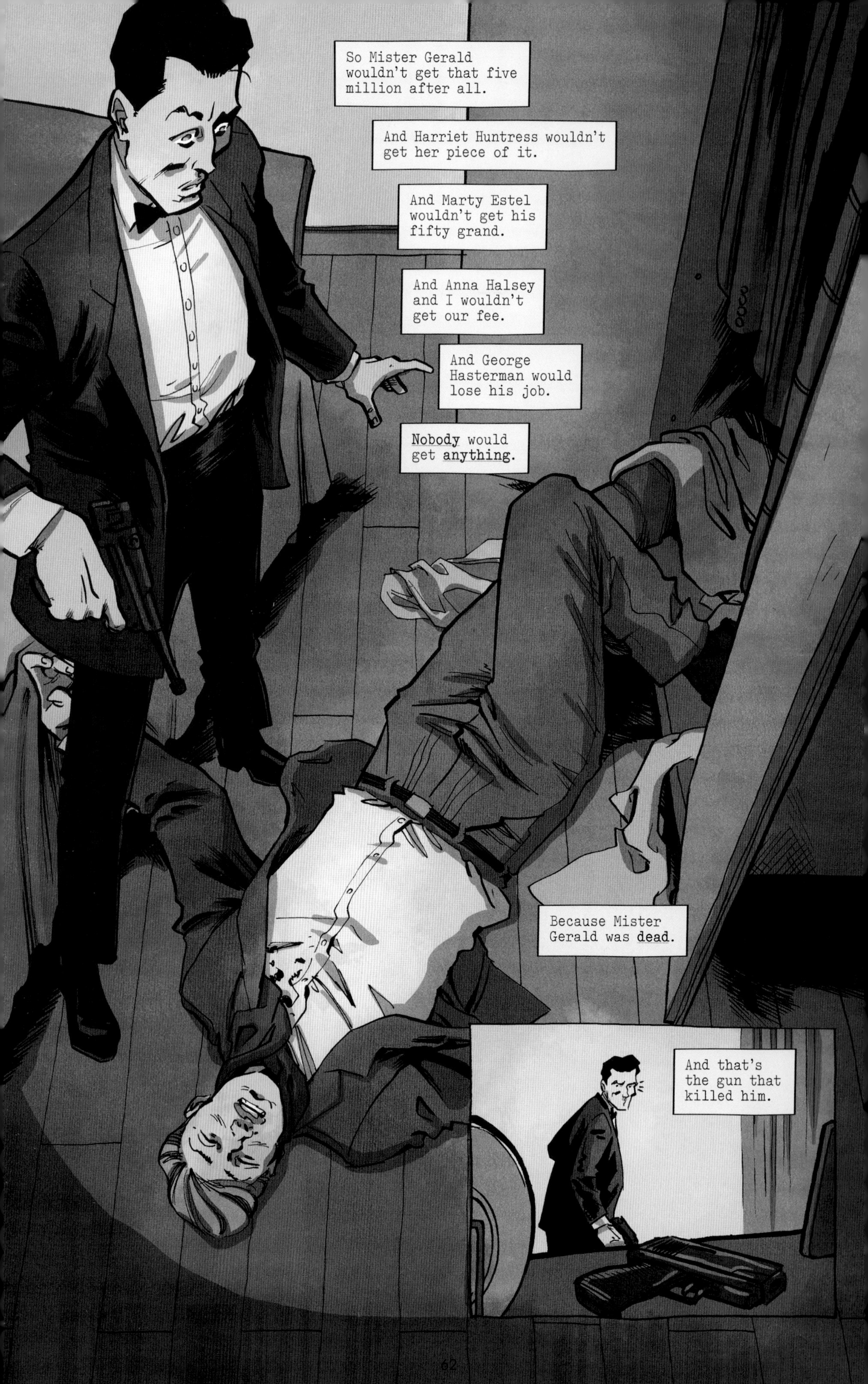
So Mister Gerald wouldn't get that five million after all.
And Harriet Huntress wouldn't get her piece of it.
And Marty Estel wouldn't get his fifty grand.
And Anna Halsey and I wouldn't get our fee.
And George Hasterman would lose his job.
Nobody would get anything.
Because Mister Gerald was dead.
And that's the gun that killed him.

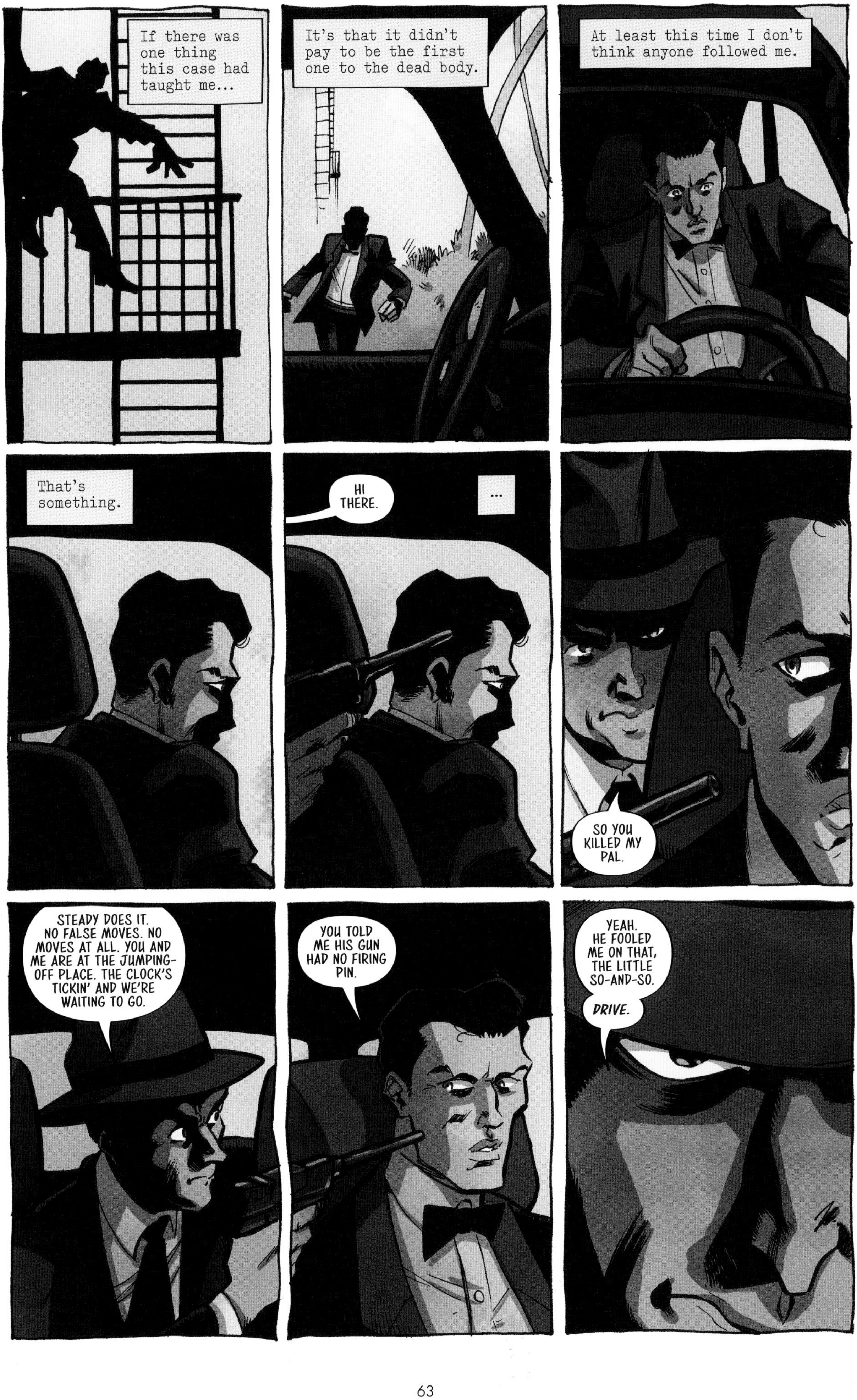

If there was one thing this case had taught me...
It's that it didn't pay to be the first one to the dead body.
At least this time I don't think anyone followed me.
That's something.
HI THERE.
...
SO YOU KILLED MY PAL.
STEADY DOES IT. NO FALSE MOVES. NO MOVES AT ALL. YOU AND ME ARE AT THE JUMPING-OFF PLACE. THE CLOCK'S TICKIN' AND WE'RE WAITING TO GO.
YOU TOLD ME HIS GUN HAD NO FIRING PIN.
YEAH. HE FOOLED ME ON THAT, THE LITTLE SO-AND-SO.
DRIVE.

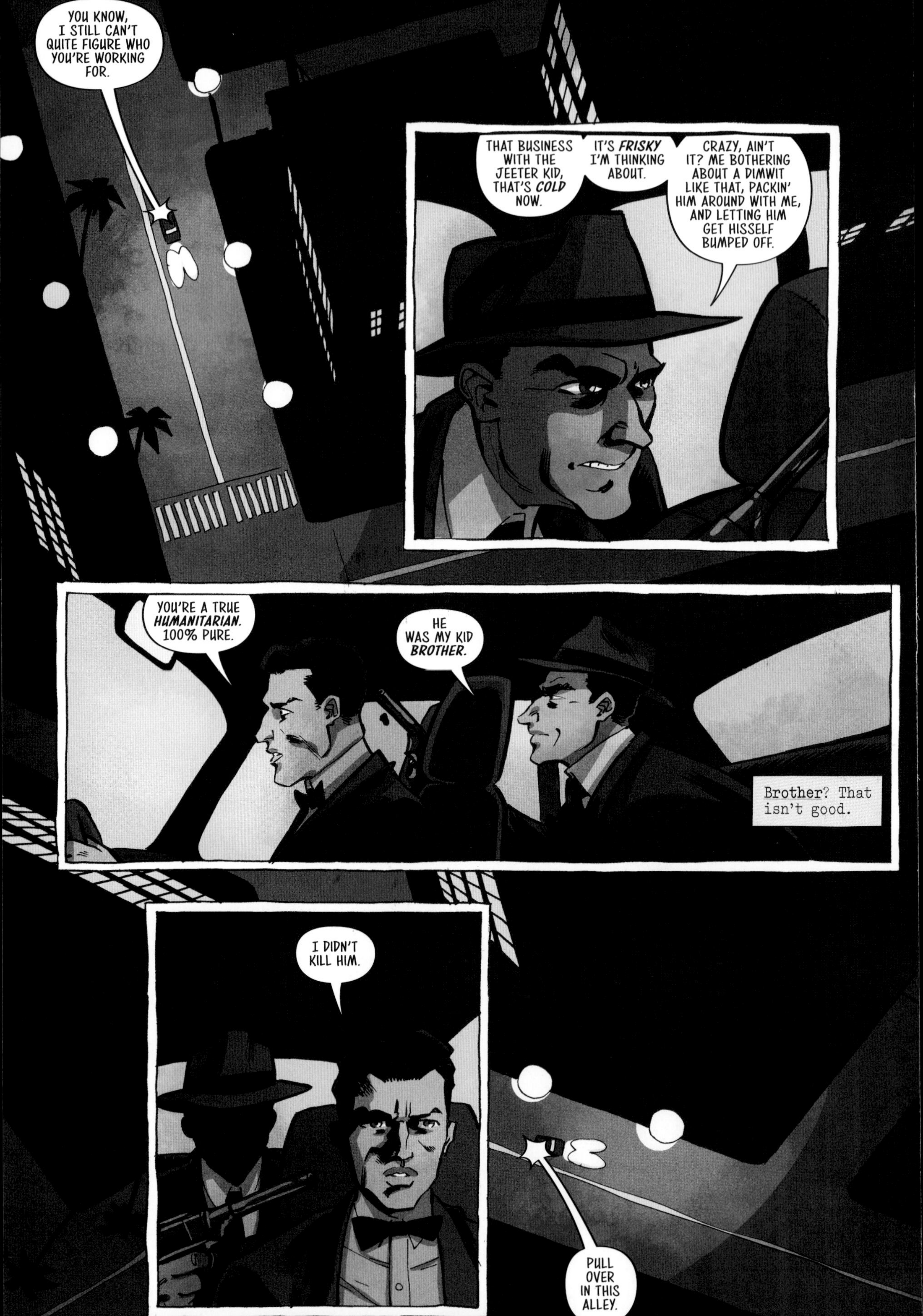
YOU KNOW, I STILL CAN'T QUITE FIGURE WHO YOU'RE WORKING FOR.
THAT BUSINESS WITH THE JEETER KID, THAT'S COLD NOW.
IT'S FRISKY I'M THINKING ABOUT.
CRAZY, AIN'T IT? ME BOTHERING ABOUT A DIMWIT LIKE THAT, PACKIN' HIM AROUND WITH ME, AND LETTING HIM GET HISSELF BUMPED OFF.
YOU'RE A TRUE HUMANITARIAN. 100% PURE.
HE WAS MY KID BROTHER.
Brother? That isn't good.
I DIDN'T KILL HIM.
PULL OVER IN THIS ALLEY.

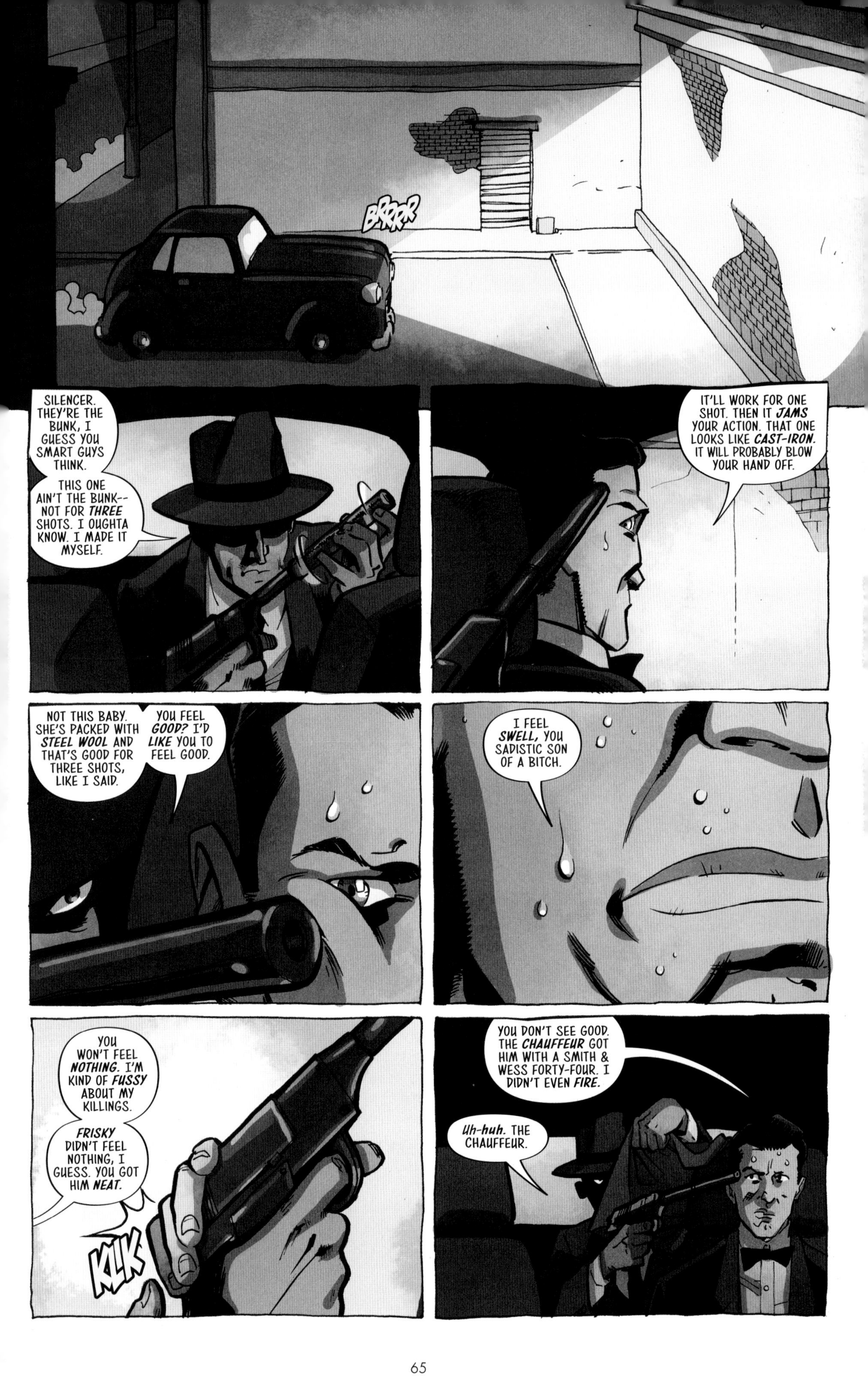
BRRRR
SILENCER. THEY'RE THE BUNK, I GUESS YOU SMART GUYS THINK.
THIS ONE AIN'T THE BUNK-- NOT FOR THREE SHOTS. I OUGHTA KNOW. I MADE IT MYSELF.
IT'LL WORK FOR ONE SHOT. THEN IT JAMS YOUR ACTION. THAT ONE LOOKS LIKE CAST-IRON. IT WILL PROBABLY BLOW YOUR HAND OFF.
NOT THIS BABY. SHE'S PACKED WITH STEEL WOOL AND THAT'S GOOD FOR THREE SHOTS, LIKE I SAID.
YOU FEEL GOOD? I'D LIKE YOU TO FEEL GOOD.
I FEEL SWELL, YOU SADISTIC SON OF A BITCH.
YOU WON'T FEEL NOTHING. I'M KIND OF FUSSY ABOUT MY KILLINGS.
FRISKY DIDN'T FEEL NOTHING, I GUESS. YOU GOT HIM NEAT.
KLIK
YOU DON'T SEE GOOD. THE CHAUFFEUR GOT HIM WITH A SMITH & WESS FORTY-FOUR. I DIDN'T EVEN FIRE.
Uh-huh. THE CHAUFFEUR.

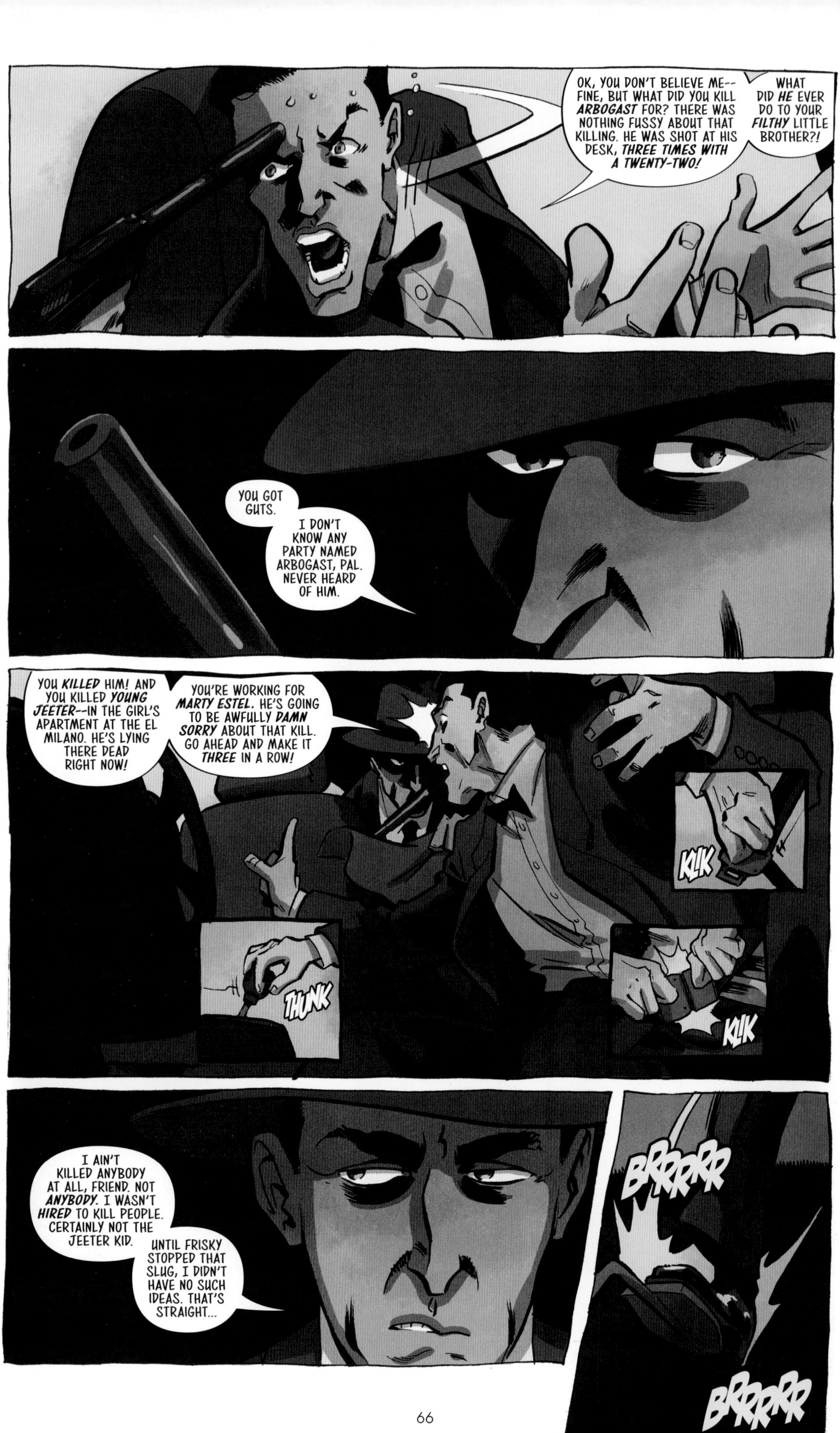
OK, YOU DON'T BELIEVE ME--FINE, BUT WHAT DID YOU KILL ARBOGAST FOR? THERE WAS NOTHING FUSSY ABOUT THAT KILLING. HE WAS SHOT AT HIS DESK, THREE TIMES WITH A TWENTY-TWO!
WHAT DID HE EVER DO TO YOUR FILTHY LITTLE BROTHER?!
YOU GOT GUTS.
I DON'T KNOW ANY PARTY NAMED ARBOGAST, PAL. NEVER HEARD OF HIM.
YOU KILLED HIM! AND YOU KILLED YOUNG JEETER--IN THE GIRL'S APARTMENT AT THE EL MILANO. HE'S LYING THERE DEAD RIGHT NOW!
YOU'RE WORKING FOR MARTY ESTEL. HE'S GOING TO BE AWFULLY DAMN SORRY ABOUT THAT KILL. GO AHEAD AND MAKE IT THREE IN A ROW!
KLIK
THUNK
KLIK
I AIN'T KILLED ANYBODY AT ALL, FRIEND. NOT ANYBODY. I WASN'T HIRED TO KILL PEOPLE. CERTAINLY NOT THE JEETER KID.
UNTIL FRISKY STOPPED THAT SLUG, I DIDN'T HAVE NO SUCH IDEAS. THAT'S STRAIGHT...
BRRRRR
BRRRRR

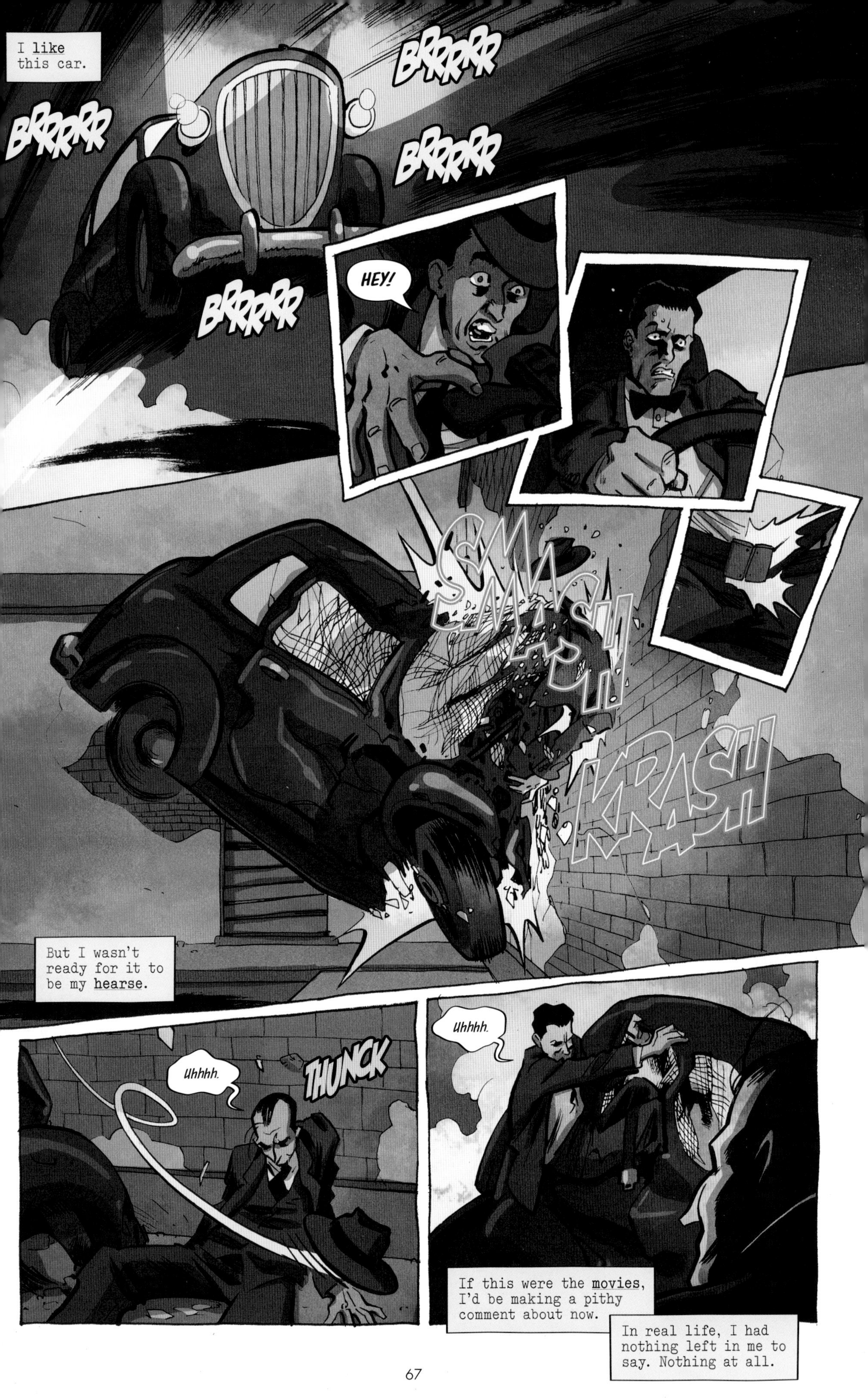
I like this car.
BRRRRR
BRRRRR
BRRRRR
BRRRRR
HEY!
SMASH
KRASH
But I wasn't ready for it to be my hearse.
Uhhhh.
THUNCK
Uhhhh.
If this were the movies, I'd be making a pithy comment about now.
In real life, I had nothing left in me to say. Nothing at all.

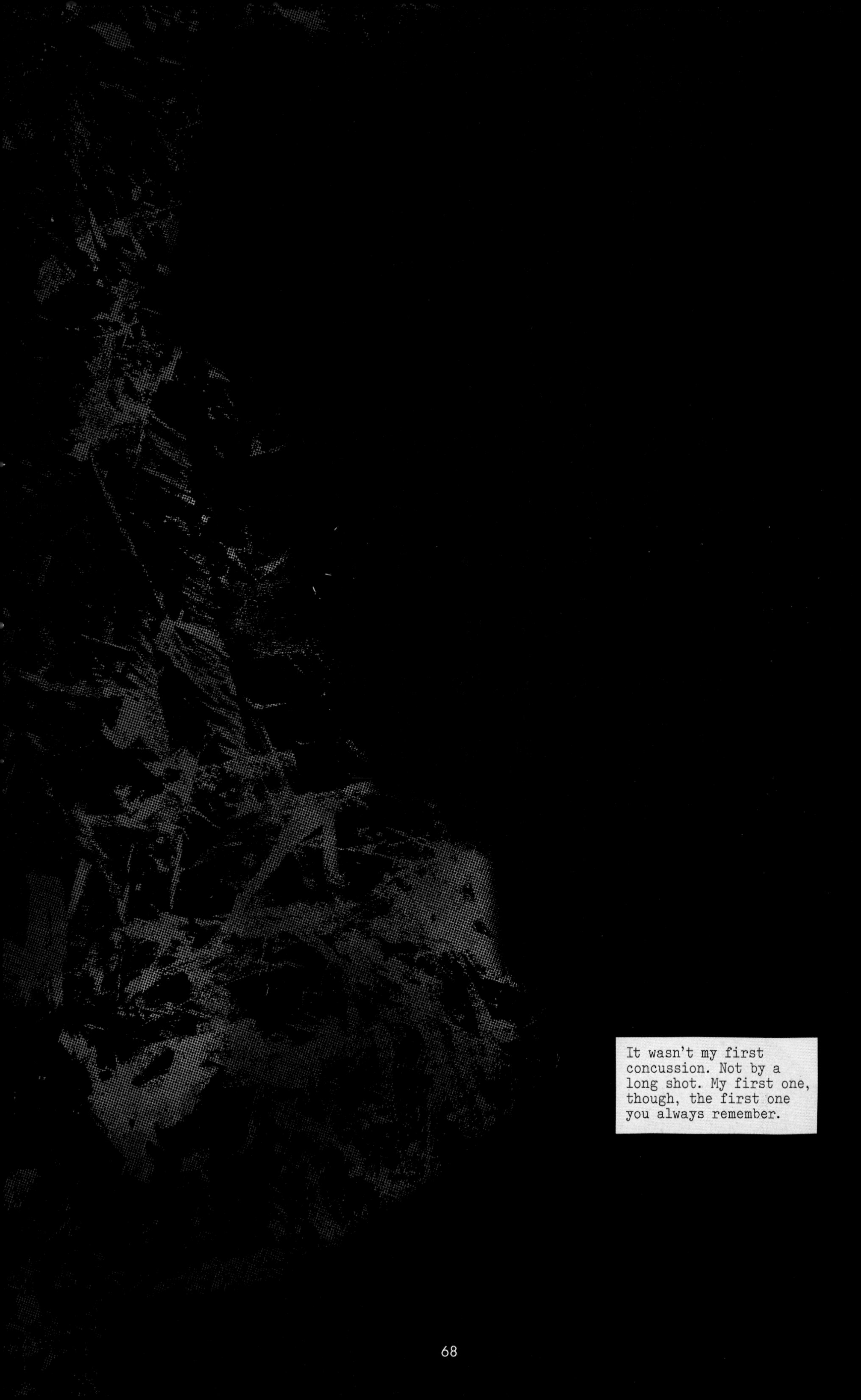
It wasn't my first concussion. Not by a long shot. My first one, though, the first one you always remember.

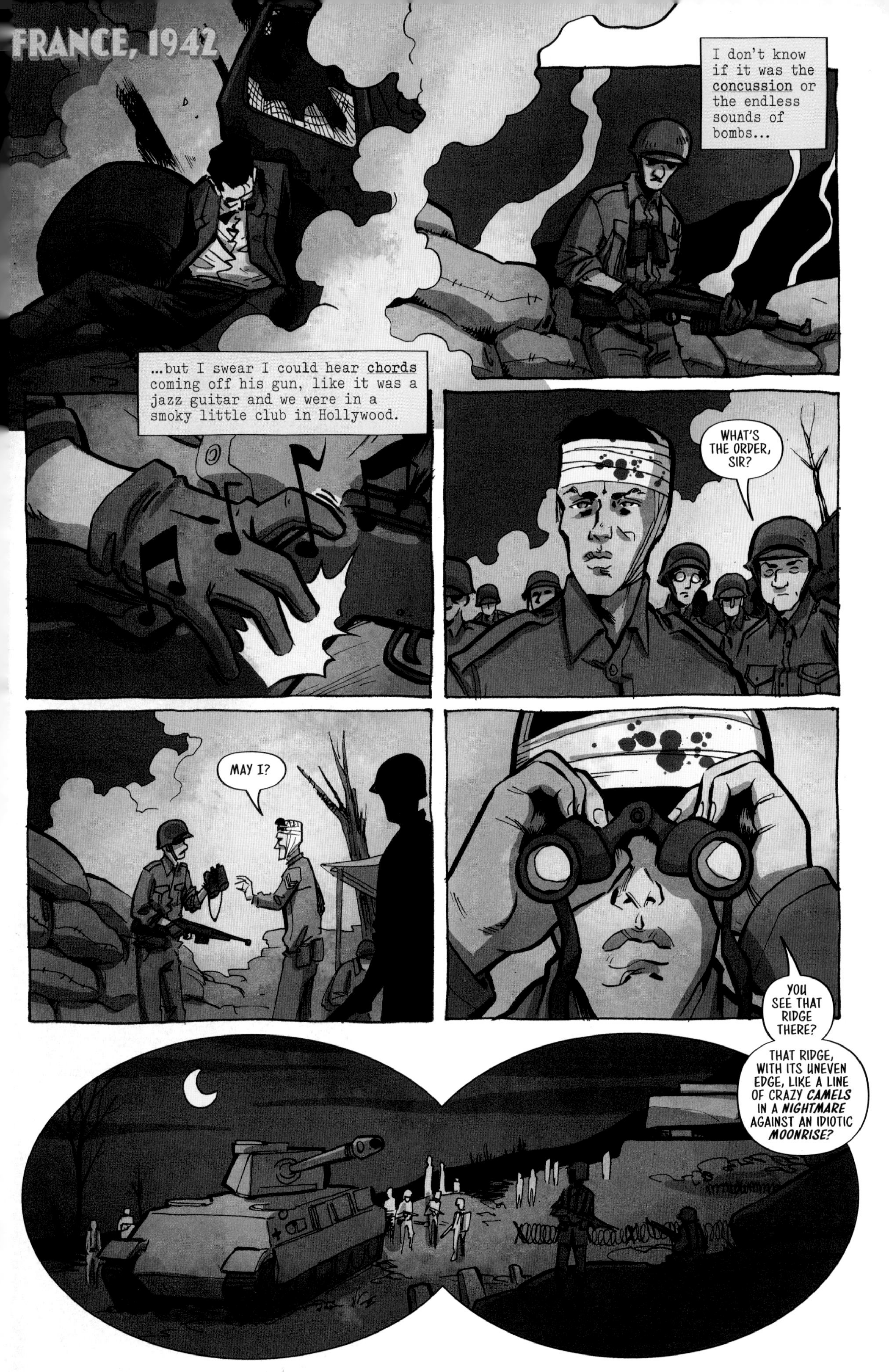

FRANCE, 1942
I don't know if it was the concussion or the endless sounds of bombs...
...but I swear I could hear chords coming off his gun, like it was a jazz guitar and we were in a smoky little club in Hollywood.
WHAT'S THE ORDER, SIR?
MAY I?
YOU SEE THAT RIDGE THERE?
THAT RIDGE, WITH ITS UNEVEN EDGE, LIKE A LINE OF CRAZY CAMELS IN A NIGHTMARE AGAINST AN IDIOTIC MOONRISE?

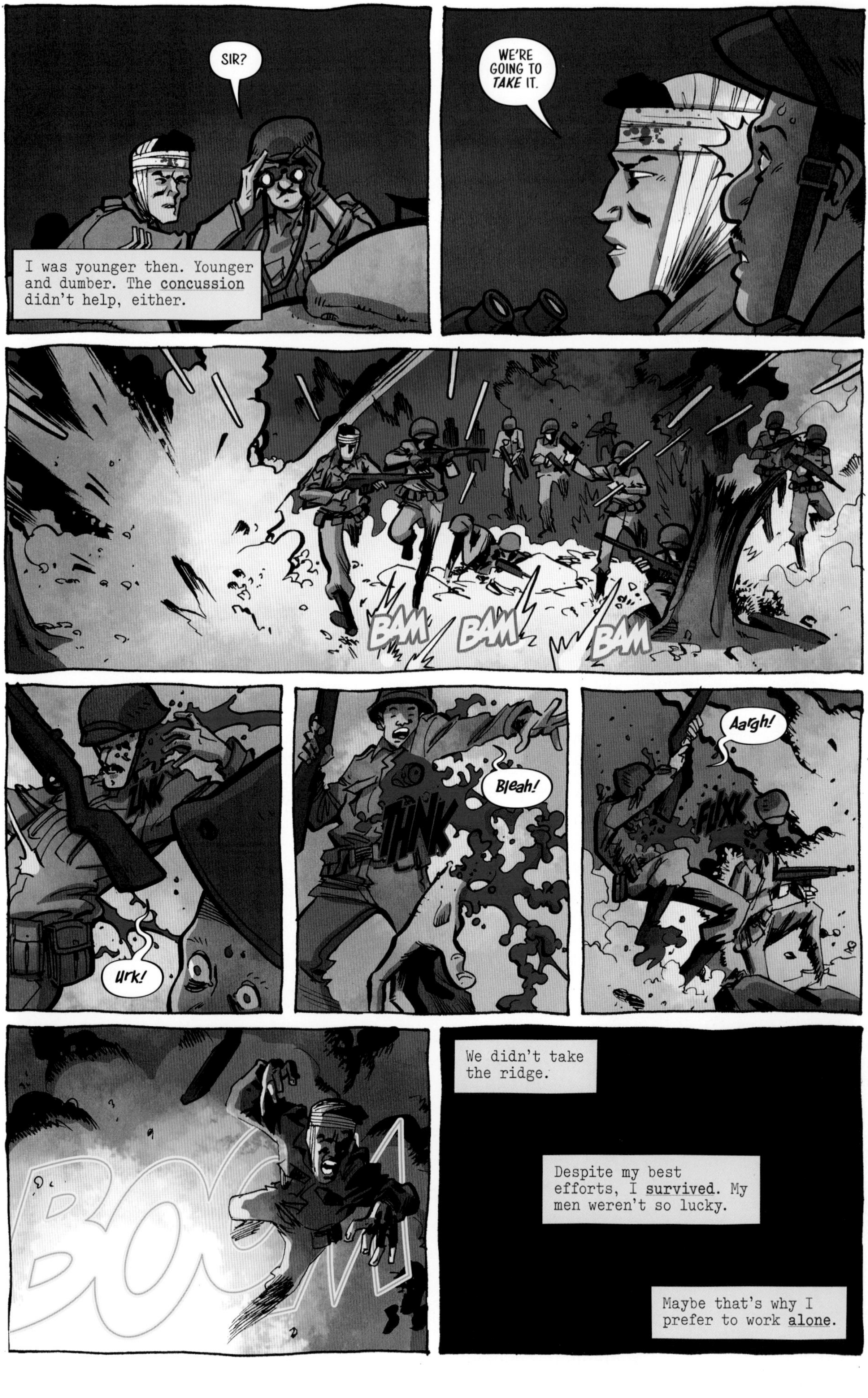
SIR?
I was younger then. Younger and dumber. The concussion didn't help, either.
WE'RE GOING TO *TAKE* IT.
BAM
BAM
BAM
URK!
THNK
Bleah!
Aargh!
BOOM
We didn't take the ridge.
Despite my best efforts, I survived. My men weren't so lucky.
Maybe that's why I prefer to work alone.

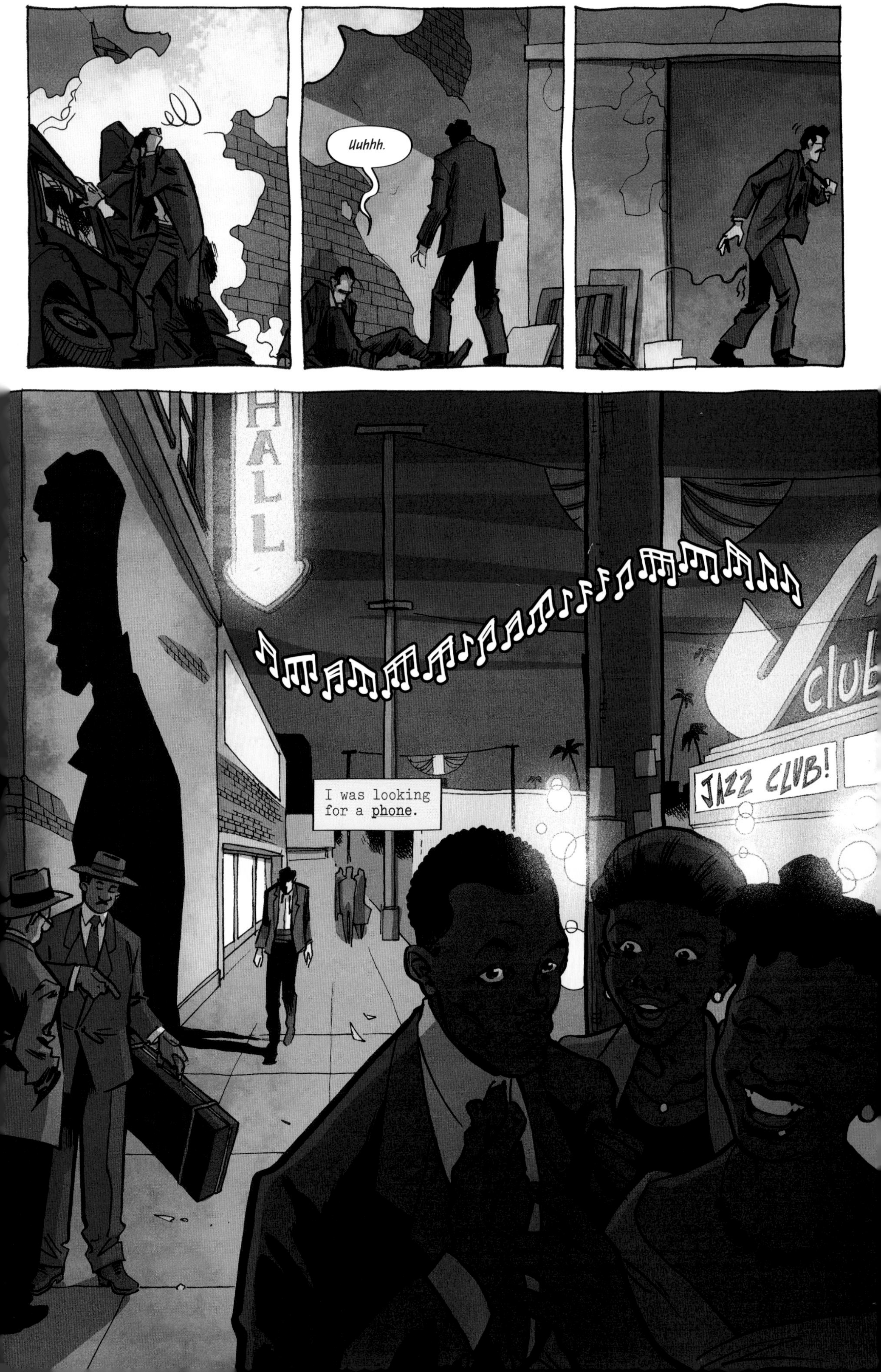
Uuhhh.
HALL
I was looking for a phone.
club
JAZZ CLUB!

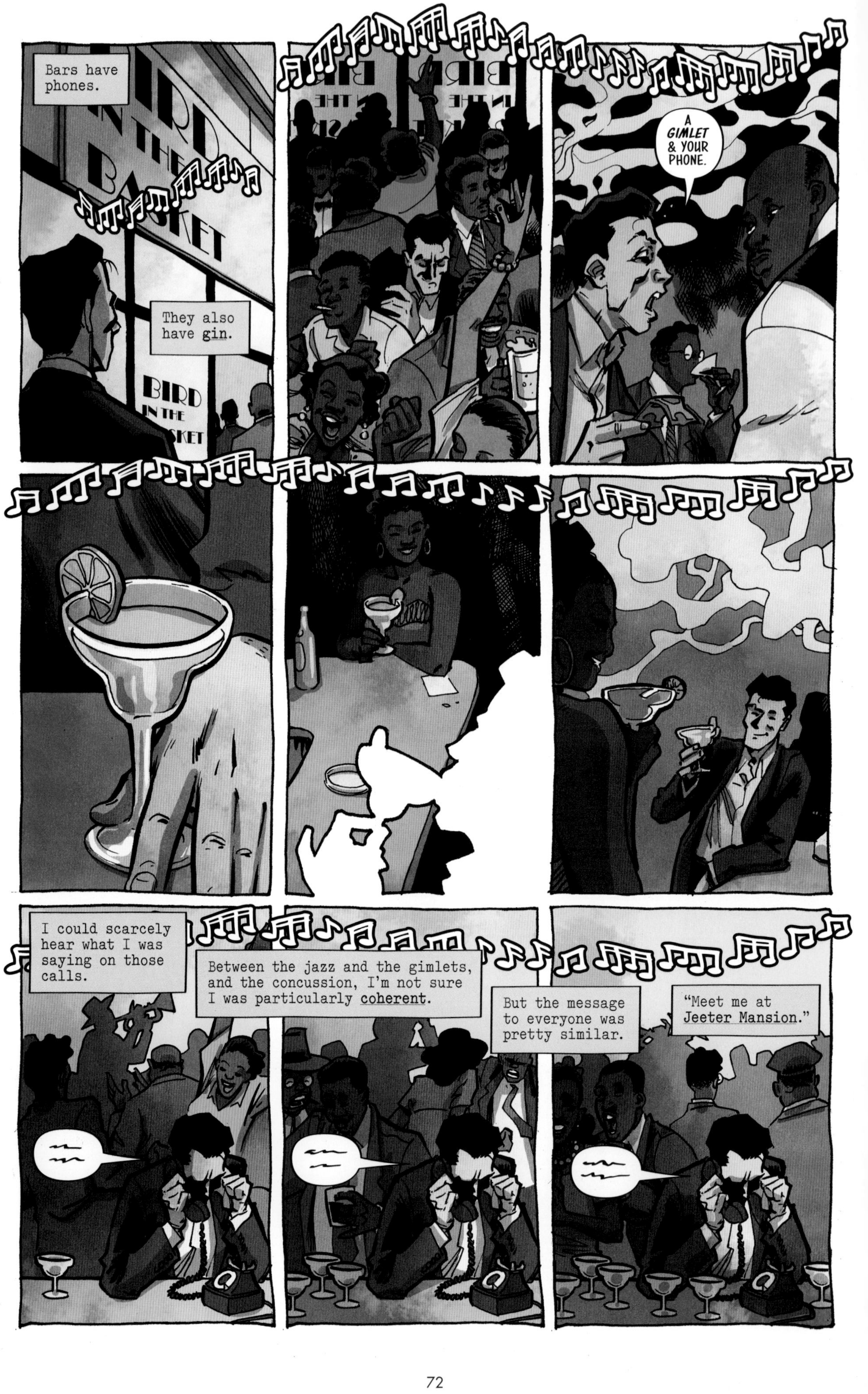
Bars have phones.
BIRD IN THE BASKET
They also have gin.
BIRD IN THE BASKET
A GIMLET & YOUR PHONE.
I could scarcely hear what I was saying on those calls.
Between the jazz and the gimlets, and the concussion, I'm not sure I was particularly coherent.
But the message to everyone was pretty similar.
"Meet me at Jeeter Mansion."

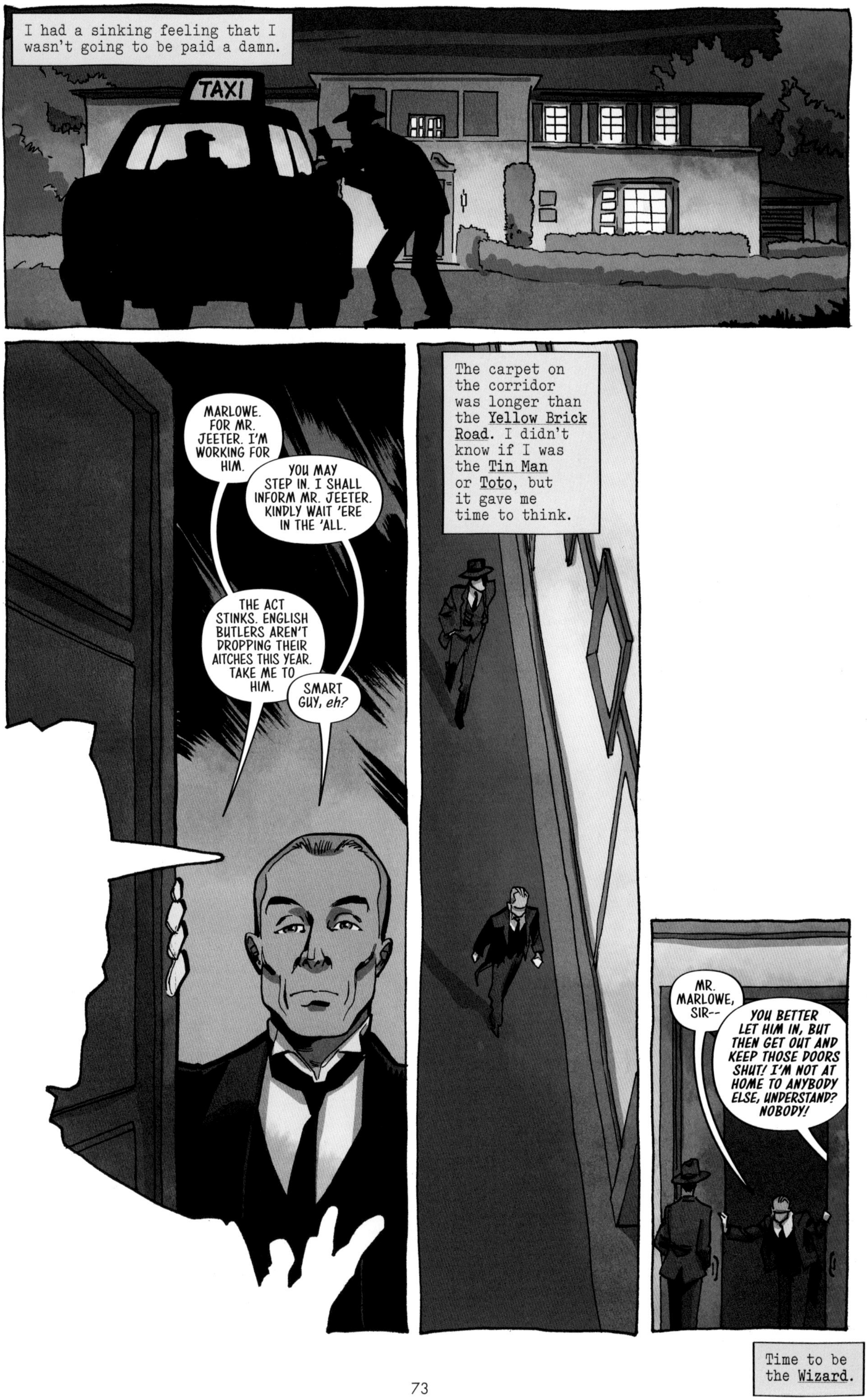
I had a sinking feeling that I wasn't going to be paid a damn.
TAXI
MARLOWE. FOR MR. JEETER. I'M WORKING FOR HIM.
YOU MAY STEP IN. I SHALL INFORM MR. JEETER. KINDLY WAIT 'ERE IN THE 'ALL.
THE ACT STINKS. ENGLISH BUTLERS AREN'T DROPPING THEIR AITCHES THIS YEAR. TAKE ME TO HIM.
SMART GUY, *eh?*
The carpet on the corridor was longer than the Yellow Brick Road. I didn't know if I was the Tin Man or Toto, but it gave me time to think.
MR. MARLOWE, SIR--
YOU BETTER LET HIM IN, BUT THEN GET OUT AND KEEP THOSE DOORS SHUT! I'M NOT AT HOME TO ANYBODY ELSE, UNDERSTAND? NOBODY!
Time to be the Wizard.

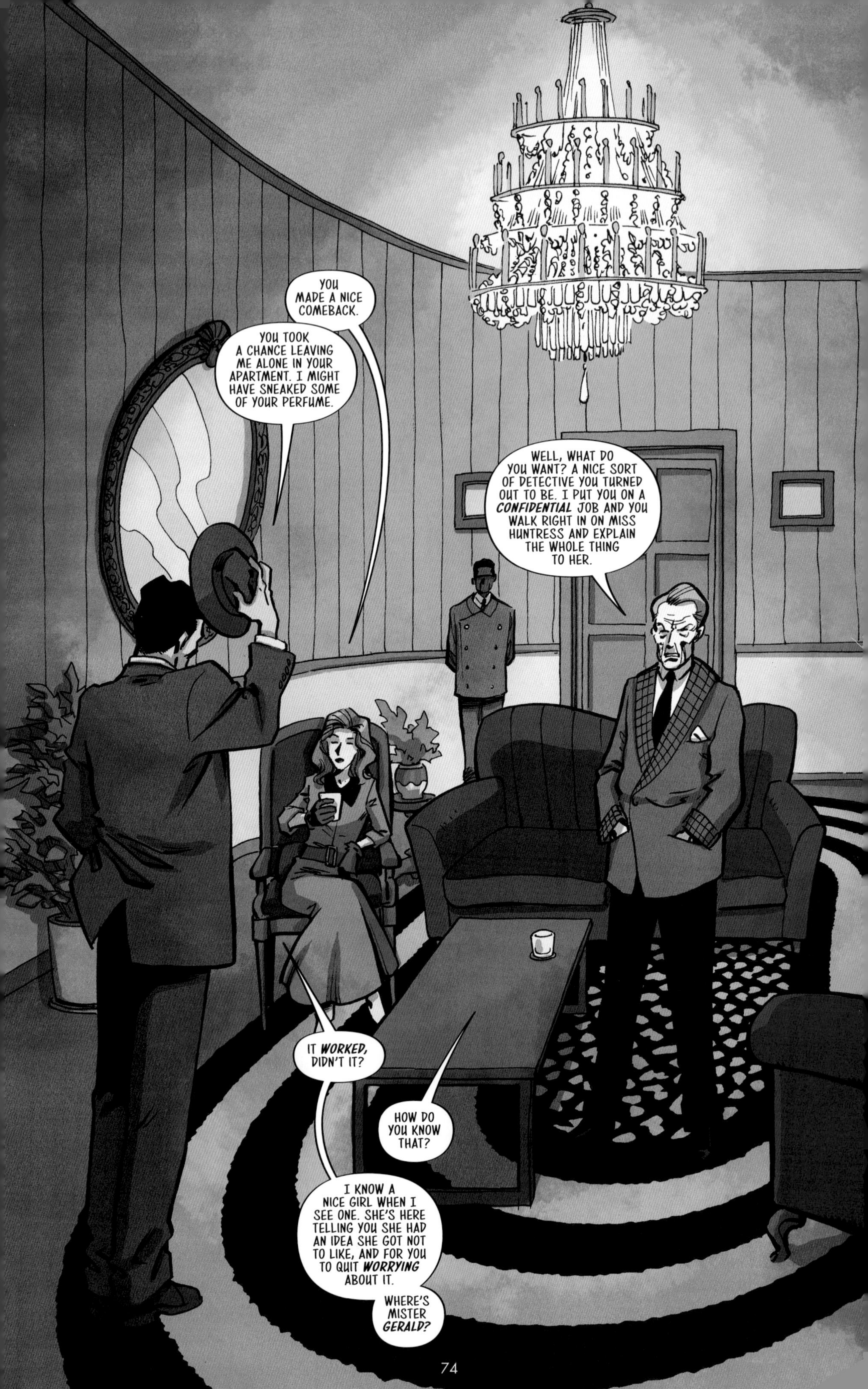
YOU MADE A NICE COMEBACK.
YOU TOOK A CHANCE LEAVING ME ALONE IN YOUR APARTMENT. I MIGHT HAVE SNEAKED SOME OF YOUR PERFUME.
WELL, WHAT DO YOU WANT? A NICE SORT OF DETECTIVE YOU TURNED OUT TO BE. I PUT YOU ON A *CONFIDENTIAL* JOB AND YOU WALK RIGHT IN ON MISS HUNTRESS AND EXPLAIN THE WHOLE THING TO HER.
IT *WORKED,* DIDN'T IT?
HOW DO YOU KNOW THAT?
I KNOW A NICE GIRL WHEN I SEE ONE. SHE'S HERE TELLING YOU SHE HAD AN IDEA SHE GOT NOT TO LIKE, AND FOR YOU TO QUIT *WORRYING* ABOUT IT.
WHERE'S MISTER *GERALD?*

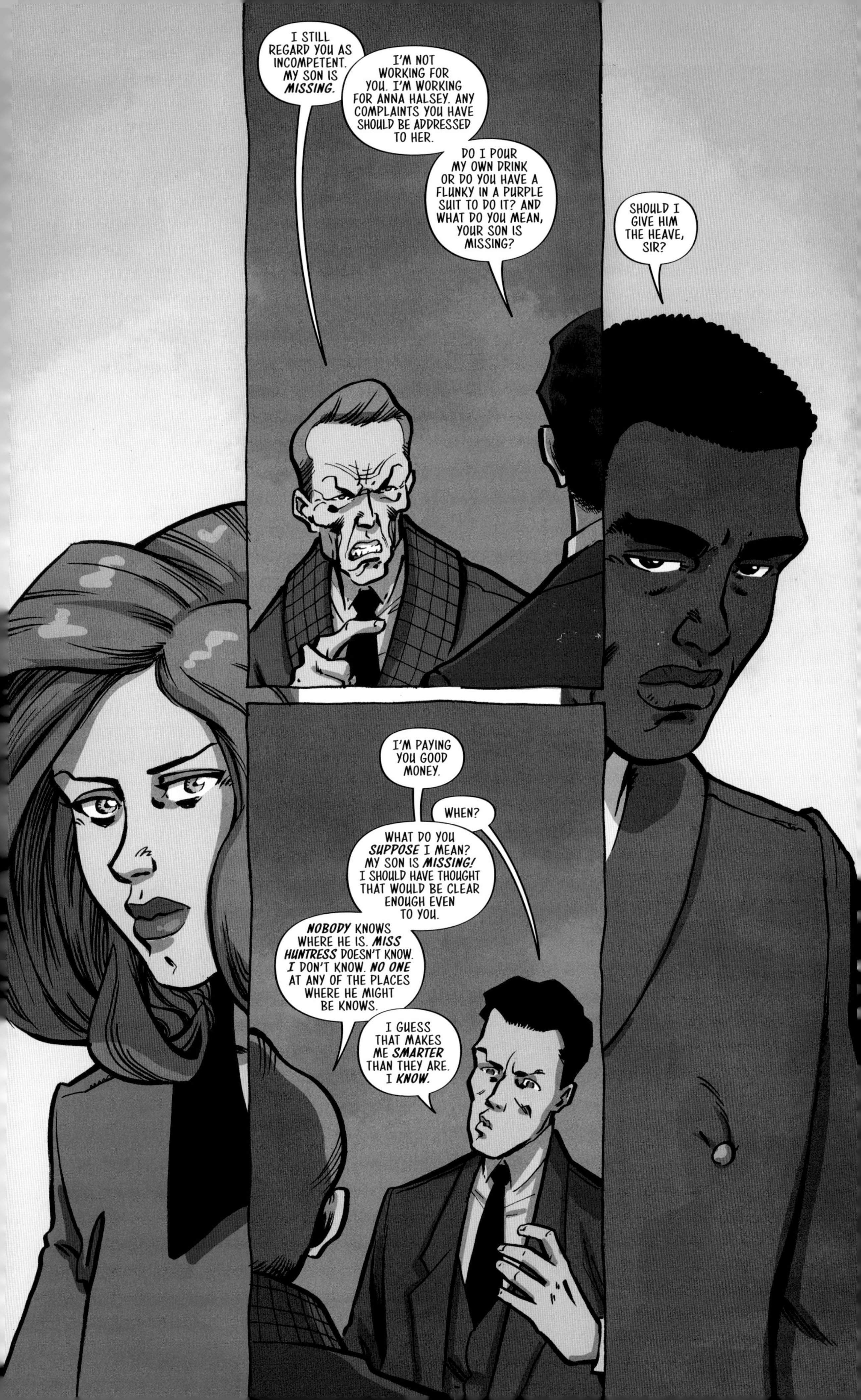
I STILL REGARD YOU AS INCOMPETENT. MY SON IS MISSING.
I'M NOT WORKING FOR YOU. I'M WORKING FOR ANNA HALSEY. ANY COMPLAINTS YOU HAVE SHOULD BE ADDRESSED TO HER.
DO I POUR MY OWN DRINK OR DO YOU HAVE A FLUNKY IN A PURPLE SUIT TO DO IT? AND WHAT DO YOU MEAN, YOUR SON IS MISSING?
SHOULD I GIVE HIM THE HEAVE, SIR?
I'M PAYING YOU GOOD MONEY.
WHEN?
WHAT DO YOU SUPPOSE I MEAN? MY SON IS MISSING! I SHOULD HAVE THOUGHT THAT WOULD BE CLEAR ENOUGH EVEN TO YOU.
NOBODY KNOWS WHERE HE IS. MISS HUNTRESS DOESN'T KNOW. I DON'T KNOW. NO ONE AT ANY OF THE PLACES WHERE HE MIGHT BE KNOWS.
I GUESS THAT MAKES ME SMARTER THAN THEY ARE. I KNOW.

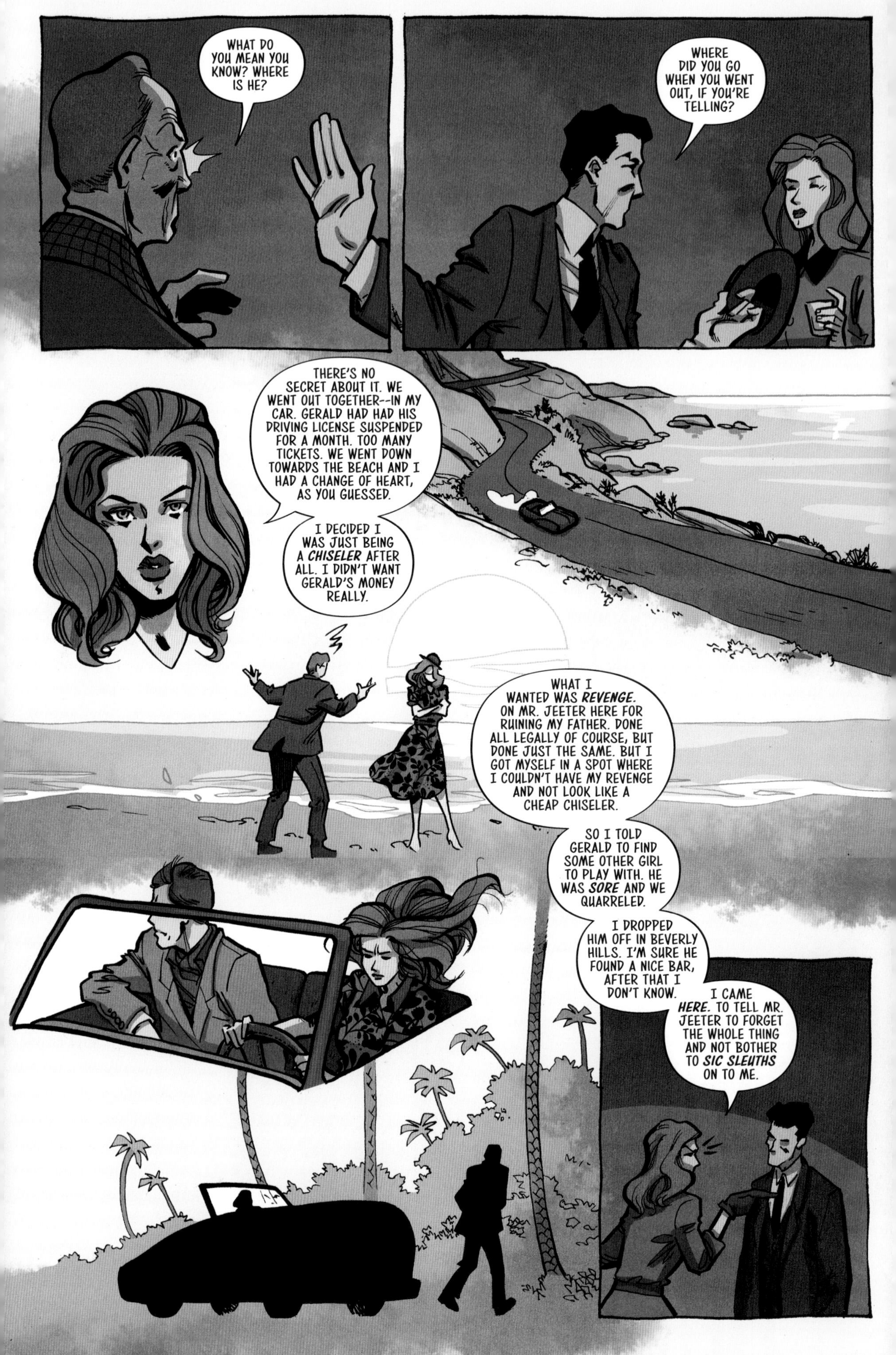
WHAT DO YOU MEAN YOU KNOW? WHERE IS HE?
WHERE DID YOU GO WHEN YOU WENT OUT, IF YOU'RE TELLING?
THERE'S NO SECRET ABOUT IT. WE WENT OUT TOGETHER--IN MY CAR. GERALD HAD HAD HIS DRIVING LICENSE SUSPENDED FOR A MONTH. TOO MANY TICKETS. WE WENT DOWN TOWARDS THE BEACH AND I HAD A CHANGE OF HEART, AS YOU GUESSED.
I DECIDED I WAS JUST BEING A CHISELER AFTER ALL. I DIDN'T WANT GERALD'S MONEY REALLY.
WHAT I WANTED WAS REVENGE. ON MR. JEETER HERE FOR RUINING MY FATHER. DONE ALL LEGALLY OF COURSE, BUT DONE JUST THE SAME. BUT I GOT MYSELF IN A SPOT WHERE I COULDN'T HAVE MY REVENGE AND NOT LOOK LIKE A CHEAP CHISELER.
SO I TOLD GERALD TO FIND SOME OTHER GIRL TO PLAY WITH. HE WAS SORE AND WE QUARRELED.
I DROPPED HIM OFF IN BEVERLY HILLS. I'M SURE HE FOUND A NICE BAR, AFTER THAT I DON'T KNOW.
I CAME HERE. TO TELL MR. JEETER TO FORGET THE WHOLE THING AND NOT BOTHER TO SIC SLEUTHS ON TO ME.

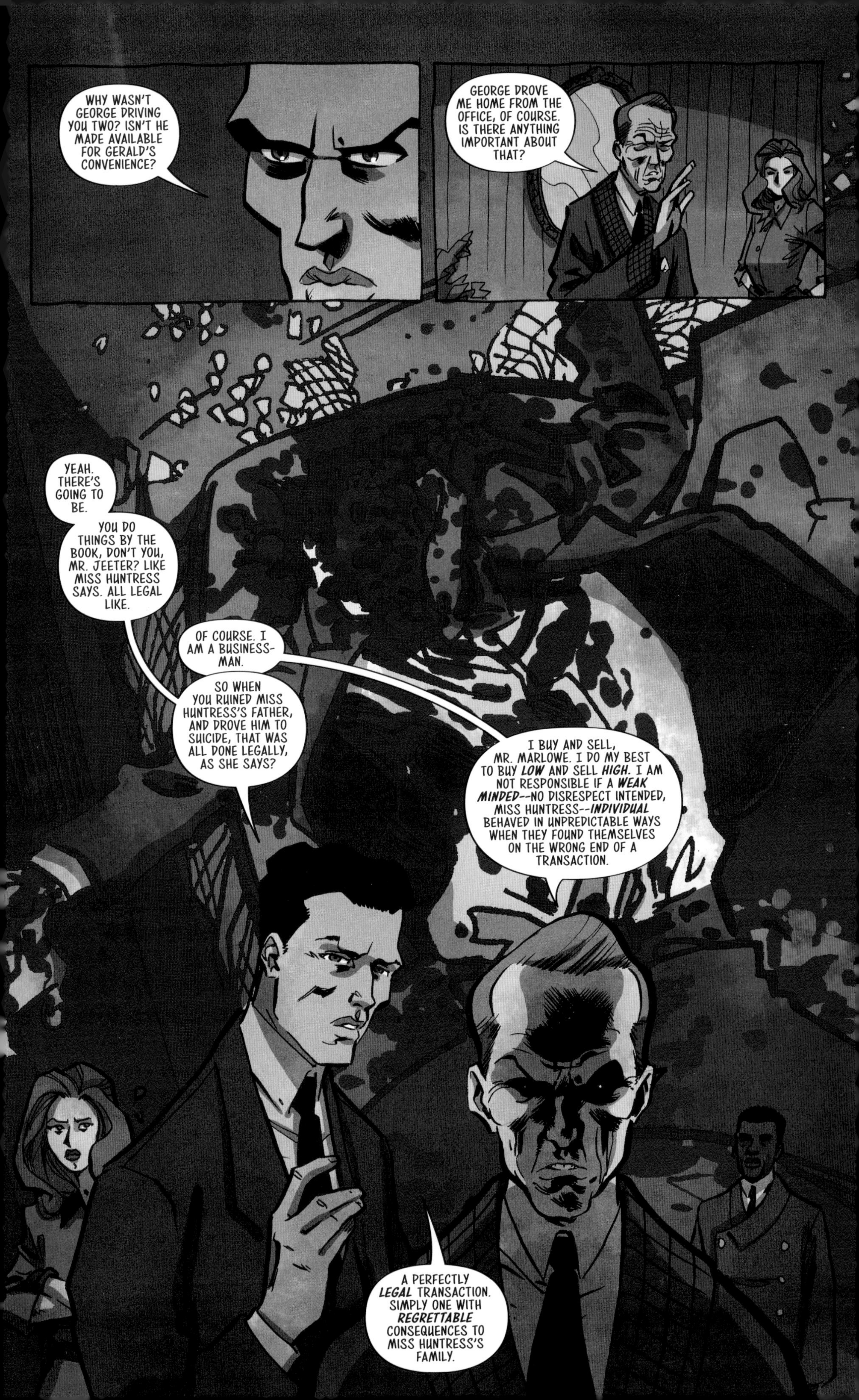

WHY WASN'T GEORGE DRIVING YOU TWO? ISN'T HE MADE AVAILABLE FOR GERALD'S CONVENIENCE?
GEORGE DROVE ME HOME FROM THE OFFICE, OF COURSE. IS THERE ANYTHING IMPORTANT ABOUT THAT?
YEAH. THERE'S GOING TO BE.
YOU DO THINGS BY THE BOOK, DON'T YOU, MR. JEETER? LIKE MISS HUNTRESS SAYS. ALL LEGAL LIKE.
OF COURSE. I AM A BUSINESS-MAN.
SO WHEN YOU RUINED MISS HUNTRESS'S FATHER, AND DROVE HIM TO SUICIDE, THAT WAS ALL DONE LEGALLY, AS SHE SAYS?
I BUY AND SELL, MR. MARLOWE. I DO MY BEST TO BUY *LOW* AND SELL *HIGH.* I AM NOT RESPONSIBLE IF A *WEAK MINDED*--NO DISRESPECT INTENDED, MISS HUNTRESS--*INDIVIDUAL* BEHAVED IN UNPREDICTABLE WAYS WHEN THEY FOUND THEMSELVES ON THE WRONG END OF A TRANSACTION.
A PERFECTLY *LEGAL* TRANSACTION. SIMPLY ONE WITH *REGRETTABLE* CONSEQUENCES TO MISS HUNTRESS'S FAMILY.

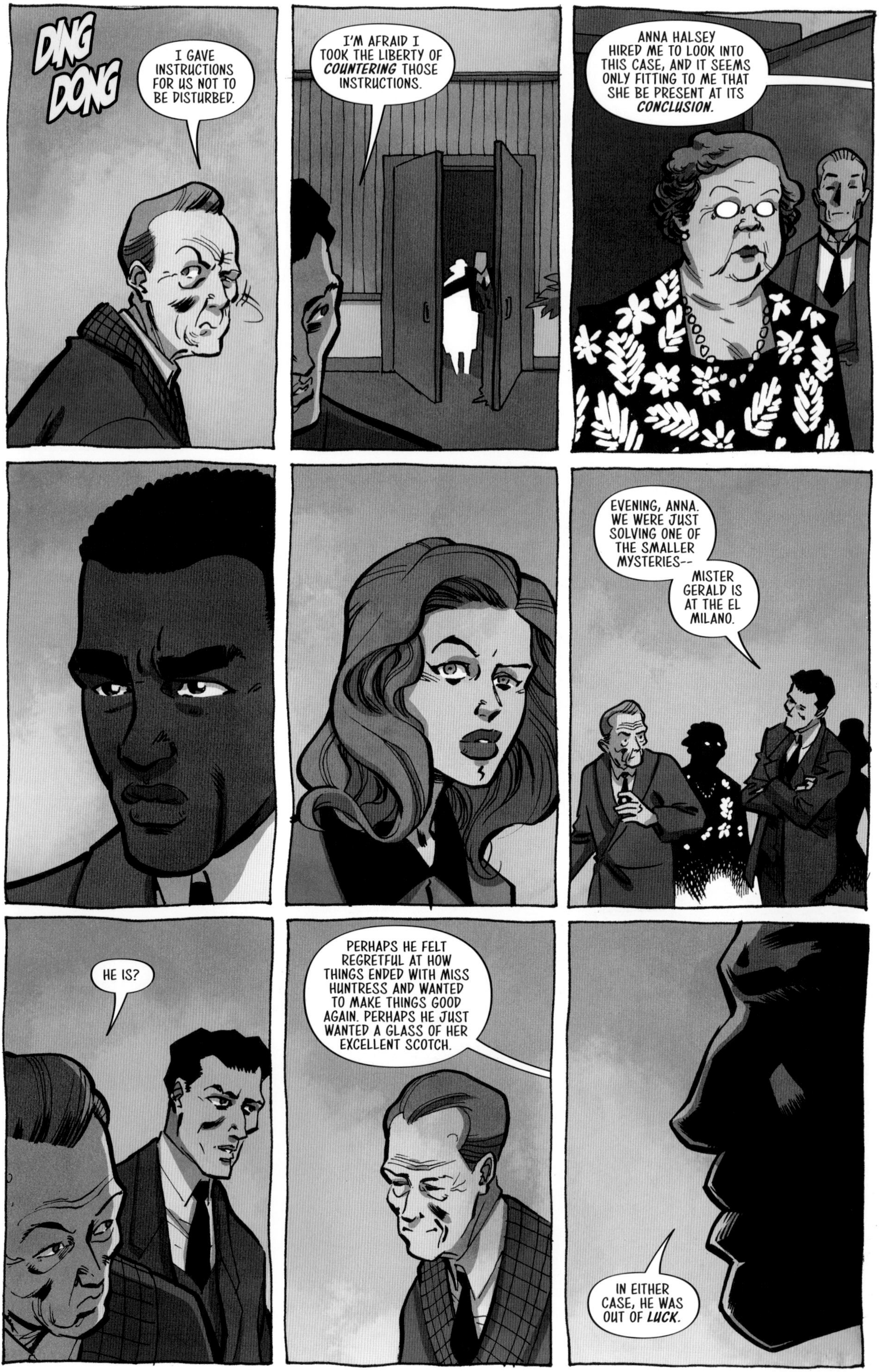
DING DONG
I GAVE INSTRUCTIONS FOR US NOT TO BE DISTURBED.
I'M AFRAID I TOOK THE LIBERTY OF COUNTERING THOSE INSTRUCTIONS.
ANNA HALSEY HIRED ME TO LOOK INTO THIS CASE, AND IT SEEMS ONLY FITTING TO ME THAT SHE BE PRESENT AT ITS CONCLUSION.
EVENING, ANNA. WE WERE JUST SOLVING ONE OF THE SMALLER MYSTERIES--
MISTER GERALD IS AT THE EL MILANO.
HE IS?
PERHAPS HE FELT REGRETFUL AT HOW THINGS ENDED WITH MISS HUNTRESS AND WANTED TO MAKE THINGS GOOD AGAIN. PERHAPS HE JUST WANTED A GLASS OF HER EXCELLENT SCOTCH.
IN EITHER CASE, HE WAS OUT OF LUCK.

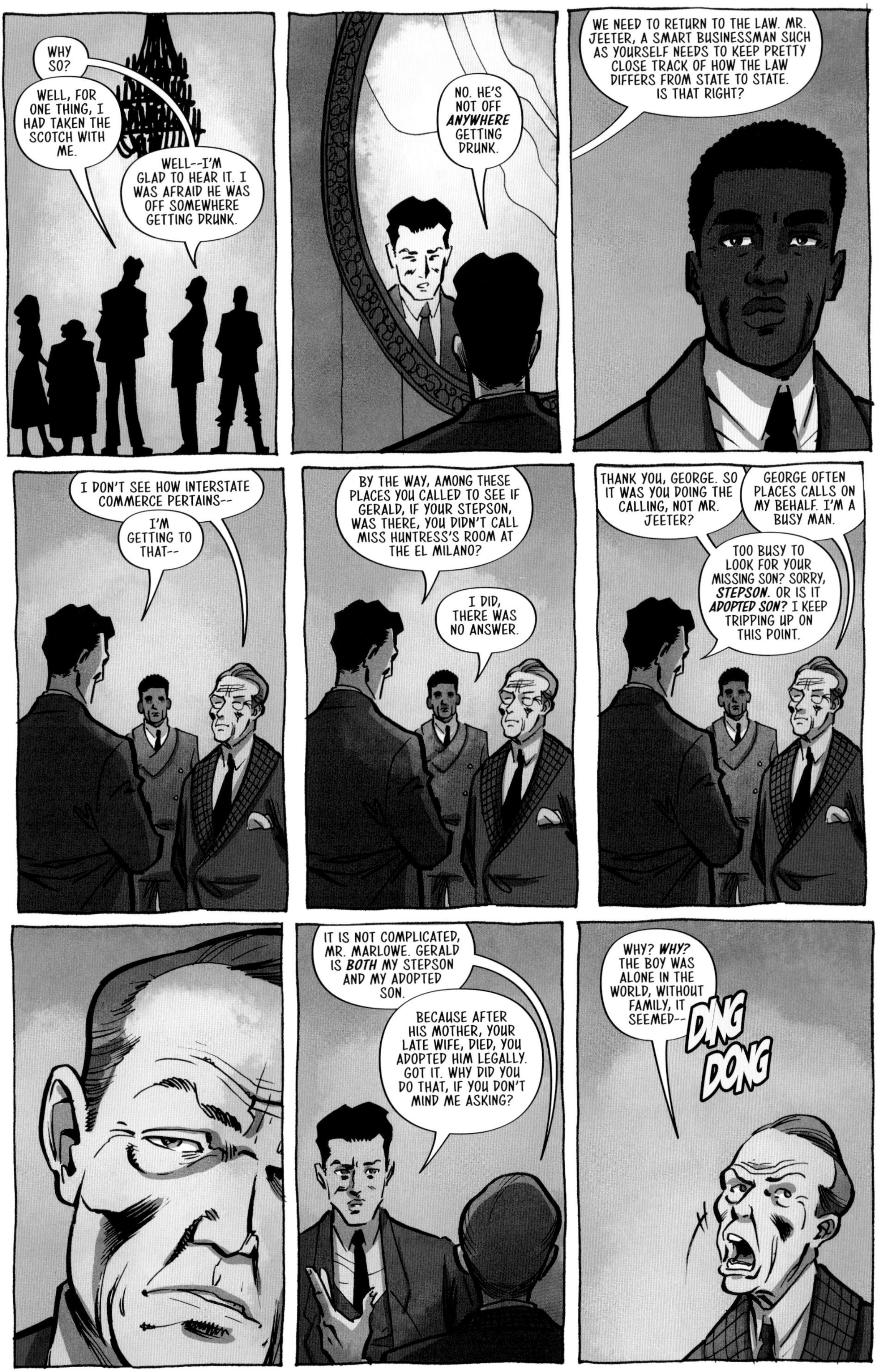
WHY SO?
WELL, FOR ONE THING, I HAD TAKEN THE SCOTCH WITH ME.
WELL--I'M GLAD TO HEAR IT. I WAS AFRAID HE WAS OFF SOMEWHERE GETTING DRUNK.
NO. HE'S NOT OFF ANYWHERE GETTING DRUNK.
WE NEED TO RETURN TO THE LAW. MR. JEETER, A SMART BUSINESSMAN SUCH AS YOURSELF NEEDS TO KEEP PRETTY CLOSE TRACK OF HOW THE LAW DIFFERS FROM STATE TO STATE. IS THAT RIGHT?
I DON'T SEE HOW INTERSTATE COMMERCE PERTAINS--
I'M GETTING TO THAT--
BY THE WAY, AMONG THESE PLACES YOU CALLED TO SEE IF GERALD, IF YOUR STEPSON, WAS THERE, YOU DIDN'T CALL MISS HUNTRESS'S ROOM AT THE EL MILANO?
I DID, THERE WAS NO ANSWER.
THANK YOU, GEORGE. SO IT WAS YOU DOING THE CALLING, NOT MR. JEETER?
GEORGE OFTEN PLACES CALLS ON MY BEHALF. I'M A BUSY MAN.
TOO BUSY TO LOOK FOR YOUR MISSING SON? SORRY, STEPSON. OR IS IT ADOPTED SON? I KEEP TRIPPING UP ON THIS POINT.
IT IS NOT COMPLICATED, MR. MARLOWE. GERALD IS BOTH MY STEPSON AND MY ADOPTED SON.
BECAUSE AFTER HIS MOTHER, YOUR LATE WIFE, DIED, YOU ADOPTED HIM LEGALLY. GOT IT. WHY DID YOU DO THAT, IF YOU DON'T MIND ME ASKING?
WHY? WHY? THE BOY WAS ALONE IN THE WORLD, WITHOUT FAMILY, IT SEEMED--
DING DONG

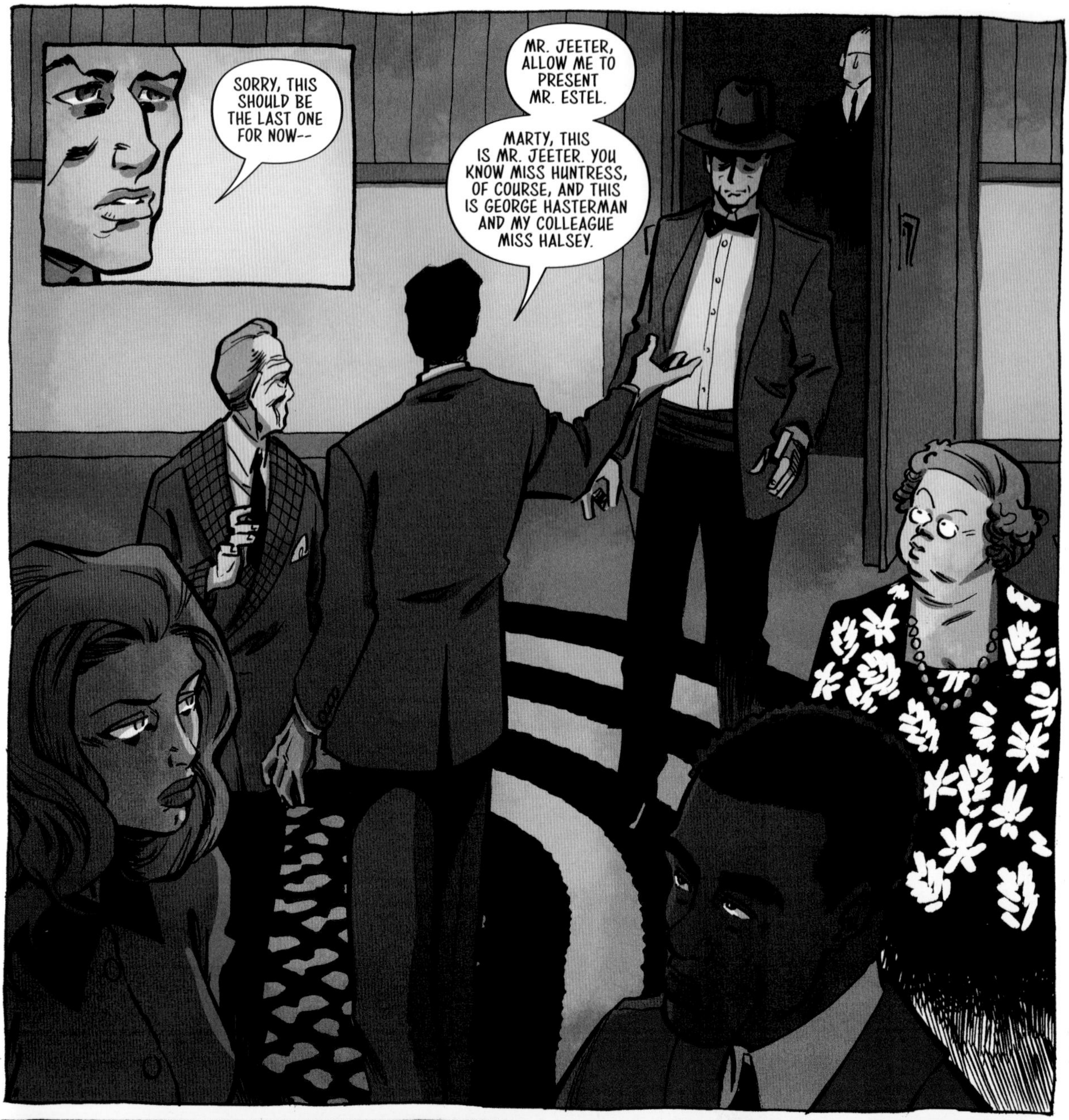
SORRY, THIS SHOULD BE THE LAST ONE FOR NOW--
MR. JEETER, ALLOW ME TO PRESENT MR. ESTEL.
MARTY, THIS IS MR. JEETER. YOU KNOW MISS HUNTRESS, OF COURSE, AND THIS IS GEORGE HASTERMAN AND MY COLLEAGUE MISS HALSEY.

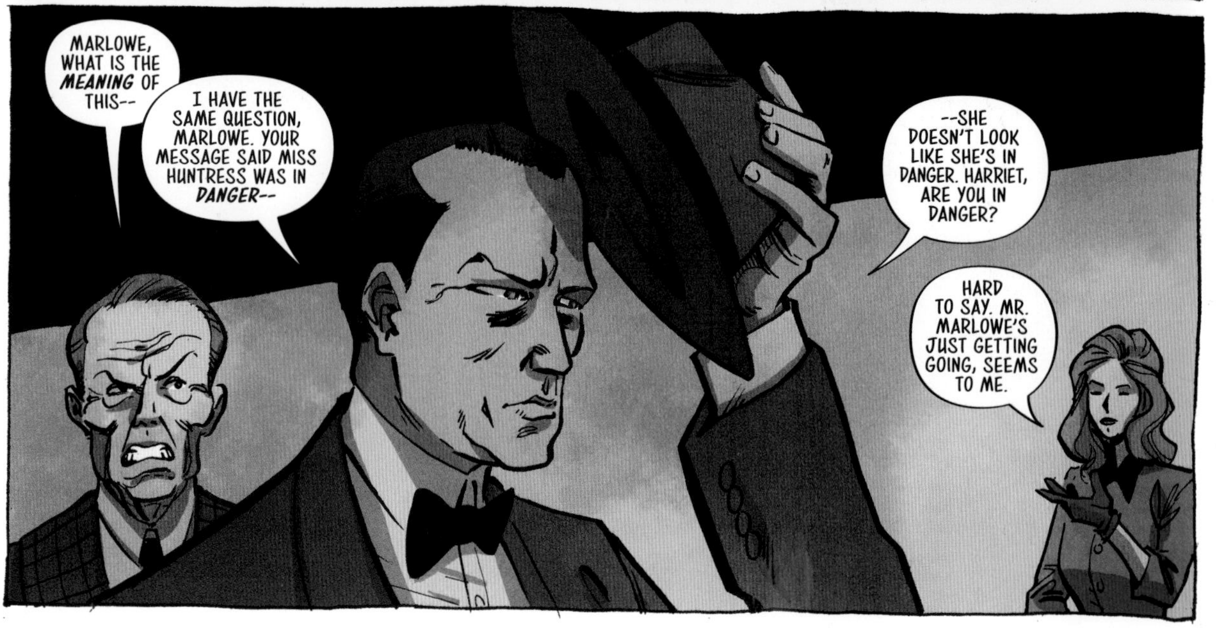
MARLOWE, WHAT IS THE MEANING OF THIS--
I HAVE THE SAME QUESTION, MARLOWE. YOUR MESSAGE SAID MISS HUNTRESS WAS IN DANGER--
--SHE DOESN'T LOOK LIKE SHE'S IN DANGER. HARRIET, ARE YOU IN DANGER?
HARD TO SAY. MR. MARLOWE'S JUST GETTING GOING, SEEMS TO ME.

SO LET'S SEE WHAT WE HAVE GOT.

WE HAVE A LOT OF THINGS THAT DON'T ADD UP, BUT I'M TOO *DUMB* TO KNOW WHAT ADDS UP AND WHAT DOESN'T SO I'M GOING TO ADD THEM UP *ANYHOW.*

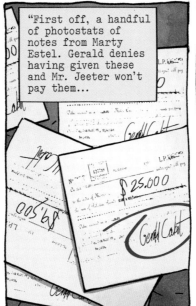

"First off, a handful of photostats of notes from Marty Estel. Gerald denies having given these and Mr. Jeeter won't pay them...

$25.000

JOHN D. ARBOGAST, EXAMINER OF QUESTIONED DOCUMENTS. PRIVATE INVESTIGATOR. ENTER.

"...but he has a handwriting man named **Arbogast** check the signatures, to see if they look genuine.

"They do. They are.

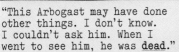

"This Arbogast may have done other things. I don't know. I couldn't ask him. When I went to see him, he was **dead**."

DEAD? MURDERED? WHY? BY WHOM?

"I haven't the faintest idea.

"What I do know is that he was shot with a *.22 caliber* pistol. We'll get to that.

"Then I went over to see Miss Huntress and we had a chat, and then Mister Gerald stepped neatly out of hiding and bopped me a nice one on the chin and over I went and hit my head on a table leg, which took me out for the count."

"WHY WOULD GERALD KNOCK YOU OUT?"

"It was the table leg, not Gerald, that knocked me out, but as for his motivations, there you have me, Mr. Jeeter.

"What I can say is when I came to, the joint was **empty**, so I went on **home**."

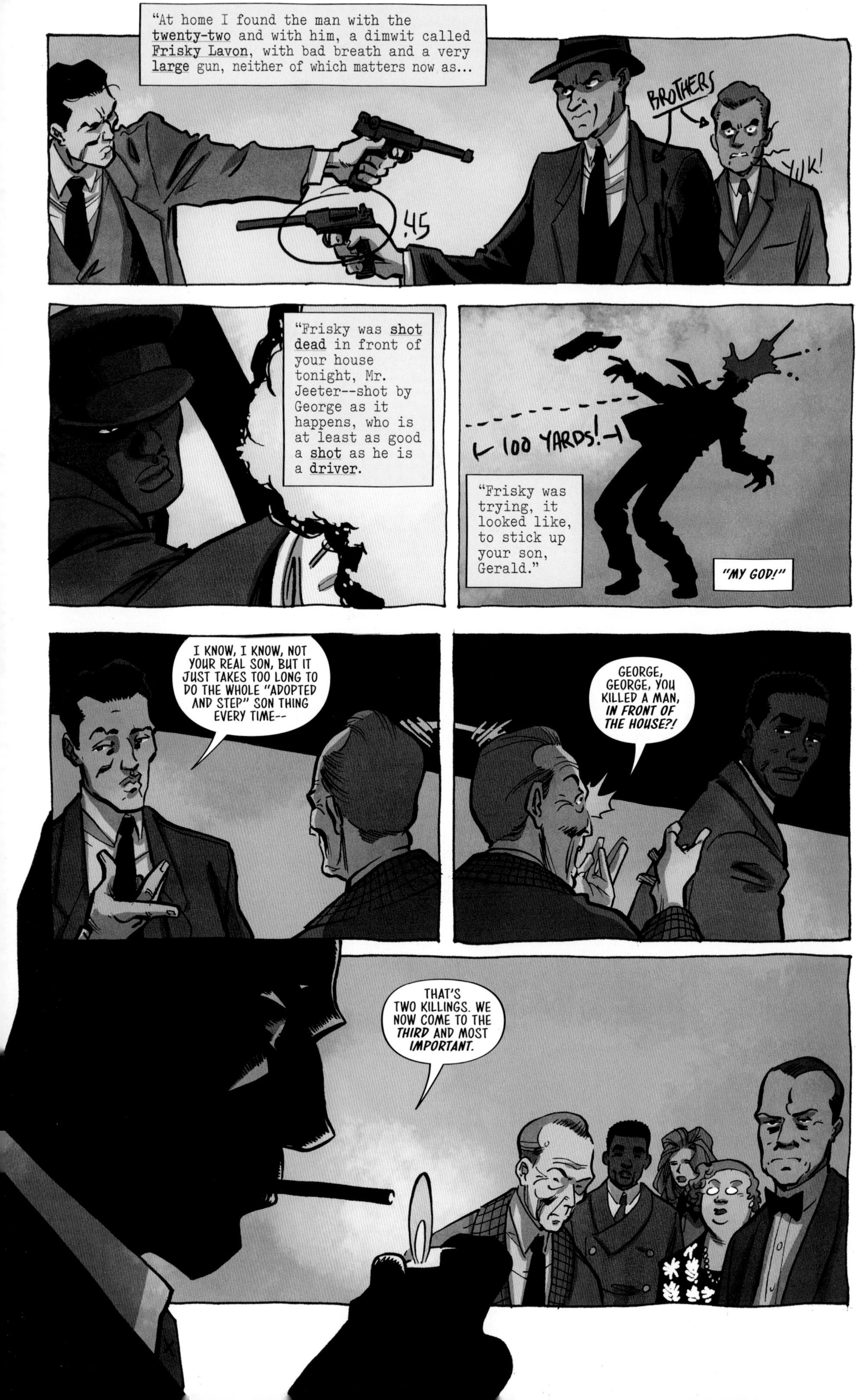
"At home I found the man with the twenty-two and with him, a dimwit called Frisky Lavon, with bad breath and a very large gun, neither of which matters now as...
BROTHERS
.45
YUK!
"Frisky was shot dead in front of your house tonight, Mr. Jeeter--shot by George as it happens, who is at least as good a shot as he is a driver.
100 YARDS!
"Frisky was trying, it looked like, to stick up your son, Gerald."
"MY GOD!"
I KNOW, I KNOW, NOT YOUR REAL SON, BUT IT JUST TAKES TOO LONG TO DO THE WHOLE "ADOPTED AND STEP" SON THING EVERY TIME--
GEORGE, GEORGE, YOU KILLED A MAN, IN FRONT OF THE HOUSE?!
THAT'S TWO KILLINGS. WE NOW COME TO THE THIRD AND MOST IMPORTANT.

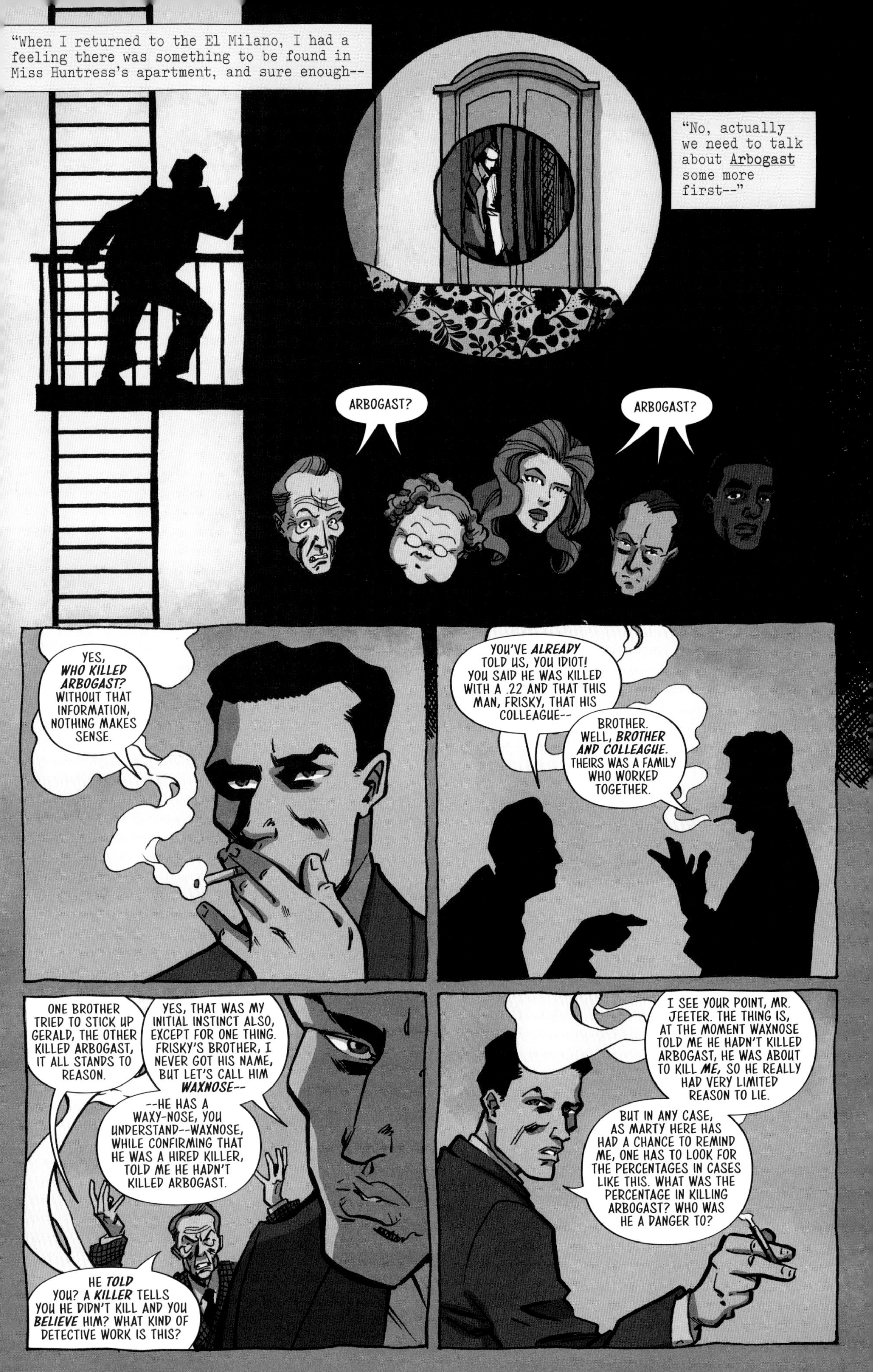

"When I returned to the El Milano, I had a feeling there was something to be found in Miss Huntress's apartment, and sure enough--
"No, actually we need to talk about Arbogast some more first--"
ARBOGAST?
ARBOGAST?
YES, WHO KILLED ARBOGAST? WITHOUT THAT INFORMATION, NOTHING MAKES SENSE.
YOU'VE ALREADY TOLD US, YOU IDIOT! YOU SAID HE WAS KILLED WITH A .22 AND THAT THIS MAN, FRISKY, THAT HIS COLLEAGUE--
BROTHER. WELL, BROTHER AND COLLEAGUE. THEIRS WAS A FAMILY WHO WORKED TOGETHER.
ONE BROTHER TRIED TO STICK UP GERALD, THE OTHER KILLED ARBOGAST, IT ALL STANDS TO REASON.
YES, THAT WAS MY INITIAL INSTINCT ALSO, EXCEPT FOR ONE THING. FRISKY'S BROTHER, I NEVER GOT HIS NAME, BUT LET'S CALL HIM WAXNOSE--
--HE HAS A WAXY-NOSE, YOU UNDERSTAND--WAXNOSE, WHILE CONFIRMING THAT HE WAS A HIRED KILLER, TOLD ME HE HADN'T KILLED ARBOGAST.
HE TOLD YOU? A KILLER TELLS YOU HE DIDN'T KILL AND YOU BELIEVE HIM? WHAT KIND OF DETECTIVE WORK IS THIS?
I SEE YOUR POINT, MR. JEETER. THE THING IS, AT THE MOMENT WAXNOSE TOLD ME HE HADN'T KILLED ARBOGAST, HE WAS ABOUT TO KILL ME, SO HE REALLY HAD VERY LIMITED REASON TO LIE.
BUT IN ANY CASE, AS MARTY HERE HAS HAD A CHANCE TO REMIND ME, ONE HAS TO LOOK FOR THE PERCENTAGES IN CASES LIKE THIS. WHAT WAS THE PERCENTAGE IN KILLING ARBOGAST? WHO WAS HE A DANGER TO?

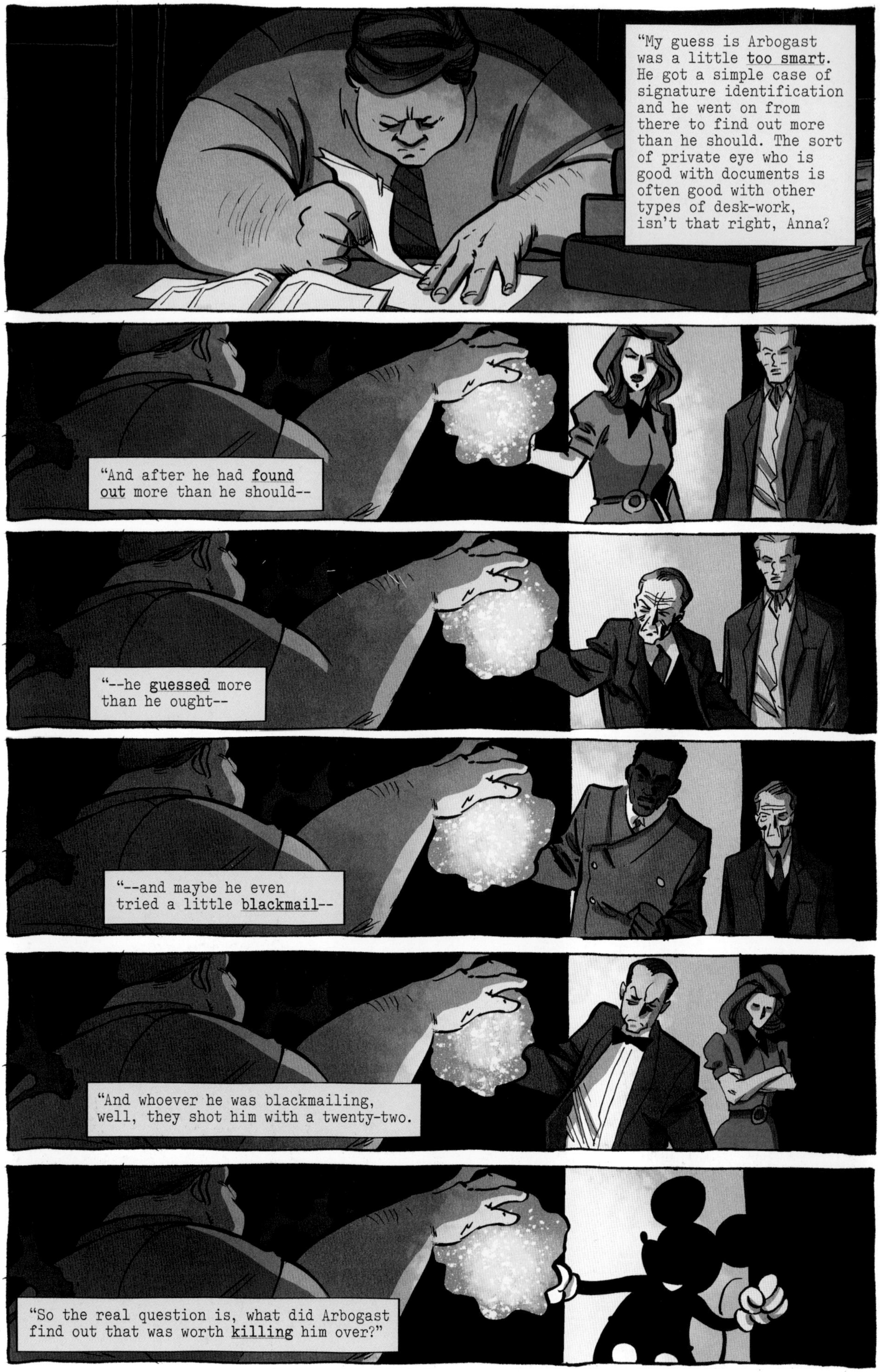
"My guess is Arbogast was a little too smart. He got a simple case of signature identification and he went on from there to find out more than he should. The sort of private eye who is good with documents is often good with other types of desk-work, isn't that right, Anna?
"And after he had found out more than he should--
"--he guessed more than he ought--
"--and maybe he even tried a little blackmail--
"And whoever he was blackmailing, well, they shot him with a twenty-two.
"So the real question is, what did Arbogast find out that was worth killing him over?"

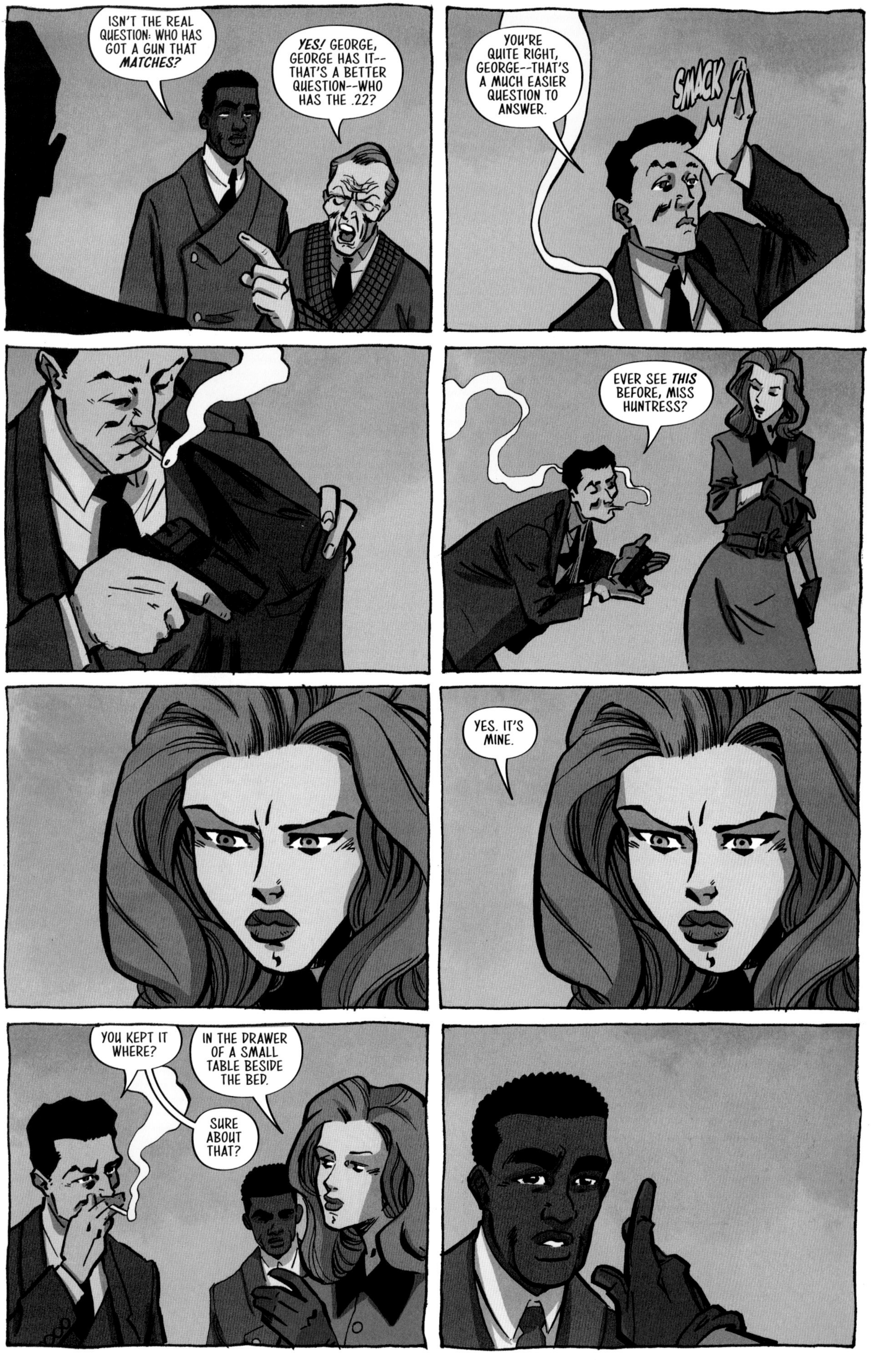
ISN'T THE REAL QUESTION: WHO HAS GOT A GUN THAT *MATCHES?*
YES! GEORGE, GEORGE HAS IT--THAT'S A BETTER QUESTION--WHO HAS THE .22?
YOU'RE QUITE RIGHT, GEORGE--THAT'S A MUCH EASIER QUESTION TO ANSWER.
SMACK
EVER SEE *THIS* BEFORE, MISS HUNTRESS?
YES. IT'S MINE.
YOU KEPT IT WHERE?
IN THE DRAWER OF A SMALL TABLE BESIDE THE BED.
SURE ABOUT THAT?

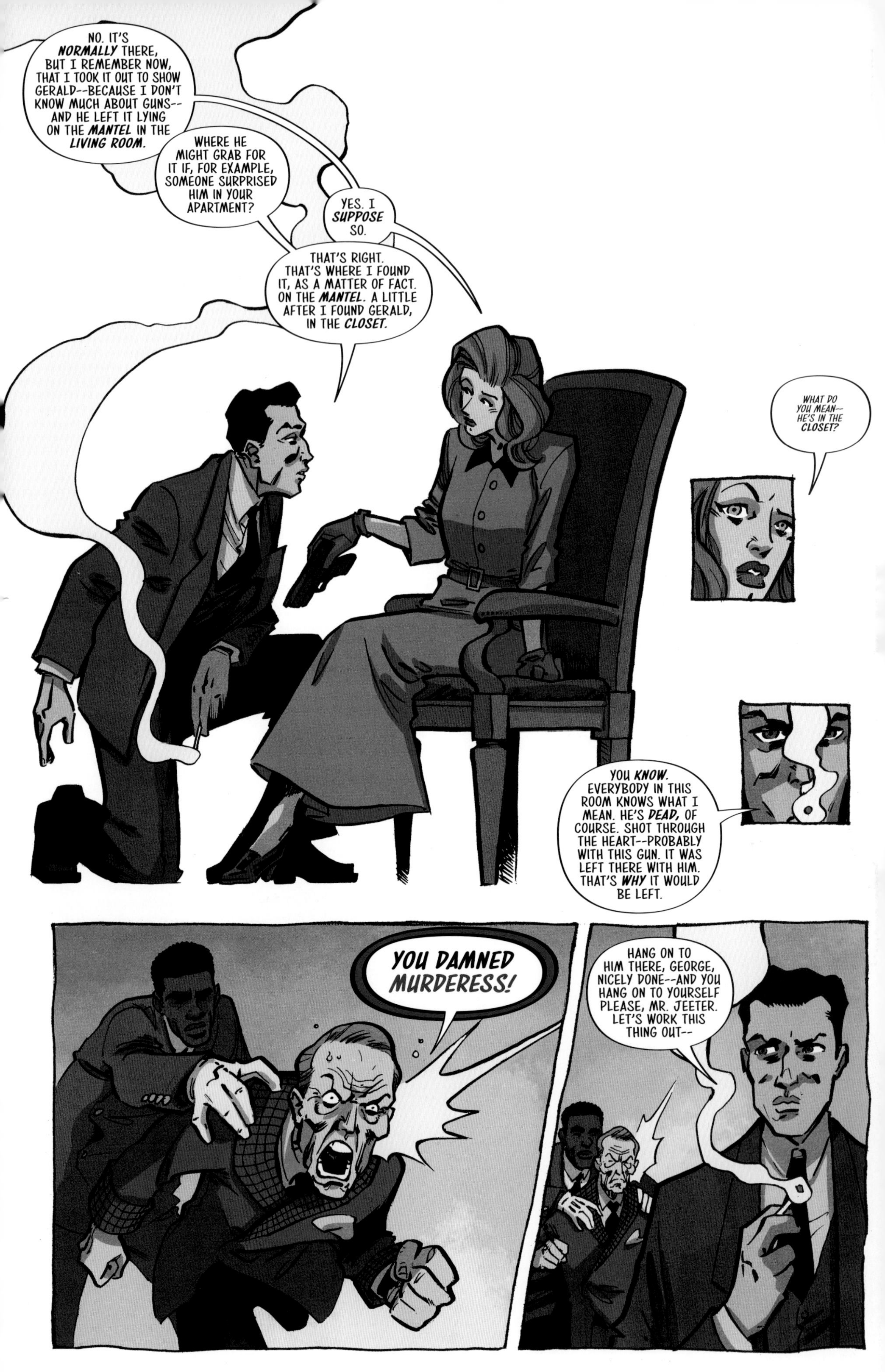
NO. IT'S *NORMALLY* THERE, BUT I REMEMBER NOW, THAT I TOOK IT OUT TO SHOW GERALD--BECAUSE I DON'T KNOW MUCH ABOUT GUNS--AND HE LEFT IT LYING ON THE *MANTEL* IN THE *LIVING ROOM.*
WHERE HE MIGHT GRAB FOR IT IF, FOR EXAMPLE, SOMEONE SURPRISED HIM IN YOUR APARTMENT?
YES. I *SUPPOSE* SO.
THAT'S RIGHT. THAT'S WHERE I FOUND IT, AS A MATTER OF FACT. ON THE *MANTEL.* A LITTLE AFTER I FOUND GERALD, IN THE *CLOSET.*
WHAT DO YOU MEAN--HE'S IN THE *CLOSET?*
YOU *KNOW.* EVERYBODY IN THIS ROOM KNOWS WHAT I MEAN. HE'S *DEAD,* OF COURSE. SHOT THROUGH THE HEART--PROBABLY WITH THIS GUN. IT WAS LEFT THERE WITH HIM. THAT'S *WHY* IT WOULD BE LEFT.
YOU DAMNED MURDERESS!
HANG ON TO HIM THERE, GEORGE, NICELY DONE--AND YOU HANG ON TO YOURSELF PLEASE, MR. JEETER. LET'S WORK THIS THING OUT--

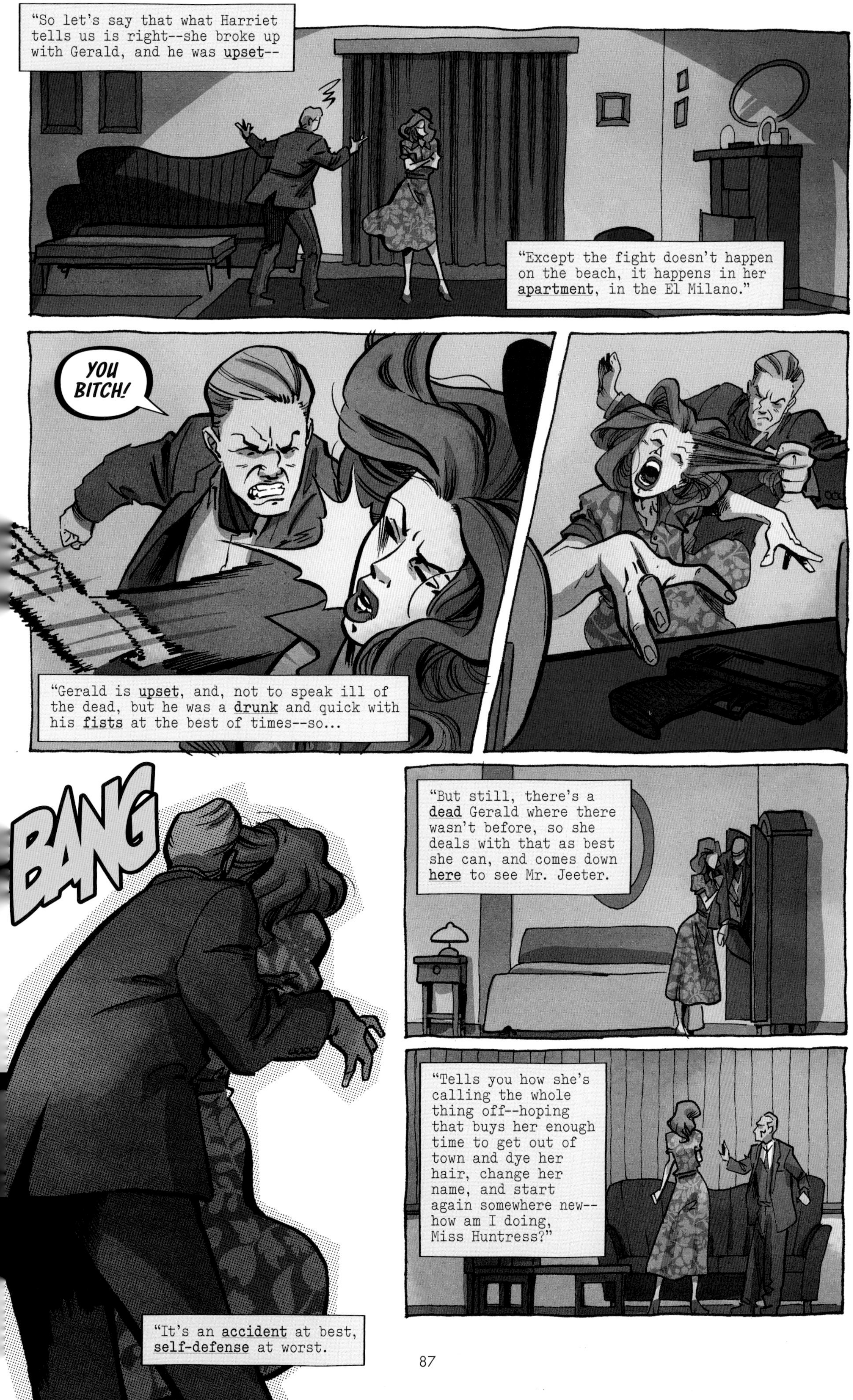

"So let's say that what Harriet tells us is right--she broke up with Gerald, and he was upset--
"Except the fight doesn't happen on the beach, it happens in her apartment, in the El Milano."
YOU BITCH!
"Gerald is upset, and, not to speak ill of the dead, but he was a drunk and quick with his fists at the best of times--so...
BANG
"It's an accident at best, self-defense at worst.
"But still, there's a dead Gerald where there wasn't before, so she deals with that as best she can, and comes down here to see Mr. Jeeter.
"Tells you how she's calling the whole thing off--hoping that buys her enough time to get out of town and dye her hair, change her name, and start again somewhere new--how am I doing, Miss Huntress?"

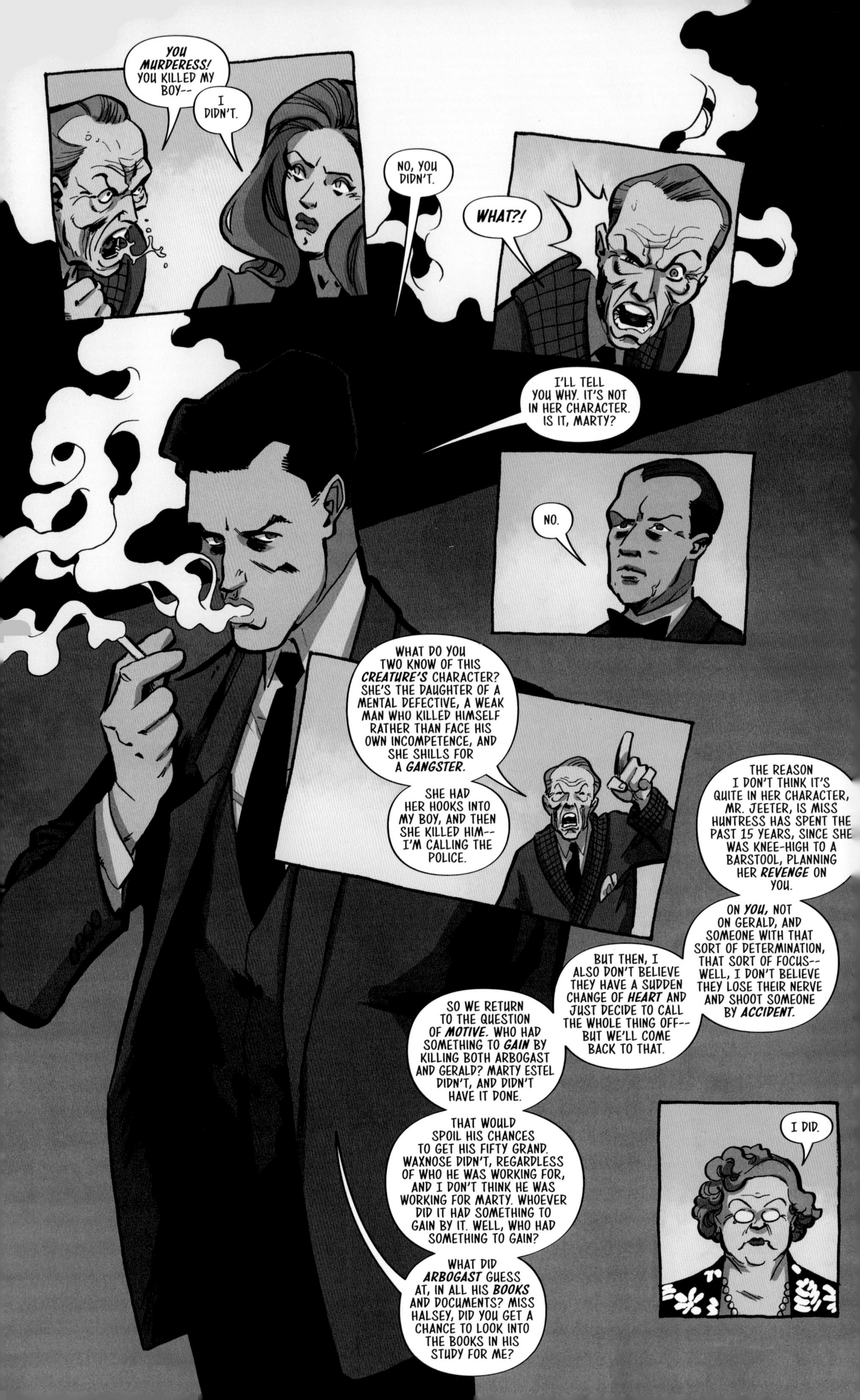

YOU MURDERESS! YOU KILLED MY BOY--
I DIDN'T.
NO, YOU DIDN'T.
WHAT?!
I'LL TELL YOU WHY. IT'S NOT IN HER CHARACTER. IS IT, MARTY?
NO.
WHAT DO YOU TWO KNOW OF THIS CREATURE'S CHARACTER? SHE'S THE DAUGHTER OF A MENTAL DEFECTIVE, A WEAK MAN WHO KILLED HIMSELF RATHER THAN FACE HIS OWN INCOMPETENCE, AND SHE SHILLS FOR A GANGSTER.
SHE HAD HER HOOKS INTO MY BOY, AND THEN SHE KILLED HIM-- I'M CALLING THE POLICE.
THE REASON I DON'T THINK IT'S QUITE IN HER CHARACTER, MR. JEETER, IS MISS HUNTRESS HAS SPENT THE PAST 15 YEARS, SINCE SHE WAS KNEE-HIGH TO A BARSTOOL, PLANNING HER REVENGE ON YOU.
ON YOU, NOT ON GERALD, AND SOMEONE WITH THAT SORT OF DETERMINATION, THAT SORT OF FOCUS-- WELL, I DON'T BELIEVE THEY LOSE THEIR NERVE AND SHOOT SOMEONE BY ACCIDENT.
BUT THEN, I ALSO DON'T BELIEVE THEY HAVE A SUDDEN CHANGE OF HEART AND JUST DECIDE TO CALL THE WHOLE THING OFF-- BUT WE'LL COME BACK TO THAT.
SO WE RETURN TO THE QUESTION OF MOTIVE. WHO HAD SOMETHING TO GAIN BY KILLING BOTH ARBOGAST AND GERALD? MARTY ESTEL DIDN'T, AND DIDN'T HAVE IT DONE.
THAT WOULD SPOIL HIS CHANCES TO GET HIS FIFTY GRAND. WAXNOSE DIDN'T, REGARDLESS OF WHO HE WAS WORKING FOR, AND I DON'T THINK HE WAS WORKING FOR MARTY. WHOEVER DID IT HAD SOMETHING TO GAIN BY IT. WELL, WHO HAD SOMETHING TO GAIN?
WHAT DID ARBOGAST GUESS AT, IN ALL HIS BOOKS AND DOCUMENTS? MISS HALSEY, DID YOU GET A CHANCE TO LOOK INTO THE BOOKS IN HIS STUDY FOR ME?
I DID.

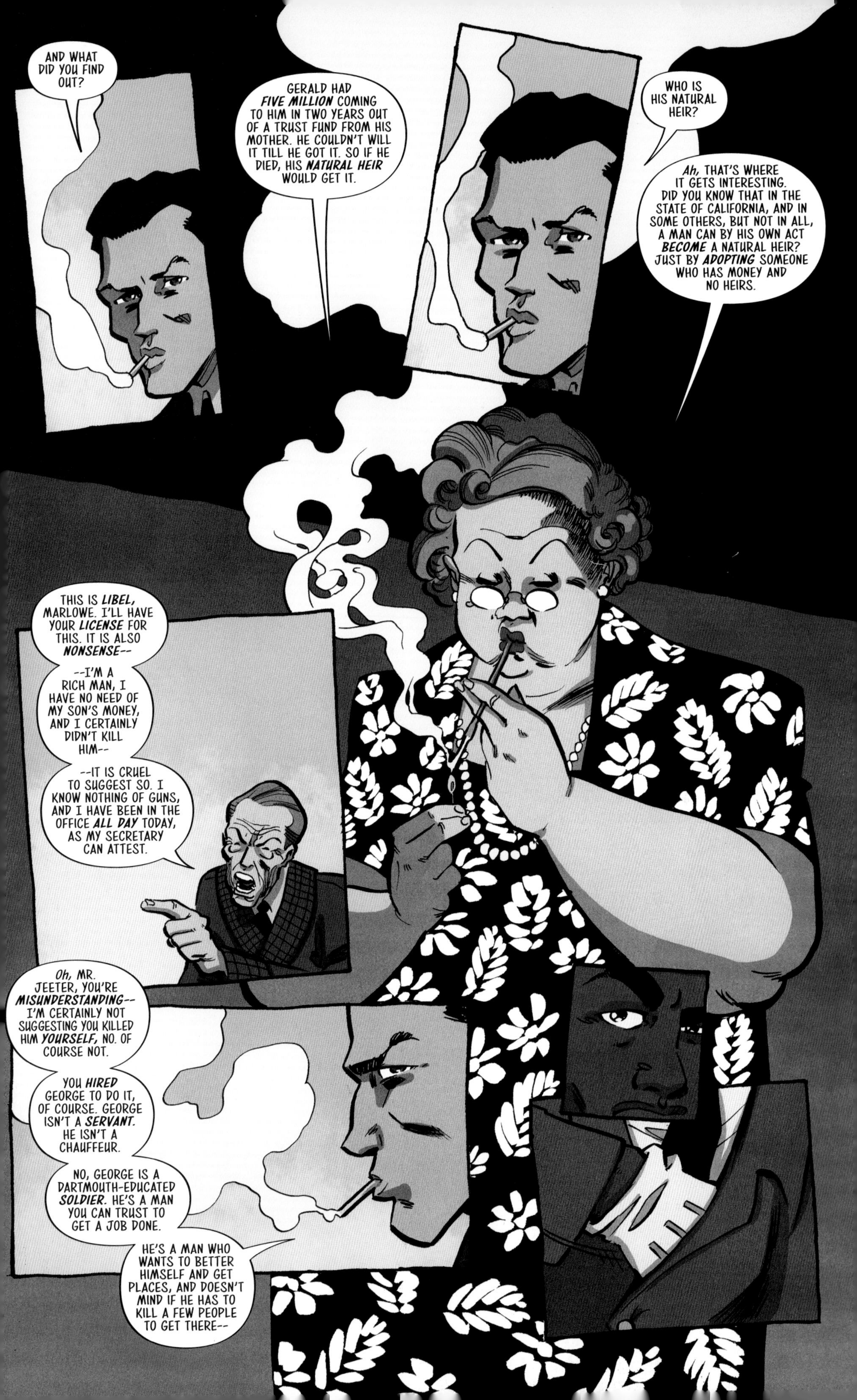
AND WHAT DID YOU FIND OUT?
GERALD HAD FIVE MILLION COMING TO HIM IN TWO YEARS OUT OF A TRUST FUND FROM HIS MOTHER. HE COULDN'T WILL IT TILL HE GOT IT. SO IF HE DIED, HIS NATURAL HEIR WOULD GET IT.
WHO IS HIS NATURAL HEIR?
Ah, THAT'S WHERE IT GETS INTERESTING. DID YOU KNOW THAT IN THE STATE OF CALIFORNIA, AND IN SOME OTHERS, BUT NOT IN ALL, A MAN CAN BY HIS OWN ACT BECOME A NATURAL HEIR? JUST BY ADOPTING SOMEONE WHO HAS MONEY AND NO HEIRS.
THIS IS LIBEL, MARLOWE. I'LL HAVE YOUR LICENSE FOR THIS. IT IS ALSO NONSENSE--
--I'M A RICH MAN, I HAVE NO NEED OF MY SON'S MONEY, AND I CERTAINLY DIDN'T KILL HIM--
--IT IS CRUEL TO SUGGEST SO. I KNOW NOTHING OF GUNS, AND I HAVE BEEN IN THE OFFICE ALL DAY TODAY, AS MY SECRETARY CAN ATTEST.
Oh, MR. JEETER, YOU'RE MISUNDERSTANDING-- I'M CERTAINLY NOT SUGGESTING YOU KILLED HIM YOURSELF, NO. OF COURSE NOT.
YOU HIRED GEORGE TO DO IT, OF COURSE. GEORGE ISN'T A SERVANT. HE ISN'T A CHAUFFEUR.
NO, GEORGE IS A DARTMOUTH-EDUCATED SOLDIER. HE'S A MAN YOU CAN TRUST TO GET A JOB DONE.
HE'S A MAN WHO WANTS TO BETTER HIMSELF AND GET PLACES, AND DOESN'T MIND IF HE HAS TO KILL A FEW PEOPLE TO GET THERE--

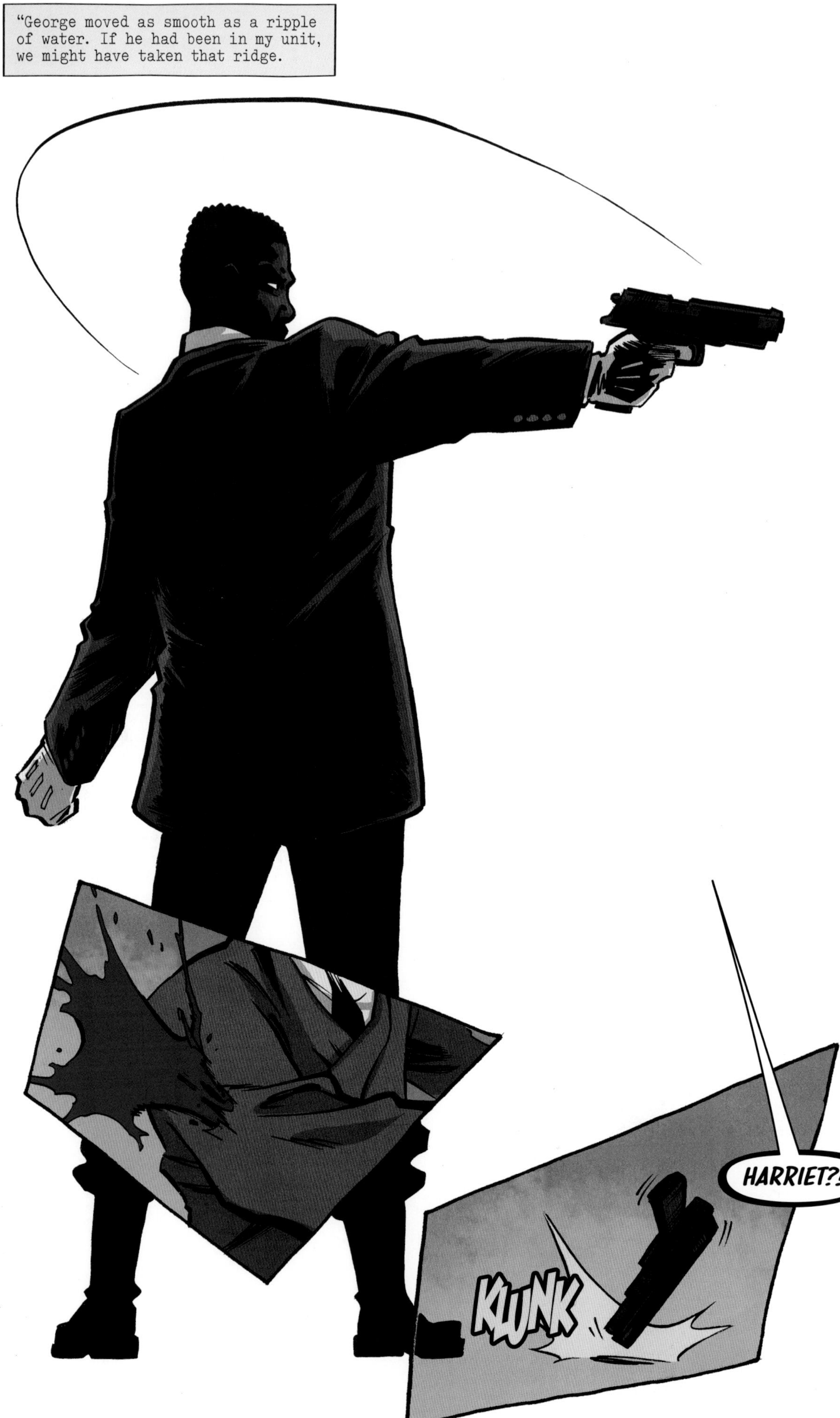
"George moved as smooth as a ripple of water. If he had been in my unit, we might have taken that ridge.
HARRIET?!
KLUNK

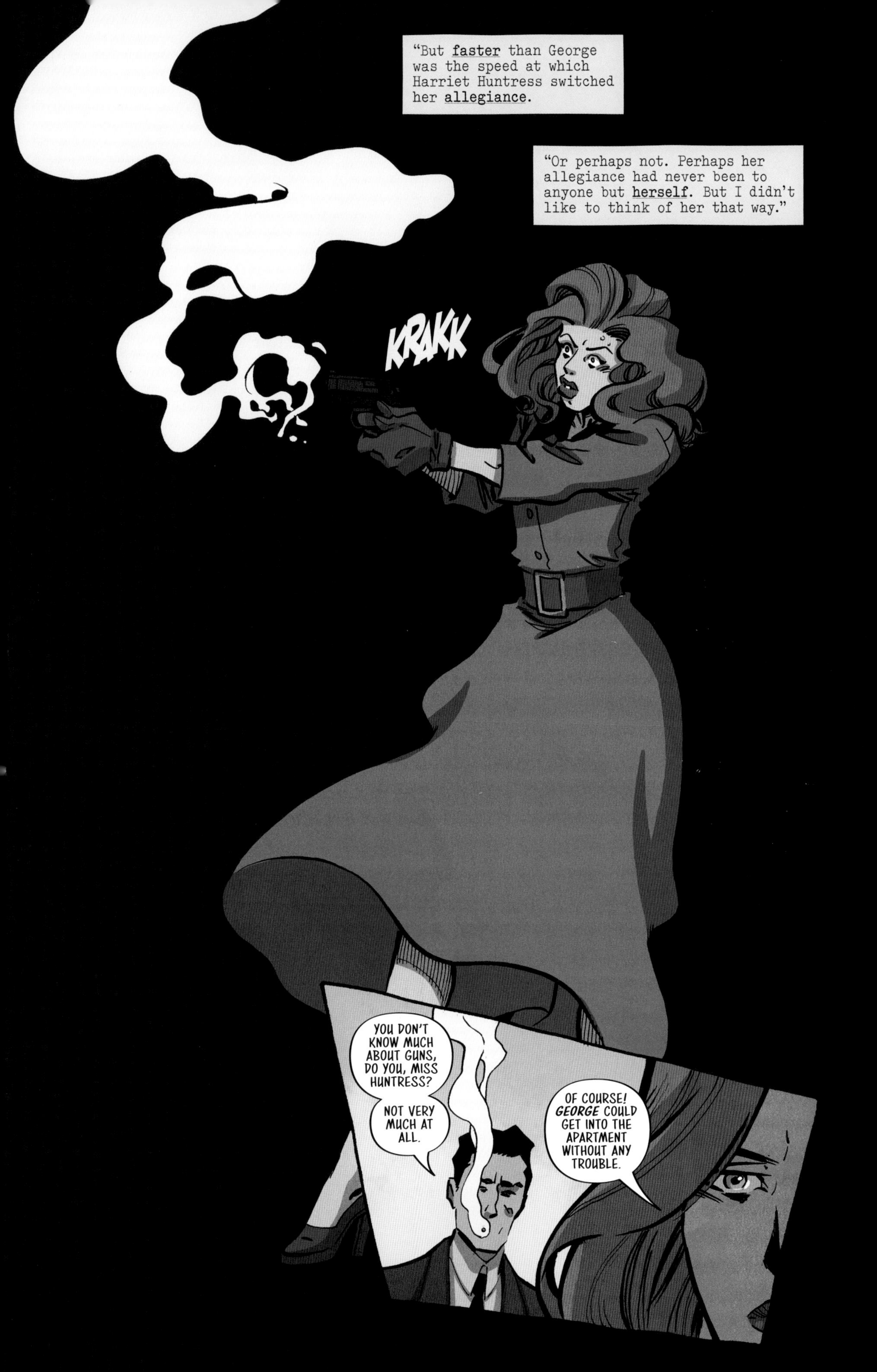
"But faster than George was the speed at which Harriet Huntress switched her allegiance.
"Or perhaps not. Perhaps her allegiance had never been to anyone but herself. But I didn't like to think of her that way."
KRAKK
YOU DON'T KNOW MUCH ABOUT GUNS, DO YOU, MISS HUNTRESS?
NOT VERY MUCH AT ALL.
OF COURSE! GEORGE COULD GET INTO THE APARTMENT WITHOUT ANY TROUBLE.

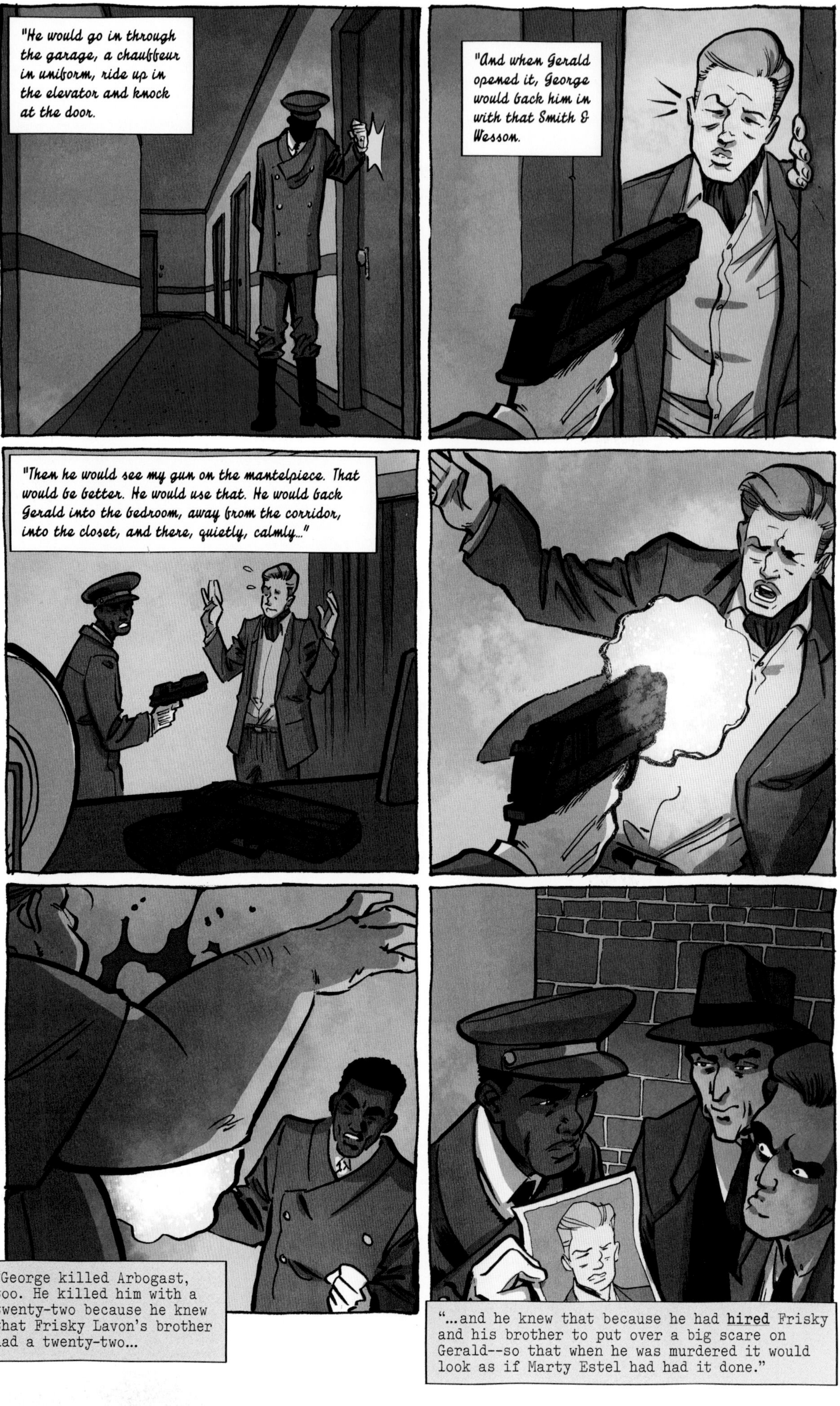
"He would go in through the garage, a chauffeur in uniform, ride up in the elevator and knock at the door.
"And when Gerald opened it, George would back him in with that Smith & Wesson.
"Then he would see my gun on the mantelpiece. That would be better. He would use that. He would back Gerald into the bedroom, away from the corridor, into the closet, and there, quietly, calmly..."
"George killed Arbogast, too. He killed him with a twenty-two because he knew that Frisky Lavon's brother had a twenty-two...
"...and he knew that because he had hired Frisky and his brother to put over a big scare on Gerald--so that when he was murdered it would look as if Marty Estel had had it done."

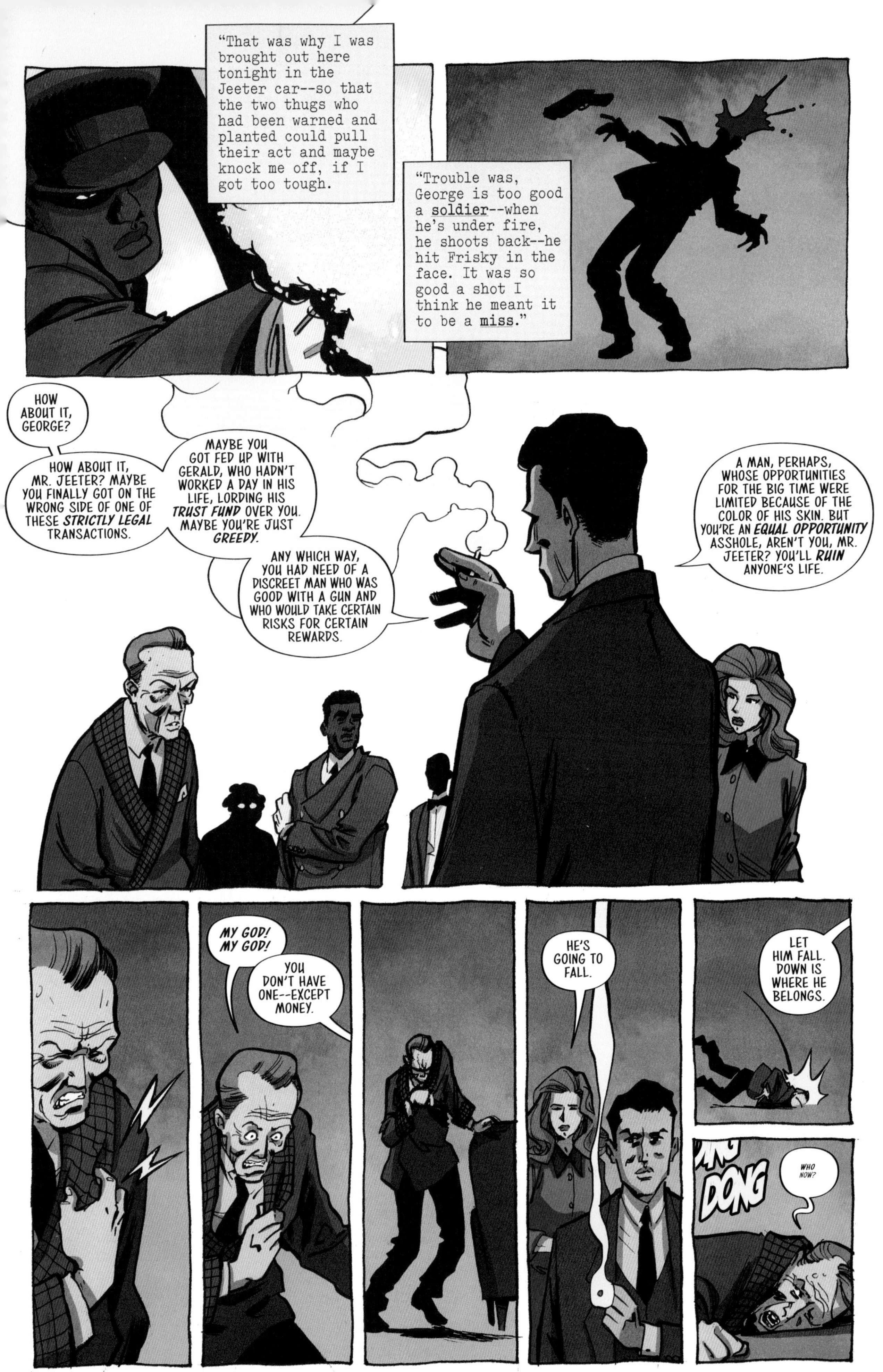
"That was why I was brought out here tonight in the Jeeter car--so that the two thugs who had been warned and planted could pull their act and maybe knock me off, if I got too tough.
"Trouble was, George is too good a soldier--when he's under fire, he shoots back--he hit Frisky in the face. It was so good a shot I think he meant it to be a miss."
HOW ABOUT IT, GEORGE?
HOW ABOUT IT, MR. JEETER? MAYBE YOU FINALLY GOT ON THE WRONG SIDE OF ONE OF THESE STRICTLY LEGAL TRANSACTIONS.
MAYBE YOU GOT FED UP WITH GERALD, WHO HADN'T WORKED A DAY IN HIS LIFE, LORDING HIS TRUST FUND OVER YOU. MAYBE YOU'RE JUST GREEDY.
ANY WHICH WAY, YOU HAD NEED OF A DISCREET MAN WHO WAS GOOD WITH A GUN AND WHO WOULD TAKE CERTAIN RISKS FOR CERTAIN REWARDS.
A MAN, PERHAPS, WHOSE OPPORTUNITIES FOR THE BIG TIME WERE LIMITED BECAUSE OF THE COLOR OF HIS SKIN. BUT YOU'RE AN EQUAL OPPORTUNITY ASSHOLE, AREN'T YOU, MR. JEETER? YOU'LL RUIN ANYONE'S LIFE.
MY GOD! MY GOD!
YOU DON'T HAVE ONE--EXCEPT MONEY.
HE'S GOING TO FALL.
LET HIM FALL. DOWN IS WHERE HE BELONGS.
DONG
WHO NOW?

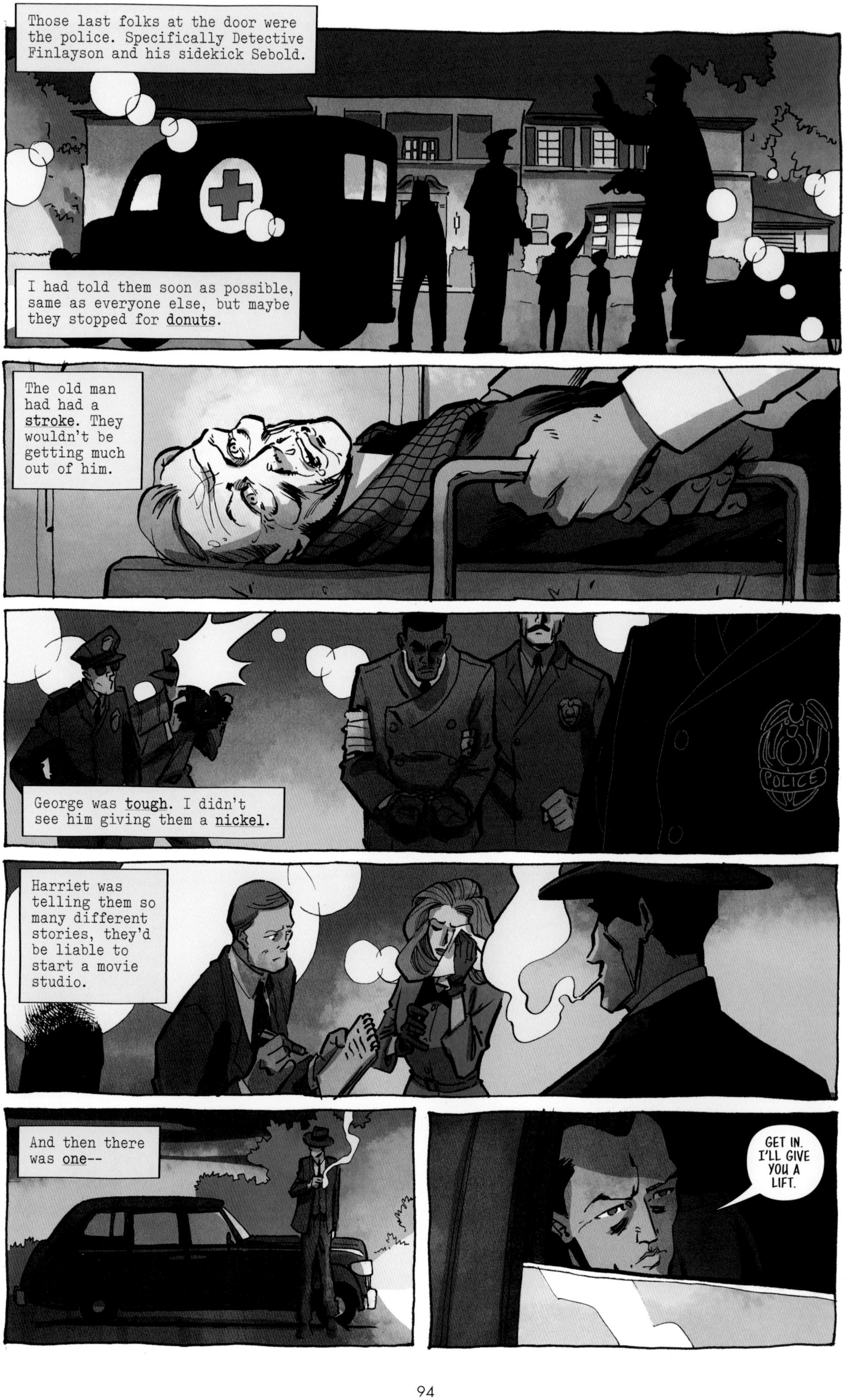

Those last folks at the door were the police. Specifically Detective Finlayson and his sidekick Sebold.
I had told them soon as possible, same as everyone else, but maybe they stopped for donuts.
The old man had had a stroke. They wouldn't be getting much out of him.
George was tough. I didn't see him giving them a nickel.
POLICE
Harriet was telling them so many different stories, they'd be liable to start a movie studio.
And then there was one--
GET IN. I'LL GIVE YOU A LIFT.

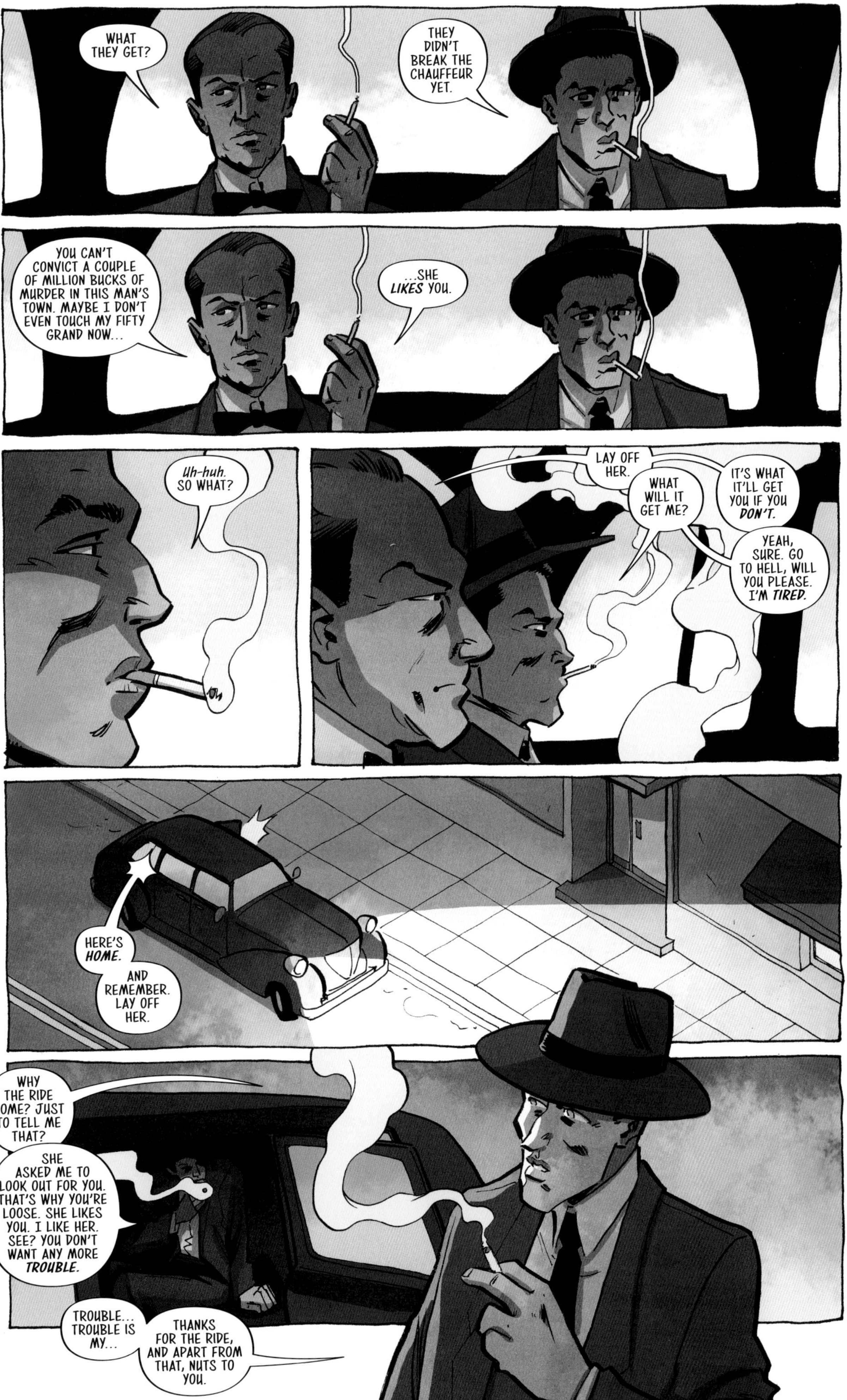
WHAT THEY GET?
THEY DIDN'T BREAK THE CHAUFFEUR YET.
YOU CAN'T CONVICT A COUPLE OF MILLION BUCKS OF MURDER IN THIS MAN'S TOWN. MAYBE I DON'T EVEN TOUCH MY FIFTY GRAND NOW...
...SHE *LIKES* YOU.
Uh-huh. SO WHAT?
LAY OFF HER.
WHAT WILL IT GET ME?
IT'S WHAT IT'LL GET YOU IF YOU *DON'T.*
YEAH, SURE. GO TO HELL, WILL YOU PLEASE. I'M *TIRED.*
HERE'S *HOME.*
AND REMEMBER. LAY OFF HER.
WHY THE RIDE HOME? JUST TO TELL ME THAT?
SHE ASKED ME TO LOOK OUT FOR YOU. THAT'S WHY YOU'RE LOOSE. SHE LIKES YOU. I LIKE HER. SEE? YOU DON'T WANT ANY MORE *TROUBLE.*
TROUBLE... TROUBLE IS MY...
THANKS FOR THE RIDE, AND APART FROM THAT, NUTS TO YOU.

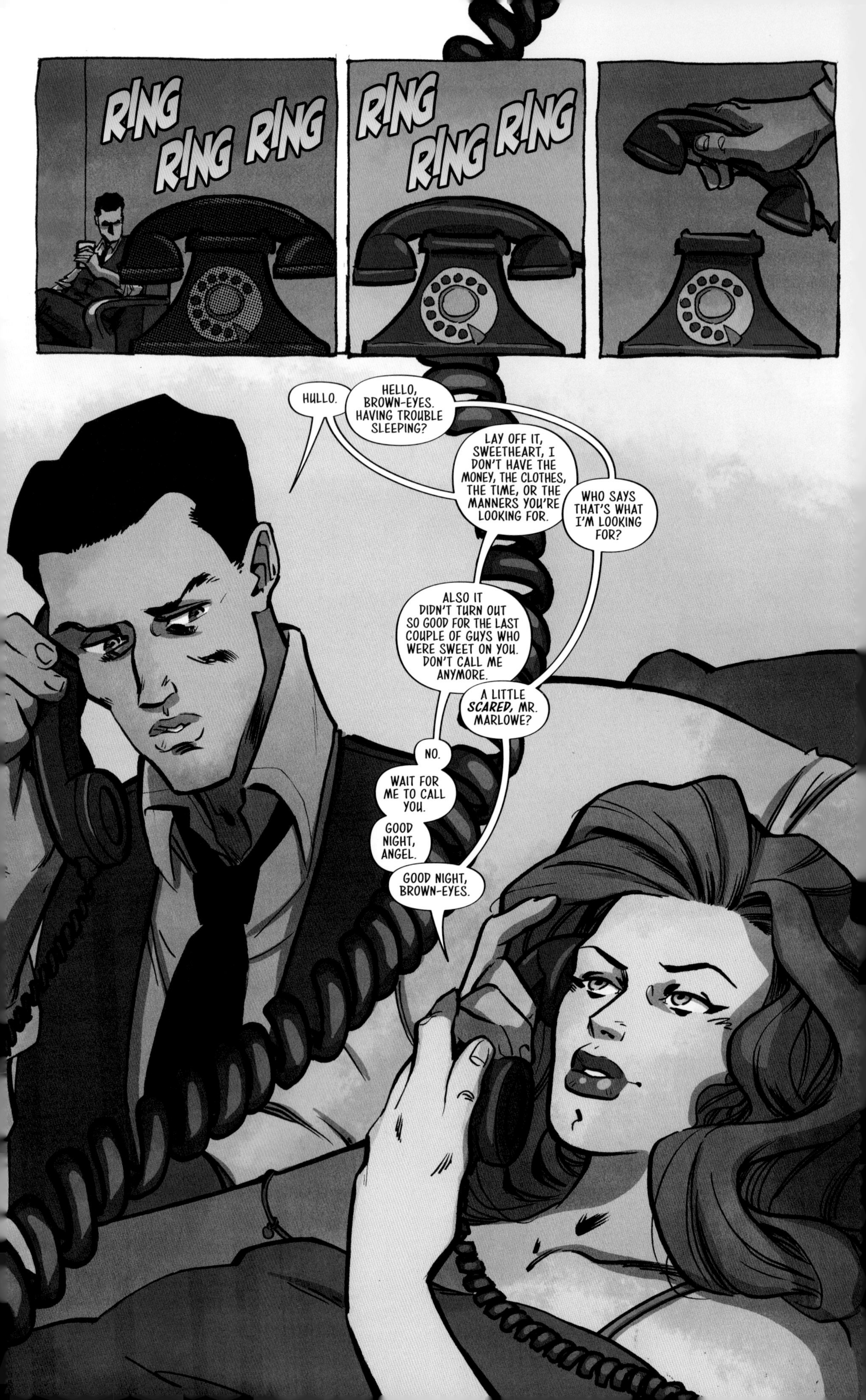
RING
RING RING
RING
RING RING
HULLO.
HELLO, BROWN-EYES. HAVING TROUBLE SLEEPING?
LAY OFF IT, SWEETHEART, I DON'T HAVE THE MONEY, THE CLOTHES, THE TIME, OR THE MANNERS YOU'RE LOOKING FOR.
WHO SAYS THAT'S WHAT I'M LOOKING FOR?
ALSO IT DIDN'T TURN OUT SO GOOD FOR THE LAST COUPLE OF GUYS WHO WERE SWEET ON YOU. DON'T CALL ME ANYMORE.
A LITTLE *SCARED,* MR. MARLOWE?
NO.
WAIT FOR ME TO CALL YOU.
GOOD NIGHT, ANGEL.
GOOD NIGHT, BROWN-EYES.

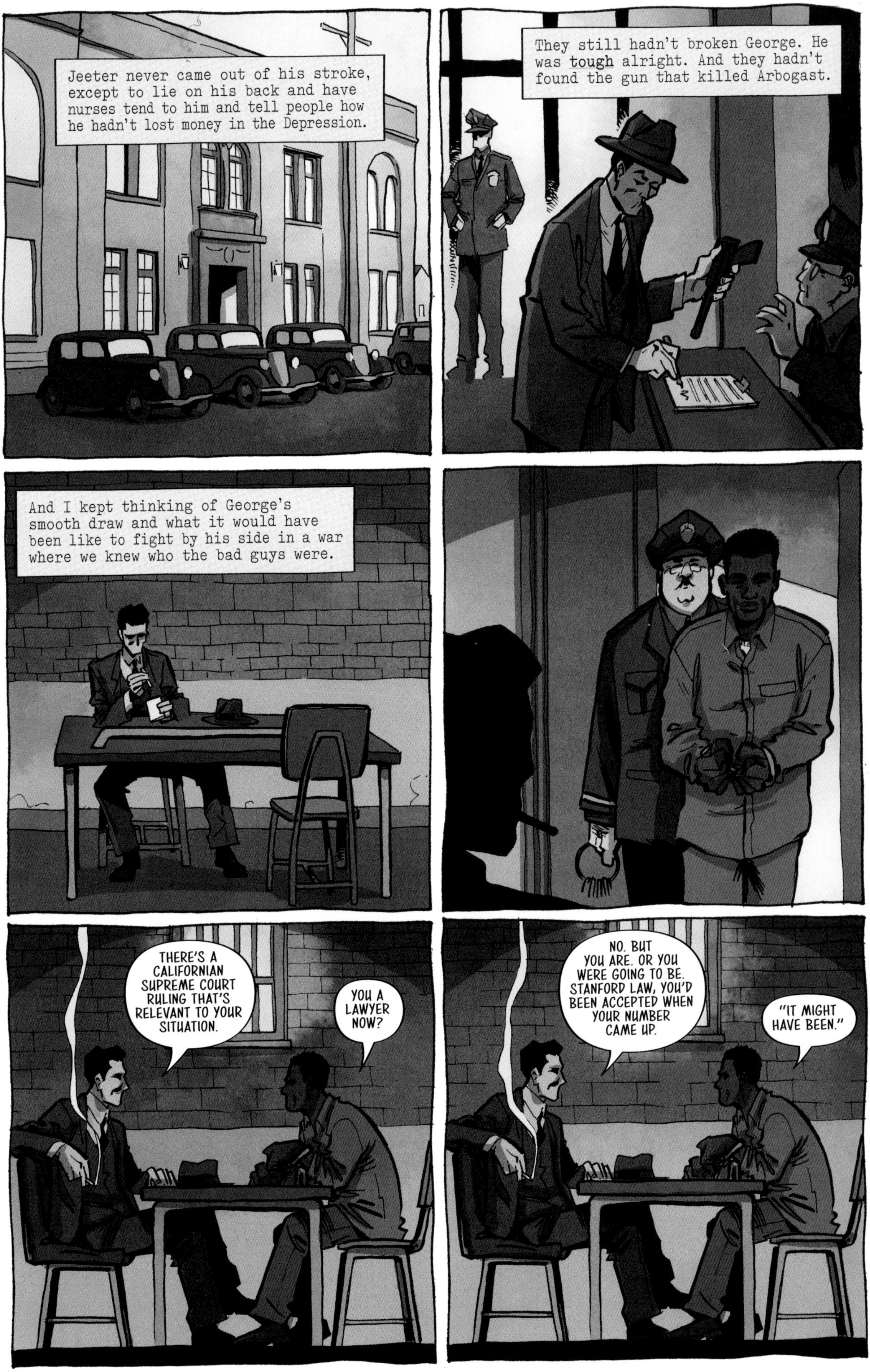
Jeeter never came out of his stroke, except to lie on his back and have nurses tend to him and tell people how he hadn't lost money in the Depression.
They still hadn't broken George. He was **tough** alright. And they hadn't found the gun that killed Arbogast.
And I kept thinking of George's smooth draw and what it would have been like to fight by his side in a war where we knew who the bad guys were.
THERE'S A CALIFORNIAN SUPREME COURT RULING THAT'S RELEVANT TO YOUR SITUATION.
YOU A LAWYER NOW?
NO. BUT YOU ARE. OR YOU WERE GOING TO BE. STANFORD LAW, YOU'D BEEN ACCEPTED WHEN YOUR NUMBER CAME UP.
"IT MIGHT HAVE BEEN."

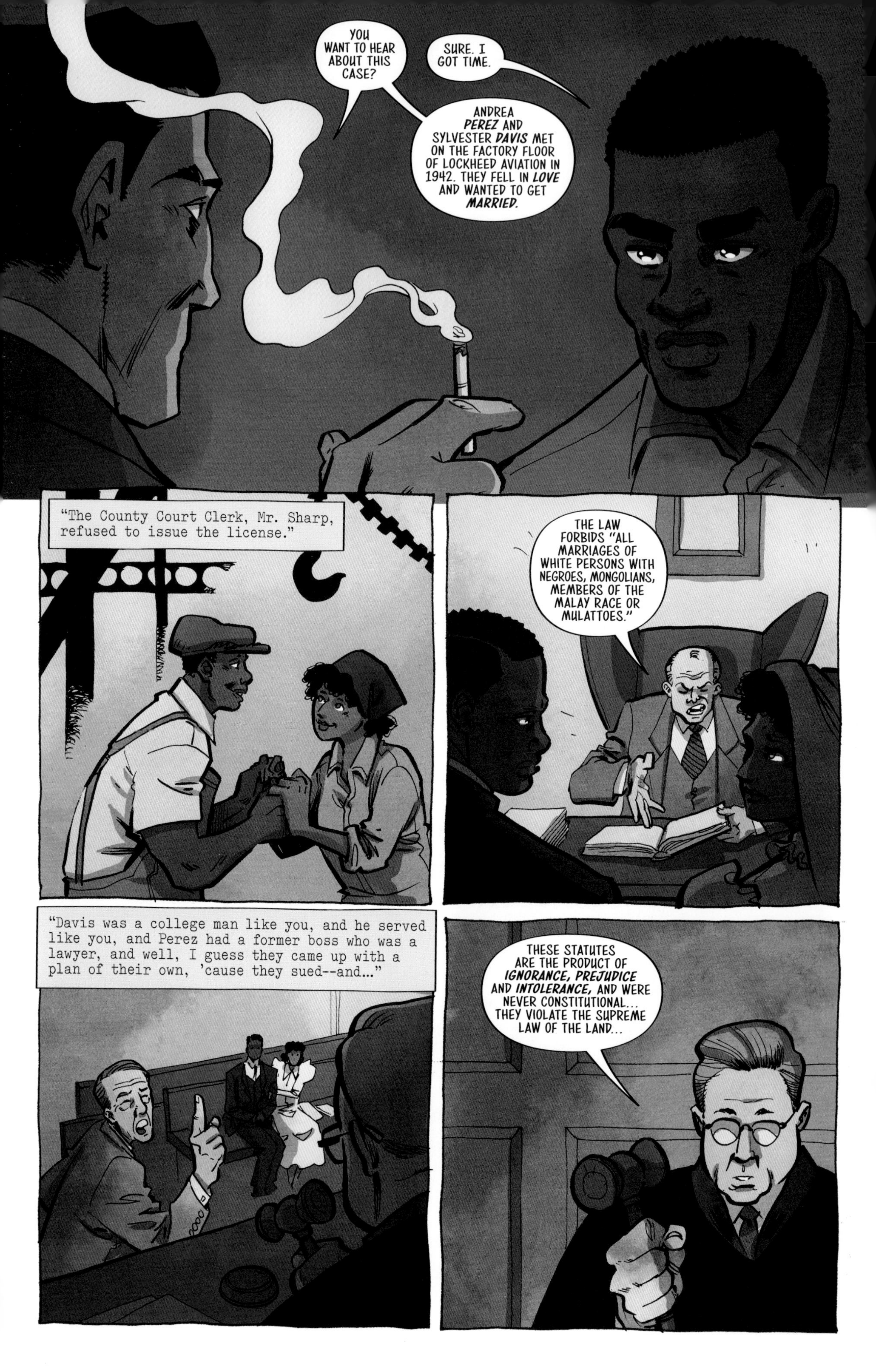
YOU WANT TO HEAR ABOUT THIS CASE?
SURE. I GOT TIME.
ANDREA PEREZ AND SYLVESTER DAVIS MET ON THE FACTORY FLOOR OF LOCKHEED AVIATION IN 1942. THEY FELL IN LOVE AND WANTED TO GET MARRIED.
"The County Court Clerk, Mr. Sharp, refused to issue the license."
THE LAW FORBIDS "ALL MARRIAGES OF WHITE PERSONS WITH NEGROES, MONGOLIANS, MEMBERS OF THE MALAY RACE OR MULATTOES."
"Davis was a college man like you, and he served like you, and Perez had a former boss who was a lawyer, and well, I guess they came up with a plan of their own, 'cause they sued--and..."
THESE STATUTES ARE THE PRODUCT OF IGNORANCE, PREJUDICE AND INTOLERANCE, AND WERE NEVER CONSTITUTIONAL... THEY VIOLATE THE SUPREME LAW OF THE LAND...

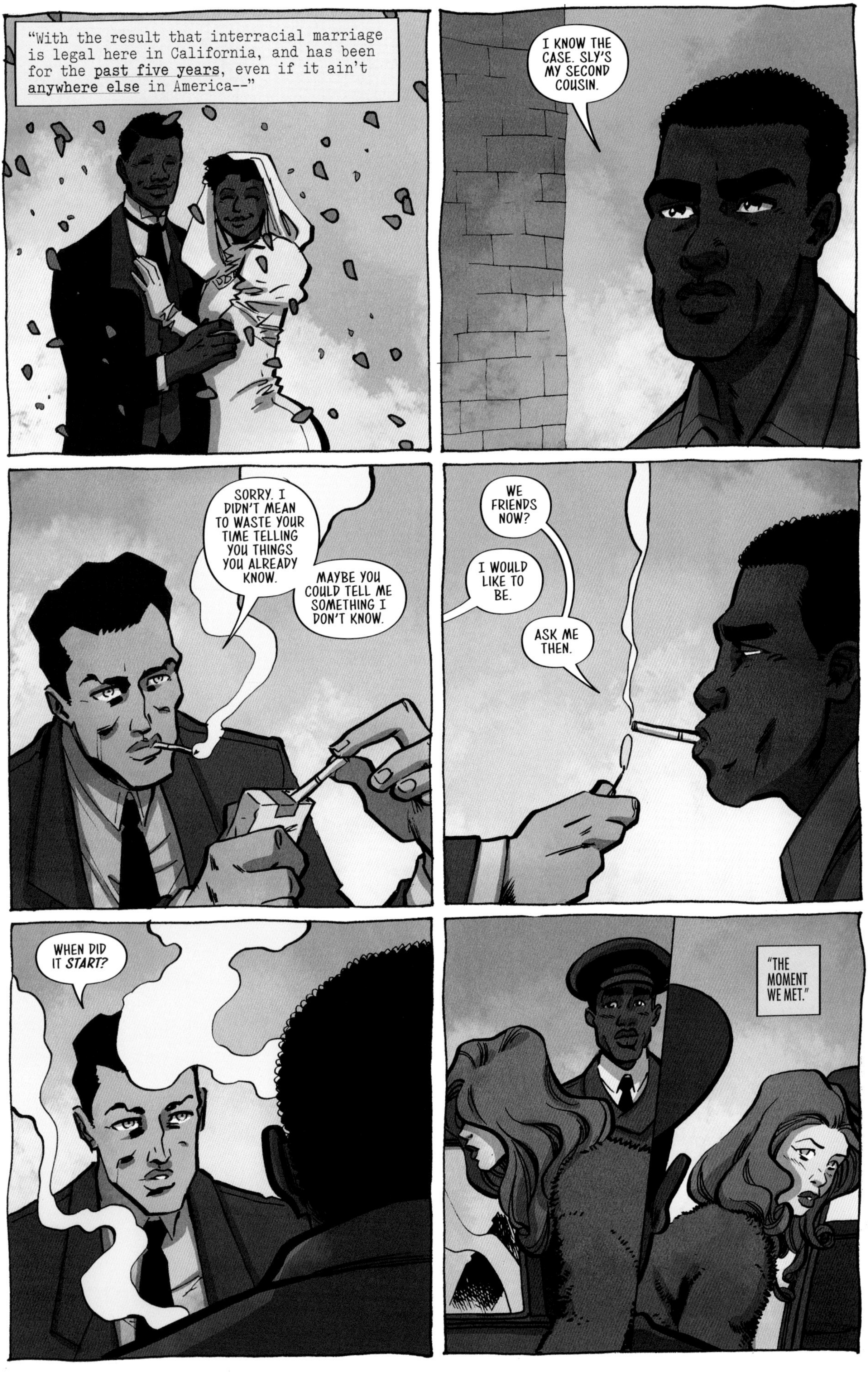
"With the result that interracial marriage is legal here in California, and has been for the past five years, even if it ain't anywhere else in America--"
I KNOW THE CASE. SLY'S MY SECOND COUSIN.
SORRY. I DIDN'T MEAN TO WASTE YOUR TIME TELLING YOU THINGS YOU ALREADY KNOW.
MAYBE YOU COULD TELL ME SOMETHING I DON'T KNOW.
WE FRIENDS NOW?
I WOULD LIKE TO BE.
ASK ME THEN.
WHEN DID IT *START?*
"THE MOMENT WE MET."

"WE WERE BOTH OWED. FOR WHAT HAD BEEN TAKEN AWAY."

"You confided in each other. She told you her plan, you told her what old man Jeeter wanted you to do. You figured together you could work both sides. Harriet would marry Gerald in secret. _Wife_ trumps _father_. She'd become his _heir_.

"Then, you'd have Waxnose and Frisky kill Gerald, but in a way that would leave a trail of bread-crumbs back to the old man. Two Jeeters for the price of one.

"It must have killed you. Having to watch Gerald drool all over her. An oaf who had never worked an honest day in his life, who couldn't hold his drink, a man who, if not for the color of his skin, wouldn't be fit to carry your water."

"I'M A PATIENT MAN."

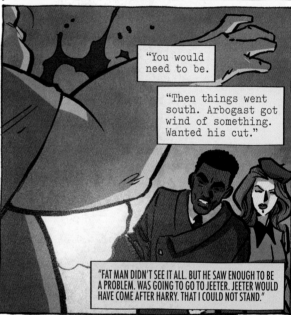

"You would need to be.

"Then things went south. Arbogast got wind of something. Wanted his cut."

"FAT MAN DIDN'T SEE IT ALL. BUT HE SAW ENOUGH TO BE A PROBLEM. WAS GOING TO GO TO JEETER. JEETER WOULD HAVE COME AFTER HARRY. THAT I COULD NOT STAND."

"When it was all done, when the Jeeters were _ruined_, when the books were _balanced_, what then?

"The two of you were going to take off to some little olive farm on the central coast, live happily ever after, raise some cute kids?"

"SOMETHING LIKE THAT. OR GO ABROAD. I WOULDN'T HAVE MINDED SEEING FRANCE WITHOUT THE TANKS."

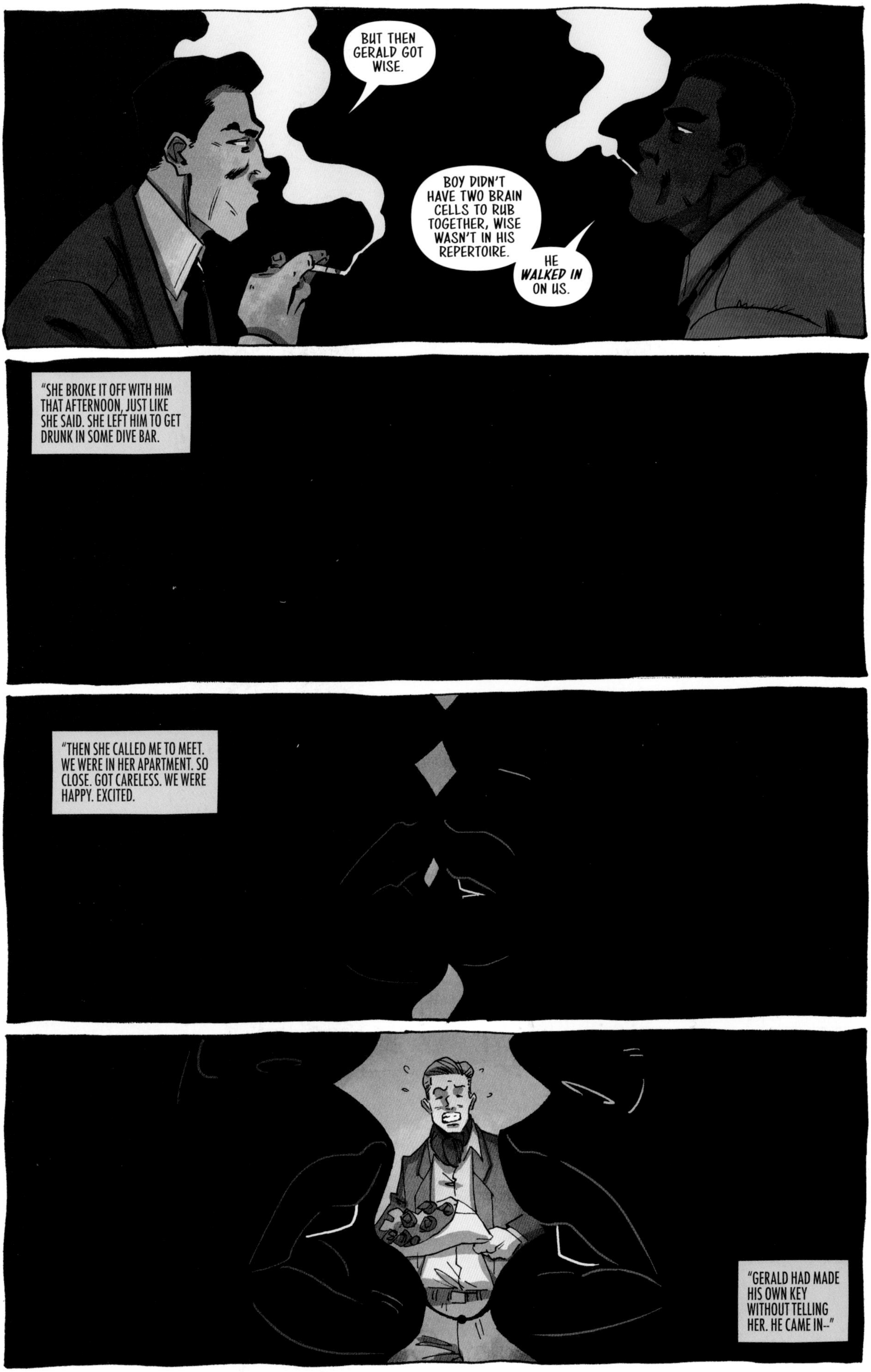
BUT THEN GERALD GOT WISE.
BOY DIDN'T HAVE TWO BRAIN CELLS TO RUB TOGETHER, WISE WASN'T IN HIS REPERTOIRE.
HE *WALKED IN* ON US.
"SHE BROKE IT OFF WITH HIM THAT AFTERNOON, JUST LIKE SHE SAID. SHE LEFT HIM TO GET DRUNK IN SOME DIVE BAR.
"THEN SHE CALLED ME TO MEET. WE WERE IN HER APARTMENT. SO CLOSE. GOT CARELESS. WE WERE HAPPY. EXCITED.
"GERALD HAD MADE HIS OWN KEY WITHOUT TELLING HER. HE CAME IN--"

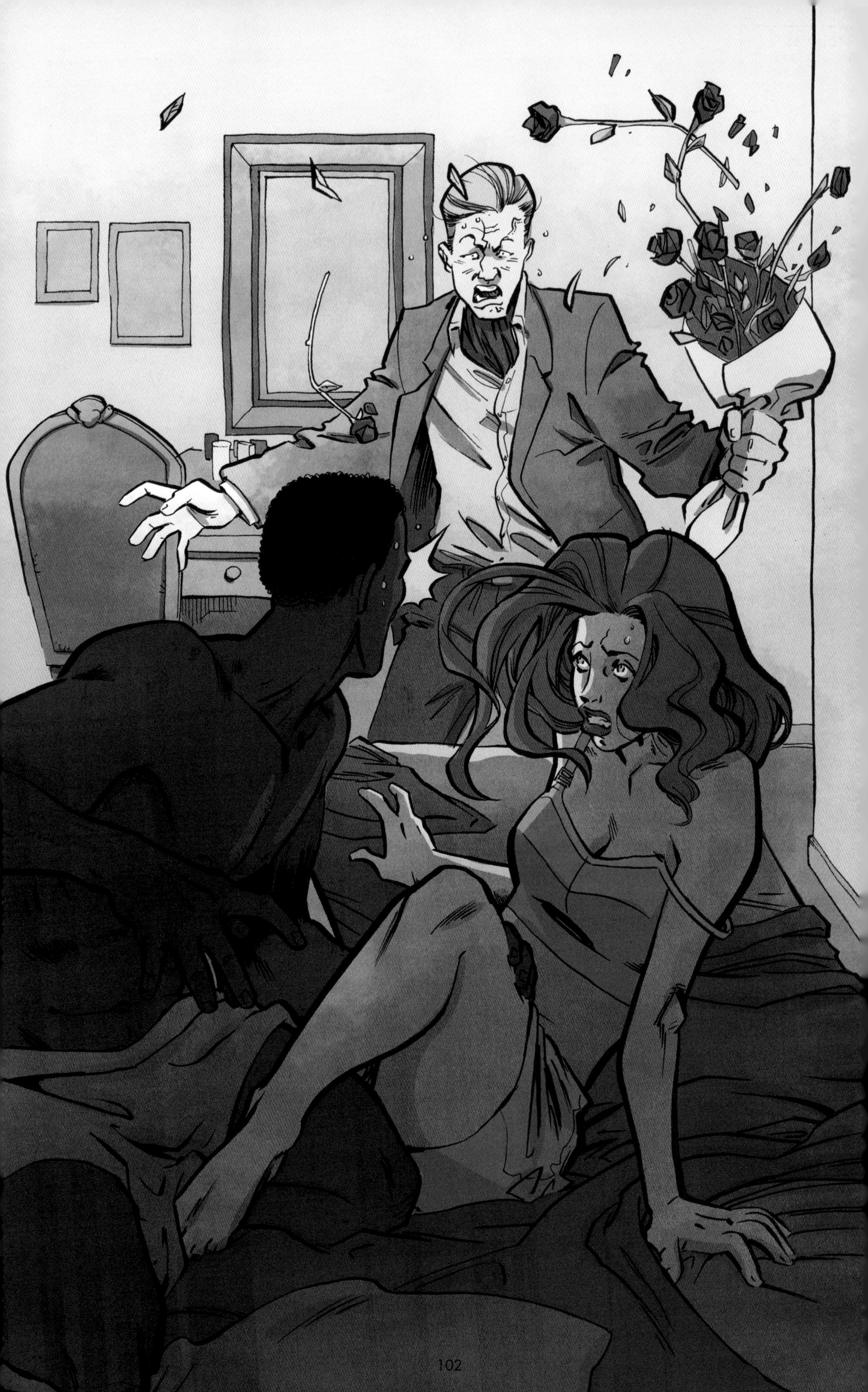

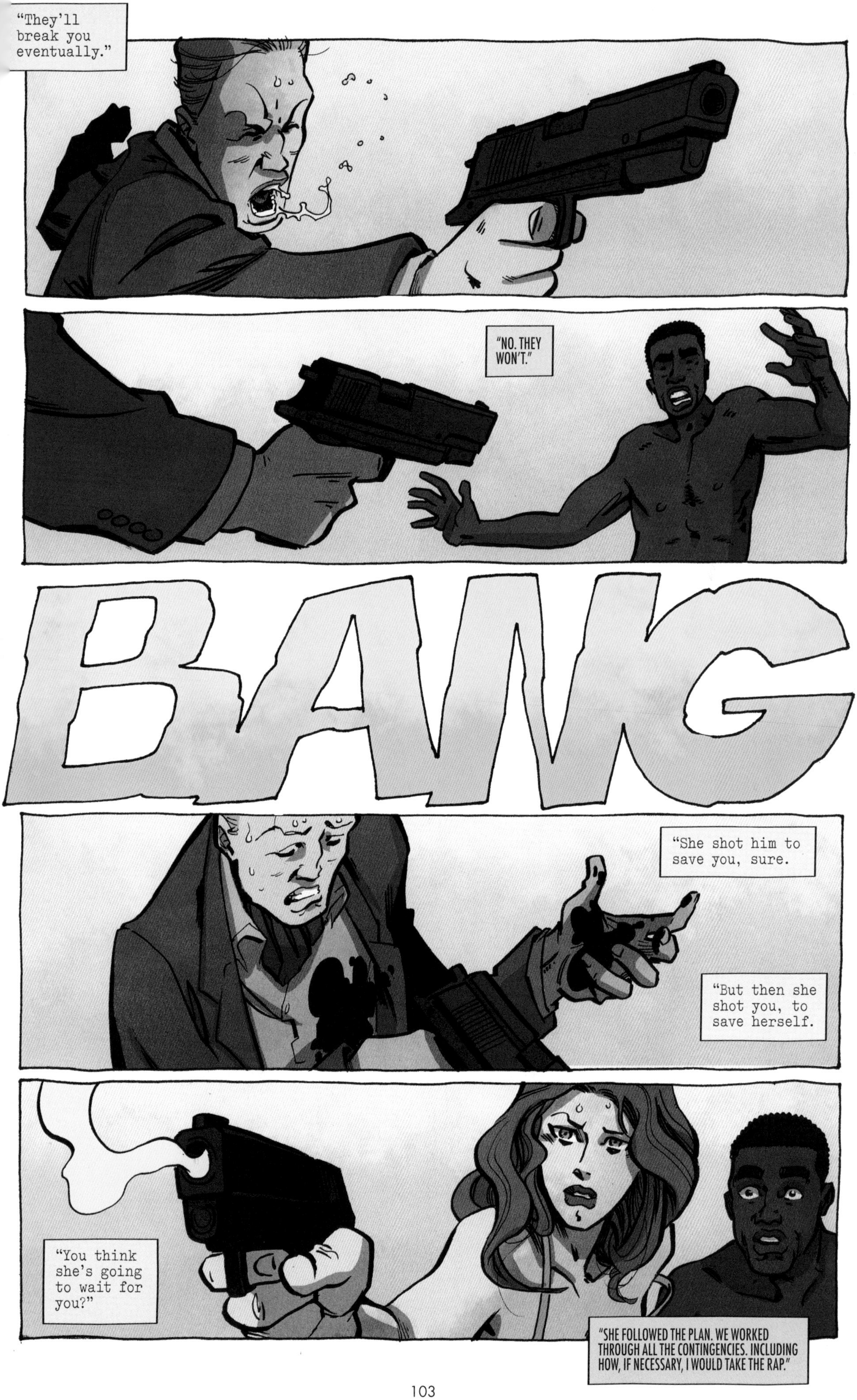
"They'll break you eventually."
"NO. THEY WON'T."
BANG
"She shot him to save you, sure.
"But then she shot you, to save herself.
"You think she's going to wait for you?"
"SHE FOLLOWED THE PLAN. WE WORKED THROUGH ALL THE CONTINGENCIES. INCLUDING HOW, IF NECESSARY, I WOULD TAKE THE RAP."

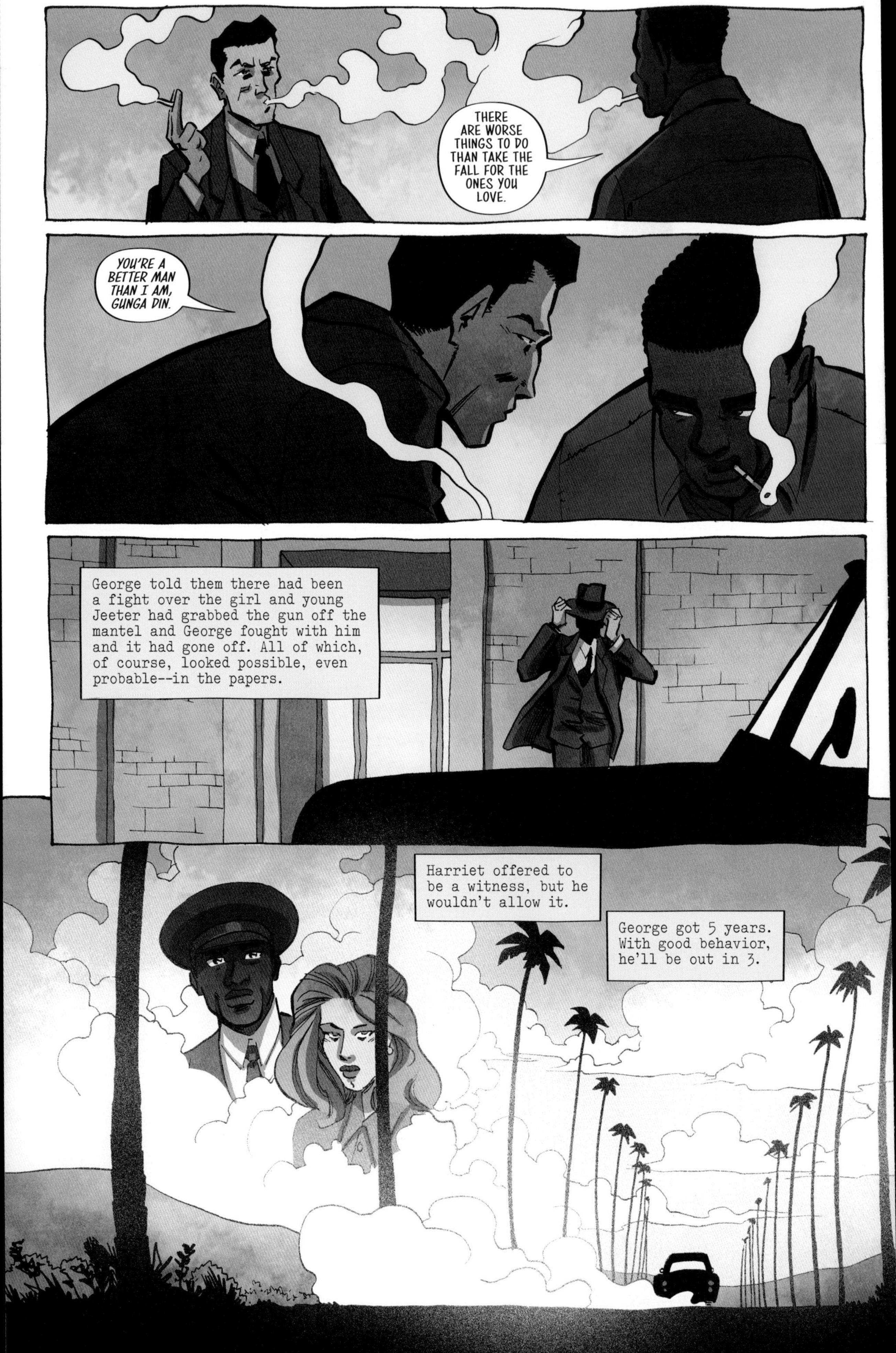
THERE ARE WORSE THINGS TO DO THAN TAKE THE FALL FOR THE ONES YOU LOVE.
YOU'RE A BETTER MAN THAN I AM, GUNGA DIN.
George told them there had been a fight over the girl and young Jeeter had grabbed the gun off the mantel and George fought with him and it had gone off. All of which, of course, looked possible, even probable--in the papers.
Harriet offered to be a witness, but he wouldn't allow it.
George got 5 years. With good behavior, he'll be out in 3.

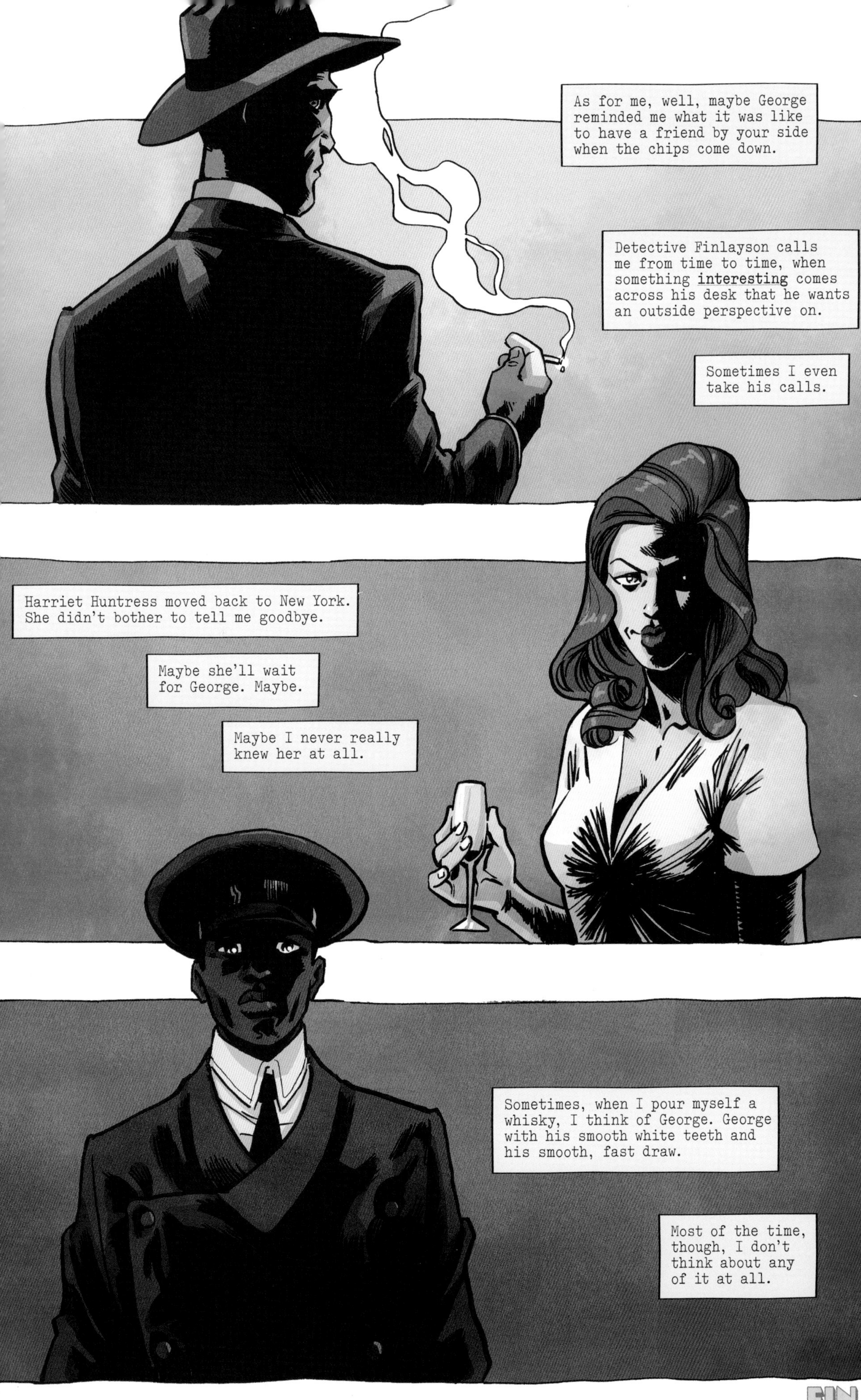
As for me, well, maybe George reminded me what it was like to have a friend by your side when the chips come down.
Detective Finlayson calls me from time to time, when something **interesting** comes across his desk that he wants an outside perspective on.
Sometimes I even take his calls.
Harriet Huntress moved back to New York. She didn't bother to tell me goodbye.
Maybe she'll wait for George. Maybe.
Maybe I never really knew her at all.
Sometimes, when I pour myself a whisky, I think of George. George with his smooth white teeth and his smooth, fast draw.
Most of the time, though, I don't think about any of it at all.
FIN

ACKNOWLEDGMENTS

Many people contribute to the making of a graphic novel, even more so than a text-only book. Here are a few of them:

Ted Adams suggested the whole thing and made the introductions and recommendations that helped it happen.

Alexander Greene, grandson of literary genius on both sides of his family tree, is a gentleman and the perfect professional heir. I hope this is the first of many cases we do together.

Ilias Kyriazis is the most gifted and generous of collaborators. He takes my writing and brings it to beautiful, dynamic life. We've done two detectives now, and I see no reason to stop there.

Cris Peter accepted my somewhat insane directive that each of the lead characters have their own color scheme, and somehow made that abstract idea a beautiful reality.

Taylor Esposito embraced my similarly cruel directive that each of them think in their own fonts and again made an abstract idea elegant and effective.

Brittany Chapman-Holman worked alongside me for many years, on many projects, through pandemics and strikes, doing whatever needed to be done without complaint and with tireless perseverance. Thank you, Brit.

Tarquin Pack, my producing partner at Prodigal, read several drafts of this book, as he now does for everything I write, and was both encouraging and insightful, as he always is.

Chris Howard-Woods at Penguin Random House was an exemplary editor—a close reader and a detailed and thoughtful note-giver. Every scrutiny of his made the book better.

Scott Kay and his team at NoRoof (Aaron Davidson, Tiffani Sarver, and Kathryn Diana) kept the trains running and the tracks safe.

My manager, Ashley Berns, has hustled for me for more than a decade; my book agent, Eric Smith, is a source of powerful positivity and smart notes; my lawyer, Richard Thompson, has navigated every new project I throw myself into with equal quantities of good humor and good sense; and Geoff Morley and Max Grossman at UTA are the latest additions to the expanding team. I owe them all more than commission.

My brother Armand is the person whose smooth right arm I trust in a fight, and is the only member of my family who loves comics more than I do. Our sister, Sheila, herself an excellent literary agent, always has helpful notes and advice which she knows to never offer unless solicited.

Odetta (aged six) is now reading and has such an appetite for detective stories that she'll be ready for this by the time it comes out. Bug, it may take a minute to realize that my love for you is the subtext of every line of this violent and dastardly tale, but look close, it's there.

Allison Caviness is my Harriet Huntress, the woman I would kill for. Thankfully, she's never asked me to. We'll have to be content with living for each other.

—Arvind Ethan David
Santa Ynez, California, 2024

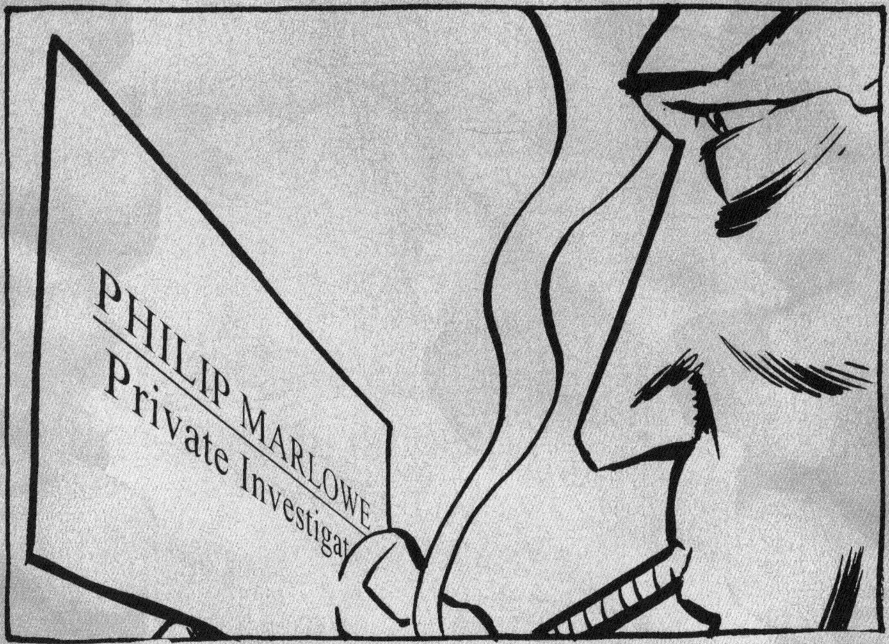
PHILIP MARLOWE
Private Investigat

Raymond Chandler was born in 1888 and published his first story in 1933 in the pulp magazine *Black Mask*. By the time he published his first novel, *The Big Sleep* (1939), featuring, as did all his major works, the iconic private eye Philip Marlowe, it was clear that he had not only mastered a genre but had set a standard to which others could only aspire. Chandler created a body of work that ranks with the best of twentieth-century literature. He died in 1959.

Arvind Ethan David's career started when he was still a student and adapted the Douglas Adams novel *Dirk Gently's Holistic Detective Agency* as a play and the great author came to see it and took the young writer under his wing. Since then, Arvind has created stories for page, stage, screen, audio, and anywhere one can tell a story. His previous graphic novels include the Stoker Award–nominated series *Darkness Visible* (with Mike Carey) and *Gray*, a reimagining of Oscar Wilde's *The Picture of Dorian Gray*, as well as three volumes of *Dirk Gently* comics (also with art by Ilias Kyriazis). Audio work includes the chart-topping Audible Originals *Earworms* and *The Crimes of Dorian Gray*. For television, Arvind was an executive producer on *Dirk Gently's Holistic Detective Agency* and is a writer on Neil Gaiman's forthcoming *Anansi Boys* for Amazon Studios. Theater work includes the stage adaptations of Lenny Henry's *The Boy with Wings* and, of course, the *Dirk Gently's Holistic Detective Agency* stage play. Arvind is a principal of Prodigal, the entertainment company where he has produced eight feature films including the Asian Academy Award–winning *The Garden of Evening Mists*, dozens of episodes of television, and several theatrical shows including the Tony- and Grammy-winning Alanis Morissette musical *Jagged Little Pill*. Follow Arvind @ArvD on Twitter/X and @arvind.david on Instagram.

Ilias Kyriazis (pencils and inks) is a critically acclaimed cartoonist based in Athens, Greece. He has drawn comics for numerous companies, including DC, IDW, Image Comics, Dark Horse, Humanoids, Rebellion Developments, and Dynamite Entertainment. *Trouble Is My Business* is his second collaboration with Arvind Ethan David after their run on *Dirk Gently's Holistic Detective Agency* for IDW. He also co-created *Chronophage* for Humanoids (with writer Tim Seeley), *Collapser* for DC (with writers Mikey Way and Shaun Simon), and *Secret Identities* for Image (with writers Jay Faerber and Brian Joines). Previous solo works of his in English are the crowd-funded sci-fi horror *Elysium Online*, the romantic comedy *Falling for Lionheart* for IDW, and the fantasy thriller *Melody* for DC, while in Greece he's best known for his iconic series *Manifesto*. His latest work is the graphic novel *What We Wished For*, published by Humanoids.

Cris Peter (colors) is a Brazilian colorist. She works mainly in the American comics market for publishers like DC Comics and Marvel Comics. She was nominated for the Eisner Award for her colors in the comic series *Casanova*. She also did the colors of Brazilian comics, such as *Astronauta—Magnetar* (with Danilo Beyruth, published by Panini Comics) and *Petals* (with Gustavo Borges, published by Marsupial Editora). In 2013, she published the theoretical book *O Uso das Cores* (The Use of Colors), by Marsupial Editora. She won the Troféu HQ Mix in 2016 and 2017, in the category "Best Colorist."

Taylor Esposito (letters) is a comic book lettering professional, owner of Ghost Glyph Studios, and teacher at the legendary Kubert School. A former staff letterer at DC and production artist at Marvel, he has lettered titles such as *Red Hood and The Outlaws* and *Harley Quinn the Animated Series, Interceptor, Heavy, Finger Guns* (Vault Comics), *Exorsisters* (Image), *Babyteeth, Hot Lunch Special, Bunnmask* (Aftershock), and *No One Left to Fight* (Dark Horse). Other publishers he has worked with include Webtoon *(Caster, Backchannel)*, Dynamite *(Elvira, Red Sonja and Vampirella Meet Betty and Veronica, Green Hornet)*, and IDW *(Scarlett's Strike Force)*.

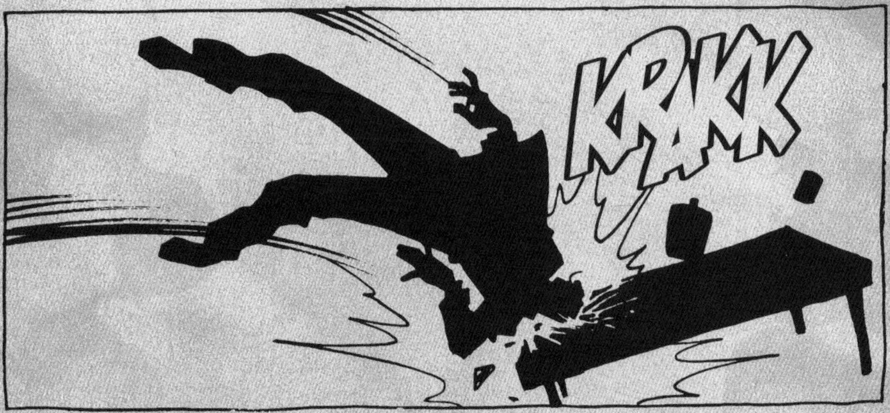
KRAKK